Pushing Bobby's Cadillac

Pushing Bobby's Cadillac

Allan Dare Pearce

IGUANA

Publisher: Meghan Behse
Editor: Marie-Lynn Hammond, Greg Ioannou, and Marnie Lamb
(www.marnielamb.com)
Proofreader: Lee Parpart
Illustrations and front cover design: Angela Vaculik
(AGP Studio: www.angelavaculik.com)

ISBN 978-1-77180-357-1 (paperback)
ISBN 978-1-77180-358-8 (epub)
ISBN 978-1-77180-359-5 (Kindle)

This is an original print edition of *Pushing Bobby's Cadillac*.

"The living have the cause of the dead in trust."

— *Osmar White*

I appreciate the forbearance shown by my family when I lock myself in my library for hours on end. Thank you for the support. Love to Mary Anne, Mackenzie, McKinley and Sullivan.

Monday, January 1, 1968
Gosfield Township, Ontario

Last night, without her, I drank too much. What the fuck else is new.

* * *

Today Aiken tramped the fields, like he needed to put food on the table, legs aching while telling himself he enjoyed the outing—a man with his hunting dog in his natural element. Sometime around 10 a.m. the black lab flushed a bird and the cock pheasant shot forth like a Spitfire roaring into battle to save the free world, flapping and thrashing, seeking to escape death. Surprised, Aiken Day yanked up the twelve gauge and fired in reflex, before pressing the weapon tight to his shoulder. The stock slammed into him, bouncing pain at him. The bird scuttled away.

"Goddamn little fucker!" Aiken threw the gun down and stuck fingers inside his coat, thrusting shirt buttons apart, kneading his shoulder, seeking to massage away the pain.

Agitation flooded the dog and she circled about, nervous. Aiken absorbed her anxiety. He beckoned her close and scratched under her chin. "Oh, for Christ's sake, dog," he said, "if you find that feathery bastard again I'll shove this gun up his arse and blow him to kingdom come." He dropped his voice, as if they were conspirators: "They'll find parts of his butt in China." The dog relaxed. *You seem quite satisfied with my ass-blowing promise. Maybe you can now disclose any knowledge you have of my wife's infidelities.*

He and the dog stood at the edge of the bean field, close to a hedgerow. Aiken retrieved his shotgun and rubbed the sore muscle again. He stumbled but recovered, settling on a tree stump just past the bean stubble. He sat down. The stump bit into his ass but he ignored it, shifting about for more comfort while fiddling out the mickey of Canadian Club from his jacket. The winter morning snapped at him, the crisp chilled smell welcome after the crumbling collapse of autumn when all things died and hope faded.

The dog circled and dropped down at his feet. Snow carpeted the ground. It was a few degrees above freezing. The air was still, crisp and silent; the outdoor sense of isolation was almost eerie, and the cold scratched into his nose. *A perfect day for outdoor hockey on a frozen pond.* He propped the shotgun against his thigh and sucked at the bottle. The charcoal-aged liquid soothed him. He rubbed his boot along the dog's flank. "Do you think my wife has a boyfriend?" he said. A tail wagged. "Is that a yes or a no? I sense that you have an opinion." A strong pull at the bottle this time and he capped it. "We need a plan to get her home and back into my bed. If she's had a hundred men, I still need her back home with me."

He uncapped the bottle and sipped a bit. "How about I tell her you have ass cancer and play the pity game?" Another wag. "So, if she buys it, you'll need a full-time nurse, someone who cares. You're black, she's black, and she cares about all blacks in need." Wag.

Later, after another swig: "But she'll have to live with your incessant farting."

Wag. Another pull, but leaving the liquid in his mouth, savouring it, letting it run down his throat slowly, teasingly.

Later: "Shit! I'm kidding. It's me that needs a full-time nurse—someone who can live with *my* incessant farting."

Aiken heard footsteps behind him, long strides of crunching snow consistent with an adult's step, but he did not rise or turn around. He let his hand move down the shotgun stock until his fingers reached the trigger.

"Can't hunt out of season," the game warden said, a sad dumpling of a man in a seen-better-days Eisenhower battle jacket, hat flaps pulled down and laced tight. He stepped in front of Aiken, waiting for an answer.

Aiken extended the bottle and the warden paused and took a pull.

"Just going for a walk," Aiken said.

"And you needed your hunting dog and your twelve gauge?"

"Man's best friend and a weapon against burglars."

"A lot of burglars out here in a crunchy soybean field, where pheasants happen to graze, on New Year's Day?"

"I heard a lion escaped from the zoo. Don't you read the fucking newspapers? Don't you want to protect your neighbours?"

"There's not a zoo for two hundred miles."

"Lions are fast, really fast fuckers. Gimme back the bottle you little prick. I could shoot you in the balls and not think twice. Your wife would pin a medal on me." The warden handed the bottle back and patted Aiken on the shoulder as he left, lowering his voice: "She'll come back, Aiken."

The sun moved and shadows shifted without Aiken noticing and he remained on the stump, ignoring the bite to his ass, which was now mostly numb anyway. He tossed the bottle and removed a second from his coat pocket. He rubbed the nose of the lab. "As a coloured dog, what do you think of coloured women? I mean the handsome black ones like my wife. Do you think a used-up white guy like me deserves a good-looking black woman in his bed? Raise a paw if you support me as a person in need of a black wife or in the alternative, eligible for racial surgery to fit in with her crowd."

The dog's head drooped, resting on her forepaws.

"Are your paws broke? Never mind, I don't care for your opinion. As a black lab dog, you are racially biased."

Aiken sipped again. "Truth be told buddy, we couldn't afford a white lab dog—have to pay for him to go prep school and then to Harvard or Yale. Buy him a Jaguar convertible and entertain his simpering white girlfriends. He'd never be able to shoot decent hoops or run off tackle with any skill. But you—Mr. black lab—we fully expected you to take out the garbage with your in-bred janitor skills and serve drinks to our guests on the lawn with a white napkin over your arm and a plastered-on smile. When the guests became tipsy, we thought maybe you'd dance up and down the stairs with Shirley Temple."

The sun slumped, a sad affair, Aiken thought. *It inches down and fails no matter what your problem. Give me a sunset that freezes in place, allows you to reset your life.* He tossed the second bottle and stood, slinging the shotgun to his side. "The liquor has split…all gone. This is a perfect place for a liquor store," he said. "Corner the market." *Where in hell did we leave the Chevy?* "Well, dog, this has been a shit-hot outing." He stepped out, cradling the shotgun, retracing his footprints in the snow. The dog loped alongside. "What a disappointment, eh buddy. Doesn't matter what a guy does, some days the fucking bird wins."

Tuesday, January 2
Key West, Florida

Duty drove him: duty to his family; duty to his country; duty to his God. And sometimes it overwhelmed his wife, thrusting love aside, pushing her into a chair at the back of a hall, or forcing her to fake-grin when consuming soggy sandwiches at a church social. It occasionally crowded a man and a woman too hard, he thought, but that was his chosen life, a life ingrained. Senator Robert F. Kennedy motioned with his hands, signalling for his family to start back to the house while he waited for his aide.

"Even on our vacation?" his wife said. He shrugged. "As if they leave you so much time to waste with family," she said. But she gathered up the children, herding them away, nestling them back to the borrowed beach house. Soggy sandwich time, he thought, as his family tramped away.

Shorebirds, American oystercatchers, skittered behind the aide, tracking in the wet sand: white bodies and round black heads, bright red-orange spike-like beaks. They stalked the aide, feet stabbing pockmarks in the sand behind him; ahead of him seagulls circled and sailed, shrieking complaints at him. Two families with seven children between them frolicked on the beach close to the water's edge, the children squealing, while the parents rested on a blanket, sipping Chardonnay from paper cups and feasting on fresh croissants, still oven-warm and spongy. It was ten past noon.

The slight northeast breeze dampened the waves down, ruffling Kennedy's swab of brown hair. His smile concealed a trace of annoyance as he waited for the young man in the gloomy suit, his staffer striding along, sensibly stepping around the beach slime, seaweed patches and blotches of shells, and avoiding the tumbling waves.

"Hallo," his aide shouted. "Duty calls."

Kennedy wore well-worn white shorts and an unbuttoned white Sea Island cotton shirt, sleeves flapped back, cloth fluffing across his chest, revealing his physique: lean, muscular. He carried sandals in his hand, the straps curled about his wrist. He sucked in the sea odour, taking pleasure in the iodine smell of sea salt, the decaying mesh of fish, clams, crabs and shrimp; he sucked in the world about him, feeling alive.

The staffer left the hard-packed beach, patent leather shoes now dutifully dredging through the sand. He carried a manila file folder. Kennedy observed the heavy wool suit on his aide and the sweat streaming down his temples. The man's white shirt was no longer crisp and the red tie nudging out from his suitcoat was twisted. His right hand clutched a file. When the aide caught up he offered the file to Kennedy. Kennedy ignored the folder.

"What's up?" he said, trying to keep annoyance from his voice.

"McNamara's out," the aide said. "We'll be getting a new secretary of defense." The staffer used four fingers to swipe sweat from his forehead. "The president wants someone who can kick the Commies in the nuts. He's leaning towards Clark Clifford."

"A hawkish choice," Kennedy said. "Very hawkish."

"Someone who can 'kick them in the nuts.' That's a quote."

"Really?"

"He's searching for a nut-kicker. That's his strategy."

A convulsing, jerking movement from the sea caught Kennedy's eye, and he saw a child's body floating face down and moving away from shore, wrenched away by the rip tide. The senator flung his sandals aside and sprinted towards the water, legs pumping hard. Two long strides into the water he dived, catching the child up in the same motion. He cradled the boy in his arms and formed his fingers around the child's mouth, fussing his lips apart, blowing into the small lungs until the child coughed and spit up. Kennedy brought the boy to his mother, but he held up a hand when the accolades started, backing away and returning to the staffer. Behind him the boy's father upended the bottle of Chardonnay, draining its contents into the sand.

"That could have ended badly," the aide said, clutching the sandals, holding them out. "If the child had drowned, your name would've been plastered all over the newspapers. They'd claim you were responsible for the death."

"And the possibility of a slander justifies not trying to save a child?" Kennedy squeezed water from his shorts and wrung out his shirttails. Water dripped from his face.

"No, no, of course not, Senator, but you have to consider political consequences...you know, sometimes."

Kennedy tugged his sandals from the aide's hand, reminding himself that a Harvard degree or even two was no guarantee of maturity or wisdom. The youngster before him was untested, even with his degrees. "Where were we?" Kennedy said.

"Yes. Our president wants a secretary of defense who can kick the commies in the balls. Surely the country is entitled to a more finely articulated strategy than a groin kick?"

Kennedy exhaled and for just a second felt a hint of weariness, but it vanished quickly.

"Perhaps that's the way they debate serious issues in Texas?" the aide said. "A Texas ball-kicking contest—winner takes all."

Kennedy headed away from the beach and his aide followed. "Lyndon has an earthy quality," Kennedy said, "and it plays in his favour on a personal level. It's often one of his strengths."

"But what does it mean for the country, Senator?"

Kennedy paused in his walk, the sounds of the sea suddenly forsaking him. After a few seconds blanketed by an unnatural silence, he turned to the aide. "It means the ghettos will continue to burn."

Wednesday, January 3
Windsor, Ontario, Canada

Dank visons of the Battle of Dieppe returned, flitting about his head, haunting his sleep: men dancing in death, friends from the Essex Scottish Regiment sinking on the stone beaches, bodies washing about, rocking with the waves. The roar of the landing craft mixed with crashing surf sounds, the crashes punctuated by the screams of the dying and pulsating rounds of gunfire showering down from the cliffs above. The stench of cordite whiffed at his nostrils, choking him. Aiken Day woke up in the concentration camp, Stalag 8B. The starvation pangs carried back the despair, and the grinding, coiling stomach cramps grated into him, thumping his guts and bowels. Foreboding and unease washed over him, blackening depression clicked in, nameless and faceless shadows hovered. He woke each morning thrown back into the camp, comprehension gradually blowing into him, overtaking him in herky-jerky stages.

His daughter, Sarah, called from her room. "Daddy! Time to get up."

He swung his legs out and dropped his feet to the floor, taking in the room as if for the first time: a bedroom with finely crafted linens, door slightly ajar, a window cracked open, curtains ruffling gently, a slight chill in the air, clothes on the chair, a nightstand, pretty with doily and delicate lamp, female touches; married, two children, living in a fine home on Victoria Avenue purchased by his wife, Paris; not captive, not hungry, not dirty, not lice-ridden, not praying for deliverance or death. Free, yet never free, from Stalag 8B.

The revolver on the nightstand jumped into focus. *What was I thinking last night?* He drew the Webley towards him, opened the nightstand drawer and stowed the pistol away. He cupped his hands over his face. *Someone save me.*

"Daddy!"

"I'm up, sweetie." *But only because drinking in bed is probably against Canadian law. And selling shoes to people with smelly feet is marginally better than staying home with a bottle of liquor and the Webley.*

In the kitchen, Aiken poured boiling water over coffee, watching the brown liquid filter down. He leaned against the kitchen sink. He rubbed his fingers against his temples, and when the coffee finished draining he trickled three jiggers of Bushmills Black Bush Irish whiskey into the pot and hunkered down at the table with a cup. *To all of you dead friends pitching in the surf, I am sorry you died and I didn't, but shove off and leave me be. Chase after someone else.*

The floor behind him squeaked.

"Poop!" Sarah said, pointing to the bottle. "I don't like that nasty habit." He shrugged. "More dreams?" she said. He shrugged again. She removed a towel from a drawer, pushed up on tiptoes and gently wiped Aiken's forehead, folding the cloth over when she had finished, setting it on the counter. She wrapped her arms around Aiken and clutched him tight. Her vanilla scent taunted him, warming him to life.

She possesses the same refined features as her mom, Aiken thought, the same deep lagoon blackness, the delicately structured face, the magnet eyes, and she has a teenager's rippling confidence in solving problems: hers, mine and the world's, but mostly mine. Her white shirt curved at the neck, forming a crisp necklace that emphasized her blackness. Her navy skirt tumbled down towards her knees without quite reaching them. She wore white socks and navy blue canvas shoes.

Aiken sipped from his cup, sweeping the steam into his nostrils. She worked in close to him, pressing against him. "Grandpa still meets with some camp survivors," she said. "They talk about what happened over there."

He passed off a lie to finish the conversation: "I'll think about it." Aiken bent over and gestured with his cup to her exposed knees. She scrunched up her face and unrolled the top of her skirt, jerking the material down until it covered her knees. He nodded. She sponged his forehead with the cloth once more.

"The booze in the coffee?" she said. "Does it actually help with the nightmares or does it just taste better than cornflakes?"

Both, dear. "Cornflakes are good."

Sarah picked up the *New York Times* doubled in half on the kitchen table and flashed it in front of him. "You don't read the *Times*," she said. "Mom does. You read the *Free Press*."

"She suggested an article about Senator Kennedy and the Vietnam War."

"Did you even read it?" she said. "Is he going to cancel the war and save the world?"

"Quite possibly."

"No, you didn't read it," she said, "of course not. 'Pigs at the trough'! Isn't that what you say about politicians? 'Pigs at the trough.'"

"Pigs can be useful," he said. "The world craves bacon but it doesn't want saving."

"Dress up if you're meeting Mom."

Aiken climbed upstairs to dress for the meeting with his wife, arthritic knees slightly wheezing with the early morning effort. He topped six feet tall and carried himself erect. He dressed carefully for the outing, choosing worn, friendly chinos and a blue oxford button-down shirt, thinking to show off his blue eyes, "blazing blues" according to Paris, spoken lovingly in better days and even better nights, when she shared his bed, shared his life. After stuffing his feet into brown penny loafers he ran his fingers through his hair. The sweats were gone, the shadows distant. *I live to fight again.* Downstairs he pushed the boozed-up coffee aside, intending to brew a fresh pot.

Sarah parked herself against the kitchen door, crossing her arms. "Shame about the rip in your shirt," she said.

"It won't show under my coat. If I remove my coat, I'll keep my arm tucked in."

"Do you ever shine those shoes? Ever?"

"As often as the cow did. Wish me luck."

"Mommy's not coming back. She'll lecture you about civil rights or the Vietnam War, or both…and it will end badly for you. Don't you know that yet?"

"So young, yet so cynical."

She lowered her head, her eyes displaying sadness, thinly veiled.

"Your mom may not dress like General MacArthur," Aiken said, "but like him, she shall return."

"Sure," Sarah said, but she said it quietly.

She hugged and kissed him and left for school. Upstairs, Aiken headed into the bedroom. He drew open the nightstand drawer, removing the Webley, swinging it about before replacing it and pressing the drawer shut. *She must come back. Be damn good practice for her. She can save me before she saves the world.*

Wednesday, January 3
Detroit, Michigan

Aiken waited in his Chevy on Goyeau Street, across from the Windsor-Detroit Tunnel entrance, idling the car, goosing the pedal on occasion, more from habit than to keep the car from stalling. He watched as Paris turned the corner two blocks away, coming off University Avenue and heading towards him. *My saviour approaches. Mind your mouth, Aiken, say whatever it takes. You need her home to survive.*

Paris was charcoal black, not beige, not milk chocolate, definitely not café-au-lait, but midnight black, the colour of his two children, more than the colour of charcoal, he thought, more like the colour of damp, glistening coal. Today she chose to dress casually, but as always, carefully, wearing blue jeans, jeans fitted but not skin-tight, a purple-and-grey sweatshirt layered over a flannel shirt, no jewelry, achieving her own distinctive style. *Only my wife could appear elegant in jeans and a sweatshirt.*

She opened the passenger door, sliding inside the Chevy in one graceful motion. She smelled to Aiken the way she always smelled, somewhat like he imagined the Milky Way to smell, or perhaps distant, swirling clouds on a fresh spring day. "Hello, Missy," he said.

"Hello Blue-eyes." He felt the urge to drag his arms around her, draw her in and squeeze her tight, but he held back knowing their get-togethers often drifted south, rapidly.

Her eyes spotted the *New York Times* on the seat. He quickly passed the newspaper to her, hoping to derail a conversation about its contents. "I thought John Kennedy was the hope for black people?"

he said. "Bobby's the younger brother who worked for Joe McCarthy, the commie witch-hunter."

"Bobby saw James Meredith into the University of Mississippi," she said. "He's done nothing but grow since. Some people grow better with age."

"Sure they do," Aiken said. *Oops. Watch your tongue, Aiken.*

She considered him for several seconds before responding. "You didn't read the article, did you?" She tossed the paper into the back seat.

"I often keep unread crap in the back seat, Missy."

"That concentration camp still keeps you a prisoner."

"Unless the trunk is open," he said. "Sometimes I chuck it in there." *Mind your mouth, Aiken. You need her home.*

The silence wedged between them until he spoke up. "Well, where to, babe? We're having so much fun already." She pointed to the tunnel entrance and he shoved the car into gear, moving into the stream of traffic heading down into the tunnel towards Detroit.

Light traffic allowed them to pass under the river and exit the tunnel quickly. They coasted up on the Detroit side, pulling up in front of a customs officer. *Bugger! Customs officers are all white and all male—a fact guaranteed to piss her off.* Aiken cranked down his window, shoving out his driver's licence. Feeling the chilled outside air blow across his face, he left the motor running. Paris twisted her face away from the officer and stared out her window.

The officer placed a hand on the door, surveying the two occupants. "You together?" he said.

Aiken cranked up a smile. "Yeah." *This could go bad.*

"I meant, pal…you two married or dating or what?"

"Yes, married."

"You," he said, pointing to Aiken, "married her." He pointed to Paris.

Paris screwed about in her seat, bending forward, speaking quietly, punching her words across Aiken at the officer. "You think perhaps I married…beneath my station?"

Oh man, she's pissed off.

"Could I have snagged a big black dude, you wonder," Paris said. "A big buck with a red Cadillac and a string of girls?"

The man's face twisted in anger. *Thank God he's not armed.*

"Show me some ID," he said. She removed a thin wallet from her purse, slid out her driver's licence and passed it across to Aiken. The officer fingered the piece of paper without glancing at it. He flung it back. It fluttered, landing on the floor of the car. He turned his back, waving them on.

Leaving customs Aiken headed his car into the side street off Jefferson, swinging it to the curb where he slipped it into neutral and yanked on the parking brake. "Always an asshole," he said.

"Shut up. You know what that was about."

"Don't let him ruin your day."

"Is he so different from your white friends who never came round after you married a coloured girl?"

We got ourselves a full-blown mood. Don't make it worse.

Her voice plunged and she bunched a tad nearer him, whispering. "So after the war, why didn't we have parties with your war-buds?"

"You know the answer. My buds are dead, still at Dieppe, still pitching about in the surf." *And that's mostly true.*

"Not because of the black faces on your wife and children? Ashamed of your black family?"

"Not true, Paris."

Her lips tightened. "A tiny bit true?"

"Not true most days," he said. "Paris, no one can be a hero three hundred and sixty-five days a year."

She turned, putting her back to him. "If I had I a wooden leg," he said, his head close to her ear, rubbing her shoulder, "or an empty eye socket, would I be sexy every day to you, or only after a bottle of wine? A glimmer of truth?"

After a few moments she grinned at his comment and turned. "With an empty eye socket, I'd call you 'Blue-eye.'"

"Or maybe 'Empty socket-eye,'" he said, binding his arm about her shoulder, squeezing lightly, in the fashion of a friend, a pal. *On track now.*

"Head to Twelfth Street," she said.

Twelfth Street? We're going to the heart of the ghetto.

Wednesday, January 3
Detroit, Michigan

The city of Detroit blossomed in the fifties, flickering hope, dragging haggard black men from the suffocating south and populating the car plants with slave descendants. The city provided proper middle-class jobs for them and in turn spawned a vibrant black community, Paradise Valley, the greatest black community in the world. But white people fleeing to the suburbs dwindled down the tax base, rotting down schools, ushering in the ghetto.

Paris and Aiken travelled through the downtown core, massive skyscrapers lunging above them. "Detroit," she said, "was once a fine city for black people, a city of hope."

Aiken dipped his head in acknowledgement, concentrating on traffic.

"Only poor black people make a home in Detroit now," she said, "people raped in spirit, people with no hope." *Yeah, "hope"—well I hope to Christ this lecture is short.*

"Drive down Twelfth Street," she said.

The car spun onto 12th Street, easing into light traffic. They drove through the riot area. Homes that once housed families now existed as burned-out shells; businesses were gutted and abandoned, foundations blackened, building walls scorched, windows broken; weeds in control between patches of snow.

After they'd travelled several blocks Paris tapped his shoulder and pointed. "Beside that park." *Your only job today: talk the wife back home.*

He swung the car next to the curb and surveyed the deadened, crumpled buildings surrounding the lot. "Probably dead centre of the riot-zone."

"Dead for sure," she said.

"Should be against the law to call it a park," he said.

"A lot of things should be against the law, Blue-eyes, but ain't." Her voice carried sadness, not anger. The burned-out foundation of a house squatted in the background behind the ancient wooden picnic bench amid fifty square feet of cinders, a bench attacked by hundreds of knives carving out statements about love or power. A stringy black kid hunkered over the bench, maybe two or three inches over six feet, mid to late teens, a goatee scruff nibbling his chin, his face heavily pockmarked, his knee twitching up and down.

They left the car and walked towards him. The kid's head flitted from side to side while his knee twitched. Aiken plopped down opposite him and Paris slipped down beside the teen, leaving the fellow several inches of space. He twisted towards Aiken at an angle to Paris, flipping open his brown leather jacket, providing Aiken a view of his .45 caliber handgun—rectangular black snout and brown grips. He sealed the jacket tight when Aiken dipped his head.

"This is Pokeface," Paris said.

Pokeface? Truth in advertising arrives in the ghetto?

"The deal?" Pokeface said.

Paris passed him a ten-dollar US bill, which he stuffed into a jean pocket while his head continued to spin back and forth, surveying the grounds.

Maybe we call him Twitchhead or Twitchpoke.

"My husband, Aiken Day," Paris said.

No acknowledgement. He really doesn't give a hoot. The deal is to answer a few questions probably; nothing said about caring or taking an interest.

"Got a girlfriend or wife?" Paris said.

"No whore."

"Mother?"

He shook his head.

"Job?" she said.

He shook his head again.

What are we here for? What's today's lesson? Mulling the kid's comments over in his mind, Aiken cast something out. "How do you earn money?"

"I sell things, Pastyman. I is what whities call an en-tren-prin-oor."

"Every day," Paris said, "he buys a container of four coffees for forty cents. A tool shop around the corner pays him fifteen dollars for the bag."

"Why?" Aiken said.

Pokeface shrugged.

"So no one bothers the cars in their parking lot," Paris said. "And no one bothers the workers going to and from the cars."

"Protection?" Aiken said, receiving no response.

"What else do you sell?" Paris said.

"Only sell what people want."

"Sometimes they want drugs," she said.

Pokeface shrugged again.

"Sometimes they want whores."

"That's why they is whores. They wanting to be sold." *Whoa! Today's civil rights lesson has arrived.*

Back in the car Aiken faced Paris, knowing another lecture circled about, ready to slam into him. Paris banged the car door shut. "The ghetto pushes black men into this."

"Paris…"

"He sells drugs, protection and whores. Think of him as the Duke of Detroit, the new royalty. His name for a girlfriend is 'whore.'"

"Paris…"

"The school system produces young men like him. They terrorize and grab what they want. They're not men unless they carry a gun to kill with. Detroit and every big American city create black men like him."

"Paris, come home with me." *Save me, for Christ's sake. Let someone else save Detroit.*

"A black male child faces three options: get religion, join the army and die in Vietnam, or sell whores."

"Slow down."

"The girl's options are worse, hateful and evil."

There is no right answer here.

"Aiken, these kids look like your kids."

He tried not to respond in anger, failing. "Those kids are not my kids."

"It's everyone's problem."

He yelled, "Our children go to good schools and do homework, get good grades. I pack Sarah's lunch every day. I send her off to school every morning." He paused. "With a hug and a sandwich. It's me that makes that sandwich and hugs her before school, not you."

"I know you've cared for our children over the years," she said. "But dead ghettos produce dead people."

"I meet with her teachers twice a year, for get-togethers called 'parent-teacher' talks; get-togethers you may have forgotten about while out saving the world. Adam goes to a fine university two hours away and is home weekends. I put him there. I arranged for his sports scholarship."

"His basketball skills put him there."

"And you, a short black woman out saving the world, had so much to do with that shit."

"These youngsters on Twelfth Street," she said, "don't have that option. No one makes their lunch, no one hugs them."

"My kids are not ghetto kids. Come back home. Save your own family."

"You don't get it, Aiken. We're losing generations. Vietnam War money should be spent on the ghetto."

"I gave at the office."

"People survive concentration camps."

"The last time I tried saving the world," he said, "the world rewarded me with three years in Stalag 8B and I dropped one-half of my body weight. I gave at the office. My goal in life is…"

"What is your damn goal in life, Aiken?" she shouted. "It's not to help people or make the world a better place."

What is my goal? Silence muzzled the space between them for several seconds. His voice softened. "Not to have a goal, I guess. To get up each day and decide how I'll piss that day away."

She yanked at the door handle, flinging the door open, jerking herself out of the car, slamming the door. "Your goal is to drink your nightmares away. Won't happen. You'll be stuck in Stalag 8B forever."

Save me, Paris. "My goal is to spend my life with you." *I'm losing it, Paris. I can't bring myself to trash the Webley.* Paris set off down 12th Street heading north, away from the river. *What would shift this conversation around?* Aiken cranked down his window and called out, "I enrolled in university."

Walking back to the car, crossing in front of the hood, she approached his window, leaning into it, forcing him to bend his head back. "Before, you always said thanks but no thanks."

"Still got some military money put aside," he said. "I'm aiming my sights on law school, eventually." *Or maybe I could be a rocket scientist, or nab a PhD in toilet technology. That would be a spicy career move— plunging plugged toilets. Your shit is my bread and butter.*

She rounded the car, pushing back inside the Chevy, but leaving the car door ajar. "You signed up for classes?" she said.

"I did, Missy." *A woman worth having is worth lying to.* "Shut the door," he said, "the ghetto can be dangerous."

She closed the door and Aiken put the car in motion, making a U-turn, heading down 12th towards the river. He saw Pokeface heading up 12th Street, traveling deeper into the ghetto. Aiken waved as they drove past. *Goodbye, Mr. Twitch-ass.*

"You as a civil rights lawyer," Paris said. "We could work with that."

Right, me as a rich-bitch lawyer! "Yeah," he said. "I'm ready for a change." *Sleeping alone chews at a man's privates. And someone should take charge of the Webley when the shadows gather.* "Aiken Day, the civil rights lawyer has arrived," he said," shining and re-shining a pair of brogues before morning coffee break."

Paris tilted her head and grinned. *Sharing humour is the first step towards physical bliss.* "It could be dangerous for you, Blue-eyes," she said, "doing civil rights."

"Not a problem, sweetie, I chase down danger. I pursue it with righteous vigour, smacking it down, strangling the sucker with a red silk tie."

She laughed. "You damn idiot."

But the real danger in being a lawyer: a monotonous daily clean shirt, monogrammed, cufflinked and properly starched, roped off by a striped tie, completing a tailored brown serge suit with double vents and surgeon cuffs, brown brogue shoes, a well-worn brown leather briefcase with brass locks and a slick black umbrella—a soul-robbing life, a life without colour. Hello, concentration camp of the soul.

He stroked a finger to his temple, pulling it away, feeling the slight dampness. She put an arm through his, embracing him, dancing fingers against his chest, acknowledging him as a male, as lover material. *How could I forget that smile, that world-smiting, wringing-sun-out-of-every-thunderstorm smile?*

"Drop me at the tunnel, Windsor side," she said. "I've an errand to run before I come home." She tapped his arm. "Take a few days at the most."

"You got it, Missy." He left her as requested, recruiting a slim smile and sending it in her direction, but she had already turned away, so he focused on her retreating figure. *Butt-saucy, as always.* She travelled away from him down Ouellette Avenue, moving briskly, heading north towards the river.

A lawyer? At my age? I learned about justice in my three years in Stalag 8B. Laws are voted on, enacted and enforced by the person jabbing the gun up your ass.

Thursday, January 4
San Francisco, California

San Francisco quakes. The epicentre of American instability is Haight-Ashbury, the canary in the coal mine of America's broken social discourse. Haight-Ashbury is a zone of apathy, of endless hand-rolled marijuana joints, of dropping acid, of good trips and bad, of glue-sniffing, and of hashish—a region of drugged contemplation, drugged conversation and drugged introspection, quicksand reflections that flitter into nothingness.

Their hair is long, Professor Harry Fortune thought, and bush-wild or braided, or maybe pony-tailed. They wear jeans, tie-dyed shirts, sandals and battle-free army fatigues; they say "fuck" out loud in the classroom; they talk of "offing the pigs"; they show up to class stoned; they avoid classrooms completely. Only a capitalist professor would demand a thoughtful essay. The walls of the University of California at Berkeley, Professor Harry Fortune thought, once heard reasoned arguments about weighty topics and soaked up the sweat of student anxiety at the intellectual challenges hurled at them. Did one truly absorb Kierkegaard; could one dispute Nietzsche? The present test of the current intellectual: In one hundred words or less, can you challenge authority in some new way using pointless obscenities? Who can fashion a new phrase that says *screw the establishment*?

As befitting a young professor of philosophy, Harry Fortune wore a brown corduroy sports coat with beige elbow patches, a clean pale green shirt with Levi's, sneakers with no socks; his blondish hair cascaded down, dancing off his shoulders. A peace symbol necklace dangled around his neck. He was in his third year as an undercover FBI agent charged with monitoring campus radicals.

He leaned his back against the classroom door. It clicked closed behind him but he didn't lock it as that might be received by the student body as a fascist act. He meandered down the hallways, aiming in the general direction of the parking lot, bobbing and weaving between the students. One of his students caught up to him and slung her arm through his. After a few steps she yanked him to a halt and spun him about, hugging him, pressing her breasts into his chest. "I loved that class today," she said. "You explain things so I can understand them."

"I always try."

She fiddled nervously with the buttons on her army jacket, dropped a hand, raising it, taking a sweep at her hair. "Um…Professor, how're things going with you?"

He bent over to hear her words better over the hallway bustle, over the clapping and sluffing of student sandals and the chatter and banter of students moving between classes. "Nothing but good Karma, Laurie," he said.

"Um, Lanie." She dug fingers into his arm.

"How you doing, Lanie?"

"Um, could I drop by your apartment later to discuss that Sartre paper…alone with you, one on one? Is that too brassy?"

"Not a problem," he said.

Her face beamed, perfect teeth flashing briefly, before moving off. "Be there soon," she said.

Fortune ambled down hallways, then moved on to the parking lot where he hunted for his yellow Volkswagen convertible. The peace symbol, stencilled on the car door by an FBI technician, jumped out at him as always. He didn't like the car or the stencil, thinking it overkill, but it wasn't his call. One didn't lock one's car; only a fascist would do so.

An hour later Fortune arrived at his apartment, observing a late model Mercedes Benz convertible in the visitor's parking spot. Lanie, having discarded her hippie attire, lingered in his lobby with a suede jacket draped over a shoulder, posing somewhat artfully in an expensive blouse and tailored slacks. He noted her lipstick and inhaled a whiff of perfume.

He inserted a key into an imposing, ornate oak door, evidence of a previous era, swinging it open. "Follow me," he said, turning to her. She shot peppermint breath spray into her mouth, quickly pocketing the petite container. She followed him up one flight of stairs to his apartment. Inside the apartment he slipped out of his jacket, pinching the shoulders around a kitchen chair, tweaking the material, adjusting it to avoid wrinkles. He removed his necklace, placing it on the side table, aligning it in the centre, cobra-coiling it. He gestured towards the couch. She sat down, unsure about what do with her coat, holding it against her leg.

"Trouble with the Sartre paper?" he said.

"Yeah. I can't get into grad school without a good mark, a really good mark."

"Focus on Sartre's concept that existence precedes essence."

"I don't know what that means."

"Well," Fortune said, "people fashion their own essence."

"So it's complicated."

"Your essence, for instance," Fortune said, "is not determined by the label 'student.'"

"It's my last year as a student unless a grad school accepts me."

The phone rang. Fortune shrugged an apology, removing the receiver. Before thrusting his ear to the phone, he offered up some advice: "Lanie, a person can choose to be good or choose to be bad." Her eyes perked up at that comment. She undid another button.

He answered the call. "It's me, Parker, your supervising agent," the voice on the other end of the line said.

Fortune cupped the phone, holding it tight to his ear. "Yes sir."

"You've become a hippie."

"What?" He glanced in the dining room mirror and saw Lanie undo a few more buttons of her blouse. She drew a small vial of perfume from her jacket pocket, dabbed a few spots of perfume on her chest and slid out her breath spray for one more quick shot. She leaned back on the couch, shifting about, fluffing her hair, positioning the open blouse suggestively. She undid the button on her slacks, tugging the zipper down a few inches.

"You're a hippie," Parker said. "You dress like a hippie. You drive a hippie car. You use drugs."

"My assignment. I never did drugs before the assignment. 'Do anything to win them over,' you said."

"You lost your piece."

"My gun? I filled out the form."

Fortune glanced at Lanie reclining on the couch. She smiled, teeth flashing.

"We're assigning you to Midwest operations," Parker said, "to Detroit."

"What?" Fortune slammed the receiver against the table, banging it twice. Lanie straightened. Fortune picked up the receiver again. "Detroit?" he said.

"Too bad you lost your piece."

"I filled out the form." The phone went dead; he replaced the receiver.

Lanie watched Fortune's face contort, his features tensing. "Professor, what is it?"

"Holy crap, I've been transferred."

"How does a philosophy professor get transferred?"

"Have you seen my gun?" he said.

"Are you with the fuzz?" She fumbled with her blouse, fingering buttons back into place. Her jacket slumped to the floor and she grabbed at it, rising, edging towards the door, struggling with the ivory button on her slacks, which had suddenly acquired spirit, thrusting back against her fumbling fingers. Her coat fell back to the floor.

Fortune jumped up, wrenching a dresser drawer open: shirts aligned on the left, his underwear on the right. He flung garments aside, emptying the drawer.

"Maybe I should go, Professor."

"Where is that freaking sucker?" He yanked out another dresser drawer, throwing the contents on the floor.

She finished jamming the button through. "I'm late for class, Professor." She backed out of the apartment, closing the door behind her.

Fortune paced back and forth. "Detroit bastards carry guns and beat people up. And a hard-core ghetto, with snow and freaking ice. I gotta find that gun. It's registered to me." He slammed his fist into the wall and pain ripped into him, calming him. He picked up the suede coat, smoothing it out, folding it neatly. He plunked down in one of the kitchen chairs, the jacket in his lap. "Who loses a piece?"

Later, when light in the apartment had faded: "Where am I gonna score weed in Detroit?"

Sunday, January 7
Windsor, Ontario

At 7 a.m. a 1953 Ford Victoria, avocado green with white hardtop, a missing hubcap and a piece of cardboard taped over the driver's side vent, pulled into the downtown bus station. The engine, in need of a tune-up and misfiring, smack-popped as it slowed down to the corner where Paris Day waited. Her friend Connie Harlan leaned over and opened the door for her.

A splash of crusted mud on the side of the car jogged memories in Paris. She recalled her summer with the preacher Vernon Johns and his wife in Montgomery, Alabama. She remembered the first Sunday at church with them. Outside the church his wife, Altona, chided Vernon. "You've mud from plowing on your shabby shoes and mismatched socks, and you aim to preach God's word to these people dressed no better than a farmer?"

"God cares more for souls than soles," he replied. And she remembered his wide smile and how that grin melted her concerns about rooming with a preacher man with shoulders wide like a truck. Vernon Johns in that short comment gave off the same comfort-feeling that her father imparted. After a few weeks Vernon called her to him. "Come close, child," he said. She was skinny and she knew she was skinny and ugly to boot. His head was large and his hands the size of shovels but she was not afraid of him, not even when he was cross. "Why did your papa, Mayhem," he said, "send you to us for the summer?"

"Papa thinks I follow a white boy too much."

"Why do you do it, child, if your papa disapproves?"

"I follow the boy's blue eyes. Something in his eyes calls out to me." Vernon waggled his head at her words, already thinking of something else. She was unsure if he even heard her. He stared to the sky and she stared at him. The whisker stubble on his chin glinted grey. Moments of silence dwelled between them. "You preach about passages from the Bible," she said, "but you never read the good book at night."

"I have my own way of following, child," he replied, "and I've poor eyes. I remember the words that stir me. I can repeat them exactly as I hear them in my mind. Words that stir me remain with me forever." He tapped a finger to his temple.

At dinner each night, Vernon offered a brief blessing but he never preached; his wife or his summer guest directed the talk. "Papa says you read Greek," Paris said, "and German and Latin as well as you read English."

"I would spend all of my days reading Greek if my eyesight permitted."

"Papa says you taught yourself without teachers mostly, that you read books while plowing."

"The mule tolerates me doing this," he said, chuckling at his own joke. He reached for a bun and stabbed his knife into the butter bowl, slabbing a chunk onto the bun. "Every minute in life gives an opportunity," he said. He munched but after a bite placed his half-eaten bun on the table. "Teachers don't always have diplomas or school credits, child. Teachers are those with something to give you. They don't charge you and you may not recognize the lesson at the time."

On one occasion she travelled with him when he rode the train north to preach. His wife tucked blocks of cheese into a leather case and packed quarts of milk on ice in preparation. "There's no service to coloured people in many places so you've only the food I'm fixing up." Altona whispered for Paris alone, dragging the child in to her. "And tend to the bathroom, at every chance," she said. Paris bobbed her head up and down. "You hear me child," Altona repeated, "at every chance."

Vernon travelled with a grocery paper bag that contained his clothes, underwear and a shirt, previously worn. Paris carried her own small suitcase, roaming near to him whenever she could, sucking in the smell of sweat and a masculine smell that comforted her. When Vernon preached, shivers cantered up and down her spine. I must remember his words, she thought. No one preaches like the Reverend Johns. But he left one lesson with her that she never forgot, a lesson taught outside of church. After one sermon they waited for a bus. When it arrived, Vernon entered the bus and purchased two tickets from the driver. Paris crowded behind him, clinging to him. The white bus driver said, "Grab a seat in the back."

Vernon set his paper bag down. "Return my money, sir. I do not wish to ride in the back of the bus." Paris froze, shrinking back, thinking they might be arrested or beaten or maybe lynched. Vernon placed his hand on the dash; it flattened out, swallowing up the area. The bus driver took note. He gave back Vernon's money.

As the bus disappeared from sight, Paris said, "What do we do now?"

"It's only seven miles to the next town, child."

"I was afraid on the bus."

"Did being afraid help you, child?"

Paris thought about his words. "Being afraid won't solve a problem," she said.

Vernon dipped his head to her and he set off down the road in slow, steady steps, spouting passages in a language she did not understand. She jumped up and chased after him. "My legs aren't so long as yours," she called after him.

In the parking lot of the Windsor bus station Paris stuck out a foot, using her shoe to scrape a chunk of mud from the Ford. She popped into the front seat, waving a greeting to her friend, Connie Harlan.

***

At 8 a.m. Aiken woke, bathed in sweat. He rolled over. His eyes focused on the bleak snout of the Webley camping on the nightstand, a few inches from his face. *What the hell?* He stowed the weapon out of sight. He fumbled his way downstairs. Nightmare gloom plastered him down but the compulsion to perform his Sunday ritual bubbled deep, a ritual he refused to discuss or acknowledge, a ritual filling something not entirely understood. He prepared no breakfast, whipping up a pot of coffee, juicing it with a few shots of Bushmills Black. He carried the pot, a cup and his Hudson's Bay blanket to the front porch. He found the Sunday edition of the Detroit Free Press wedged between the railings. He adjusted the Adirondack chair slightly, plopping down into it. He wiggled his butt to get comfy and snuggled up in the blanket while wrestling out the sports section. He pressed the newspaper against his nose, sucking in the inky-wood smell of newsprint before rifling up stories about the Tigers or the Red Wings. *Show up, you church-going bastards, I'm ready for you.*

Church-goers passed by his front porch every Sunday, making their way to their various places of prayer. Parade by me you peckers, he thought, seek out those church-blessed green stamps or saviour credits or whatever they give you in church that's redeemable when you pop a gasket and exit this world. Most people fit into two groups, he thought: the save-the-worlders, which his wife, Paris belonged to, and the save-my-own-assers, which the church-goers belonged to, a group that Paris maintained he also belonged to. Actually, he thought, I harbour no real fondness for either group. There must be a third group, my genuine group, the don't-give-a-rat's-assers group. I don't give a rat's ass about most junk. Paris thinks I never asked friends over because my family was black. Maybe I asked but they begged off. With help from Paris's teaching job we bought a house on Victoria Avenue and I moved in my black family. Surprise, neighbours! Your house values just tanked, so that might explain the cork up your ass. But even so, who among you sanctimonious people welcomed my family, my black family.

Oh right, no one.

Today I see mixed-race couples, he thought, and a measure of tolerance. But not after the war, not in '45 or '46. Black was black, white was white and the two mustn't mix. Sitting on the porch, he felt the prison camp sweats swinging in, clouting him down. Gloomy shadows hovered over but the sweats kept him warm in the chilled air. *Let the parade begin.* No longer able to make out the printed words jumbling about the page, he fiddled the newspaper closed, collapsing the mess over his lap.

At 9 a.m. the first pilgrim family arrived, the bloke marching properly on the curbside, mustache precisely waxed, pink cheeks glistening, wearing a tightly stretched, fading, three-piece brown suit with a vest firmly buttoned to control a pitching, bobbing stomach. His white trench coat flapped, snapping—a subversive, warning sound.

I hear you, Mr. Churchgoer.

His wife followed a dutiful stride behind, modest black hat tilting, veil fluffing, imitation fur coat to the waist, ass-slamming girdle in place, restraining her buttocks, her flabby asscheeks firmly under control for the morning's outing. Both parents shone with perspiration so bountiful that it defined them. Three meek children, all boys, followed, with brown clothes and worn coats, unpolished shoes, hair greased and cowed down, totally slickered up and grim-faced.

The couple spun their heads, bobbing politely to Aiken as they crossed in front of him. The Black Bush kicked in. He waved a greeting, lip-ends moving upwards, imitating a smile. "Good day to you," Aiken said. *Good day, fat Mister, and to you, the fat Missus who will never blow away in a windstorm and good day to you, three future hoodlums.* "Good praying day," Aiken called out. "Good praying day for tolerant people everywhere." *Yes, black people reside here.* Both parents dipped their heads to him again. The oily boys drummed along behind in silence, faces down.

You religious people plod up and down the street on your way to your churches all clean and spanky, all scrubbed to the nines, a big factor in having souls saved. Where were you people of the cloth when Paris and I sought friends after the war? Who among you allowed your children to play with my black children? Was God on vacation in '45? Not yet back from the war?

I know the awful lesson from Dieppe. In the beginning some men in Stalag 8B held hope, praying to God, thinking God was listening, thinking God would act, some men keeping hope even when the months stretched into years. Maybe God just needed some time to sort things out, so much happening in the war and all, still thinking God would save them. But with the hours and months wearing on, buddies dying, buddies dying, buddies dying, came the knowing, the awful knowing. We were alone in Stalag 8B. There is no God, just survival, eating the food you scratch up. Alive on Monday? Don't count on Tuesday.

Uncork the wine, down snorts of liquor, sleep with someone, anyone, grab someone's ass while your fingers still function, before your dick degenerates to pus and gangrene. Play grabby-ass. In time the grabbing ceases, the digits rot and fall off, chucked into garbage cans, transported to the city dump by Union City workers unhappy with their lot, just killing time. He tugged his head up and down as another family spun into view. "Good praying day!"

Christ, Aiken: Could you be more depressed? Where in hell is Paris?

At 10 a.m. the '53 Ford parked across the street. The engine fired off a pop that sounded like a gunshot. Aiken remained on the porch steps wrapped in the blanket, quietly now, sweats banished, the newspaper's sport's section spread across his lap, blanket tucked tight. Paris dropped out of the front passenger door, leaving two women inside the vehicle. When he saw his wife, Aiken's heart perked up. But instead of her usual jeans and sweatshirt she wore an unbuttoned, pearl-grey wool overcoat, and underneath a dark grey skirt and a fine silky blouse. And she wore heels. Not a real typical Paris Day outfit, he thought.

As she closed on the porch he noted the string of pearls, the matching earrings. When she was a young girl, he thought her pretty, extraordinarily pretty, but now she showed not so much pretty as noticeable, still attractive, with bold features and darting eyes, eyes always searching; more like a filled-out woman now, handsome but an anchor. *She fusses down the pretty these days. A political strategy?*

The sky darkened with sombre clouds rumbling about. Snowflakes appeared. Her fingers twisted in a wave to him as she approached the porch. Aiken dumped the newspaper to the side, pulling himself up and bumping down, dragging the blanket with him, plopping his butt down to a lower tread. She paused in front of him. Crispness in the air ate up the sweat on his brow. *She smells like saltwater toffee should smell but doesn't.* "Gussied up for a funeral?" he said.

"Saying your normal Sunday hello to all of our religious neighbours?" She held out a palm, catching snowflakes, whiteness melting into darkness. "Be home in two or three days, Blue-eyes."

"Not tonight?"

"Got business in Michigan, that's all, but I'll be home soon. Now you've escaped Stalag 8B we must make plans." Her eyes wandered the yard but quickly spun back to him, whirl-pooled into his blue eyes. For a few seconds he thought she might discard her plans. The two figures in the car were hidden from him, shadowy silhouettes only. She tapped his arm, rubbing it, preparing to leave. "Lay in some wine, Blue-eyes."

"Coals to Newcastle, woman. Your friends in the car have time for a beer?"

She bit into her bottom lip. "They're fine. They're tough."

Tough? "Why tough?"

She swept a finger down her pebbled wool coat. "It's a white, white world. Black people need to be tough, tough and vigilant, always vigilant. But things improve. This year might be a good year for serious change."

"And maybe pig-shit is tasty as hell."

She flung back another one his maxims: "And I bet it's a good praying day." Silence drifted over them, stretching between them, failing to comfort him, leaving him with a spot of anxiety. *What's going on, Missy?*

"The children fine?" she said.

"Yeah, fine. Come home for Sarah. One parent is only half enough."

"I should get to know her better. She needs a full-time mom."

"And the nonstop, red-hot sex?"

She slapped his leg at that comment. "Yes, Blue-eyes, nonstop and red-hot. I miss you."

"Can you delay this business?"

"Attending university is a good beginning for you."

"We can talk about school, Missy," he said. "Can you put off this thing?"

She started back down the sidewalk. "I've committed," she said, "In Grosse Pointe tomorrow morning. Won't be long."

He called after her, "Could they do this without you?"

She twirled about. "We can talk about it?" she said. "That's what you said."

"Ah, Paris…"

She stepped towards him. "Show me your class schedule."

"What?"

"If you signed up, you'd have a class schedule."

"We'll talk about this."

"You lying bastard," she said, "You never intended to enroll." She stomped towards the car.

She's traipsing back to her world of civil rights, back to her two tough black women. He felt an urge to chase her down, but didn't. Waste of time, he thought. *She's got to save the goddamn world. A knitting Penelope she is not.* He rustled up the newspaper and blanket, dumping the remaining coffee over the side of the porch. *Fight shadows on your own, Aiken Day. Give the Webley away; donate it to a suicide-prone youngster who can't afford a gun. Here, kid, have a good praying day. Throw some papers down so your mom doesn't have to clean up brain splatter.*

Thursday, January 11
Federal Building, Detroit, Michigan

The Federal Building on Gratiot Avenue housed Detroit's Internal Revenue Service. The directory on the first floor listed the various departments and occupants, showing an empty fourth floor. The fourth floor, in fact, housed agents of the Federal Bureau of Investigation operating in the City of Detroit. Roland Feeber, Agent-in-Charge, ruled an empire of twenty-three covert agents, all white males. A bulky, aging jock running to flab, large hands scarred with battle-flattened knuckles, he ruled with minimal oversight, reporting directly to J. Edgar Hoover and no one else.

A thin woman cautiously wormed into Feeber's office carrying a box of donuts, flipping the lid up, inviting him to choose. He plucked a Boston cream. She shuddered once more at the sight of his knuckles, pointing, finally gaining the courage to ask. "What happened to those?"

He bumped down the doughnut before answering. "They sorta grow like that when you begin as a prison guard keeping slime-bags under control." She turned away with the donut box. "I didn't buy them for the office," he said.

"I used petty cash," she said.

"Park the box and go file some files or type a few words, whatever you do all day."

She left the box, slamming the door behind her. Feeber's phone rang and he crammed the receiver into his ear. His fingers snaked out towards the box, grabbing a second Boston Cream. He stuffed it, python-like, into his mouth with a finger, munching with purpose but in no hurry. When the donut choked down, he crabbed into the phone, "What?"

"Rizzuto here, Chief. That black chick on our radar…"

Feeber used a knobby finger to swab chocolate from his lips, sucking on it briefly.

"Yeah, Paris Day. You locate her?"

"Had a blow-up in a Grosse Pointe bank…her and two other black girls. One girl blown away, whole face shot off."

Feeber reached out for another donut. "Burr-heads in a Grosse Pointe bank?"

"Civil rights bunk. Our agent panicked. Paris Day may be alive, maybe shot, can't say for sure, several shots banged off, people screaming, diving for cover. No one knows jack shit. I'm guessing here: she's probably in hiding or bleeding to death in someone's basement."

"I run Detroit," Feeber said. "No one does civil rights shit here. Kick their butts down to Georgia for that crap."

"And Chief…"

"What else?" Feeber said.

"That new long-haired agent from Haight-Ashbury is covering."

"Harry Fortune?"

"Yeah."

"Fuck the scene up good and proper," Feeber said, "so no one knows what happened." He sorted through the donut box, tossing a donut with sprinkles into the garbage can. "Spread the news that Paris Day died," he said. "Who can tell one burr-head from another? Put a contract on the broad and offer up some decent money."

"The list?"

"Yeah, add her to the list."

"Consider it done, Chief."

"And keep that dipshit in the dark," Feeber said, "until I decide if he's a hippie."

* * *

Special Agent Rizzuto hung up the phone and turned about, facing Harry Fortune. Rizzuto's beefy face lit up and he smiled at Fortune. Fortune plucked at his wool pea coat, fingers twitching, scratching at the buttons. "What'd the boss say?"

Rizzuto's lips cut deeper. "He says cut your hair, Miss Pussy, before one of the real agents tries to fuck you."

"Holy crap. I've been undercover at Berkeley for three freaking years."

"Go look for clues, Miss Pussy."

Saturday, January 13
Windsor, Ontario

At 7 a.m. when Aiken awoke, the weather outside blew stink, and windows clattered from bursting wind gusts, causing him to shiver; he dragged on a sweatshirt and sweatpants in hopes of more warmth. He hauled on wool winter socks, socks too thick and itchy to wear in warm weather, and he crammed his toes under the bedroom radiator, placing his hands above it, bending over, keeping his fingers inches above the rad. Gazing out the window, his eyes wandered about the street and fixed on the small car parked across the way. The grim light spinning from the streetlight slanted across the automobile, casting outsized sharp shadows, making the vehicle look bleak and foreboding in the swirling snow. The heat from the rad suddenly scorched his feet. He withdrew them, tucking on slippers. Downstairs he opened the inside front door, removing the damp, wedged-in morning *Free Press*. He observed the small car, a Volkswagen Beetle, still parked across the street, its motor running, exhaust smoking.

Weaving through the living room, Aiken smelled the acidic taint of last evening's fire wisping from the fireplace, tickling his nostrils. In the kitchen he plugged the kettle in, dumping coffee into the filter, hauling out the Bushmills. He heard Adam moving about upstairs and on an impulse slid his fingers across his brow; they came away sweat-free so he tucked the Bushmills back in the cupboard and plopped down at the kitchen table and sipped coffee, hickory flavoured with a hint of vanilla. He scanned stories on the front page, cupping one hand over the mug, sucking in the heat.

The stairs squeaked as someone bundled down, thumping the steps. Adam, six foot three and one-half inches tall, grunted a morning greeting to Aiken and wrapped fingers around Aiken's neck and bent over him.

Hello world, this is my son, Adam: a husky sort, with his grandpa Mayhem's shoulders, only taller, maybe four inches taller. He sucks the light out of every doorway he passes through, causing a brief doorway eclipse. But does he possess Mayhem's steady demeanor, his composure under fire? Doubtful at his age.

Adam sniffed the air in front of Aiken, testing for the smell of alcohol as he normally did, not offending Aiken. *He does it for me. Checking out how my day is going.*

"No sweats today, Pops? Bushmills all tucked away." His snowplow-sized hands rubbed Aiken's neck, messaging it for a few seconds.

"I might live for another day," Aiken said. "No babysitting needed." He slapped a hand against Adam's back, more of a caress than a guy-slap. *I'm a lucky bastard. I have a kid who'll shoot baskets with me or whip a baseball back and forth on the days that the devils plough in. He gives up his life for mine on those days.*

Adam popped four slices of white Wonder Bread into the toaster before sprawling across one of the hardwood kitchen chairs, causing the chair to mostly disappear. He wore a sweatshirt from the University of Western Ontario and busted-in blue jeans. After a few seconds the musty smell of toasting bread drifted over to Aiken.

"Gonna make first string?" Aiken said. A first-year student at Western might not make the starting lineup or even the team. "'Less they brain-dead," Adam said. "Been hitting better from the line. Coach not shooting daggers at me."

"Classes going okay?"

The toast popped. Adam buttered the slices before smearing peach jam thickly on each piece. Each piece of toast dwarfed down as his hand scooped it up. He could dominate a room because of his size but always chose not to; his infectious way of smile-speaking usually accomplished the same thing. When he grins you forget he's a giant, Aiken thought. *God, but you remind me of Mayhem some times.*

"Acoustics bad in here?" Aiken said. "Toast fog your brain? Are classes going okay?"

"I'm not Mom and I'm not Sarah. I'm more like you and Gramps. Learning stuff isn't easy—doing stuff is easier. Classes is just something you gotta do to stay on the team, Pops. That's all."

"Do you have a plan for your life?" Aiken said.

Adam finished the fourth piece of toast and sucked on his finger, licking crumbs and jam away. "Do you have a plan, Pops," he said, "for your life?" He dropped more bread slices into the toaster.

"The topic of this conversation is you," Aiken said.

"After you raise us two up, what are you gonna do, Pops? Spend your days and nights sweating to death, hoping for help in a bottle?"

"After university...what?"

"Mom ain't coming home," Adam said, "and your ass-kicking nightmares ain't gonna go away unless you get help or find something to do with your life."

"Let's keep this conversation about you."

"There's time yet. They can drop someone on the moon; they can get me a decent job."

"If you don't get a decent education, don't worry, you can still inflate basketballs for a living as an assistant coach of tobogganing, or pump gas."

"Don't know what's worse," Adam said. He stooped over the toaster and waved heat into his face. "You with straight coffee or you with boozed coffee."

Sarah spun into the room, jumping onto Aiken's lap, slinging an arm around his neck, pecking at his cheek, smelling his breath. "Morning, Daddy." Her vanilla smell drifted into Aiken. Like her brother, she wore jeans and a sweatshirt. Adam cuffed his sister on the head playfully and rubbed her neck. The toast popped. He buttered and jammed up the second set. She slipped into a chair. "Some for me?"

"Growing boy here, sis." But he smiled, reaching out, pressing a piece of toast towards her. The toast shrank back to normal size in her hand. She chewed on the slice slowly, shooting for dainty, not quite achieving it, settling for girlish.

"Be warned," Adam said to Sarah, "Pops has no sweats today. Gonna fix up the world beginning with you and me. You probably gotta quit school, get a job in construction." Sarah moved back to Aiken and threw her arms about him, kissing him on the cheek. "I could build beautiful houses," she said. *I should do sober at breakfast more often.*

* * *

Outside their house snow flurries continued to beat down, sweeping against the Volkswagen, snow collecting on the hood but not on the car side panels, the stencilled peace sign still visible. The snow dappled into water against the windshield. Fortune hunched inside the car with the heater blasting, the wipers switched off, occasionally glancing at his watch. Water trickled through a tear in the convertible's roof, splattering on his shoulder, cold splashes bouncing against the side of his neck, unfelt. A canvas bag balanced in his lap. His fingers gripped it tight and he slid the contents back and forth, producing a rasping sound. He paused and fingered out pearl earrings but quickly threw them back into the bag.

"You get this," he muttered out loud, "from a freaking dead coloured girl who tried to rob a bank in a rich white suburb." He dropped the bag onto the seat, swiping at the ice drips on his neck for the first time. "And exactly where in the hell do you get good grass in Detroit if you work for the freaking FBI?" He slammed his fist against the dash and decided to break the news about Paris Day to her family.

* * *

The doorbell to Aiken's home rang and Adam tumbled out to the front hall to answer it, returning in a few seconds. "Guy on the front porch with a tie, Pops," he said. "Alert, Pops: guy with a tie, guy with a tie." He grabbed the orange juice bottle from the fridge, uncapped it and drank straight from the bottle, juice sluicing down his chin. He swiped his face dry with the arm of his sweatshirt. *I should probably make some sort of parenting comment here.*

"What're you gonna do with someone who owns a tie, Pops?" Adam said. "Make him into a banker after Sarah finds a job in construction?"

Aiken crossed through the dining room and front hall, reaching the door, observing the figure on his porch. Both kids remained behind him. He opened the inside door but left the outside door latch on. The wind slammed into the storm door, rattling it, making snapping noises.

"What is it?" Aiken said. He noted the attire of the man before him, seeing a classic, starched-up authority figure: trench coat belted against the weather, dark suit, spanking new white shirt poking out, striped tie neatly tucked in, blond hair clipped short, almost a brush cut, his face tanned, with a whitish band of pale skin circling the hair line. A muscle twitched in his neck.

"Can I come inside, sir?" Snow flurries danced in the air behind him. "Please let me inside, sir?" *What the hell are you selling? Jehovah's Witness? Mormon?*

"It's freezing out," Sarah said. "Invite him in."

Aiken unlatched the door and the man skipped inside. Aiken smelled cologne, the cheap imported type a barber might slap on a freshly-barbered neck. Sarah ignored her two male family members, taking charge, leading the way into the living room, taking a chair, motioning the stranger to a chair, indicating that he should be seated. *Taking charge: shades of Paris.*

The man glanced at Aiken, who shrugged. The two men found seats. Adam reclined against the kitchen doorway, munching on a last piece of toast.

"I'm trying to find the husband of Paris Day."

"Paris is my wife," Aiken said.

"No, this Paris Day is a black woman."

Silence buckled over the room. Aiken watched as Fortune suddenly took note of the presence of two black people. His face sagged.

"Paris is my wife," Aiken said.

"I'm Agent Harry Fortune. I'm in Detroit from Berkeley."

"We have insurance."

"FBI agent," Fortune said. "I should speak to you privately."

"What do you want?"

"It's bad news."

Aiken saw Adam straighten up. The doorway behind him shrunk.

"Bail money for Paris?" Aiken said. "Some sort of civil rights protest?"

Adam's face muscles tightened. "You hunting for my mom?" The toast in Adam's hand crumpled as his fingers turned into a fist, the withered crusts dropping to the floor. Unease trickled into Aiken, suddenly sharpening; knifing into him. "Tell me," he said. His words rasped out.

"FBI agents," Fortune said, "shot and killed your wife in Grosse Pointe, Michigan, during an armed bank robbery."

"What?" Aiken said. *You killed Paris.*

Adam shouted, "You lying bastard." He flew at Fortune who started to rise. Adam knocked him out of the chair, wrestling him to the ground, straddling him, clamping his hands around Fortune's throat, clutching and choking him. "You damn liar!"

Sarah jumped on Adam's back, wrapping her arms about his neck. "Adam, don't!"

She's dead? Paris is dead and this bastard killed her.

Fortune's face turned red. Adam pressed his fingers tighter and tighter. Spittle dribbled from Fortune's lips and his leg twitched, slamming up and down against the floor. Sarah jumped up and slapped at Aiken. "Do something, Daddy."

Yeah, do something, Aiken. Aiken knelt down and cloaked himself around Adam, placing his hands over his son's hands, prying away a thumb, bending and jerking at it until he broke the hold. Adam's fingers whipped away uselessly and Fortune snaked out from under him, scrambling out the front door. Adam pushed up, spilling Aiken to the floor.

"They killed Mom," Adam said. "I should've killed him, Pops. He ain't a good guy just because he's white." *What?*

Sarah flopped down on the floor, crying.

"Sarah," Aiken said, "Call your grandpa Mayhem." *He'll know what to do.*

The crumpled piece of toast caught Sarah's eye. She hunched over, scraping jam off the floor using a tissue from her pocket, scraping at it for several seconds with her finger, and the scratching sounds dominated the room. "Mom can't be dead," she said. She cupped the tissue with jam and toast crumbs in her palm.

Adam finally plucked the tissue away from her, chucking it into the kitchen garbage. He returned and fell down into one of the living room chairs, hands on his face, elbows on his knees. "What'll we do, Pops?"

"We sit tight," Aiken said. "If it's true, we deal with it."

"You mean maybe he was lying."

"Or mistaken."

Adam rubbed his thumb. "You might've broke my thumb. Can't make first string with a broken thumb."

"You can't kill people," Aiken said, "not even FBI agents. A stupid rule, sometimes, but still a rule."

"Mommy's not dead," Sarah said.

"We call Gramps," Adam said. "We should call Gramps."

Aiken rubbed a hand on his son's knee, patting it. "Yeah, that's good. I'll call Mayhem." *How do I tell him that his only daughter might be dead?*

Aiken dialled Mayhem's number. It rang repeatedly but no one answered. He tried throughout the day but still no answer. The three of them remained captive in the house, the day overspread with gloom.

"Shouldn't we do something?" Adam said, not for the first time.

Aiken pressed the receiver down again. "Not without your grandpa."

Aiken's sweats picked up but he left the Bushmills in the cupboard. Sarah wiped his forehead occasionally with a towel. At six o'clock the phone rang and Aiken picked up the receiver.

"It's me," Fortune said, "Agent Harry Fortune. I have your wife's belongings. I'll meet you somewhere without that freaking big dude."

Multiple thoughts blasted through Aiken but after a few seconds he reined the dangerous bubbles in. "The Bridge House Tavern, by the university, in fifteen minutes." *I used to go there with Paris.* He lowered the receiver down gently. *I've never been there without Paris.* Aiken cuffed Adam on the shoulder in a mechanical motion and kissed Sarah on the forehead. "Keep calling your grandpa," he said, "I've an errand." Sarah cried, sobbing into the towel reserved for Aiken's sweats. *This FBI bastard knows something about Paris.*

Saturday, January 13
Bridge House Tavern, Windsor, Ontario

The University of Windsor, established in 1857 as Assumption College, a Catholic oasis in Anglican Upper Canada that would later rechristen itself Assumption University, banged up against the Detroit River to the north. Two windowless taverns relied upon the student body for patronage, one to the east of the campus, one to the west, each separately owned and operated by men named Syd.

To the west stood the ancient Dominion House Tavern, a historic structure established in 1878, possessing a kitchen, putting up meals—burgers, fried fish and chicken dishes—flapping out tablecloths and housing an array of beers, fine liqueurs and numerous wines. The "DH" Syd wore sports coats with neckties. He functioned as a greeter, a welcoming soul, summoning wait-staff, arranging tables, scrutinizing the preparation of food and the delicate dispensing of wine.

To the east of the university lay the Bridge House Tavern, an establishment possessing no kitchen, serving chips and snacks, pickled beets, hardboiled eggs, and beef jerky. Waiters circulated among the cramped sea of laminated two-foot-square tables and plain-functioning chairs, balancing trays of regulation glasses, each standardized glass filled with one imperial pint of draft beer. This tavern operated under the watchful eyes of the other Syd, a man who worked in a short-sleeved shirt and durable permanent-press slacks. He perched behind the counter, biceps bulging, minding the bar, hovering over the cash box.

During her tenure as a professor of political science, Paris favoured the Bridge House, routinely rejecting the westerly choice. "The Bridge House is a working-class saloon," she explained, "no pretense, no dishing up triple-stacked burgers with melted cheese, fake friendliness and tossed salads slopped about with bottled dressing. It's a draft beer joint run by a publican who watches that you pay your tab and doesn't give a whit if you like him. What you see is what you get. I empathize with that. The same thing drew me to you, Blue-eyes."

Aiken parked his car on Bridge Avenue, sliding it into a spot a block away from the hotel. The street, wrinkled in snow-blots, possessed only one functioning streetlight, which stood close to the tavern. Outside the hotel, three men mixed it up in the pale light, their puffs of breath visible in the chilled air. Boots and fists flew, the fight ranging back and forth. Aiken heard muted combat sounds: few words, heavy breathing, occasional wheezes, feet slapping and scraping against the pavement as the men lunged forwards, then backwards.

A heavyset man, sporting thin legs for such a stocky fellow, weaved side to side, bobbing like a prizefighter. "Come to Papa, Moon Doggie," he said, grumbling these words at a slim, long-haired student in a greasy sweatshirt who danced about, trying to avoid fists. "Woof, woof! Come to Daddy!"

As Aiken watched, a new sound dominated. The prizefighter's partner, a shorter man wielding lawn shears, jabbed the scissors at the slim student, snipping at him.

Does he mean to cut his hair or chop up his face?

The blades opened and snapped shut, time after time, metal against metal, harsh grinding snips that Aiken heard but tried to ignore. "Move a little closer, hippie," the shorter man said, "the barber wants you." The shears sliced, just missing the hippie's face. "The barber wants to shave you."

Two against one, and the hippie is about played out.

A strong yearning flooded Aiken's whole body, urging flight, urging him to climb back into his car and escape, to bolt the squalid scene. *I need to know about Paris.* He opened the trunk of his car, rummaging for a weapon in case the men tried to drag him into their fray. The sounds of snipping clanked up; the steel snaps ate into him.

The trunk contained a toy bat, about fifteen inches long, given to Adam years ago. Aiken stroked the bat, a hardwood affair with a smooth satin finish. *Not even a real bat—finished up more like a furniture piece. Who stole the stupid tire iron?* He closed the trunk and the lid snapped tight. His eyes wandered back to the fight scene. The prizefighter landed a solid blow; the hippie staggered back. Aiken strode towards the tavern, keeping the bat at his side, out of sight, moving to the side of the street away from the fight. The snips kept grinding out a message that he ignored.

The fight shifted to the sidewalk, where Aiken paced with the bat still concealed, strung down aside his leg. "Help me out, pal," the hippie called to Aiken. Aiken shook him off but his eyes fastened on the garden shears, still snipping away. *Not my affair, you long-haired freak.*

The fight lurched sideways, drifting towards Aiken now, blocking his path. *Get away from me, assholes.* The hippie danced to the side, avoiding a blow.

The prizefighter turned to Aiken. "Don't stick your dick in this," he said. The man's eyes, dark and cold, reinforced the warning. He stumbled towards Aiken pushing close. Aiken smelled garlic and squelched the urge spit out at the stench. The man swung at him, his fist bouncing against Aiken's chest, knocking him back. In a reflex action, Aiken struck back with the bat. The prizefighter clutched his head, falling down to the curb. A large purple lump appeared instantly and swelled, widening out, visible between his spread-out, fleshy fingers. The man blubbered nonsense, words unintelligible to Aiken.

Why did I hit him so hard? Aiken shushed him. "Quiet, sport, you'll draw the cops."

The hippie seized the remaining assailant, flung the shears aside, grabbed the man's throat and slugged away at his face with his free fist until the man broke free and ran, his face showing cuts and blood.

The blubbering in front of Aiken continued. *Whoa! The cops! Hide the evidence. He might die.* Aiken ran back to his car, stowing the bat into the trunk behind the spare, discovering the tire iron. *Where were you, Mr. Goddamn Tire Iron, when your help might have saved me, you damn coward?*

When he revisited the scene of the battle, all three men had vanished. *Wasn't there some sort of battle here? Am I in some sort of* Twilight Zone *episode?*

***

Ontario, the virtuous heartland of Canada, retained antiquated tavern laws and customs, outmoded standards to many, positively archaic compared to Michigan's loose ways. Taverns retained a "Ladies and Escorts" side, where a chap could sip a beer if accompanied by a woman, and a men's side. The Bridge House possessed a common area in front of the bar, a no-mans-land, gender-wise. Behind the bar Syd minded the taps, guarding the cash box, as always. Aiken proceeded into the Bridge House. He entered through the mixed side, as if with Paris. The room, as always, screamed *ugly* to him. *Did no one ever think to change the wallpaper or buy a Tiffany lamp? Could you throw a stupid rug down somewhere or hang up a Picasso print? Here's a thought: put a heating vent in the men's john or maybe paint the urinal fluorescent orange so the drugged-up hippies aim better. Relax Aiken, it is what it is.*

Room navigation was slow and meandering, snake-like. Privacy arrived courtesy of room buzz and of people focused on other things: law students arguing case law; poli-sci majors debating politics;

students flirting, with some craving flirtation, some tolerating it. Those without parents of means caged drinks or nursed them. Those with parents of means bought rounds; everyone overindulged. The jumbled smell was the smell of every student pub: people chewing and smoking, reefer-smoke drifting from the toilet areas, beer flatulence, student sweat, uncertainty—an ocean of uncertainty.

Aiken's hands shook. He crammed them into his coat pockets, balling his fingers into fists, crushing his fingers until pain struck, seeking to rid himself of the shakes before he met the FBI agent. He drifted between tables, aiming towards the front in zigzag fashion. Harry Fortune was alone, sitting at a table a few feet from the bar. He wore jeans and an unbuttoned navy pea coat, with an orange silk scarf spun about his neck, snaking artfully down his chest. A man roosted on a bar stool with his back to Fortune three feet away.

Aiken dropped down into a chair, facing the agent. An American ten-dollar bill lay on the table, placed squarely in front of Fortune. The waiter balanced a tray of beer, giving off no greeting. "Syd charges ten percent on Yank money," he said. Fortune nodded. The waiter bent low, scooped up the bill, dropping two glasses of draft, dropping Canadian change in coins and bills. Fortune pushed one beer at Aiken, leaving the other one standing before him. The foam settled, the beer level creeping up but not quite reaching the etched line on the glass, something to trigger the law in years past. Fortune did not notice; Aiken ignored the travesty.

"Holy crap, man," Fortune said. His voice croaked. Aiken noted the slim river of red bruising showing under the scarf. "That was frightening. I'm never gonna deliver bad news again. That freaking dude wanted to kill me."

Aiken sipped beer. The taste of cold pea soup blasted into his mouth, the second sip moderating, improving the taste. He sipped a third time before responding, the beer now sweet, and a familiar friend. "What's the world coming to," Aiken said, "when people get riled up when you kill their family?"

"I never killed anyone," Fortune said. "Never even fired a gun."

"My wife's belongings?"

Fortune lifted up the canvas bag, sliding it across the table to Aiken. "I fired at targets but wasn't good." He licked his lips. "Just enough to qualify."

Aiken's fingers brushed across the pebbled canvas bag, feeling fabric bumps but also the lumpy contents. He found the zipper unwieldy, stiff. He worked it back and forth until it slit open. Peering into the bag, he tilted the satchel up, moving it back and forth. The contents bounced about. He dipped inside the bag and fingered a pearl earring, holding it up to the light.

Fortune sipped his beer, eyes on Aiken. "If she had money," he said, "or real expensive stuff, someone scooped it before I got to the bag."

Aiken dropped the earring back into the bag. "So, someone maybe stole her things, but not you." Fortune nodded. "Tell me," Aiken said, "tell me how my wife died."

"Bank robbery, two other gals got away, maybe shot up...blood everywhere, bank statements all over the freaking floor."

"A stickup gone bad?"

Fortune looked away. "A real freaking bad situation."

"Your name again?"

"Harry Fortune."

"Where's my wife?"

"Wayne County Morgue." Fortune sipped at his beer. "But it's messy...unpleasant."

"Unpleasant?"

"Don't view the body. Someone else should do that."

Aiken peered into the bag again, his fingers dipping inside once more, sloshing the contents about. "So we bolt down the casket lid."

"Yeah." Fortune bent his head away. "I'm sorry about this." The few seconds of silence between them appeared to bother him. "I miss Berkeley," he said. "I hate goddamn Detroit."

"She never robbed banks," Aiken said. But another thought occurred to him. "You find a gun?"

"No, I didn't. But I gotta go." Fortune scooped up the money from the table, checking the bills and coins, frowning when he noticed the Canadian bills.

"Good anywhere in Canada," Aiken said, "not so much in the Belgian Congo."

Fortune fussed out a wallet and arranged the bills neatly inside it, leaving the change on the table. He wrapped his scarf about, adjusting it, hiding the bruising, and did up the buttons on his coat one at a time. "Sorry about your wife, but robbing banks is dangerous."

Aiken sipped on his beer, the liquid level dipping to the bottom third of the glass. "Nice scarf." He swiped foam from his lips with his tongue. "A strangling sort of scarf. Very pretty."

Fortune froze for a second. "The kind of clothes sold in Haight-Ashbury," he said.

Fortune poked the last button tight. The scarf nudged over his collar, a gently choking necklace of orange silk. He left. When he disappeared, Aiken swept the coins off the table. They clattered on the floor.

The man sitting in front of the bar, making conversation with Syd, swung about, grabbing the chair vacated by Fortune. "Who was that turkey?" he said.

What? After a few seconds, Aiken said, "FBI agent."

"Can you believe him? The FBI kills your wife and he pops for one dog-fart beer." He jabbed out his hand to Aiken.

Aiken recognized the long-haired hippie from the fight outside. "You're Moon Doggie."

"Actually, I'm Chester. I'm in law school." Aiken reached, grasping the outstretched hand and, when Chester winced, rolled it over, seeing blood on his knuckles. Chester caught the waiter's eye and stuck up two fingers. "You are...?" Chester said.

"Aiken Day."

"You're real hero material, buddy—the way you waded in when you saw me in trouble."

Aiken drained his glass. "No problem, Moon Doggie."

"You saved my bacon."

Chester appeared to be in his early twenties. He wore jeans and sandals, with hair hanging down to his shoulders. An exhausted grey V-neck sweatshirt clung to his chest, the material haphazardly displaying stains and blots, some quite large. Aiken fingered a large red spot on his sweatshirt. "Blood from the fight?"

"Tomato sauce," Chester said, his eyes glazing over. "From shrimp scampi linguine."

"A law student?"

"Yup."

"No dress code for law students?"

"Burned it, years ago."

Aiken pointed to another stain. Chester jerked the shirt apart from his chest for a closer view. "From making mustard," he said.

"Mustard?"

"You know: brown sugar, paprika, turmeric…"

"Mustard?"

"You don't make your own mustard?"

"A friend, Heinz," Aiken said, "makes mustard, ketchup and relish for me…a triple threat player."

The waiter placed two glasses of draft beer on the table and waited for payment. Chester rummaged about, popped a wallet from his pocket and snagged out a thin piece of plastic, shoving it to the waiter. "Use this," he said. "Have Syd run a tab."

"A Chargex card?" Aiken said. "A student with a charge card?"

"Courtesy of a wealthy father. I get no bread, so everything I buy goes on the charge card and his accountant rags at me once a month."

"Shouldn't you be studying, cracking books at the law school?"

"Why? I could never pass."

"Why are you enrolled?"

"I don't care about law school," Chester said. "My old man will fund a human rights chair and lobby for the dean's appointment to the Court of Appeal. He figures they'll grant me a diploma for those things."

Aiken sipped his beer. "That's your plan B?"

"That's my dad's plan B. My plan B is to hang on until I inherit and then squander it—piss his fortune away."

Aiken drained his beer. "I gotta get back to my children," he said. "Thanks for the beer." He pushed himself up from the table.

"You got children and a dead wife. Monster bummer!"

"A question for you," Aiken said, sliding back down into the chair.

"Lay it on me, Mr. Hero."

"Why would a woman wear pearls, Sunday church-going clothes and nylon stockings to a bank robbery?"

"Stocking over her face?" Chester said.

"No."

"Wow…a monster dog-fart question."

"Paris didn't much care for guns," Aiken said. "She wasn't afraid of anything but she didn't much like guns, and I don't see her with a gun no matter what."

"All good points," Chester said. "Time for another round?"

"Gotta go…the children."

"Ferry me to the Dominion House?" Chester said. "They give me access to their kitchen. And the western Syd wears ties and carries a gold watch in his vest pocket. He's the classy Syd."

"Paris liked this Syd," Aiken said. "He serves beer and minds his own business."

Chester waved for the bill and cash-box Syd sent it over promptly, along with Chester's charge card. Chester pencilled in a tip and signed.

"Your father discover plutonium?" Aiken said. "Maybe inherit Rockefeller money?"

"Better...he put a girl on a ballpoint pen. Her clothes fall off when you tilt the pen upside down. Sells millions." Chester leaned over, reached down, producing the garden shears used in the fight outside. "Battle of the Garden Shears is already a legend now, someday be a movie. You'll be famous—Windsor's King Arthur. Want a souvenir?"

"Souvenir? Aiken said. He rattled the canvas bag back and forth. "I got pearl earrings for a souvenir." *And two black kids in a white, white world.*

Monday, January 15
Windsor, Ontario

Mayhem Chase, Aiken's father-in-law, owned shoulders built for transporting Hannibal's thirty-eight elephants across the Pyrenees and the Alps, shoulders built for lifting up the stuck ones, un-trapping them and cleaning the beasts off for the march down abrupt valleys into the productive plains of Italy. Aiken paced behind Mayhem, marvelling at those shoulders once again. *My son inherited those strapping, Samson-like shoulders.*

"Is her body there?" Aiken said.

Mayhem, speaking to the Wayne County Morgue, cupped the phone to his shoulder. "It is." Mayhem covered the phone, clasping it against his chest. "If I hang up does it make this nightmare true?" he said. He kept the phone tight to his chest, putting his back to Aiken. Dots of sweat appeared on his brow. He slowly returned the phone to its cradle. "Another battle," he said.

***

Another battle for Mayhem, Aiken thought. He recalled Mayhem Chase at the Battle of Dieppe, how Mayhem Chase chose to be there. When Essex County white boys began signing up in the fall of '39, joining the Essex Scottish Regiment, Mayhem decided to join up as well, for his own reasons, and he knew the person to approach.

Every summer Sunday a sizable crowd turned out in Windsor's Wigle Park for baseball, one of the few instances where the races mixed. Black ballplayers including Mayhem Chase, members of the Chatham Coloured All-Stars, former all Ontario champs, hitched up from Chatham. They lined up against the best white players in the county along with the occasional Michigan ballplayer. The quality of play was unmatched, save perhaps in the major leagues. Black people camped out on blankets along the sidelines, generally wearing Sunday church clothes; white people hogged the stands, dressed more casually. Older, infirm black people might sit in the stands, tolerated. No law and no park rule proclaimed this arrangement. That's the way it was.

The recruiting officer for the Essex Scottish played ball on most weekends. Mayhem plunked down behind the plate as the recruiting officer stepped up to bat. Mayhem bent close. "I need to join up, Bud," he said. He said the words quiet-like so the umpire would not pick up on them. The officer swung, a practice cut while checking to ensure no one overheard. "They'll be black Regiments with the Yanks," he said, "But not 'til they join the war. Join with us and they'll make you a dishwasher. You know the way things are."

"Play ball," the umpire shouted, moving in, crouching behind Mayhem. The pitch came and the officer clouted a stand-up double. When the inning finished he trotted over to Mayhem, saying nothing until they stood alone. "Whatta ya want to join a white regiment for, Mayhem? That'd be hard time. You know the way things are."

"My daughter fancies a boy in the regiment," Mayhem said. "And I aim to keep an eye out for him. Don't know where she'd be if he didn't survive."

The officer's voice quietened. "Mixed marriages are legal in Ontario but ain't so popular with some."

"You got three offspring," Mayhem said, "and one of them has a black friend, a 'friend' she lives with in Detroit."

"That's so, but we don't advertise it...it upsets some. Got two grandkids from them too."

"You know me as a good man," Mayhem said.

"You're a clutch hitter." The officer checked again for people within hearing distance. "Don't you do some praying with people on Sundays?" he said. Mayhem nodded. "Look me up some time."

Mayhem understood, knowing the way things were, what could be done, and what couldn't. Mayhem Chase signed on as the regimental chaplain for the Essex Scottish. Grumbles about a black clergyman were minimal. Most Essex County men knew him as a steady sort and men going into battle worried about other things, things about life and death.

Mayhem Chase landed at Dieppe with the regiment, jumping off the landing craft without a firearm. When the awful killing parade started he cast aside his bible-thinking. With no weapon but dogged determination he lugged a wounded soldier across the beach under fire and pitched him into a landing craft. He saw that Aiken had waded through the surf and was now crouched down on the beach but alive. Over the next several hours Mayhem dragged four more men, and on the last trip, played out, men dragged him aboard. But he saw Aiken Day still alive, still hunkered down on the beach. He wept, saying a prayer for him as he shipped back to England. The concentration camp Stalag 8B sucked in the Scots remaining on the beach, collecting the survivors as prisoners of war.

"Had you been white," Aiken once said to him, "they'd have pinned medals on your front and back, right down to your ass for what you did on the beach that day."

"Pieces of ribbon, Aiken," Mayhem replied, "pieces of dang ribbon. They don't tell the measure of a man, bud. Those who actually earned medals prefer not to wear them, probably tuck them away out of sight, in a bottom drawer. And those that preen with medals, you take those dang men in small doses, Aiken. Mark my words. As for not getting medals for doing what I chose to do, that's just the way things were, the way things are."

***

"One more battle," Mayhem repeated. "I'll be going over to that morgue," he said. "I'll see to bringing her home."

"We'll see to it together," Aiken said.

Mayhem arranged for the funeral man from Chatham to follow them to Detroit with the Mercury station wagon used for black funerals in Chatham.

"Whites on the first floor," the morgue attendant said. "She's down in the basement level in the coloured section."

"Yeah, in the coloured section," Mayhem said. "Where else would she be?" He headed towards the basement stairs but the attendant's comments angered Aiken, who seized the man's arm, dragging him along.

"They separate dead whites from dead blacks?" Aiken said. "Afraid those white women corpses will jump off their slabs taking after those dead black men?"

Mayhem pulled on Aiken's shoulder but Aiken refused to release the man's arm, hauling him along. "Please, mister," the man said.

"We're here for your wife, bud," Mayhem said. "Not about race relations." Aiken released the attendant's arm and followed Mayhem down the stairs to the basement. The stench of formaldehyde blasted into Aiken, gagging him. *Christ! The stink of death.*

When the sheet flipped back, Mayhem flinched at the sight, bending away. He bobbed his head to Aiken, who remained rooted, refusing to look at his wife, needing to remember her as she had been. Mayhem, shaking his head, fingering away tears. But, business-like, he rallied, arranging for the body to be brought back across the border. "An awful mess," he said to Aiken. "A godawful mess."

***

In Windsor Aiken phoned about a burial plot, sending over an envelope with one hundred and thirty-five dollars in cash to the cemetery director. Two days later, forty-three people, with a sprinkling of white faces, attended the funeral service in Chatham at Mayhem's church. A guest preacher spoke of Paris; a gospel singer rendered an artful solo of a piece Aiken didn't recognize.

I guess a regular church-goer, one bouncing with faith, would recognize such a sad, mournful tune. It's probably called the "dead wife" song or something similar. He draped his arm around his daughter and she folded into his chest, sobbing. On the other side of him Adam, sitting bolt upright, kept his emotions to himself.

After the church praying and weeping, most of the people followed to Windsor for the burial. They trucked her body using the same Merc wagon to the Grove Cemetery on Giles Boulevard, chosen by Aiken as it was only a few blocks from his home. Sarah and Adam would be able to visit their mom when they craved comforting.

A slim chap, a man with sweet-potato tinting, stood beside Aiken, head jerking towards Mayhem Chase, then towards Adam. "Either of those fellas could sling her casket alone."

Aiken ignored the comment mostly because he couldn't remember the man's name, not knowing how he knew Paris. But he really didn't feel like making small talk. Only the man was dead on, he thought: a matching pair of million-dollar shoulders.

"Had he been white," Sweet Potato went on, nodding to Mayhem, "he'd have played for the Tigers and made those fans forget Cobb." Aiken placed him now, a pitcher out of Dresden, a small Kent County town with a race track, a man who loved the ponies and, when young, owned a dipsy-doodle curve ball. *Yeah, just the way things are.*

Aiken left Sweet Potato, seeking out Sarah, tugging her in, dragging an arm about her, offering comfort but unsure of the result. Sarah spent the time trying not to cry, without noticeable success. His eyes tracked back to Mayhem Chase; steady, even today, when burying his only child. The death-gloom crept over him. *I'm putting my wife in the ground. I remember a skinny girl following me about our Division Road farm. I remember her graduation from Spelman. I remember the way her closet smelled: the cachet of Chanel and calamine.* Focus on Mayhem, he thought. Be rock steady like him. He noticed Adam, apart, grim-faced but silent and composed. *He's more like Mayhem than I thought.*

The funeral grounds held snow, freshly fallen, icing the grass, frosting the stone markers, but the driveway was clear, two lanes flattened from previous cemetery traffic. A cold wind buffeted the grounds. The Merc paused at the cemetery gateway, waiting until people parked their cars and gathered behind, and then it led a slow, chilled funeral march. Snow scrunched underfoot, a sad symphony to the followers. The Merc threaded through the rows of granite stones until it reached the freshly dug hole. Frost-lined chunks of sod surrounded the grave that marked her final place of peace. Snippets of snow whooshed about and clouds hid the sun. People gathered around the site dressed in the bleary browns and blacks of funeral-goers. Ropes laid into the hole telegraphed the agenda. Men struggled the box out of the wagon, faces red from exertion, dumping the container beside the cavity in the ground.

The cemetery director hovered about the site, thin and wiry, with a face pasty from the winter but displaying a precisely trimmed mustache. Battle ribbons clung to his tattered navy blazer, the coat showing wrinkles and frayed sleeve ends and covering a gray wool turtleneck. Grungy wool mittens insulated his hands and he tugged at Aiken's arm, dragging him aside, out of earshot. He brushed at his battle ribbons in an unconscious gesture. Pieces of ribbon, Aiken recalled Mayhem saying, "pieces of dang ribbon."

"Lot of coloured people in your party," the director said. "Almost all coloured in fact."

"Against the law, is it?"

"There's cemeteries that welcome coloured folks but this ain't one of them. It's the way things are. You ought to have known that."

Aiken pointed to the ribbons on his lapel, tapping a finger to them. "You saw combat?" *Pieces of dang ribbon.*

"Second Battle of El Alamein. I was there."

"Tank commander?"

"No."

"Gunnery man, were you?"

"Cook. Kept the men fed."

"El Alamein was a tank battle. Guess you had time to spare."

"Bloody hot in those kitchens."

Aiken pulled him behind a larger monument, out of sight, taking out his wallet. "Maybe there's a way to solve this problem."

The director perked up, lips showing blistered pink. "Maybe there is." He took a mitt off, reached into an inside pocket, and removed his own wallet.

Aiken slugged hard, without warning, whacking the director in the stomach, pushing at him as he crumpled down. After a few seconds mewing sounds spewed up from the ground. Aiken fished out a five-dollar bill, bent low and jabbed the bill into the director's jacket pocket. He stomped on the man's chest with his shoe. "A deal is a deal," he said. *But it's my wife, and today I just don't care for the way things are.*

At the grave Sarah slung her arms about Aiken, weeping into his coat, while the preacher spoke words about Paris and about heaven. When the words finished, Adam, Aiken and Mayhem roped the pine casket down into the hole, snaking the ropes back up. People, one at a time or in small bunches, begged off, mumbling polite comforts. The worker assigned the dirt-moving waited to the side, parka zipped up over jean overalls, wool hat respectfully held in front. Aiken stuffed five dollars into the pocket of the man's parka. "We'll throw the dirt down ourselves," he said. The man put his cap on and left.

Adam still spoke no words.

Aiken picked up the shovel, bent into it, slinging dirt on top of the box. When he paused for breath, Mayhem spelled him, then Adam, then Aiken again. Sarah picked up the occasional chunk of sod, flinging it down, splatting it on the coffin.

While Mayhem worked the shovel, Adam pulled his father aside. "Mom was a hero," he said.

"She did civil rights, so you and your sister could live in a better world."

"You miss the point, Pops. She robbed a bank. She drifted from Martin Luther King Jr. to Malcolm X and at the last switched over to Stokely Carmichael with a gun."

What? "Paris didn't do things without a reason," Aiken said.

"Mom got tired of demonstrating, tired of convincing people to sign petitions that accomplished nothing. She turned radical, Pops."

"She wouldn't do something without good reason."

"Maybe you don't see the reason."

"What reason is that?"

Adam pulled the shovel from his grandfather and pitched down dirt. Twenty-five more minutes of effort filled the grave. After the dirt-filling, Adam gripped Aiken's elbow and pinched hard enough to make Aiken flinch. "It's because she was black," Adam said. "They're not killing white women in Grosse Pointe banks."

***

In the morning Adam's bedroom stood deathlike cold and empty. The bed neatly made, tight hospital corners, the dresser drawers abandoned, empty but shut, the duffle gone, the Detroit Tiger baseball cap centred neatly on the dresser. All these things reached out and tapped Aiken down, seeping into him, sinking his spirits. Sarah pressed by him, taking in Adam's room. "Why did he leave?"

Because saying "it's just the way things are" becomes harder and harder to sell.

Wednesday, January 17
Detroit, Michigan

The sun dipped below the horizon. Three or four minutes of quiet, soft daylight remained. She descended slowly, moving down the crude stone staircase, treading carefully over the seven steps, avoiding the three capsized ones with their heaved-up, spiky edges. Professor Constance Harlan carried a brown paper bag, mouthing "Rats be gone, rats be gone," praying for rats to hear and obey. She opened the wooden door, which had no lock, no handle, and it creaked, sharp squeaks catching her by surprise once again. The elderly white-haired gentleman kneeling beside the cot turned to the door at the squeaks. The room was stiffly cold, sparse, and decidedly rancid, its floor hard-packed, without a single floor board. It lacked plumbing. The single lightbulb hanging from the ceiling spun off paltry light, the potbellied stove barely emitted heat, and the one basement window was partially snared in by the tin flue snaking up from the stove, flanges crudely nailed into the window frame.

Paris Day lay on the cot, sweat rippling her face, dried sweat crusting her eyes, sealing them shut, a bandage plastered on her forehead, woollen blankets wrapping her tight. Aside from the cot holding Paris, the only furniture in the room was a small, scuffed, square kitchen table and two wooden chairs. The calendar on the earthen wall, permanently nailed opened to December 1957, showed a circle pencilled around day 29. The calendar edges were browned and frayed, curling in spots.

Connie passed the bag to him. "Only on Twelfth Street would this dirt-bottom room be called an apartment," she said.

"Your momma and poppa lived in worse. It's the ghetto, Connie. That's the ghetto. You make do. People make do. Everyone makes do." He removed packets of gauze from the paper bag, setting them on the table, thrusting them about.

"You're just fidgeting" she said. Bloodied bits of gauze lay on the floor by the cot. Connie squatted, scooting the bits into the empty bag, careful not to let her knees touch the floor.

"Did she wake up?" Connie said. The old man shook his head. "Is she in pain?"

"Don't appear to be."

Connie dusted off the chair before sitting. "Will she live?"

"I'd say so, but I work in a drugstore…not a doctor."

"But she's not going to die?"

"Can't say, Connie. The skull wound's not bleeding but there's blood coming out of the stomach hole."

"Will she wake up?" Connie said.

"If she dies, they'll be blaming me."

"She won't die," Connie said. "She wouldn't give them the satisfaction." Connie's fingers stroked Paris's face. "But she might not wake up."

The old man bent to Paris, wiping sweat from her face with a clean white handkerchief.

"Should we call someone?" Connie said.

"If she lives she can call whoever she wants."

"And if she doesn't," Connie said, "what? We skedaddle? Is that your plan?"

"They'll be needing to blame someone…I'll travel south, Georgia maybe."

"The peckerwood spotted Paris," Connie said, "and right afterwards shot up the whole bank."

They faced each other across the table, the old man balancing on the edge of his chair, worn creases charting his face, fingers tapping lightly along the table top, right foot involuntarily twitching up and down without warning. Occasionally he bent and arranged the strips of gauze on Paris's face. Connie sat firm and upright in her chair, silent.

"You plotting us out of here?" he said.

She nodded. "Thinking things out." Her bristled hair was swept back, her dark-wool sensible skirt tucked in tight, but her white blouse showed sweat stains and wrinkles and her nylons displayed a small ladder in one leg. Her face remained composed, even tranquil. She suddenly noticed the calendar and pointed to it. "Do you wonder what happened on December 29, 1957?"

"Lions won the championship," he said. "People celebrated."

"What? Nobody living here ever had reason to celebrate. Not ever."

"People raise families in worse rooms. Families celebrate things, even a white football team."

"Should we take her to a hospital?" Connie said.

"If the FBI shot her, they'll be watching hospitals."

"Across the border then, back to Windsor?"

"Can't say if she'd make the trip. And what'll you say to border guards with an unconscious, bleeding, coloured woman in the back seat?" He stood and edged towards the door. "I'm gonna collect more wood. Keep us from freezing."

"What's the plan," she said.

"If she lives, we make a plan."

"Yeah, and if not we skedaddle, just leave her?"

"I'll bring some food," he said. "Keep an eye and see she don't skedaddle her blankets off."

Saturday, January 27
Division Road, Essex County, Ontario

The symmetry of their garb was dictated by function. Both men wore aging, drab, olive canvas hunting coats. Their jeans concealed long johns and wool socks stuffed down into worn leather boots: twelve-inch Greb Kodiaks, steel shanked, water-proofed by each man in case they decided to shake out for duck season. But duck-shooting involved sitting and cold-ass hunching down and the two men far preferred pheasants or rabbits and the tramping of Essex County fields. The boots cost more than either man could afford to spend on footwear only pulled on three, maybe four, times a year but Kodiaks wore best of all, so they indulged their feet. And the wool socks were always new, not darned, never darned, a lesson from the Essex Scottish, an infantry regiment: *protect your feet, they carry you into battle and home again.* Aiken carried a single-barrelled twelve gauge and Mayhem a marked-up pump. Like Mayhem, Aiken wore a glove on his left hand but not the right, keeping his trigger finger free. Like Mayhem, he balled his fingers from time to time, blowing to warm them.

The black lab froze. Her left ear twitched; the two men took note, pausing, shoulder to shoulder. Aiken said, "Go Gus." The lab charged, flushing a cock pheasant, a bird exploding in front of them, beating his wings to death seeking escape. Neither Aiken nor Mayhem raised a barrel in the bird's direction and in a few seconds it busted out of range. The dog craned her ropey neck, eyes watching Aiken, searching. "She thinks we're dotty," Aiken said.

"Explain that it's out of season," Mayhem said, "and tell her why you named her Gus."

"If you talk to dogs," Aiken said, "things goes south. Maybe you begin taking advice from cows instead of Ann Landers."

The dog trotted back to Aiken, rubbing against his leg. "Why are we out here?" Aiken said.

"We have to find a new normal, bud, and it means going back sometimes. We buried her."

"Yeah, we did." Aiken rubbed the dog's neck, scratching behind her ears.

"You have a plan going forward?" Mayhem said.

"Gonna keep on. I got kids to raise."

"And some kind of purpose beyond that, Aiken? Like Paris had a purpose."

"Her purpose got her dead."

"Drinking to ease the pain is not a purpose."

Aiken pressed fingers against his nose and squished tears away. "Raising two up is my purpose, my only purpose."

"Adam's a man full grown and Sarah will be a woman soon enough."

"She's a child."

The conversation over, they kept on. Snow flurries dotted the air, the frozen ground bumpy and unyielding. "You don't seem sweat-up much today," Mayhem said.

"Some days are good, some not so."

"That's what other Stalag 8B survivors tell me."

"Nope…no chance. I ain't a joiner by nature."

"Just asking," Mayhem said.

The day was crisp, near to eye-stinging, with just enough weather to make both men feel alive. They crossed farmers' racked-out corn fields and crunched across stubbled-down soybean pitches. The black lab led by twenty to thirty feet, ranging back and forth, nose to the ground, tail working harder than a Spitfire propeller. The dog moved slower in the bean fields, the stubble biting her paws. The lab barked once and a jackrabbit spun out.

Aiken shouted, "Go Gus." The dog lunged out, chasing the jack as if the gold at the rainbow's end was in plain sight for taking up. The dog would never catch the jack, the men knew. Whenever she got close, the jack twisted out, darting away, swinging the dog wide, but the dog's arc brought the jack back in range. The men kept their weapons ready. Aiken tapped Mayhem on the shoulder and dropped his own shotgun down, pointing to the ground. Mayhem acknowledged with a nod. When the jack raced far enough in front of the dog, Mayhem flipped the pump to his shoulder. In one quick motion he blasted the rabbit. The shot boomed, followed a split second later by a *ta-chunk* as Mayhem pumped another shell into the chamber. The jack tumbled head over heels, dead in the air, collapsing and spreading flat on the snow. The lab quickened to the body, sniffing vigorously but not chewing or touching the carcass. Blood spurted dark maroon, staining the icy ground, and she shoved her nose to it.

"She's good these days," Mayhem said. "A well-trained hunter."

"Takes a while to bring them along," Aiken said. "But her eyes are failing. She's aged."

"Eyes are overrated," Mayhem said. "Training and instinct last better." He wrapped his fingers around the rabbit's neck and lifted it with little effort. Blood dripped from the limp torso, wetting the frosted turf, staining it claret. The dog sniffed aggressively, nose puffing, still seeking out the blood. Aiken slung open the game bag. Mayhem dropped the rabbit inside and Aiken tossed the bag to the ground. The dog continued sniffing at the bag until Aiken shoved her aside with his boot.

"Should we keep on?" Aiken said.

"Nope. Enough for a meal and a stew, unless you care for some."

"Nah." They lingered, leaning on fence posts, cradling shotguns, puffs of white breath whipping into the air. "In lean years," Aiken said, "you fed yourself and Paris with that pump."

"A man with half an eye and a weapon," Mayhem said, "should never apply for pogey." Mayhem ejected the remaining shells out of his pump, banging each shell out and catching it before the shell hit the ground. Aiken broke his gun, removing the shell, shoving the cartridge back into his pocket. They removed right-hand gloves from their pockets, working them on over crusty, cold fingers.

Aiken bent down and retrieved the game bag but Mayhem held still, so Aiken laid the bag back down, thinking Mayhem needed to talk.

"What about the nightmares?" Mayhem said.

"Back to that?…Fine. No problem."

"If I put the same question to Sarah?"

Aiken paused, considering before he responded. "She'd tell you she was worried at times."

"You still think about the beach and the killing?"

"You were on the beach but you escaped. You missed the Death March. Because the Nazis were trying to hide evidence of their crimes, they marched us in bitter cold from Poland into Germany. At that time we slurped a bowl of thin soup only for maybe three months, nothing else. Men trapped rats and ate them but they died from dysentery. No proper clothing for the winter but they marched us away from the Red Army. The fucking Siberian wind chopped you to pieces during the day and if you fell, a bullet got pumped into your head but most killings happened at night, from the cold. If a man died you tried to grab his boots, sometimes frozen solid to his feet. Boots are for the living. Like clothes. We stripped the bodies in the morning and divvied up the clothes so we could live. But now I wonder: Why did I survive, why not someone else? "

"I still meet with the Stalag 8B survivors," Mayhem said. "To talk about anything that helps."

"Did talking ever drop a rabbit into the pot?" Aiken said. The lab bounced against his leg and Aiken bent and stroked her behind the ears to compliment her on her efforts. "It's a good praying day," he said to the lab "You did good pal."

"I'm going to spend time away," Mayhem said.

"Away where?"

"In the South with King," Mayhem said, "helping with the struggle for civil rights."

"Is this about Paris?"

"Something I must do, that's all," Mayhem said, "but yeah, maybe a bit about Paris." Mayhem strung his weapon down and picked up the game bag, slinging the strap over his shoulder. "And your drinking," Mayhem said. "Does the drinking help or just camouflage the problem?"

"I survived Stalag 8B. I'll survive nightmares and my drinking is my drinking. Go home and stew your rabbit."

The hunt over, they walked together, weapons pointed down, close enough to each other that they bumped shoulders occasionally with neither one noticing. The dog trailed, tail down, disappointed, sensing the game was finished and her skills no longer in demand.

"Come with me," Mayhem said. "Meet Martin. He's a good egg. Puts on airs with no man."

"Go home and cook up your dinner."

"Might help with the nightmares."

"And maybe pig-shit is tasty as hell."

Saturday, January 27
Kennedy Compound, Hyannis Port, Massachusetts

The television set, tuned to Johnson's State of the Union address, dominated the room, fixating the people. When the president finished, Pierre Salinger clicked the set off. Salinger and Kennedy lingered in the room as Kennedy's family filed out. Kennedy relied on Salinger for practical no-nonsense advice. Salinger, Jack Kennedy's former press secretary, was a family friend and confidant, a jowly man with wavy black hair, about Bobby Kennedy's height but carrying an extra hundred pounds on his torso, chomping forever on a fat Churchill-sized stogie, slurping it across his mouth side to side, removing it, stabbing it in the air to make a point.

"Johnson speaks of peace," Kennedy said, "but continues to carpet-bomb Vietnam."

"Bob, one of the two hundred body bags unloaded yesterday carried a high school friend."

"I'm sorry, Sal."

"A New Yorker," Salinger said, "with two children in school."

"I'll send a letter of condolence," Kennedy said. Anger flashed across his features. "I hate this insane war!" Salinger slipped over a note with the widow's name and address.

"Johnson's boxed in by the war," Salinger said. He stabbed again with the cigar, his voice rising. "Bob, let's announce and take him on!"

"Not yet, Sal."

"While we sit on our butts, the ghettos burn away. Shootings every night..."

"Ending the war is our first priority," Kennedy said, "so that money goes to the inner cities."

"To throw a punch at Johnson, you must climb in the ring with him."

"Johnson is drowning," Kennedy said. "Drowning men are dangerous."

"Okay, for now we stay mum."

Kennedy gave a short nod; the conversation was finished. After a few seconds he jumped into their running joke, seeking to lighten the atmosphere. "You still smoke cigars?"

Salinger glanced at Kennedy, tilting his head, eyes squinting. "Weren't you going to sprout up a few inches before the election? I've taller weeds in my backyard." He waved his stogie in Kennedy's face.

Kennedy slumped into an easy chair, fiddling with a copy of the *New York Times*, flipping over pages, searching for the editorials. He glanced up. "Don't you light them anymore?"

Salinger left the room, calling back, "Who knows? The surgeon general may be right about that lung cancer crap."

Salinger crossed the house to the sun room, where Jason Bartlow Morgan, known universally as JBM, stooped on the edge of a chair, elbows on knees, clutching the same newspaper, eyeballing the front page. JBM wore a sleeveless navy wool sweater-vest, white shirt, frayed cuffs, sleeves folded back, displaying his wrists. He had brown hair and plain glasses. The stub of a cigarette was wedged between two fingers, fingers tobacco stained one-half inch from their tips, fingers impervious to cigarette heat. He butted the stub, rising as Salinger entered the room. The newspaper on his lap fell aside.

"Are we jumping in?" JBM said.

"Close JBM, very close." Salinger pinched out a slim package of wooden matches from a pocket, fired up his cigar, sucking hard, rasping until the glow satisfied him.

"But is it a go?" JBM said.

"Line people up," Salinger said, "but keep things on the quiet for now."

"You put Bobby in the seat of a Cadillac," JBM said, "and I'll push it by myself if I have to."

"More like a Chevy," Salinger said.

"A Cadillac says class."

"Chevy says man of the people."

JBM pulled his overcoat on and buttoned it up, punching buttons through their spaces slowly, one at a time, with finality. "It's time," he said. They shook. Salinger followed JBM to the front door, squeezing his shoulder by way of farewell.

When the door closed behind him, JBM puckered up his collar against the wind. "Class," he said. "I aim to push Bobby, in his Cadillac, to the top of the mountain."

Monday, January 29
Federal Building, Detroit, Michigan

The wall outside Roland Feeber's office held a single picture, a framed photo of a heavyset man of serious countenance, a slightly balding chap with a widow's peak, wearing a grey suit and dark tie. An illegible signature was scrawled across the bottom of the photo. Harry Fortune glanced at the secretary a few feet away. She paused from her typing, eyes rotating to Fortune.

"Senator McCarthy," she said. He shifted over until directly in front of the photograph, inspecting it once more, turning back to her again.

Her lips curled down. "Joe," she said. "Not the other one. Not the poet."

Fortune mouthed "Oh" and rapped on Feeber's office door.

Feeber's voice shouted, "In."

Fortune stepped inside. "Sir."

The walls in Feeber's office carried no mementos, showed no family photographs and displayed no decorations. A shabby rug cowered under a scratched-up desk and his office chair was squat, functional.

"Fuck you been?" Feeber said.

"Sorry I'm late, sir."

Feeber arched back in his chair, the chair squeaking, bleating complaints as he shifted his weight. His service revolver bulged on his left shoulder, Sam Browne leathers crossed his chest and stomach, and his white shirt was sweat-stained at the neck and armpits. His suit coat hung on his chair, dragging on the floor, slithering about the ground when he leaned back. He pivoted in the chair, stretched out his feet. His right pant leg rode up, revealing a pistol strapped to his ankle. Feeber noted Fortune's eyes staring at his backup piece. "It's like a woman's tit, Fortune: it ain't good for squat if you can't grab it and wring the bitch whenever you need to."

Harry Fortune jerked upright at this statement, pausing before moving towards a chair.

"I tell you to park your ass?" Feeber said. Fortune straightened up.

"Okay, sit," Feeber said. Fortune pressed down into the chair, sliding to the back, keeping his body ramrod straight. "You look over that dead girl's face," Feeber said, "all shot up?"

"Yes sir."

"Shoot up Paris Day the same way."

Fortune said nothing.

"You lost your piece."

"I filled out the form."

"How you gonna do wet work without a piece?"

"Sir?"

"You partner with Rizzuto. Learn from him."

"Sure."

Feeber's chair squawked as he dipped forward. His lips cracked upwards, not smiling but not unhappy. "Rizzuto's an artist at wet stuff, a real goddamn artist."

Tuesday, January 30
Windsor, Ontario

The white panel van crouched outside Aiken Day's home had squatted in the same spot for the past four hours. Camped inside the van, Rizzuto, black curly hair clipped close, slouched behind the wheel, perpetually sweating, tapping his maroon nightstick—a scuffed-up, nick-laden, oft-bloodied rod—slapping it against the wheel, beating to a rhythm only he could hear. The nightstick froze, its dance paused. "A war vet," Rizzuto said, "a war vet who marries a coon who drops out coon kids. I gotta say it: the fella's screwed up somehow, swimming upstream. No sense to salt and pepper marriages."

On the other end of the bench seat, Fortune butted up against the passenger door, right knee compressed, foot tight against the dashboard. "Dude, we're on a stakeout in a foreign country."

"Don't sweat it," Rizzuto said. "Cops in Windsor speak white, just like us."

"What's the stick for?"

Rizzuto flipped it about, his fist tight to it, rubbing it, faking masturbation, an obscene ballet. "We get a chance, Miss Pussy, we do payback to the big coon who choked you. Hammer his skull until the big maroon splashes red on the dirt." He jabbed the nightstick into Fortune's chest, twice, hard enough to make Fortune wince.

"Feeber only targeted the guy's mother."

"We find that pretty little dame..." He patted the gun in his shoulder holster. "We bang off a few rounds inside her skull."

"But her boy?" Fortune said.

"Icing, Miss Pussy…just icing."

"We can't kill anyone in Canada."

"You couldn't kill anyone," Rizzuto said. "You lost your piece."

"I filled out the form."

Rizzuto set the nightstick aside, stuffing it alongside his butt. He removed a pack of Pall Malls from his shirt pocket, jerking cigarettes to the top, slitting one to his lips, extending the pack to Fortune: a peace offering. Fortune declined but reached into his own pocket and snapped open his Zippo, clicking it a few times in front of Rizzuto. Sparks flew but no flame.

Rizzuto's eyes focused on the sparks, the constant sparking, flashes and flashes; his eyes rolled upwards, the cigarette fell. He convulsed, arms and legs shaking; white foam appeared on his lips, body banging against the seat. The seizure lasted for half a minute, maybe a few seconds more. When it finished, Rizzuto slithered down quietly against the seat, sweat clumping his forehead. When his strength seeped back he removed his pistol from his holster, facing Fortune, pointing the gun at him, forcing the weapon closer and closer. "Between me and you," he said. The cold steel barrel tapped down, drilling into Fortune's forehead, at first gently but then harder, sending shoots of pain, raising a headache, bouncing fear into Fortune. "Yeah," Fortune said, "Partners…always partners. We cover for each other. 'Till death do us part,' 'thick and thin.'"

Rizzuto's weapon slowly sank until it settled on the seat. Rizzuto mopped spittle from his lips. "Right!" he said. "Partners."

**

Inside his home, Aiken Day delayed getting out of bed, the full enormity of Paris's death now soaking into him. *Paris is dead and buried; time to move on; definitely time to move on.* Eventually he swung his legs out and his feet fell to the floor, but he delayed pulling himself upright. He splayed his fingers across his cheeks, rubbing his chin, feeling stubble. *Maybe I'll shave tomorrow. Moving on tomorrow is good. But no point in rushing it.* He rose and shuffled to his closet, eyes skimming over the clothes that cleaved to hangers, the garments screaming chaos to his mind, a jumble of sundry colors and unknown textures, costumes ready for occasions not yet booked, invitations not yet received or mailed. He slid hangers from side to side and back again, determined to choose something. *Does it matter a rat's ass what I wear? I'm not gonna meet the Queen today.* He picked up the rumpled slacks and the reeking shirt bunched on the floor, pulling both on for the third day in a row. The phone rang and he picked up the upstairs extension.

"A panel van has been parked on your street," Mayhem said. "Two gents inside. Michigan plates."

"Why're you watching my home?"

"Friends of Paris called me, that's all, bud. Just keeping an eye out for the in-laws."

"Who parks outside my home?"

"FBI, bud," Mayhem said. "But I'm guessing. What was my daughter up to?"

"Same old civil rights crap."

"Right! Same old civil rights crap. Mr. Empathy himself."

"Rat's ass, Mayhem, don't get involved in the same shit that got Paris killed."

"Paris lived before she died, bud. Can you say the same?"

After the call Aiken forced his leaden legs and groaning knees into action, climbing down the stairs, slitting open the curtains, peering at the white van parked across the street. *Be gone FBI; Don't ruin a good praying day.*

Downstairs Sarah hunched over the kitchen table, elbows on the top, cereal untouched. Aiken checked out her bowl. "Should I sprinkle sugar and dump in some milk?" he said.

"What?"

"Sugar and milk?"

"I'm going to school today."

Well, I'll stay here, dear. No urgency about shaving today; no harm in a brief pause before moving on. "That's good, honey," he said. *Real good. At school you'll be out of harm's way if the FBI decides to attack our home and shoot someone dead.*

Wednesday, January 31
Windsor, Ontario

At 8 a.m. banging erupted on Aiken's front door. The sudden noise bolted him upright in bed. He flung blankets aside and jumped down the stairs followed closely by Sarah, whose nightie flapped as they descended. Two steps from the door the realization that Paris was dead blotted out everything for him. Terror overwhelmed, slowing him, and Sarah smacked into him. The banging continued, relentless. Aiken opened the door, failing to recognize the long-haired fellow on his porch in front of him. *Did we phone in an order for crazy? Does crazy do home delivery?* Aiken glanced down the street. "The van is gone," he said, turning back to the chap in front of him. "Who're you?"

"Chester from the Bridge House Tavern. You know: 'Charge Card' Chester."

"What do you want?"

Chester wore an olive-coloured Eisenhower jacket, the tunic in poor condition, jacket flaps open, displaying a mottled, food-stained sweatshirt. A tear in the right knee of his blue jeans showed a slick of white, hairy knee. At the end of his too-short jeans, his ankles displayed white sweat socks on top of reclaimed rubber-soled sandals. *Who chooses to dress like a spaced-out beatnik?* Aiken gestured to the army jacket. "You in the service?"

"Don't shit me," Chester said. "Army-navy surplus."

"You're the law student," Aiken said, "who doesn't study."

"You fought in the war?" Chester said.

"Briefly."

"You spent three years in a concentration camp."

"I did."

"And in a major downer," Chester said, "the FBI Cossacks shot and killed your wife." He held up a file folder, flapping it back and forth, sending an ice-cold breeze across Aiken's face. "It's chilly on the porch," Chester said. *Next time bring an oven.* Aiken didn't reply.

Sarah reached into the hall closet, grabbing her overcoat, pulling it on.

"You find it chilly out here?" Chester said.

"Get to the point."

"My father's lawyers sent me a dossier."

"A dossier?"

"They compile a dossier on everyone I meet…still fixated on that Lindberg killing."

"Shove off."

"Daddy…" Sarah said.

"Sorry," Aiken said, turning and smiling at his daughter. "What can I do for you, fine sir?"

Chester reached out, squeezing Aiken's shoulder, blowing beer breath into his face. "You need a sidekick in your fight with the FBI: Pancho to the Cisco Kid, Jimmy Olsen to Clark Kent, Norton to Gleason."

Aiken drew back, seeking relief from the breath. "I'm fighting the FBI?"

Chester leaned over, reached back, placing the file folder on top of a case of Heineken, twisting, swinging the case up waist high. "A get-acquainted gift," he said.

"Poop," Sarah said. "Just what this house is lacking—more alcohol. Why don't we just live in a liquor store?"

Chester considered her comment for a few seconds, shrugged, moved past them into the house, correctly guessing the way to the kitchen. They followed him. In the kitchen, Chester set the case on the floor, opened the fridge and shifted things aside to make room for the beer bottles. He read labels and tossed expired things into the kitchen garbage can. Some things he pronounced *funky* or *tacky* and tossed those items as well. Eventually, he fit the entire case of beer into the fridge.

"Maybe we should just eliminate the food?" Sarah said. "Chuck it all into the trash."

"Not everyone *eats to live*," Chester said. He pulled a Swiss army knife from inside his jacket and popped open two beers, giving one to Aiken. "You are definitely in a fight with the FBI," he said. "There's a note in the file here." He bent, arranging the last of the bottles in the fridge, pushing them into neat rows.

"Saying?"

"Note says," Chester said, "that FBI agents messed up the scene of the crime."

"Why would they do that?"

Chester lowered his voice to conspiracy level. "FBI Cossacks lie about everything," he whispered.

Aiken put his beer down untouched.

"Show me your wife's belongings," Chester said. Aiken collected the canvas bag from the hall closet and brought it to the kitchen, passing it over to Chester, who tipped Paris's belongings onto the table.

Sarah sorted through the contents spread out in front of her. She held up the pearl earrings. "The FBI stole Mom's good earrings," she said, "and left us these imitation ones."

Aiken removed the watch from the table. "Rat's ass!" he said. "Paris wore a Timex."

"Told ya," Chester said. "FBI are lying liars."

Sarah sorted through the items on the table, shoving things back and forth. "These must belong to someone else."

"With me as your sidekick," Chester said, "we could kick FBI butt." He picked up Aiken's beer and sipped on it. "What we have here, Kemo Sabe…is an FBI cover-up."

Thursday, February 1
Windsor, Ontario

In the night the temperature spun upwards. Freezing rain pounded against Aiken's bedroom windows, the rain chilling to snow as the temperature flipped, falling quickly, blanketing Windsor streets with a treacherous layer of ice but imparting a lovely crisp whiteness that cloaked the danger. At 2 a.m. the city trucks banged into action, scraping and salting during the remaining night, hoping to counter the hazardous conditions, clanging and chugging down every city street. Aiken sweated in the night, restless with ugly dreams of the past, waking often at the outside clanking noises. Each time he awoke he found himself staring at the Webley. *Paris, why did you leave me?*

At 8 a.m. he heard unusual noises downstairs, dragged on his housecoat and slippers and cupped his hand over the Webley. He sneaked down the stairs, peering into the kitchen. Sarah perched primly on a kitchen chair, snuggled up in housecoat and slippers, her hands smoothing away imaginary wrinkles, occasionally reaching out and adjusting ever so slightly the position of a glass of orange juice perched in front of her. Her eyes followed Chester as he clattered about. Clad in worn Levi's and sandals with white socks, Chester knelt down in front of a bottom cupboard, his food-stained sweatshirt riding up on his back. He rummaged, seizing pots and pans, chinking and clinking them, tilting, examining, thrusting each aside in turn. He skirted over to another cupboard, rummaging through it. He flopped down when Aiken entered the kitchen. Aiken lowered the Webley, pointing it down, keeping it tight to his leg.

"Your crêpe pan is missing," Chester said. He reached for an apron, pulling it from the broom closet, looping it about, tying the straps behind his back in one effortless, well-practised motion.

"What're you doing here?" Aiken said.

Chester pointed to the two large army duffle bags against the far wall of the kitchen. "I'm moving in for the battle."

"What battle?"

"Your crêpe pan?"

"Probably pawned it," Aiken said.

"We have to buy a new one for Chester," Sarah said.

"Call him Uncle Chester," Aiken said. "It's more respectful."

"A good kitchen requires a really good crêpe pot, Daddy." *Crêpe pot? Sure, what's a crackpot in the kitchen without a decent crêpe pot?*

"It wasn't her watch," Aiken said. "She wore a Timex."

"No problem," Chester said. "We'll use my pan until you buy one." *Turn around and bend over pal and I'll show you the proper place to store a crêpe pan.*

Chester bounced over to one of his kit bags, rummaged inside, plucking out a round iron pan, chipped and battered. He showed it to Aiken, spinning and flipping it about with practised ease.

"Really," Sarah said. "We must buy a new one."

"Crêpes," Aiken said, "always a big hit in the prison camp…or maybe Bananas Flambé first thing in the morning, right after a strip search and a flogging."

"I fully appreciate sarcasm," Chester said, "…in appropriate situations."

"You're here because?" Aiken said.

"To help you battle the FBI."

"They leave me alone, I leave them alone."

On the table in front of Sarah, precisely arranged, were a dozen eggs, a quart bottle of milk, a pound of unsalted butter, a two-pound package of all-purpose flour, a package of granulated sugar, a petite jar of vanilla, and a bottle of maple syrup. Aiken picked up the bottle of syrup and rolled it over: 100 per cent pure Quebec syrup, the expensive sort. "Where did you get this?" he said.

"Had it delivered," Chester said.

"They accepted a charge card?"

"They did." Chester hauled the card out of his pocket, waiving at Aiken. "I'm a true pioneer. Lewis and Clark material, Radisson and Groseilliers up the butt."

"They accepted a piece of plastic instead of greenbacks?"

"They did," Chester said.

"What about law school?"

"My father's dream—he'll see to it." Chester placed the pan on the element, cranked the heat up, dumped eggs into a bowl and one at a time whisked in milk, flour butter, sugar and vanilla. He opened the utensil drawer, claiming a kitchen whisk, rolling it about in his fingers, grinning; grinning and grinning more. *He's savouring this moment for some reason.*

"In crêpe-making," Chester said, "the whisk rules supreme." He held it up. He started beating the whisk against the glass bowl, clacking monotonously, commenting as he worked. "The secret to magnificent crêpes: we whisk away every last lump. Smooth, smooth, smooooth." To Aiken: "Did you know that?"

"No cooking classes in Stalag 8B."

"Pity." Chester placed the whisk aside and clicked the element higher. When the pan was heated he bounced a few water droplets off it by way of testing and started the process of crêpe-creating. He poured batter over the pan, tilting it so the batter unfurled and expanded evenly, flipping a finished crêpe off every thirty seconds or so, building a sizable pile on each of three plates. He drizzled maple syrup over each pile. Chester stared at Aiken for a few seconds, moving his eyes to catch Aiken's eye without speaking. Aiken acknowledged the look, placing the Webley on the table beside him, covering the pistol with the cloth napkin. Chester beckoned, inviting them to dig in.

Aiken doubled over the first crêpe, dumping on extra syrup, munching it into his mouth in burger fashion. The crêpe crumbled in his mouth, the bouquet from the maple sauce rushing at his nose, the syrupy smash dissolving down his throat. *Christ, but this weird freak can cook.*

"Savoury," Sarah said. She dabbed the white cloth napkin delicately to her lips.

"Yeah, very savoury," Aiken said. *Whose cloth napkins are these?*

"I can pay rent," Chester said, "if you accept charge cards."

"I don't. So pack up your kit bags."

When he had finished eating, Aiken picked up the Webley, keeping the napkin tucked about it, and placed it on top of the fridge.

"Humph," Chester said, "pity." He plucked two crystal glasses from the cupboard and opened the fridge, removing a bottle of champagne, laying the bottle in his hand against his arm, showing Aiken the label, offering him an opportunity to comment.

"Champagne?" Aiken said.

Chester bit his lip. "Not just champagne, Kemo Sabe: Piper-Heidsieck Champagne." *He brought champagne and his own crystal?*

Chester twisted the wire, winding it off slowly, ritualistically. He popped the cork.

"Can I try some?" Sarah said.

"A taste," Aiken said.

"I will now demonstrate," Chester said, bending towards Sarah, "how a sophisticated person appreciates champagne." He removed a pristine white napkin from the drawer. *He stores his napkins in my kitchen drawer?*

"A proper champagne goblet," he said to Sarah, flashing the glass, fiddling it out for examination, "is a bit larger than a flute, permitting us to experience this nectar on multiple levels." Sarah nodded, focused on Chester.

Just pour the shit.

He tilted the bottle, pouring slowly. "We dispense the liquid gradually, not disturbing the wine until we experience it." When the first glass was filled, Chester filled the second one in similar fashion. He raised the second glass up as a priest might offer up the chalice at mass. "Note the rising bubbles, Sarah." Sarah squinted, peering at the glass.

"While the bubbles rise," Chester said, "we inhale, seeking to discover the three levels of experience." *Snobbery, name-droppery and bull-shittery.*

"The primary flavour," Chester said, "is lemon with a delicate hint of apricot." He inhaled, sipping. "The secondary flavour is of cooked fruit, maybe strawberry-rhubarb." He inhaled again. "The tertiary flavour absolutely screams: walnuts, glorious walnuts."

He slipped the goblet in front of Sarah, who inhaled and tasted. "It's worse than ginger ale," she said. Chester passed the glass to Aiken.

"Get changed for school," Aiken said to Sarah. She left the kitchen, climbing up the stairs to her bedroom.

Chester raised his glass. "To my new job as sidekick," he said.

"To a good praying day," Aiken said. He raised his glass and guzzled it empty. "This crap would be good with a beer chaser," he said. Chester's face tensed. He filled his own goblet again but made no effort to re-fill Aiken's.

"What do you want?" Aiken said.

"I'm craving some purpose to my life: to help you in this battle."

"Battle?"

"Why did they kill your wife?"

"Maybe they wanted to burgle her earrings or maybe an agent was short one Timex?"

"You can't let the FBI slap you around."

"Don't care," Aiken said. "My wife mixed it up with them and she's dead. I have two kids to feed and selling shoes barely covers expenses."

Chester tipped more champagne into Aiken's goblet. "Kemo Sabe," he said, "my life works because of a naked girl on a ballpoint pen, those stupid, downer, dick-wad pens. I can make a difference. And another bonus…"

"What?"

"I buy all the goods for the house with my piece of plastic. You reimburse me fifty cents on the dollar."

"Why?"

"It gives me hard cash," Chester said, "coins in my pocket that jingle. You can't buy everything with a charge card…but your offspring would eat magnificent steak." He crossed the room and picked up the Webley off the fridge, pulling off the napkin. "I'll assume charge of the cannon for you."

You're not as pretty as Paris but you might keep me alive for my kids. Chester spit into his hand, Aiken did likewise and they shook to seal the deal. Chester tucked the Webley in one of his kit bags and hefted the bag over his shoulder.

Sarah came downstairs and collected up her schoolbooks, giving Aiken a quick hug. "About Mom's watch and earrings," she said. "We should do something."

"Yeah," Aiken said, "of course."

"No, we should definitely do something."

"Sure, we can do something." She left for school. *I'll call the Dead Wife department of the US government. They'll know what happened.*

"Which room is mine?" Chester said.

The one with the Webley. Mine's the one with the dead wife.

Thursday, February 1
Windsor, Ontario and Grosse Point, Michigan

Chester followed Aiken to the front door, drying one of his crystal glasses, fogging it with his breath and rubbing it clear. "I'll dig up a bottle of decent Bordeaux for dinner," he said. *Thank God, I'd hate for the world to explode.*

The day was cool, slightly below freezing but sunny, when Aiken crossed the border and travelled down Jefferson Avenue heading east. His Chevy entered the serene village of Grosse Pointe. A police car slowed, checking him out, so he twisted about and waved so they could observe a docile, white man. Aiken understood from Paris that a police department telegraphed loads about a community, maybe everything. He knew, for instance, that to be a police officer in Grosse Pointe, you must be a white male over six feet two inches tall, with enough accumulated muscle to bulge out a uniform shirt. You had, or quickly acquired, the skill of conveying disdain, without speaking, to people of limited incomes, to left-wing college professors, and to hard-rock musicians. No women, blacks or Asians need apply for law enforcement positions in this community.

Ancient trees loomed overhead; broad streets and ageless mansions imparted an aura of prosperous peacefulness. Another police car slowed to check him out. He turned once more, keeping his face visible.

Nothing in Windsor compares to Grosse Pointe. If they flipped the finest house from Victoria Avenue into Grosse Pointe, it would fill with rats from nearby St. Clair Shores, collapse in a pool of sweat and urine and slither down the closest sewer drain.

Aiken entered the bank through mammoth doors. The bank blended perfectly with the surrounding neighbourhood: granite exterior, rich polished counters, oak desks and chairs dotting the room, engraved glass panels and brass bars partitioning off the tellers.

Most of the tellers are of the aging, blue-haired, woollen-sweaters and hankies-tucked-into-a-sleeve type. They smile without conveying warmth; they only reluctantly agree to accept deposits. I should have dressed better, maybe rented a tuxedo.

One teller was young, maybe twenty, twenty-one, standing out because of her youth—a pretty girl, dressed neatly but conservatively. Aiken angled about, lining up in front of her. The person before him left and he stepped up.

"How can I help you, sir?" she said.

"Nice bank you have." *I'm stalling.*

"Thank you, sir. How can I help you?"

"Been here long?" Aiken said. "You seem rather young."

"One year, still on probation, sir." *How long before you become snotty and fit in? Is that why you're still on probation? Failed the snotty test?*

"How can I help you?"

Aiken hesitated, fumbling for words, but finally just blurted it out. "My wife was shot dead in your bank. I'm trying to make sense of what happened."

The teller lowered her voice and shuffled papers back and forth in an effort to mask the conversation. "I spend my lunch break in the public library down the street…two blocks. I could speak with you then, sir."

***

Aiken sat at a polished walnut table in the library, a table identical to six others, all surrounded by sturdy leather chairs tacked with brass buttons. He glanced at the *Wall Street Journal* neatly aligned on his table, as on all the others. *In case someone with money suddenly decides to change his order: Buy IBM, sell 3M, invade England.*

At exactly five minutes past noon, the young teller slipped smoothly into a chair across from him. She unfolded a clipping, pressing the edges down, smoothing them, treating it with reverence. "From *Life* magazine," she said. "It shows Vietnamese General Nguyen Ngoc Loan, executing a captured Viet Cong officer in Saigon."

Aiken pulled the clipping close.

"Notice the man's brains blowing out the side of his head," she said. Aiken examined the glossy paper, thinking it might somehow relate to Paris.

"We're involved in an illegal war we can't win," she said, "and this killer represents America abroad."

Aiken said nothing, unsure of her point. "This is not my America," she said.

It's journalism. The shot could be posed by a clever poser. Might be fake brains—maybe cold porridge done up as brains. And rats-ass, it's somewhere on the other side of the world.

"The killing of your wife was horrible," she said. "Three young coloured women, all nicely dressed and all polite....They called the leader Tanya."

"And Tanya pointed a gun at you?"

"I didn't see a gun," she said. "They lobbied the manager to hire a black teller. What nonsense! The first black person employed in this bank will be an underpaid janitor."

"They had no guns?"

"A man in a brown wrinkled suit shot your wife and one of the others, spraying bullets everywhere. Later, the FBI, with all their evil, arrived at the bank wearing their freshly pressed suits."

"But no guns?"

"The FBI discovered a note demanding money. Absolute nonsense."

"Why did the FBI shoot her?"

"The FBI came later. I didn't recognize the shooter. He's not a regular. I don't know who he is."

What! "Not FBI?"

"Blood all over the floor." She held her stomach, face whitening, and he wondered if she was going to faint.

"None of this was in the newspaper," Aiken said.

She stowed the clipping back in her purse. "Mr. J. Edgar Hoover decides what goes in the newspaper," she said. "Any moron knows that."

Aiken removed a photo of Paris from his wallet and set it on the table. The girl glanced at it but said nothing, sliding it back to him. *Sure, I get it. Black people all look alike unless you're in love with one.*

"The man in the brown suit killed your wife," she said. "Not the FBI. They did the cover-up." She stood, her face closing up. *She's mentally preparing to resume work, rounding up her emotions and filing them away until quitting time.* "Sorry about your wife," she said. She started away but spun around and clinched his arm. "Those FBI people take evil to a whole different level."

Thursday, February 1
Windsor, Ontario

Harry Fortune parked the Volkswagen outside the Bridge House, leaving it running. He switched the radio off, checking his watch. After a few seconds of silence, he clicked the radio back on. He checked his watch again, wiping sweat from the side of his cheek. He turned the radio off again. He slammed his fist against the dash. "Just make sure, Harry, she's not some undercover agent." He shut the car off.

Fortune entered the tavern, bearing right, moving into the mixed side of the tavern, and quickly scanned the room. Sitting alone at a table, a girl with blonde, stringy hair and dressed in a flowery peasant's dress, fiddled with a beaded necklace. She lifted a finger up off the table, crooking it back and forth a few times. Fortune nodded. He wound through the tables, pulling up a chair across from her.

"I'm Harry, we spoke," he said. "You must be Joni. No one else in the room fits."

"I don't sell anything," she said. "I don't do drugs and we've never spoken."

"But you're Joni?"

Rings looped each of her fingers. She tapped them against the table in an unconscious gesture and they knocked out a bizarre beat that irritated Fortune after a few seconds.

"Joni," she said. "But I got nothing for sale."

"Understood." He flapped open both sides of his coat. "No wire," he said.

"You seem pretty straight to me," she said. "You could pass for Eisenhower's son."

"Job requirement."

"How fucked up is that."

Fortune leaned forward and dropped his voice. "I gotta score some weed."

"Sure." Her fingers tapped nervously along the table again and the clanging resumed. "Your usual...*friends*...away or maybe busted?"

Fortune squirmed in his chair. "I'm from the west coast," he said, "...new in town."

Her fingers paused and rose, swaying above the table and bestowing silence while she digested this information. "Jeepers, the west coast," she said. "Perry Como performs in LA. He's Mr. Casual. Ever watch him on TV? He wears those sweaters."

"Perry Como?"

"Any other kind of music on the west coast?"

"Sure, checking credentials," he said.

She waited, fingers dancing against the table top, hurling out a crazy rhythm once more.

"The Grateful Dead," he said, "Big Brother and the Holding Company."

The tenseness in her face vanished. "Tangerine trees and marmalade skies."

"Cellophane flowers of yellow and green," he replied.

She rolled her fingers into fists and stood up. "Go to the men's side and buy a beer," she said. "I'll be in the men's can in five minutes."

"You'll meet me in the men's washroom?"

She jostled in close, whispering. "I never peek. How fucked up is that." She left the table, scratching her fingernails across the back of his neck on the way by. He jumped at the touch. He shifted over to the men's side, finding an empty table, ordering and paying for a beer. He left it untouched in front of him. He counted twenty-one men in the room, sitting mostly alone, and a few small groups. No windows, so the only way a person knew dark from light outside was when someone entered or left. He checked his watch again.

When the five minutes were up, he moseyed slowly towards the men's room. A long-haired man in his twenties wearing a camouflage hunting coat and red wool toque crossed in front of him, pushing into the washroom ahead of him. Fortune hesitated, pausing a few seconds. He swung the washroom door open in time to see Joni pass the man a baggie and accept money. The hippie crammed the baggie into his coat and shoved into one of the stalls. A few seconds later he heard the sound of racing pee blasting into a toilet. He pushed into the washroom and held up bills to Joni. She passed a baggie to him. The stall door opened and Chester emerged, still zipping up when he saw Fortune.

"Christ, almighty," Chester said, "you're that dick-wad FBI guy."

"FBI!" Joni said. She flung the money on the floor towards the urinal and it fluttered, flapping and landing in haphazard fashion on the bathroom floor.

"No, no, no, not me," Fortune said. "That's Narcotics. My group does political crap."

Chester pressed fingers into Fortune's chest. "Like shooting down black wives," he said.

"Not me," Fortune said. "I've only been in town a week. I had to score some weed."

"Piss-stained bread," Joni said, bending down and picking up the bills one at a time, in jerking, angry motions. She spread them out on the sink and patted them down with paper towels. After the patting, she gathered up the bills and crammed them down the top of her dress, fussing the material smooth.

"Good doing business with you," she said to Chester. To Fortune, she said, "Thanks for pissing up my bread."

"No father pays your way," Chester said to her.

"Tried whoring," she said, "but it didn't go down well."

"But you tried it?"

"Yeah." She adjusted the peasant dress one last time. "How fucked up is that."

Thursday, February 1
Windsor, Ontario

Snow flurries swirled about as Chester left the tavern and scurried down University towards Victoria Avenue. Harry Fortune left in the other direction, moving towards his Volkswagen. Joni followed Fortune.

"Hey Eisenhower," she called out. He spun about. "And you a son-of-a-bitchin' FBI agent," she said.

He pulled his pea coat tight while slitting the buttons into their holes. She wore no coat, just her peasant dress gripping generous curves, oblivious to the chilled air.

"And you a son-of-a-bitchin' drug dealer," he said.

"Hitch a ride?"

"I guess." He drew open the passenger door for her. Inside the vehicle he shivered in the cold interior. He started the car, shoving the transmission into first gear while holding the clutch in, revving the engine to jumpstart the heat. "Where to?"

"Let's sit here awhile."

He shifted the car into neutral, releasing the clutch, revving the engine once more.

"Guards and cops—men in authority," she said, "have always been my downfall." She slipped an arm through his and he left it there, keeping still.

"It's not like I have the clap," she said. Her fingers made the sign of a cross over her heart. He smiled at that. "You let me play with your weapon," she said, "and I'll give you some high-grade acid." She unfolded her fingers to display her palm and a small piece of blotter paper that held several white tabs. Her tongue flicked out, licking her forefinger. The finger dabbed down at a tab and it stuck. She jutted her tongue up, positioned the tab underneath it carefully. "Under the tongue is faster."

"I lost my piece," Fortune said.

"Not your only weapon, Eisenhower."

Fortune licked a finger and plucked a tab, placing it under his tongue.

Friday, February 2
Windsor, Ontario

Chester bounced back and forth at the kitchen counter, hovering over the sink, humming quietly while meticulously scrubbing out a pan. The vigorous scrubbing raised sweat on his forehead but he kept at it, occasionally swiping the beads away. The duck's ass end of marijuana joint perched on the edge of the sink, weak smoke-stream looping upwards. He reached down, sucked on the joint and resumed scrubbing. When he heard Sarah's footsteps squeak on the stairs, he butted the joint out, swallowing the quarter-inch remains. He flapped a dishcloth in the air.

"What do I smell, Uncle Chester?"

"Burning extract of vanilla—a recipe that never panned out."

She plopped into a kitchen chair. "Still in pajamas?" he said.

"Not going to school. The teachers hate me and no one eats lunch with me."

"I'll make you some breakfast," Chester said.

Sarah sobbed. Chester dried his hands. "Tell me, sweetie?"

"No one includes me," she said. "I don't look like them."

Chester spun the apron about his waist and knotted it. "It's very important," he said, "to personalize one's breakfast, the most important day of the meal."

"What?"

He opened the refrigerator door. "First we pick out sausages." He sorted about, locating a package in the fridge and retrieved it. He unfolded the brown, waxy butcher's paper, revealing a dozen pinkish sausages. He pushed the paper in front of her and positioned the sausages, adjusting them up and down until they lay in a perfect line. "Choose the first one, please," he said.

Sarah pointed to a sausage. "That's Peter," Chester said. "Good choice. The other sausages hate Peter but he would die if he could make a pretty girl happy. Choose another." Sarah pointed to another sausage.

"That's Frieda. She has hair trouble and is hoping to be warm…next to Peter. You've a knack for this."

He gestured, waving over the sausages. "Pick one last piglet for the pan." She selected one more. Chester baritoned his voice: "The perfect trio." His voice dropped further: "This one sings bass."

Sarah's face lightened. Chester cranked the element beneath the fry pan on high and it soon glowed. He removed the egg carton from the fridge, flipping it open. "Everyone loves a good egg," he said. Choose two." She chose two. "Frank and Ernest," he said. "Perfect. You can be Frank and I'll be Ernest. Oh no, hold on, we did that yesterday. Today I'll be Frank and you'll be Ernest." He broke the eggs and carefully put the sausages into the pan. He dropped down on one knee in front of Sarah. "Let me be frank with you, Scarlett, you're a wonderful breakfast companion." Her face gleamed.

He stirred the pan while humming. "What are you humming?" she said.

"Picture a world," he said in singsong, "with tangerine trees and marmalade skies."

"Such a pretty thought, Uncle Chester." She stood and twirled about. "'Tangerine trees and marmalade skies,'" she sang. "What else?"

"How about 'cellophane flowers of yellow and green.'"

He grabbed a plate from the cupboard, spun it about and served her breakfast. He packed her lunch for her while she dressed. He walked her to school. She waved goodbye to him, running to a friend. At the bus-stop bench across from the school he produced a baggie and cigarette papers. "Time for another pick-me-up, Tonto." He rolled a joint.

Friday, February 2
Windsor, Ontario

Mayhem Chase phoned Aiken at 9 a.m. and Aiken handled the call on the upstairs extension, still in bed. "I'm leaving for Washington, D.C.," Mayhem said. "To warn you, bud—a head's-up: I'm going to the CALCAV march and you may have to bail me out."

"What's CALCAV?" Aiken said. He was still fully clothed: still wearing yesterday's clothes.

"A group of clergy," Mayhem said. "Ministers, preachers, priests and rabbis who are against the war."

Sorry I asked. "Why fart about with that? Waste of a good praying day. We can chase up some rabbits with Gus."

"The landscape is changing about the war."

"Sure it is. Maybe they'll outlaw guns and bombs, imprison anyone with a switchblade."

"Mr. Sensitivity, as always."

Aiken swung his feet out, dropping them on the floor, sitting up, kicking his shoes off. He undid the buttons on his shirt. "Went to the Grosse Pointe bank yesterday," he said.

"And?"

"Paris wasn't robbing a bank," Aiken said.

"Well I know that."

"How do you know that?"

"I know my daughter," Mayhem said. "How do you know it?"

Should have thought of that. "Been talking to a bank teller."

"And?"

"It's a cover-up for something," Aiken said.

"No matter the reason, she's still dead…. I'll be doing more civil rights work."

"The stuff she did…"

"Yeah, the *stuff* she did." The phone went dead.

Aiken found Chester washing dishes in the kitchen while humming, spinning each plate, buffing it for several seconds before filing it in a now sparkling cupboard. "Here we go little plate-ee," Chester said, "join your groovy brothers."

"What's that smell?" Aiken said.

"Burning extract of vanilla…a recipe gone bad."

Chester removed another plate from the dishwater. "What's next, buddy?"

"Gonna find someone on Twelfth Street. A guy who might be dangerous. You in for backup?"

Chester continued to buff the plate. "About your wife?"

"Yeah, *stuff* about my wife."

"You miss your wife," Chester said. Another perfectly polished plate funnelled into the cupboard, gently and perfectly placed on the pile. "Behind every great man stands a woman."

"And if he's a lucky bastard," Aiken said, "she's fondling his butt while trying to peel off his undies."

"Whoa, no bitterness in this room."

***

Together they crossed the border, pulling up before customs on the American side. Chester leaned across Aiken, shoving a pen at the border guard. "Now, tilt it upside down," he said. The guard waved them through without asking for ID, flipping the pen up, then down, then up.

One hour later on 12th Street, Chester hunched down in Aiken's Chevy, the car crammed in between a clapped-out pickup truck and a new Mercedes, directly across the street from an automotive tool shop—*Progressive Detroit Tool Shop*, one of the few buildings in sight unmarked by the riot. He slouched down in the front seat, trying to remain warm without running the engine so as not to draw attention to the car. He smoked a joint, fogging the windshield over. He sorted through the contents of Aiken's glove box, separating the papers from assorted nuts and bolts and a sommelier's corkscrew. He rubbed the box clean using tissue paper, humming while he worked.

Inside the building Aiken Day waited in the small reception room. The waiting room was professionally decorated, some sort of modern art on the wall, soft pastel-coloured wallpaper, a statue on the coffee table that struck no bell with Aiken. *A hunk of jerked-up metal must be "art" now.* Aiken perched in one of the six expensive leather chairs, keeping the day's *Free Press* up in front of his face, but not reading, dropping it down a tad to peek when people entered the room.

Occasionally automotive engineers, wearing the brown, stained and rumpled suits they favoured, left the shop floor through the office on their way outside, bobbing to the blonde receptionist as they left, ignoring Aiken. When the door to the shop opened, the cutting sounds from the shop floor blazed in, the whining of the lathes and the grinding, grating crunches of the Bridgeport vertical mills. The smell of cutting oil drifted in, offsetting the perfume of the receptionist who poked at a typewriter, crimson fingernails tapping the keys one at a time, delicately, purposefully. *She's probably a whiz at Pitman speed dictation. Miss World Stenographer of 1960. Maybe built that typewriter herself in shop class.* The woman paused often, rubbing her fingers, holding out her nails for inspection. She spoke again to Aiken, the only person in the waiting room. Her practised, quiet voice, polite yet borderline syrupy, floated over to him: "Sure you won't have something to drink, sir? We stock all the name brand liquors and ice."

"Going to meet someone," Aiken said. "Good for now."

At 11 a.m. Pokeface bustled through the door and placed a tray with four coffees in styrofoam cups onto the countertop. The receptionist stepped towards him with studied indifference, passing over an envelope. He pushed it into his pocket and tapped a finger to his wool cap. Aiken drew the newspaper down. "So, Pokeface…still in the en-tren-prin-oor business?"

Pokeface put a hand inside his jacket before turning. Recognizing Aiken he leaned back, perching against the counter, taking a minute before answering. "I is in fact, Pastyman."

Aiken folded the newspaper, dropped it on the chair and gestured to the door. Pokeface followed him outside. Aiken pointed to the scribbled word *Soul* on the side of the building. "Nobody torched this building in the riot."

Pokeface shuffled back and forth on his feet. "Owners get what they pay for. Nothing wrong with that. People got to earn a living."

"Their own private insurance policy during the riot?"

"Whatch'ya doin' down here, Pastyman?"

"You hear about the three black women sticking up a Grosse Pointe bank?"

"I had nothing to do with that." His hand shoved inside his coat, withdrawing a weapon, the same .45 calibre handgun, black rectangular snout and brown grips, as before. "Who's pointing a finger at me?" He backed Aiken up to the wall, poking the gun barrel into Aiken's stomach.

Aiken held up his hands. "No one. My wife was killed in the bank. You remember my wife, Paris?"

"I told you, Pastyman. I had nothing to do with that."

Aiken withdrew a fifty-dollar bill from his wallet, stretched his hand out slowly and poked the bill into Pokeface's jacket pocket. "Another hundred bucks for the location of anyone involved in that shooting. They'll be holed up in some rat-trap on Twelfth Street. Paris knew Twelfth Street inside and out."

Pokeface dropped the weapon, keeping it alongside his leg, barrel down. "How do I find you, Pastyman?"

Aiken held up a piece of paper, poking it into the same jacket pocket. "My phone number."

***

Aiken jumped back into Chevy. "Blast the heat up," Chester said, "my ass is frozen to the seat."

The pungent smell in the car smacked into Aiken. "That burnt vanilla smell follows you about."

"More to the point: Can he locate Tanya?"

Aiken wiped his forehead, mopping beads of sweat aside. "What a dangerous asshole that guy is. He yanks that gun out like a Dodge city sheriff on Saturday night."

"Downer," Chester said. "Keep away from that turkey."

Friday, February 2
Detroit, Michigan

In July of 1967, the riot sparked up first on 12th Street, blowing up with the police raid on a blind pig. Forty-three people, mostly Negroes, died, including three young black men summarily executed by white officers at the Algiers Motel. Before the riot, the street had already seeped and crept into ugly, a commercial strip surrounded by brick homes with fading hedges and sparse, browning lawns. Now, over one hundred gutted blocks cursed out each side of the street, mocking the elegant city of years gone by. Across the street from the basement unit hiding Paris Day, a burned-out gas station crowded close to the wrecked shell of a furniture store. The cindered building above her unit was no longer inhabited, but mustiness, tainted with the smell of scorched wood, persisted, drifting down to the unit below. In the basement Paris Day balanced on one of the two chairs, sitting erect. Professor Connie Harlan poked with the makeup brush, sweeping lightly over the thin, wiggly white scar on Paris's forehead. "Perfect…doesn't show but hardly at all, girl. It'll fade."

"I'm not sitting at the back of the bus," Paris said. "Give back my money. Do you hear me?" The white scar suddenly showed vivid, almost winking.

"We hear you, girl. You'll get your money back."

The old man moved behind Paris, extending his hands outwards, flipping them towards Connie, motioning to her. Connie responded by placing her fingers on the collar of Paris's blouse, pressing the ends down flat, her fingers gently massaging the material and Paris's neck. She spoke quietly, close to a whisper: "Do you know who you are, girl?"

"Vernon Johns," Paris said. "My grandfather killed a white man, a white man who deserved to die, as white men do…Grandpa cut him in two with a scythe. But they hanged Grandpa and threw his body away in the trash. They buried the white man properly, I expect."

"Girl…"

"I speak German, Latin, Hebrew and Greek."

"Did I mention, girl," Connie said, "…that you have a husband?"

"Don't speak nonsense. A man can't have a husband."

The old man flipped his hands again, pacing back and forth behind Paris.

"And two children," Connie said. "You have two fine children." Her fingers fell away from the blouse, and she bent down until she could look directly into Paris's eyes, locking into them. Paris glanced upwards. "I'm not sitting at the back of the bus."

The old man repeated b the gesture with his hands and Connie bent close to Paris once more, speaking quietly. "The thing is, Paris, your husband is a white gentleman."

"Don't talk gibberish."

Connie left Paris's side, sliding over to the old man, speaking in a low voice. "Will this memory thing fix itself up?"

"Oh yeah," he said, "I heard it does."

"If it doesn't?"

"She joins Barnum and Bailey and tours with the circus."

"For God's sake!"

"Well, I don't know."

"But you're a pharmacist, not a doctor."

"Then make up your own answer, Connie."

"But the FBI…" Connie said, wiping Paris's brow. "Those peckerwoods want her dead." She tugged at Paris's shoulder again. "They really hunting for you serious-like, girl."

The old man spoke up: "So, what's the plan, Connie?"

"We skedaddle out of this area," she said. "Paris, or Vernon, comes with me and we engage in some low-profile civil rights work far away from Windsor and Detroit, far away from those FBI peckerwoods." Facing Paris, she lowered her voice again. "When your memory finds its way back, girl, we work out a plan for your family. Now we just skedaddle off the radar."

"I might do some preaching," Paris said. "I'll prepare a few sermons."

"Sure, we'll do some preaching too." Connie touched Paris's forehead. "Listen to me, girl! You is burning hot and you must stay out of sight and cool off. You'll eventually come 'round to my way of thinking...eventually, girl." Connie rubbed Paris's shoulders; the thin white scratch dimmed somewhat.

Tuesday, February 6
Arlington National Cemetery, Virginia

Twenty-five hundred people, mostly religious leaders, including Martin
Luther King Jr., gathered at the Potomac River, milling about, bused
there by CALCAV, intending to march to the Arlington National
Cemetery and hold a church service. A young man in a dark suit raced
across the bridge, legs pumping hard, jerking to a halt in front of King.
The man, a lawyer, doubled over, wheezing from his effort, clutching a
few pages in his hand. "Just out of court," he said. "The court granted
the government an emergency injunction against our march."

"Tell me exactly," King said.

"A national cemetery can't be used for partisan purposes."

King pulled the papers from his hand and scanned them.

"We should call off the march," the lawyer said, "and play it safe."

King rocked back and forth on his heels, huddling with others
before veering back to the lawyer. "A march to the cemetery, to
observe a moment of silence, breaches no order."

"Maybe," the lawyer said, "and maybe not." He gestured to the
rows of uniformed men. "They want an excuse to beat us down."

King glanced at the police, his eyes roving up and down the lines.
"Everyone knows the risk," he said. King wrapped his arm around the
man. "Either way we make our point."

"We are cancelling our religious service," King called out to the
crowd. "But we will march to Arlington and observe a few moments
of silence."

Mayhem Chase, near the front, stamped his feet, seeking to warm
his toes as he listened to those words. A young white clergyman,

clerical collar poking out from his coat, stood beside Mayhem, taking his cue from him, stomping his feet up and down, but chatting nervously. "Hundreds of young black men," he said to Mayhem, "die in Vietnam every month."

"Hundreds upon hundreds," Mayhem replied.

"They joined up because they've no jobs or prospects in the ghettos."

"I heard."

"We save them, we save America."

"You're preaching to the converted," Mayhem said.

"I'm scared. The police are waiting to attack us."

"Don't worry over it before it happens."

"I've never been in a fight, never been hit. I know what a headache feels like, no more than that."

"The police might hold back," Mayhem said, gesturing towards the reporters camped together on the street sides. "There are a lot of news cameras hanging about."

The march commenced. Twenty-five hundred people marched together, a silent procession, eight abreast, Jews, Catholics, Presbyterians and others walking to the Tomb of the Unknown Soldier to observe six minutes of silence. Mayhem Chase tugged his wool cap tight to ward off the chill, marching in the third row beside the young clergyman, whose teeth now chattered and whose forehead bubbled sweat. "Stick close to me," Mayhem said. "If there's trouble, I'll help you." He received a quick nod in response. Reporters kept their distance, keeping to the street sides, careful not to be caught between the marchers and the police.

The clergyman, lips trembling, mumbled to Mayhem, "Are we violating the restraining order? Will they attack us?"

"Stay steady," Mayhem said.

The group marched slowly, without speaking, the only sound being the slap of leather on pavement. Police officers on either side fidgeted but kept their ranks, maintaining their stations, most gripping their batons tightly. The marchers halted before the Tomb, the atmosphere still tense. Martin Luther King Jr. called out: "In this period of absolute silence, let us pray."

The clergyman's knees crumpled and he peeled off, falling towards the line of police officers. The nearest officer swung his Billy club and Mayhem stepped into it. The club bounced off Mayhem's shoulder as he swept up the clergyman, hauling him back into line, holding him up. A sergeant reeled in the officer, and the incident finished with only a few people aware of the disruption. Mayhem and another marcher propped the clergyman upright and Mayhem gently massaged his face until he regained consciousness. The silence continued. After six minutes Rabbi Abraham Heschel called out: "My God, my God, why have you forsaken me."

Tears filled Mayhem's eyes at Heschel's words. "Has God forsaken the black soldiers in Vietnam?" he said to the clergyman. He rubbed his shoulder muscle, sore from the blow. His eyes sought out and found the soldier who had assaulted him, a man glaring hatred at him, restrained by his sergeant's presence. "Are we to turn the other cheek forever?" Mayhem said.

"I thought there'd be trouble," the clergyman said, "but I was wrong." He suddenly bubbled with chatter since the danger was gone. "I was scared during the whole march," he said, tugging his collar. "I was really scared. I don't believe in fighting."

Mayhem rubbed his sore muscle once more. "You did well," he said. "You were rock steady."

"I just don't believe in fighting."

Tuesday, February 6
Chicago, Illinois

Six B-52 bombers flying in formation, releasing bombs from thirty thousand feet, could obliterate all life within an area one mile wide and two miles long—approaching the potency of a nuclear weapon. Up to forty of these planes flew on any given day. The planes launched from a base in Thailand, flying thousands and thousands of such sorties against North Vietnam. In spite of this carpet bombing and in spite of five hundred thousand US soldiers, on January 30 eighty thousand North Vietnamese Communist and Viet Cong troops slashed across South Vietnam, striking at 113 cities and towns, unleashing carnage. They launched the attack on Tet, the Vietnamese New Year.

Robert Kennedy, scheduled to speak at a book signing for his recently released book of essays, wandered back and forth in a small room at the Chicago Sun-Times Building. He reviewed his speech, sipped ginger ale, resting the glass on a side table, scribbling the occasional note. Pierre Salinger entered the room and thrust a copy of the *New York Times* at him. "Holy Christ, Bob, read about this Tet Offensive."

Kennedy pushed his notes aside, flipped open the paper, reading the article while standing. Pierre Salinger plopped into a chair, flamed a match and lit a stogie, sucking on it until it was going.

"Eighty thousand soldiers," Kennedy said. "Is this true, Sal?"

"I confirmed it with a source at the Pentagon. It's gospel."

"It means that Johnson lied about the war," Kennedy said. He flung the newspaper aside and threw his fist into the wall, one vicious, quick blow. Tiny splats of blood clung to the pastel wallpaper where his fist had struck the plaster. Salinger passed over a white handkerchief and Kennedy used it to swab at his knuckles. He retrieved the paper, reading it again while pacing.

"Those reporters out there," Salinger said, "will be seeking your thoughts on this Tet Offensive."

"My opinion: the president lied about the conduct of the war."

"Bob, you can't call the president of the United States a shit-faced liar."

"I never cared for Johnson," Kennedy said. "But I never thought him a liar until now."

"Beware, Bob, he is a crafty and dangerous son-of-a-bitch, a politician's worst enemy."

"I'm not up to lying about this."

"But not yet," Salinger said. "Not yet, Bob. Just stall. Let someone else call him out first. You don't need to be on his shit list. Just think about it for now."

"I'll think about it."

They moved into the adjoining room. The signature table was ready, the podium in place. Well-wishers and reporters gathered to hear him speak.

A short, flabby, red-haired reporter leaned into the newsperson beside him. "We're gonna get fluff today," he said. "Vietnam just exploded but we're gonna get polite political bullshit."

Wooden collapsible chairs placed in neat rows contained thirty or so people but many lazed along the walls. One black reporter from *Ebony* stayed near the back of the crowd and a black woman with her young daughter occupied seats in the front row, but the rest of the audience was white. The girl wore a crinkly, cream-coloured dress and a layered crinoline, a hooped petticoat affair from an earlier time. She sported long white stockings and black patent shoes, and her legs swung back and forth while she waited for Kennedy. Her mother passed Kennedy's book to her and gently thrust her towards Kennedy when he entered the room.

Seeing the girl, Kennedy passed by the podium, accepted the book from her and dragged the girl's chair out, hoisting her up into his lap. The smell of fresh lemon from her hair teased into him. She poked a finger into the whiteness of his cheek and he left it there. He asked her name, wrote a note in the book and signed it. He helped the girl off his lap and lifted her chair back, and she climbed back on, clinging to the book. Her legs resumed swinging. Kennedy glanced down to his knuckles, noting the scuffs and splashes of blood. He studied the girl and her swinging legs, legs swinging in innocence, he thought. He returned to the podium but paused for a few seconds before beginning. He thought about the child, about all children and about the innocence displayed by those swinging legs. The room hushed into a sticky silence. This girl is America's future, he thought.

"We owe it to the young people of America to be truthful," he said.

Reporters scratched notes. "Forty thousand American soldiers are dead in this Vietnam War," he said. "And another two-hundred-and-fifty thousand wounded." His eyes wandered down to the child again. "It is time to kill some dangerous illusions."

The red-haired reporter murmured, "Still third page copy, Bobby boy. Spice it up."

"We must destroy the illusion," Kennedy said, "that our bombs have destroyed the will or the morale of the Viet Cong. Carpet-bombing has failed."

The same reporter muttered, "Holy Christ, he's breaking with Johnson. His career is plunging into the toilet." The reporters scribbled in frenzy, seeking to capture every word.

"We must kill the illusion," Kennedy said, "that we can win this godforsaken war. We cannot." He paused, forming his thoughts into words, speaking slowly as they rushed to him. "We owe a duty to the American people to tell the truth," he said. He glanced at the child once again. "We must seek a peaceful settlement and allow the Viet Cong to participate in South Vietnam."

Salinger's cigar tumbled to the floor and he slowly dipped down to scoop it up. "We're in the shithouse now," he said to no one. "We just fired a torpedo at the president of the United States."

After the speech Salinger pushed his fingers around Kennedy's tie, clutching it, straightening the knot slightly. "He's gonna really be pissed."

Kennedy rolled his wrists over, observing the slight shaking in his hands. "This war has driven a stake through the soul of our country." He felt bleakness but he thrust it aside. "Crank up some stuff, Sal, but low key for now."

Kennedy's speech, reported verbatim in the *Times*, was delivered to the president by an aide who quickly scurried away. The president swore and stomped about for fourteen minutes. After venting he called his senior secretary in for dictation. "A memo to General Westmoreland," he said. "Tell him he's got another ten thousand five hundred combat troops for Vietnam." His voice rose in anger. "And tell him to stop pissing soldiers away."

"May I suggest, sir," she said, "that we rephrase that slightly?"

"Rephrase it if you choose but don't change a fucking word."

"Yes, Mr. President," she repeated, "'Stop pissing soldiers away.'"

He rose from his chair, his face dropping. "Ah, Christ, rephrase the damn thing. Pretty it up."

"Yes, Mr. President."

"What a little shitass that Kennedy is, a goddamn pipsqueak."

"Yes, Mr. President."

"Why couldn't he just keep his mouth shut?"

She closed her steno pad and rose, dipping her head down to him before she left.

In the evening Salinger finally managed to contact JBM by phone. "Mobilize a few troops," he said. "Kick it up a notch." He hung up the receiver, not hearing JBM's response.

"I'll tune up the Cadillac," JBM said.

Tuesday, February 6
South Carolina State College, Orangeburg, South Carolina

President Johnson's decision to end draft deferments for all graduate students except those in medicine seeped out of the White House, bleeding from university to university, hemorrhaging unease, wringing unrest at every college. Students at the University of South Carolina, an exclusive haven for whites, brooded over the president's decision. But at the black university, South Carolina State, the campus cauldron festered and boiled more about civil rights than the war.

Moving about the campus proved easy for Adam Day, just one more young black man among the large black student body. He read the scribbled note of directions once more and crossed the campus looking for Lowman Hall. The small, fading building sign, neatly lettered, was tacked up to the porch overhang, the sign tilting at a slight angle, screwed on in rusty exhaustion. He stalked down ancient oak floors to a well-preserved stairway and climbed to the third floor, another student trudging up the stairs in front of him. At the top of the stairs he paused. His eyes watered as he thought of his mother.

A slim young woman standing sentry at the door held a pen and a clipboard; her long, slender fingers flicked away as she checked off names on her list, tapping the pen against the clipboard between students. The student in front of him greeted her. "Peace, Kendra," he said. She bent over the clipboard, checked off a name, indicating the student could enter. Adam faked a quick smile. Her face was the colour of a fudge brownie and her hair was plucked back, gathered up by a green bandana. Her face displayed nothing; she made no effort to acknowledge him but she stuck the back side of the pen to his cheek, underlining the tears. "Come back to the revolution in a few years, we've no use for a momma's boy."

Anger drove into him and he thrust his right hand out, wrapping her throat, pinning her against the wall. She froze. The kerchief flittered to the ground. The fragrance of spicy nutmeg sifted into him, the female aroma goring into his heart.

"Release me, you gorilla," she said, still without struggling. He dropped his hand. "Courage counts more than muscle," she said.

He bent down, rustling up the kerchief, pinching it by an end, stringing it over her shoulder, careful not to touch her again. "Grieving my mom," he said. He gave his name and she made a mark, allowing him entry.

Inside the room Adam counted eleven students: eight males, Kendra and two other females. The students and the decor showed stark contrast, the furniture ratty in appearance, chairs beat-up and scuffed, with worn armrests and threadbare, shabby cushions. But every student was dressed neatly, almost immaculately: no jeans, no sweatshirts, no Afro haircuts; starched white shirts and blouses for all, dark slacks and pristine skirts. The only flash of colour in the room was Kendra's green kerchief. Adam, the tallest in the room by several inches, wore jeans and a sweatshirt, and he stood out for his casual dress as much as for his height. He slumped into an empty chair, slouching down to minimize his bulk. Chipped mugs passed about; he accepted one and a girl filled it with coffee from a worn pot. He nodded thanks. Kendra declined coffee and settled into the chair beside his. Her scent bounced into him once more, softening his heart. The students spoke in measured tones, the southern dialect pronounced, accents exotic to a man raised in the Windsor-Detroit area. He kept his own voice low, addressing Kendra. "Are we getting weapons?"

"I don't know," she said.

"Cops carry weapons."

Her face contorted, "We didn't have them before. But…it didn't go well either."

A slim man, somewhat older than the students, with furrowed forehead and serious countenance, entered the room. Conversation abruptly ceased. The man's cardigan sweater covered a faded white shirt; his seasoned face sported a neatly trimmed mustache with traces of milk showing. He wiped at his lips. "Call me George." After a few seconds, he added: "Expect some danger."

"So we get weapons," Adam whispered to Kendra, who ignored his comment.

George unzipped a binder, removing a few sheets of paper. Kendra bent forward, tendering the student list to him, dropping back down into her chair. The radiator on the wall cranked off. Kendra, sitting close to it, reached for a monkey wrench from the radiator top and banged the rad hard. The clanging ceased. "Radiators at South Carolina don't act up," she said.

"Our goal," George said, "is to integrate the All Star Bowling Lane."

Adam jumped up; his size shrank the room. "A bowling alley?" he said. "This is about bowling?"

"In a town of twenty thousand people," George said, raising his voice, "and the only source of recreation is reserved exclusively for whites."

"We could open our own bowling alley," Adam said, "or take up fly fishing." He remained upright, facing off against George. "Maybe we surround the police station or do something dramatic."

"There will be drama," George said, "plenty of drama."

"What about weapons?" Adam said.

"You talk like a northerner."

"South Detroit."

"Mr. Detroit, we've been at this a while."

"South Detroit," Adam said quietly, dropping back down into his chair.

"It's about bowling but also about balls," Kendra said into his ear. "Some people have them, some don't."

"I'm in for the bowling alley," Adam said to George.

"Glad to see that your years of civil rights work brings you around to our way of thinking, Mr. Detroit." He stuffed papers into his binder, zipping it closed, ending the meeting. The students mingled but George left quickly, slamming the door behind him.

The radiator cranked again and Kendra hammered the monkey wrench against it once more. "I never heard of South Detroit," she said.

"From Windsor, Canada…. It's actually south of Detroit."

"Never got to be a Mountie? Down here to compensate?"

"The FBI killed my mom. Got off on the wrong foot with George, that's all."

"You don't realize the danger in the South." The radiator sounded off again and she crammed the monkey wrench into his stomach. In reflex he grabbed hold of it. She left the room and he whacked the rad hard, silencing it.

Alone in the room, the wrench felt cold and heavy in his grasp. "We are the weapons," he muttered. He flipped the wrench onto the top of the rad. "I'm the damn weapon."

Wednesday, February 7
South Carolina State College

The sturdy, historic, Dukes Gymnasium with its five-bay brick arcade, orange brick and red-tile roof commanded respect, oozed reverence and dominated the campus. Inside the gym, Adam watched the basketball team run drills. The room smelled of guy-sweat, leather and saddle soap, and the canyon-like hall amplified noises: coaches shouting sharp commands, feet slapping down, sneakers screeching at cuts and fake-outs, jock-grunts regularly bursting out.

Adam promoted a ball and received directions to an outside court, a court showing no signs of recent use. The rusty hoop held no string; the court surface was hard-packed dirt. The sawtooth oak tree with its patches of mottled green moss had dumped acorns about the court and he brushed them aside with his foot, clearing a space for play. The temperature, cool by South Carolina standards, was quite acceptable by Windsor's. Adam breathed in the tangy salt smell of the South Carolina winter air and flung his jacket to the side. As he started to play, the sweat gathered, warming him, until it was slopping down his temples, soaking his cheeks, sopping his T-shirt. When he missed a shot he charged after the ball, scooping it up, whipping around to shoot again. Few of his first shots missed, and when they did, his follow-up toss always clipped in. After one shot sank through the hoop, movement attracted his eye. George rolled towards him at a brisk pace. Adam retrieved the ball and moseyed towards him.

"She's in jail," George said.

Adam held the ball, palming it down. "Kendra?"

"She struck a cop at the bowling alley," George said. "Smacked him in the face."

"You struck the bowling alley and didn't tell me?"

"Telling you now."

"Why?"

"Told ya, she's in jail." Adam swallowed at that, the taste in his mouth suddenly dry, acidic. He spun the ball lightly. "Nothing to me." He twisted about and sent the ball up with his fingers, drifting a shot; the ball bounced off the rim and he jumped, fetching it, sauntering back to George.

"It won't go well for her," George said. "Her mouth never quits working."

"As I said, nothing to me." Adam bounced the ball twice and shot again, missing. He retrieved the ball, moving in slow cadence, faking nonchalance.

"Lawyer's in the cafeteria," George said, "collecting bail money for those arrested. She's the only girl."

George waited and after a few seconds Adam abandoned nonchalance and flung the ball against the backboard. It ricocheted back to him and he grabbed it on the first bounce. "Son-of-a-bitch!"

"She's a good sort," George said, "but maybe too lippy for a girl."

Adam left the ball under the hoop and returned to the dorm room he shared with several others. George followed him. Adam hauled out bills from his wallet and suitcase, counting the limp pieces of paper twice, then a third time. His counted a tad over three hundred dollars; money earned working farms during summers and harvests in Essex and Kent counties and converted to US bills by the bank. "How much does bail cost?" he said.

"Not sure."

"I got what I got," Adam said. "If it means bank robbing, I can do it. Mom did it, I can do it."

George, at the door, did not answer. "I gotta drum up money for the others," he said, closing the door behind him.

"Who knows," Adam said, "bank robbing might be an inherited skill."

The lawyer controlled a table in the centre of the cafeteria. Students milled about but men and women too old to be students also waited to sit with him. Two women, wearing white aprons, circulated with platters of fresh buns, and Adam inhaled the smell of squishy bread. The lawyer, a balding man in his 40s, wore a wrinkled suit and a faded white shirt finished off with a limp brown tie. He gathered in money and scribbled careful notes with a pencil about each dollar received. Students threw in small bills; coins tinkled on the laminate tabletop. Most of the students dropped money without giving a name but the older folks, parents and grandparents, those with cracked, tear-stained cheeks, gave their money for their particular relation. When the commotion lessened and people drifted away, Adam dived in beside the lawyer and shoved his money bundle over. "For the girl, Kendra," he said.

"Last name?"

"Don't know it."

"And you being such good friends, you don't know her last name."

"It never came up."

The lawyer's eyes drifted up, staring at Adam, squinting. "Can I assume she's a looker?"

"Assume whatever. Just get her out."

"Only one girl in custody," the lawyer said.

Adam pointed to his stack of bills. "You gonna use all that?"

The lawyer squinted at him again, counting the money. "This'll bail her out and leave enough for my new Cadillac, maybe a vacation to Rome to meet the Pope."

"Sorry."

"Cheaper to get a girl bailed. Men judges don't think a girl can do much damage to a two-hundred-pound cop. Not sure I agree with that premise but it's hanging out there all the same."

***

The following day Adam arrived at the courthouse at first light. He waited by the granite stairs, pacing back and forth for several hours. Kendra made bail first. She wearied down the steps, one at a time, moving like molasses on a winter day. Her blouse hung limply, untucked, showing streaks of dirt, and her skirt boasted a tear. When she closed on him he smelled staleness and sweat. "No showers or perfume," she said. "Don't be near me."

"Finally we agree on something," he said.

"Where'd my bail money come from?"

"Maybe Rockefeller heard you was in trouble?"

"Why did I make bail first?" she said. "Guys beat up and bleeding, lying on cell floors, in worse shape than me."

"Women and children first?"

She glared, taking offence at the comment.

"If a pleasing disposition was the test," he said, "you'd never see the light of day."

"I won't participate in a sham trial. Someone should consider that bail money toast."

"I crawled on my knees picking tomatoes in muggy August," Adam said. "I suckered tobacco for those bills."

"Your money?"

"I pitched bales of hay till my back broke."

"Never asked you for help."

He clenched his fists, squeezing hard. The muscles on his jaw tightened. She walked away, her fingers clasping the green scarf, letting it trail beside her, and it flipped back and forth, fluttering in the breeze. As she drifted away from him, the stale smell should have drifted with her, but instead of fresh South Carolina air, sourness rushed over him.

Thursday, February 8
South Carolina State College

In the late afternoon, two students fired up a small bonfire at the front of the campus while others, at first only watching, eventually huddled about. Someone dismantled a bannister, breaking it apart, feeding the railings into the fire.

At 6 p.m. a police car approached and parked several hundred feet away. The two officers remained in the car. The students around the fire stood up, one at a time, facing the police car. One of the students bent and picked up a railing, holding it behind him, hiding it.

In the cafeteria, forty or fifty students milled about tables, but instead of normal chatter, a sultry silence hung over the room. Students discussed the recent arrests and the injuries sustained. Adam munched on a squelchy cafeteria sandwich, sitting alone. Kendra dragged out a chair at his table. The squeaking of the chair across the hardwood floor made him glance up. She dropped into the chair, facing him.

"Why are you still here," she said. She wore jeans and a sweatshirt and her green bandana wrapped her hair.

He pushed his sandwich aside and wiped his lips. "The million dollar question: Why are you still a bitch?"

"We didn't know you, Detroit. We thought you trouble."

"All done with the bowling alley?"

"No, next time maybe you go with us."

"In case you need bailing out?" he said. "Costs a heap of money to be your friend."

"We're not friends," she said. "George says we might go tomorrow or the day after." Her foot jiggled up and down. She removed a paper napkin from the table's container, shredding it while taking in the room. "It's quiet here," she said, biting her lip. Her eyes moistened and a melancholy look scuttled across her face. He pulled his chair closer to hers. "I heard screams in the cells," she said. She balled the paper up, tossing it aside, and dragged out another napkin, shredding it in similar fashion.

Chairs scraped, then crashed to, the floor; angry shouts filled the room. Two students shoved against each other. One punched out a fist that failed to connect and more shoving ensued. Kendra watched quietly while other students broke up the fight. "People are scratchy after the arrests," she said. "Let's pop outside, there's a bonfire."

"Sure," he said, "maybe we roast up some chestnuts."

She smiled, and seemed to jostle aside her melancholy. "Is that what they do in South Detroit? Roast chestnuts?"

"Some people have nuts, some don't."

***

A few hundred students now huddled about the fire. Kendra and Adam, elbows propped, lay on a blanket with another couple. Adam's feet stretched off the blanket. Students pitched more firewood into the fire, and flames jumped, flashing three or four feet in the air, with sparks flying. Students forgot about the police car opposite them, chatted with others, discussing and flirting, and the tension of the last few days dissolved.

At 7 p.m. a second police car drove up, parking alongside the first, and four state police officers left their vehicles and lined up in front of the cars, as if standing parade for inspection.

Kendra sat up. "Is a bonfire suddenly against the law?"

The officer on the far right checked the load in his weapon, snapping the breech shut. He holstered his weapon, and the officer beside him checked his load and snapped the breech closed as well, holstering his weapon. The other two officers followed suit, in sequence. Adam wiped a trace of sweat from his cheek. Those students lying down or sitting slowly came to their feet. Talk ceased and the crackling sound of the fire dominated. Other police cruisers arrived, and officers in ones and twos climbed out of their vehicles until nine officers lined up, facing the bonfire. The newly arrived officers checked their loads. Now they withdrew shotguns and carbines from car trunks, brandishing these weapons in addition to standard-issue revolvers.

Two hundred feet separated the police from the students. An agitated Kendra shifted back and forth on her feet. "Go back to your pigsties," she screamed. "Po-leece be gone." Others joined in, shouting curses and insults at the officers. Adam edged nearer to Kendra, keeping her in hearing distance, as students now shouted and yelled nonstop. He smelled apples, fresh picked apples from the orchard, and he resisted a strong, sudden urge to touch her. "We should charge at them, Detroit," she said.

"Picking apples beats suckering tobacco," he said. He dipped his head and put an arm to her shoulder.

"What?"

One student flung a bannister rail, hitting an officer, knocking him to the ground. Other officers helped him into the back of a cruiser and tended to his cuts.

"We should charge now," she said, "before they get ready."

"We don't need to provoke people with guns," he said.

The police officers reformed their ranks. Another student pitched a brick towards them but it bounced short. Students hurled stones and officers ducked the missiles.

A brick whipped close to one officer and he fired a warning shot into the air. Eight South Carolina marshals opened fire using their shotguns, rifles and pistols. Students screamed and ran. The shooting barrage lasted fifteen seconds. Three bodies crumpled down dead, one of those students blown completely out of his shoes. Students ran in every direction. Twenty to thirty students suffered wounds, mostly shot in the back, and these students struggled, trying to drag themselves away. Kendra lay on the ground face down. A small, dark stain appeared on the back of her sweatshirt, widening, circling larger. Someone rushed by Adam, bumping into him, and he tripped over Kendra's body. Police officers waded into the students, clubbing at random, knocking people down and cuffing them. Adam hauled Kendra upright, staggering under the load. She recovered, helping with the weight, and his load lightened. "I'm shot, Detroit," she said. They lurched towards the infirmary.

Students crammed into the one-room infirmary. Blood and gauze littered the floor. The doctor beckoned to Kendra as they entered and she moved to him. He spun her about and wrenched up her shirt, revealing a pristine white bra. Below it a red slash dripped blood and she winced when his fingers probed. He splashed antiseptic on the wound and she jumped. He reached for gauze and tape, shoving them towards Adam. "Flesh wound. You deal with this. We need the space." Adam tore off a strip of gauze with his teeth, wadded up a patch and banded the tape around her, stretching it around her body. He noticed beads of sweat across her skin. His fingers dabbed at the sweat and he touched a finger to his lips, tasting her.

"Staring at my underwear?" she said. Her face rippled in sweat. He rolled her shirt down.

"All done," he said. "But…"

"But what?"

"I'm sorry I called you a bitch."

She tugged her green bandana from a pocket. Anger slashed across her face. "They killed us," she said, "because we had no guns." She brushed at her clothes, angrily jerking at her sweatshirt, fingers chipping at dirt no longer present, and lastly twisting fingers into her green bandana, fussing with it, adjusting it about her locks.

"That's not exactly Aunt Jemima's bandana," he said.

"Are we travelling together now?" she said.

"We could."

"Paris Day," she said, "believed in non-violence."

"My mom cranked it up to bank robbing."

"Piss on non-violence and piss on the po-leece," she said.

They left the campus together, toting their possessions in knapsacks. In a black-owned café on the outskirts of Orangeburg, they heard the first reports from the white press on the radio. The reports indicated that black power activists fired on police, who responded with their own fire. Adam stirred his cup of coffee, the spoon clicking against the chipped porcelain cup. "No one cares about the truth," he said.

"Dead black students don't matter," she said. "Dead white students—now that would get news people and politicians riled up."

Thursday, February 22
Detroit, Michigan, Federal Building

They waited in their office for a summons from Feeber. Rizzuto stretched his feet across a second chair, plaid polyester tie looping backwards to his neck, tie-end strung over his shoulder, his white shirt stretching. Lumps of pale skin and black, curly tuffs of hair stiffed out between his buttons. He munched on a banana and threw the skin towards the garbage can but it fell short and landed on the floor beside another skin. He kept his nose buried in the sports section of the *Free Press*, reading an article on the Tigers, lips moving while he read.

Harry Fortune wore a dark suit and maroon silk tie. "Does the room smell of garbage cans or raw sewage to you?" Fortune said.

Rizzuto did not reply.

Seated behind his desk, Fortune read the editorial page of the *New York Times* with the page nipped in, halved and quartered, subway rider-style. "The *Times* still supports the war," he said. When there was no reply, he twisted to stare at Rizzuto. "Every conversation does not necessarily involve hookers, tits or runs-batted-in," he said. "Shouldn't someone challenge the president at this point?"

Rizzuto lowered the *Free Press*, paper crackling. "Communism ain't no fantasy," he said, spitting off to the side on the floor.

"This office is our home, dude. Would you defecate in your living room?"

"It's why God created cleaning ladies," Rizzuto said. He spit off to the side again. "Can't let commie bastards into any country," he said. "They never leave. Don't need no college degree to figure that out, Miss Pussy." He raised the paper back up to his face and his lips jiggled up and down once more. But suddenly he jerked the paper back down, crunching it again. "Gossip says we got to follow political ass-wipes around. Any thoughts, Miss Pussy?"

"Maybe Feeber is seeking to educate you in politics, dude…so you can render a pithy opinion on the pros and cons of the Vietnam War."

Rizzuto's top lip twisted into a sneer. "Right…college grad. You spent how many years in university?"

"Six."

"And yet here we sit, each with the same job," Rizzuto said. "Ever think you pissed those six years away?"

Fortune lifted the *Times* back up, reading again. "Not since I met you."

Rizzuto rattled the *Free Press* again. "Doped-up hippies should be sent to the front lines instead of Marines."

The door to their office banged open and Feeber barged in. Rizzuto yanked his feet off the chair and both agents quickly dropped their newspapers aside. "Paris Day is with a Professor Connie Harlan," Feeber said.

"Gotcha, boss," Rizzuto said. "Connie Harlan."

"And this Harlan dame," Feeber said, "does politics up the ass."

"Gotcha, boss," Rizzuto said.

"The politicos running for president…" Feeber turned to Fortune. "You know them?"

"Black activists would support McCarthy or Kennedy."

"When you find Connie Harlan, you find Paris Day." Both agents nodded.

"And Rizzuto," Feeber said, "when you unearth the bitch, you deal with her."

"Gotcha, boss."

Fortune coughed politely. "Any word on my request for a transfer, sir?"

Feeber strode out of the room. The conversation was clearly over, but he called back. "You lost your piece."

The smell of garbage cans and raw sewage flooded the room, stinging its way into Fortune's nose.

Monday, February 26
Windsor, Ontario

Pokeface phoned Aiken early in the morning. "Pastyman, the Tanya whore and another one left for New Hampshire with some muscle. Don't know more. You hear me, Pastyman?"

"I hear you."

"You owe me, Pastyman. Send me some money." *Cheque's in the mail, asshole. May all your whores fill their crotches with cement.*

Friday, March 1
State Prison of Southern Michigan, Jackson County

Folks called it Jackson Prison, sometimes Jackson State Prison, because it was located in Jackson City. The largest walled penal institution in the world housed 5,237 inmates, including 1,605 in the maximum-security cell block. A wretched graveyard slouched within sight of the prison. A man dying in prison without funds, most likely a black man, was dropped without ceremony into a hole in this pauper's field, his grave marked with a wooden cross. Unless a man of the cloth happened to visit the prison on the put-down day, nobody said words over the body. Even in death the prison watchtowers, overlooking the ditching ground, controlled the prisoners, minding the bleak crosses and the few small stone slabs.

Beverly Turner insisted on stopping at the graveyard to say words over her deceased husband. The austere graveyard held spots of snow in the midst of coffee blotches outlining the white stick crosses and the few stones. Sprigs of hair poked out from her round hat and they rocked with the breeze. She drew the hat down tighter and gathered her thin coat tight, attempting to marshal warmth. The patches sewn into the coat trowelled in the cold. Her husband had been under ground for seven years but the tiny stone was only three years old, costing eighty-seven dollars, money saved by her out of welfare funds. She placed a kerchief on the ground and knelt in front of the headstone, wiping the stone face with a tissue. The small stone held no room for an epitaph or bible saying. It showed his name and his dates.

"I've suffered nine pregnancies," she said, hovering over the stone, "losing three, carrying six full term, raising them on Twelfth Street, both before and after you died on me, two sons shot to death, one son killed with a knife, two daughters married with children but no man, and Percy jailed for killing the man with the knife." She carefully laid the small bundle of leaves and flowers on the grave. They blew away because they hadn't been tied, but she failed to notice. "Percy's most like you, John…wild streak but craving to do what's right."

Professor Connie Harlan and Paris Day waited in the car with the engine running. "Why're we here?" Paris said.

"Give her a bit to report to her husband."

"I meant, at a prison? Am I to give a sermon to the prisoners?"

"We are skedaddling," Connie said, "and some muscle might keep us safer."

"Can't see wasting time in a cemetery," Paris said, "People in heaven are doing all right, seated in the company of the Lord."

Connie surveyed the bleak grounds in front of her, the disfigured landscape of crosses, mounds of chunky dirt with the occasional weathered headstone. "This is a dusky dumping ground, girl. Scarcely any white bodies buried here. Is there a special heaven for black people?"

Paris curled about, listening, but made no reply.

"Whether in heaven or not," Connie said, "many of these folk were just guilty of being black."

***

Inside the prison a guard banged a nightstick on Percy Turner's six-foot by ten-foot cell, unlocking the gate, allowing Percy to file out. He wore standard prison garb: faded dungarees, undershirt, blue shirt, tennis shoes with no laces, no socks. "Visitor," the guard said.

His mother sat across from her oldest boy, a man whose strapping size dwarfed the table between them.

"It's hard to pretend prison visits are normal meetings," she said.

"I know, Ma."

"It's hard to pretend this is a kitchen table."

"I'm glad you came, Ma."

"You are being released today," she said.

"I heard."

"Professor Harlan made sure of it," she said, "and you owe her for that. She's outside, waiting for your help."

"Yes, Ma."

"You gonna mend your nigger ways and obey the law?"

"You know why I did what I did."

"Your cousin Tanya is gone missing and my sister worries. She's probably dead but people should know one way or the other."

"OK, Ma. I'll see to it."

One hour later, Percy presented himself to the bullpen outside the warden's office. Two beefy guards, already inside, sat on the institutional chairs. Percy waited in silence until they spoke to him. The senior guard spat on the floor. "So Percy—jumping out of the pen, are we? Your last asshole opera?"

Percy stripped off his shoes, socks, pants, shirt and underclothes, dropping them one at a time, a rockslide heap of prison garb.

"No newspapermen or TV cameras in here," the senior guard said. Percy shook his head up and down, having heard the warning almost daily.

"You mess with us in here and it'll be a hard way to die, a real hard way. Don't matter it's your last day." Percy nodded, acknowledging the threat.

"Do the asshole opera, Percy."

Percy faced the wall, stretched his arms up and flapped them, and after that lifted one foot high up, then the other. He reached around behind him and pulled his ass cheeks apart to confirm nothing was hidden there.

"Okay, Percy."

Percy opened his mouth and tugged his tongue from side to side.

"No need to run fingers through your hair, Percy. Is that why you keep it so short?"

Percy nodded.

The guard sorted through Percy's clothes, dropping each article to the floor after examination.

"Myself," the younger guard said, "I can't believe they even locked you up since it was only a nigger you killed." Percy flashed a quick smile to indicate that he understood the humour.

"See you in church," the senior guard said. Percy pulled his trousers on.

***

They left Beverly Turner at her home on 12th Street and drove down the interstate system to a church on the outskirts of Cleveland, arriving after dark. Paris slept in the back for the entire trip. When they arrived at the church, Percy carried Paris inside with little effort. She was feverish and her words garbled, making no sense. The church basement held two rooms, seven cots in one room and a few tables and assorted mismatched chairs in the other. Eleven people huddled around the tables. The nun's whiteness shone out, contrasting with the others. A loaf of bread and slices of cheddar cheese waited for them on a card table along with quarts of milk and several worn glasses. Percy sat Paris on a chair and held her upright.

The nun greeted them warmly. "We use the cots in four-hour shifts."

"Except for this one," Percy said, nodding to Paris. The nun waved a finger to the other room and Percy carried her there, laying her down in a cot, smoothing a blanket over her, waiting until he heard regular breathing. The early arrivals filed into the room for a cot. Connie and Percy slabbed together sandwiches, sitting around a square wooden table. Percy sluiced down a glass of milk. "Who are these dusty rabbits?" he said.

"People skedaddling," Connie said. "Either on someone's radar or trying hard not to be."

"The age of the men, Miss Harlan..." Percy said. "Maybe draft dodgers making their way north to Canada?"

She eyeballed the men in the room. "Perhaps."

"Which way are we heading, Miss Harlan?"

"New Hampshire," Connie said. "Gonna help some politician who's against the war."

Percy ran his tongue around his mouth, scrubbing out the last of his sandwich, and his cheeks puffed in and out briefly. "Political shit." He grabbed another slice of bread, sticking a piece of cheese on it, munching while speaking. "Why are you needing me?"

"We're not so popular right now. You'll have to dig up some sort of weapon."

"What's the matter with your friend?"

"She'll be fine in a few days," Connie said.

"Where's Tanya?"

"Dead by the same people hunting us."

"Dead?"

"Dead and buried under the wrong name."

"Dead is dead," he said. "I'll send word to my aunt."

"Yeah," she said, "dead is definitely dead."

Saturday, March 2
Madison, Wisconsin

Students from the University of Wisconsin at Madison inhabited most of the houses on Mifflin Street. Political rallies against the war ran nonstop, fuelled by rampant drug use. Adam and Kendra bunked in one of the smaller houses, the one with the handwritten sign on the porch: *Off the Pigs.* She read the sign once more. "Damn straight," she said.

"They totally hate the police," Adam said, as they shoved past the sign, moving into the building's shadow. The moist, rank smell between the houses whacked into them; they trod carefully on the chunked-up sidewalk, threading into the backyard. The weed-crammed yard contained no shrubs or trees; the uncut, untended grass bent over like slivers of avocado. A faded mattress lay against the fence, pinned flat; another mattress lay crumpled on the ground in front of it. Concrete blocks, arranged in a makeshift fireplace, supported a large iron pot, the sole sign of communal life.

The chap who taught them basic karate moves a few days ago now held up a Coke bottle, rotating the spiralled glass about in his fingers. "A Molotov cocktail," he said, "that doesn't off a pig is a wasted effort." His eyes drilled into Kendra. "Girls piss away a lot of opportunities."

Kendra hefted the bottle but before she tossed it, he shunted her forward, pushing her to within five feet of the fence. She threw the bottle and it whacked against the mattress. He collected the bottle and backed her to ten feet, then fifteen, and she flung the bottle again and again, hitting the mattress each time. At the end of thirty minutes, she hit the mattress consistently from across the yard.

The man offered the bottle to Adam. He paced off the entire length of the yard and probed about for a target. He flung the bottle at the iron pot and it smacked into it, shattering, with shards spreading, plummeting about. "Baseball," Adam said. "Good practice for throwing anything."

"Just a bottle-chucking maniac," Kendra said.

Saturday, March 2
Windsor, Ontario

In the evening, Aiken answered the phone. "You okay, Pops?" Adam said. "Got a phone number for you. We'll be bunking here a while."

"We?"

"Yeah…we. Uh, with some people, that's all." He read the phone number to Aiken, who scratched the number down. "I've been worried for you," Aiken said.

"I'm fine."

"Students are fleeing to Canada to avoid the war. You ran in the wrong direction."

"Sort of like Mom always did, eh?"

"Come home," Aiken said. *Please come home, son. Toss a ball around with me or nag me about my drinking or just spend the day farting about.*

"Doing fine," Adam said. "At the University of Wisconsin."

"Studying there?"

"Does learning how to toss a Molotov cocktail count as studying?"

"Why do you hanker for that skill?" Aiken said.

"For the same reasons Mom robbed a bank."

"She never robbed a bank," Aiken said. "Some sort of misunderstanding."

Adam paused a few seconds before speaking. "So the pigs killed her for no reason."

"No one knows what happened."

"The pigs killed her, that's what happened."

The dial tone clicked in, ringing about Aiken's head, sounding louder and louder until he forced himself to lay the receiver down. His temples throbbed. He unscrewed the cap from a quart bottle of Canadian Club, tossing the cap away, moving out to the back porch, ignoring the black lab, who sought attention. He drank from the bottle and the dog flopped down across his feet, glancing up, slobber spilling over Aiken's shins. When the bottle emptied, he crawled up to the bedroom and ripped off his shirt and pants and collapsed into bed.

A nightmare drove Aiken back to the shadowy beaches of Dieppe. Burning fever and sweats carted over him. The killing of the Essex Scottish commenced once more. German soldiers on top of the cliffs began a fine killing day, pumping bullets, shells and grenades down onto the Scottish. Men died as they jumped ashore and others jumped over the bodies to be shot down a few feet farther on. Aiken heard shouting and woke to Sarah, sitting beside him and shaking him.

"It's fine, Daddy. The war's over."

He sat up, swinging his legs off the bed, sliding his feet into slippers.

Sarah wore a mauve nightie with bushes tattooed across the material, tiny bushes, dancing as she shifted about. His T-shirt and shorts dripped in sweat even though coldness stank up the room.

"I'm okay, sweetie. Go back to bed."

She stood but he reached out and caught her shoulder. "Sarah," he said, "I'm going to New Hampshire for a few days, and you'll stay with Grandpa Mayhem."

She plopped down beside him. "Why, please?"

"Searching for Tanya…the girl with your mom at the bank."

She remained on the bed, digesting his words. "We'll talk about it later," she said. "Do you think Adam is okay?"

"He's strong and smart. He'll be okay."

"Go back to sleep, Daddy." She squeezed a final hug to him and left the room.

But a guy tossing a Molotov cocktail might wind up dead.

Saturday, March 2
Madison, Wisconsin

The kitchen showed peeling wallpaper and torn-up patches of linoleum flooring. Mucked-up dishes lay over the countertop and filled the sink.

"What a junkyard," Adam said.

"Who cares," Kendra said. She wore black jeans that wrapped tight to her butt, green scarf tucked into the back pocket, and a loose blouse tailored like a man's dress shirt. Adam wore jeans and a sweatshirt. He plucked a cup from the sink and twisted the faucet on. The water burst forth with spurts and bubbles. He let it stream a little before he rinsed out the cup. He inspected the cup carefully before filling it with tap water. He leaned against the countertop and it creaked under his weight. Kendra spun a kitchen chair about, plopping down on it.

"No one owns the dishes," he said, "so no one washes them."

"Say what you mean."

"We should leave this place," he said. "Maybe aim south."

"Why?"

"I don't care for this group living."

"Collective," she said. "A collective is the pattern for the future. No private property and no capitalism."

He tweaked at his shirt. "So I don't own these clothes..." He tugged again at his shirt. "Even though I'm wearing them."

"Everyone in the collective owns them. You wear the clothes you require."

"But no one person owns these jeans I'm wearing?" He plucked at his jeans.

"That's why they call it a collective," she said.

"And no one washes the clothes because no one owns them."

"The point?"

"I'm not taking off this shirt and these pants until they rot away and I ain't ever wearing someone else's underwear that no one washes because no one owns them."

"Calm down," she said.

"And it applies to sex?" he said.

"We finally arrive at the point. You don't own me just because we slept together."

"Just another night in the sack for you?"

"They invented monogamy to enslave women," she said. "We won't be fully admitted here until we share our bodies."

"There's diseases and things like that," he said. "Maybe gonorrhea."

An exasperated look spun across her face. "You'd be able to screw every girl here."

The muscles on his back stretched tight, bunching under his shirt.

"That redhead's body is nice," she said, "and she watches you."

"Don't care."

"Do you think she's pretty? A nice, sultry little white girl to keep you warm. You could make her squeal."

"Don't care."

"She's looks at you, follows you about with her eyes."

He yelled: "I don't care." Rising up, he thrust his hands underneath her arms, lifting her to her feet. "I ain't sharing underwear and I ain't sharing you and I ain't sharing the redhead."

"Calm down."

"That ain't me and I'm out of here if that's you." He dropped her down in the chair but towered over her. She slumped lower.

"I could do it with anyone," she said.

The veins about his temples flared up, his muscles tensed. "Choose."

She pressed against his shoulders, standing and shoving him down into the chair. She spread her legs, crawling over him, legs wrapping him, rubbing his neck. He smelled lemony-orange-preserve and felt light-headed. "Maybe we head south or maybe east," she said. "Why learn to throw a Molotov cocktail and not actually toss one."

Sunday, March 3
Windsor, Ontario

Aiken shaved and scrubbed up while slugging down a naked shot of Canadian Club, chasing away a slight hangover. He decided to proceed with a resolution formulated over the past day or so. *Get back in the saddle. You can do this, Aiken.* He dragged on his Assumption University jacket, a melton and leather affair, a gift from Paris during her teaching days. *Days when she felt she could save the world by teaching political science to dolts, un-dolting them one at a time.* He parted the drapes and checked the wind, opting for a scarf as well.

Outside, the whipping wind hurled spring freshness with a remaining dash of the hardness of winter into his face. He tugged his scarf tight and hoofed it to Pond's Drug Store at Giles Boulevard and Ouellette Avenue. He sorted through the newspapers for sale. *What sort of papers would discuss an election in New Hampshire?* He scooped up the local Detroit papers—the *Free Press* and the *News* out of habit, and snatched the *New York Times*, the *Washington Post*, the *Globe and Mail*, and the *Toronto Star*. He set the most recent issue of *Time* magazine on top of the pile and slapped a twenty-dollar bill down on the counter. The clerk, reading the sports section of the *Free Press*, cast an eye over the pile of papers. "Just discover how to read?" he said.

Hello dolt. "Just discovered my first asshole of the day," Aiken replied.

The clerk rang up the sale, packaged the purchase in a brown paper sack and slammed Aiken's change down on the counter. "Just making conversation, pal."

"You've no flare for it," Aiken said. "Do something else, *pal*. Or join a monastery and consider a vow of silence."

"Screw you."

Outside the door he recapped: *That went well. Get rid of the nut-cuttin', Aiken. Slow down…Pretend to be Perry Como and buy one of his sweaters. Farting about America and New Hampshire figuring out what happened to your wife might be good for you…quality time away from the Webley.*

***

At home Aiken hijacked the dining room table and arrayed newspapers about. Out of longstanding habit he flipped to the *Free Press* sports section seeking news of the Tigers or Wings, casting aside the other sections as he normally did. But he quickly found himself agitated, flipped the sports aside and grabbed the first section of each paper, reading the hard news, then the editorials, before moving on. His fingers smudged ink and he scratched notes with a pencil, the newspapers releasing a pleasant, acidic smell that reminded him of balsamic. *The New Hampshire election pits an underfinanced, somewhat disorganized poet, Senator Eugene McCarthy, against President Johnson.* He re-read the *Times* article again. *And the president is a crafty, ruthless son-of-a-bitch, a mean bugger you shouldn't piss off.*

He reached for the *Toronto Star*, skimming photos from a west coast university demonstration. *Everybody in America is pissed off, and apparently the solution is to wear ratty-ass clothes, forgo shaving and refuse to cut your hair.* The *Wall Street Journal* showed photos of the "Clean for Gene" students: short hair, pleated skirts and navy sports coats, and slacks capable of carrying a crease. *Students should dress like this.* He dropped the newspapers to the floor. *Two different Americas are duking it out—the same crap that killed Paris.* He crumpled up the paper, balling it up, heaving it towards the fireplace.

When the paper bounced off the ash-covered grate, the burnt-out, dead smell of the fireplace slagged into him.

He knelt down and sorted through the pile of papers until he found the sports section of the *Free Press. Give this political shit a rest. It killed Paris. If Denny McLain has a good year, the Tigers may go all the way.*

Chester entered the room, beating some liquid in a bowl. He booted aside some of the papers with his foot. "Opening a newsstand?"

"Boning up on New Hampshire politics."

"And?"

"I've changed my mind," Aiken said. "Dead is dead. She's not coming back to life, so why chase after Tanya in New Hampshire?"

"I ken what you're telling me," Chester said. He stuck a finger into the bowl and popped the finger into his mouth, sucking it clean. "You've a daughter to raise up."

"Exactly, I've a daughter to raise up."

"You can't traipse around New Hampshire," Chester said, "seeking answers about your wife's death."

"Exactly."

"Even if your two children deserve to know the truth about the woman they loved."

Leave the nut-cuttin' to professionals, Tonto.

Sarah trudged into the dining room. "Hair time," she said. Her voice carried an edge and Aiken knew the tenseness was caused by *"hair time."* He followed her into the kitchen. She shooed Chester out of the room.

The hateful tools wait in a row: comb, hair dryer, bowl of goo, curler, butter bowl and the scorched piece of leather a few inches wide. He knew the function of each item. He pointed to the butter. "We won't need butter this time," he said.

Her face simmered with impatience. "We'll need it, Daddy. We always need it."

He cleared a space. Using the chair she climbed onto the counter and stretched out so that her neck dangled on the edge of the sink, her hair strung down, a few inches from the tap. He draped a towel around her neck and shoulders, wetted her hair and applied shampoo. An apricot scent drifted up from the shampoo. He rubbed the shampoo into her hair before rinsing, repeating the process two more times. She winced whenever the shampoo dribbled into her eyes but voiced no complaint. After the third rinse, she climbed down and sat straight in the chair while he towelled her off. He applied conditioner and a similar smell wafted into him. He rubbed slowly, massaging the conditioner thoroughly into her hair. He clicked the dryer on low. She reached over and clicked it on high with an irritated gesture. "Hold it close," she said. He did as instructed, and after a few minutes her sweats started. At this point he began to brush, pulling her hair away from her head towards him, stroking it continuously, a practised movement, repeated endlessly. His arm tired but he kept on. She grimaced as he removed some of the tangles, but she kept quiet.

"Now the goo," she said. He scooped his fingers into the paste-like substance and applied it to her hair, untangling the hair as he rubbed it in. She wrinkled her nose at the rotten potato-like smell. "Boys say mean things about Mommy," she said.

Oh man! "The boys at school?"

"Yes. Now the stove," she said. He clicked the element on. She spoke sharply: "Switch it on high, Daddy."

He cranked the element on high and placed the pressing iron on the stove element. After a while it glowed. He bunched up some of her hair and glided the piece of leather under it, then flattened the iron against the hair. "This part might hurt," he said.

"You have to find out about Mommy."

"It won't bring her back," he said. "Maybe we should leave it lie."

"Straight hair is prettier," she said. He kept ironing her hair with the iron against the leather. When she flinched, he slathered butter on the burn. "You don't get straight hair without burns," she said.

"All done."

He passed the hand towel to her. She rubbed it against her forehead, dabbing the sweat away. "Mommy did not rob banks."

He stowed the hair utensils under the sink and in cupboards. When he was done, she led him to the hall and from the closet removed a cleaning bag containing his grey flannels and his shirt. "All clean and mended," she said. "Wear your tweed coat and pretend to be a teacher. They won't check."

"A teacher?"

"And you join the Clean for Gene group that Chester spoke about."

"For political stuff?"

"Uncle Chester will pick you up at noon in his Morgan sports car." *Chester drives a Morgan? What kind of idiot drives an English sports car in Canada?*

He twirled the hangers, rotating the trousers and shirt back and forth, but he hesitated.

She squeezed her arms about him. "People should know that Mommy did not rob banks."

Monday, March 4
Detroit, Michigan

Rizzuto lugged a medium-sized duffle and a leather case, the case four-foot long and twelve inches wide. Harry Fortune carried a small, frayed cloth suitcase. Followed by Rizzuto, Fortune pushed through the doors, out of the building that housed Detroit's FBI squad. Sleet banged against his uncovered head, stinging his face, and goaded by the weather he fled quickly, opening the door of the first cab in line. Rizzuto plucked him back, walking him to the third cab, shoving him into the back seat. They crammed their luggage between them. Rizzuto waited until the vehicle merged into traffic before giving a destination.

"Go through the tunnel and drop us on the Canadian side," he said. The cab exited the tunnel and drifted up to Canadian customs. Rizzuto flashed ID and held up the leather case.

"Nothing to declare," he said. "Just moose hunters making our way to northern Ontario." The officer waved them through. "Black moose," Rizzuto said to Fortune, chuckling at his witticism. "Black moose," he repeated.

Outside the tunnel exit they left the cab and walked the few paces to Ouellette Avenue. They found a few Windsor cabs in line outside the hotel, the operators clustered and smoking in an alcove, out of the wind and snow. Rizzuto chose the second one in line and a cabbie hustled into the front seat. Again, he waited until the vehicle glided into traffic before giving a destination. "Windsor Airport," he said.

The taxi left the two men at the entrance to the single airport terminal. "Do we check in somewhere?" Fortune asked. Rizzuto didn't reply. He thrust his way into the terminal, pushing out through an unlabelled door onto the airport tarmac. Fortune followed. A de Havilland Twin Otter parked about thirty feet away, propellers whirling, emitted a raspy, grunting sound. A thin man in overalls carried crates from a forklift and stowed the boxes one at a time in the plane. Rizzuto climbed the three-step metal staircase and Fortune followed. Both men tumbled into the single row of seats at the back of the plane. The pilot fussed the boxes about in front of them and strapped them down. When he finished he removed the overalls, shoving them aside, and jerked on a brown leather jacket, dropping into the left-side pilot's seat. He revved the engine; the noise rose loud and sharp. The plane taxied and lifted into flight. The engine sounds reverberated throughout, making conversation strained. There were no other passengers. Their luggage pressed against their feet, bunched up against the crates.

"What's in the boxes?" Fortune yelled.

"Wheaties," Rizzuto said.

"Too heavy for cereal."

"Weapons to some people in the Carolinas. People with a civil rights problem."

"White supremacists?"

"Lucky guess, Miss Pussy, lucky guess."

They flew across Lake Erie just above the waves, landing at a small airfield in New York State to refuel. Fortune left the plane and found a grubby washroom. Rizzuto stayed in the plane. Fortune lit one of the three joints in his jacket pocket and sucked furiously until it was finished.

Back in the air Rizzuto opened the leather case and assembled a rifle with scope. Fortune put a cigarette to his mouth and clicked his Zippo several times. Rizzuto stared at the sparks. His eyes rolled up and his limbs shook. White spittle appeared on his lips. After a moment he recovered from the trance, saw Fortune watching him and grabbed his pistol, but Fortune quickly whipped his hands palms-out.

"Between us," Fortune said. "We're partners."

Rizzuto focused on his rifle. He clutched the bolt, turning it, tugging it free from the weapon, blowing across it, blowing into the breech; he wiped the innards with an oily cloth and reassembled the mechanism. He removed a box of shells from his duffle and slapped one shell in the rifle chamber, sighting it briefly, aiming it at the back of the pilot's head. He mouthed the word "bang" to Fortune. He retrieved the shell, placed the rifle back in the case and the single shell back into the box, and returned the box to his duffle.

They landed at Pease International Airport in New Hampshire just before dark. Rows and rows of military planes gleamed in the final rays of light. "Is this some sort of military airport?" Fortune said.

"The blue-grey planes," Rizzuto said, "are Air National Guard F-16 Fighting Falcons and the camouflage ones are Air Force F-4 Phantom fighters."

"In case someone attacks New Hampshire?" Fortune said. "Or maybe New Jersey."

"Keeping America safe, Miss Pussy," Rizzuto said. He held up his leather case and rapped his fingers against it. "Same as us."

Fortune felt about his jacket pocket until he located one of his two remaining joints. He rolled it about with his fingers. Calmness settled over his face. He lifted his hand from the pocket. "Do we rent a car?" he said.

"No tracks, Miss Pussy. There'll be a car waiting for us."

"And then?"

"We stake out the McCarthy headquarters in Concord and see who shows up."

"And if someone does?"

"If we locate a certain black woman," Rizzuto said, "we won't be dishing up tea and cookies." He held up his leather case again, rapping his fingers against it.

"Why?"

"She's on Roland Feeber's list," Rizzuto said.

"List?"

"A list of people who use up too much air, take up too much space."

Tuesday, March 5

Concord, New Hampshire

Aiken's forehead bubbled sweat, trickling droplets down his face. The German soldiers commanded the Dieppe high ground. Death pranced among the Canadians, uprooting them one at a time, sometimes with a bullet to the body, sometimes in the back, sometimes a gut shot, but no one escaped the butchery. Aiken rolled over, grabbing the iron bedframe, shaking it, banging it against the wall. Someone pounded from the adjoining room, waking him. He sat up, swinging his legs out, feeling about for his slippers. The boarding-house room measured twelve feet square; austere, with faded, ancient wallpaper and a few pieces of mismatched wooden furniture strewn around. A half-drained bottle of Canadian Club sat on the nightstand, its recent comrade, a glass, empty and bleak. The age-old pair of wall lamps had no central switch, each one needing standing-beside for clicking on or off. He snapped the knob on the nightstand table lamp, but the dead click produced no light, so he remained in the dark. *Those guys are dead and I'm not.* He rotated the alarm clock towards the curtained windows, catching light from the false dawn filtering in. The wind-up clock read 7:05.

When the chill bit into the sweat on his face, he reached for the cardigan sweater crumpled on the floor, dragging it on. He plonked two fingers of whiskey into the glass and swallowed it down in one gulp, followed by another two fingers, wiping the sweat from his face with his sleeve. He carried the glass to the window, parted the curtains, and looked down at the rooming houses across the street. A figure emerged from the building across the way, glancing about cautiously, filing between the two buildings and flaming a match to light a cigarette. Aiken remained watching. *He's not smoking a cigarette. The constant sucking…he's doing drugs. Marijuana! He's smoking a marijuana cigarette at seven in the morning.* The sky lightened and the figure shifted out from between the houses. *That's the FBI guy, Fortune—Harry Fortune.* Aiken slumped down on the bed, the bedsprings creaking from his weight. He sipped whiskey. *Why would a Detroit FBI agent be in New Hampshire for a political campaign? Are they hunting for Tanya?*

Aiken stumbled down the creaking stairway, making his way to the kitchen. Chester gently waved a fry pan slowly back and forth across a heating element. "Flank steak," he said, "rubbed down with cocoa and coffee and sautéed with wild mushrooms and preserved cherries."

"It's breakfast," Aiken said. "Nothing wrong with cornflakes."

"Nothing wrong with jerking your pants down and shitting in the bushes either."

"Agent Harry Fortune is rooming at the house across the street."

"Curious. You start work with the McCarthy people, commencing this morning."

"How did you arrange that?"

"With my no-limit credit card—a form of poetry similar in effect to the first time a man sees a naked woman."

Yeah, my grandma; nightmares for years!

Another thought crossed Aiken's mind. "Maybe Tanya is working for Johnson," he said, "not McCarthy."

Chester set the pan down. "A black woman in 1968 would not work for Johnson over McCarthy. Dog-fart guaranteed." *A sneer is not required, sidekick.* "You hunt up black campaigners, Kemo Sabe, I'll food-shop and cook."

"Do you even know where the supermarket is, Moon Doggie?"

"I know the name of every three-star chef in the state and which restaurants sell out of the back door and who accepts charge cards. What use would I have for a supermarket?"

"Agent Harry Fortune," Aiken said, "smokes illegal drugs."

Chester set the pan down and slapped his forehead. "And him an FBI agent."

* * *

Just past noon, Harry Fortune left his rooming house, removing his last joint from a pocket, filing into the space between the buildings. Chester waited there, leaning casually against a wall with a joint of his own propped in front of him with two fingers clasped about it, showing it off to Fortune. "On me," Chester said.

Fortune pocketed his own joint. He grasped Chester's joint, flipped it around in his mouth, moistening it, striking a match, sucking in hard as the joint caught fire. "Running low," he said. "Any idea where to buy weed in Concord?"

Chester toked up. "I'll check around," he wheezed out.

"In New Hampshire for the weather?" Fortune said.

"Political doings," Chester said. "You?"

"Chasing someone on a hit list." Bleakness spun briefly across his face. "Bad karma stuff."

"Hit list?"

"I gotta find my way back to California," Fortune said. The joint burned low and and they pinched at it with their fingers. Chester produced a roach clip, grabbing the dwindling joint, passing it back to Fortune, who finished it.

Chester fumbled around his pockets and, magician-like, popped a weed baggie, giving it over. "To keep your spirits up. It's not often I get to toke up with a man sworn to uphold the law."

"Thanks, man," Fortune said, pocketing the bag. He started away, waving, but suddenly reversed. "Why does the freaking Detroit FBI," he said, "get to decide who lives and who dies?"

Tuesday, March 5
Kennedy Compound, Hyannis Port, Massachusetts

On February 29 they released the Kerner Report, commissioned by President Johnson after the Detroit riot. The blunt conclusion: white racism caused urban violence. Cities should hire more diverse police forces; governments should invest billions in housing to break up *de facto* segregation. "Our nation is moving toward two societies," the report said, "one black, one white—separate and unequal."

A copy of the report nestled in Pierre Salinger's briefcase and another copy was flipped open in front of Kennedy. The report formed the focus point of their meeting. Kennedy's copy was dog-eared and marked up. The men sat across from one another in the basement sipping room of the compound. A platter of cheddar cheese slices and an open bottle of Chablis sat on the table between them. Kennedy tipped wine into two glasses, passed one to Salinger and sipped. "What did King say?"

Salinger reached for a sheet of paper in his briefcase and perused it. "He called the report a 'physician's warning of approaching death, with a prescription for life.'"

"King has Churchill's gift for phrasemaking," Kennedy said. "What's Johnson's response to the report?"

"You mean His Evilness?"

Kennedy smiled at that.

"Johnson expressed the view," Salinger said, "that members of the Kerner Commission 'painted their asses white in order to run with the antelope.'" Salinger paused. "Texas humour. I love it."

"I'm surrounded by phrasemakers," Kennedy said.

"I'm not understanding Johnson's thinking," Salinger said. "He appoints a commission but ignores the recommendations?"

"When cities burn and people are killed, the real issues blister into focus. People do what's right. Later, the politics steal back in."

"Nixon issued a statement," Salinger said.

"And?"

"The report, according to him, blames everyone except the rioters."

"Red meat for his political base."

Salinger fingered a piece of cheese and took a tentative bite. "What's your opinion on the report, Bob?"

"If we ignore those recommendations, ghetto problems will overwhelm the country."

"So why don't we announce now?" Salinger said. "We launch your campaign focusing on this report."

"Not yet," Kennedy said

Salinger dropped the sheet of paper back into the briefcase. "You mean we hold off until after New Hampshire?"

"Right," Kennedy said. "Work behind the scenes and give McCarthy his day of glory."

Wednesday, March 6
Concord, New Hampshire

"Icy sidewalks screw people over," McCarthy's point man said. "We got crotchety dogs out biting asses, sub-zero weather, blistering snow storms and butt-freezing rain." He sucked his cigarette down to a nub and crushed the butt into a smoldering ashtray, an ashtray where dozens of butts already mushroomed over the side. The rotting-weed smell curled into Aiken's face, forcing him to lean back.

"Sure," Aiken said, "sometimes canvassing is a bitch."

"Nice slacks," the point man said. "Pants should always carry a crease."

"Any black people work for McCarthy?" Aiken said.

The point man paused, not answering, lighting another cigarette. "Everyone meets up here in the evening after canvassing."

"I'm available today."

"I can dig up a partner for you."

Aiken picked up a bundle of McCarthy flyers, waving them back and forth. "I'm okay on my own. I've been doing politics for years." *In Stalag 8B I ran for class president.*

At 9 a.m. Aiken knocked on the first door. The man answering wore a ratty white tank top and faded jeans. "Whaddya want?"

Aiken held up a McCarthy flyer. "Canvassing for Senator McCarthy."

The man slammed the door. The next person slammed the door in his face as well.

When the third door opened, Aiken rammed a flyer at the woman. "Read the goddamn thing," he said. He walked on. *Political canvassers should carry firearms to make their point.*

At 5 p.m. Aiken returned to the rooming house. Chester was humming in the kitchen. "Canvassing means you play kissy-face with strangers," Aiken said. Chester responded by wrapping his arms about Aiken, squeezing tight, slapping his hands against Aiken's back. *What? Dipping into the cooking sherry?* "Your apron is on backwards," Aiken said.

Chester made the Jackie Gleason "going away" move. "Not so," he said. "My body faces the wrong way." He laughed and sang out, "Tangerine trees and marmalade skies." He withdrew a white tablecloth from a kitchen drawer, snapped it open, waved it in front of him and snapped it once more. He floated it across the table, organizing it, fussing, making subtle adjustments until satisfied. He produced two platters from a warming shelf and set them carefully on the table.

Chicken and what? Some sort of root things?

Chester waved over the platters. "Roast chicken with truffles," he said.

Aiken examined the platter, sniffing it. "Truffles?" *More like angry, rogue potatoes or thalidomide carrots?*

"Magnificent fungi," Chester said.

"Fungi? Like athlete's foot, or jock itch?"

An ugly expression slashed Chester's face for one brief second. "Imported from France," he said. "Bought them from a most exclusive restaurant."

A wine bottle on the side table drew Aiken's attention, the cork drawn, nestling alongside, with two crystal glasses on standby duty. Chester poured a few inches into each glass, slid a glass to Aiken and held his glass to his nose, inhaling, inviting Aiken to breathe in as well.

The smelling thing again?

"Somewhat spicy with a strawberry leaf smell," Chester said. "It's Beaujolais—one of the original ten crus."

Aiken sipped at the wine and it tingled pleasantly in his throat. *With enough alcohol I could chug down a fungus, and with a second bottle, maybe a dirty sweat sock.*

After dinner Aiken walked to the campaign headquarters and read newspapers as the students drifted in from canvassing. No black person showed. At 10 p.m., he gave up and walked back to the rooming house alone, keeping his coat tight in the blowing snow, his face smarting from the wind. *Why do I really care how Paris died? Is this quest to find Tanya part of my moving on from Paris? That must be it. This is me moving on.*

* * *

Banging on the door to his room stirred Aiken out of bed. He stumbled to the door, flinging it open, finding Chester, shirt unbuttoned, hair hither and thither, haystack-style. He held his apron, wringing it nonstop. "The LSD bitch," he said, "makes you think you have unlimited options."

"What?"

"Aiken, could I survive without those downer pens? Without those naked figures?"

"What?"

"Every day we grow inside," Chester said, "but our outsides die a tiny bit. That's what LSD does, Aiken. You comprehend things that people weren't meant to know."

Aiken opened the door wide to allow Chester inside. "No black people work for McCarthy," Aiken said.

"Feed me a warm beer or a shot of something, buddy. I crave some reality." He glanced around the room. "Oh for Christ's sake, who makes wallpaper this ugly?"

* * *

Professor Connie Harlan and Paris rented digs in the black area of Concord but occasionally ranged throughout the state. Connie enlisted the black press on behalf of Senator Eugene McCarthy, who was unaware of her efforts. She solicited support for him from black fraternities, black women's clubs and religious organizations, engaging as many people as possible on the senator's behalf. She spent her days phoning and talking to the residents of Concord and her evenings meeting Manchester residents in a schoolhouse on the edge of the city. Paris followed her about while making copious and curious notes in a journal she carried, speaking rarely and rubbing her forehead with her fingers, soothing the scar.

They waited at the school not knowing how many would show. "Our conversations follow a predictable pattern," Connie said. "The senator has no profile in the black community. They just don't know who he is." A short chestnut-coloured man entered the room, removing his hat, and bobbed his head at each woman. He wore a plaid shirt and work overalls and sat down in front of Paris, who ignored him, continuing to pen entries into her notebook. He spun the chair around to face Connie Harlan.

"We're canvassing votes for Senator McCarthy," Connie said.

"Know that. Things are better now than before. I never ate food in a restaurant with white people until 1939. Now I can do that in New Hampshire."

Connie tried to contain her anger. "Well if that ain't the acid test for the good life," she said, "then, mister, I don't know what is." She rose and paced, stalking the room. "So let's do our sums," she said. "We have puke schools, absolute puke." Her voice struck a higher note and her arms splashed about. "We're crammed into ghetto neighbourhoods…couldn't buy a suburb home even if we had the money, and poor black men join up to die in Vietnam because that's their best option."

"Just saying," he said, "things are better now than in the past."

Connie stepped to the table and grabbed up the Kerner Report. "We can't do what this report says the country needs while we remain at war in Vietnam." Connie dropped a chair next to the man, crowding his space, and he arched back a bit. "McCarthy is our pony in this race," she said, "that's all we're saying. We're asking you to vote McCarthy. Not asking you to demonstrate or to kill anyone, just show up and cast one stinking vote."

"Might do that." He bowed respectfully before he left the room.

"Every person is a hard sell," Connie said. "Black people want Nelson Rockefeller or Bobby Kennedy in the White House. They don't know McCarthy from the man in the moon."

Paris snapped shut her notebook. "I may mention that in my sermon this Sunday."

Connie wrapped her arms about Paris, clinging to her for several seconds. "You do that girl. Tell me your name again."

"You know it's Vernon. Don't tease me so."

Thursday, March 7
Windsor, Ontario

Thunderous pounding on the front door roused Sarah from her homework. Peeking through the curtains she saw two figures huddled together to ward off the chill.

Her brother, Adam, kept banging and gesturing at her. "Cold out here, sis!"

She sprung the lock, allowing them to enter, and tolerated a nippy hug from Adam.

"Washroom off the kitchen," Adam said to Kendra and she headed towards the back of the house. When she was out of sight, Adam tapped his sister playfully. "Kendra's pretty, eh?"

"Trampy pretty," Sarah said. "Maybe attractive to someone who was desperate for a girlfriend."

"Don't be like that."

"She smells like a sewer."

"Good thing this'll be just a short visit," Adam said. "A person can stand only so much bitchy at a time." He leaned their knapsacks against the wall.

"Grandpa," Sarah called up the stairs, "Adam's home," and in a lower voice, "for *just a short* visit."

Mayhem Chase lumbered down the stairs and immediately wrapped Adam in his arms, lifting him off the ground before setting him back down. Mayhem gave off a toothy grin.

"Being taller," he said, "still don't make you bigger than me." Adam introduced Kendra when she returned and Mayhem responded with a warm handshake, his two large hands smothering hers.

In the silence that followed, Adam shuffled back and forth, one foot to the other. "Gramps knows Martin Luther King," he finally said. "Met him at college."

"Crozer Seminary," Mayhem said. "Martin was the cream, top of the class. People were surprised they even offered me a diploma." The grin again: "Could've been a mistake."

"Why attempt something," Kendra said, "if you don't aim to be the best?" She jammed her kerchief into a back pocket.

Mayhem's face froze in place. "There's some truth to that," he said.

"Grandpa's very smart," Sarah said, "at the important things."

Mayhem hustled them towards the kitchen. "I'll make us some chow," he said. He draped on an apron, opened three cans of Heinz beans and dumped them into a pot while Sarah removed a package of wieners from the fridge and sliced it open. Both moved about the kitchen smoothly, brushing past each other with tender touches as they shifted back and forth. She nudged fingers into his back and put water on to boil. She chopped the wieners and dropped the pieces into the pot.

"Beans and franks?" Kendra said. "That's what you got?"

"We have beans and franks a lot," Sarah said, "only because we like beans and franks." Mayhem smirked at that comment.

After dinner Mayhem washed up the plates and opened a beer while Adam helped himself to a tall glass of milk. They gathered about the dining room, leaving Sarah at the kitchen table working on her homework. Mayhem produced some of Paris's magazines: *Time* and *Newsweek*, a few copies of *Life*. He stacked them in front of Kendra and she browsed, flicking the pages with a slender finger, touching her index finger to her lip, wetting it before each flick.

Mayhem dragged out the checkers box and the two men hunkered down at the table. Aiken's cherry dining room suite was in fair condition, showing well, but the pockmarked wooden checker box missed one hinge, and the board only worked by pushing parts together because the binding had frayed away years ago. Mayhem raised an eye to Adam while putting the pieces in place. "Have you mastered this game yet?"

"How long has it been," Adam said, "since you swooshed a shot through a hoop? Years maybe? And thirty years since you last cracked a home run?"

The checker game clicked on. Mayhem kept track of their games on a scratch pad, a single stroke underneath the winner's name at the conclusion of each game.

Somewhat later Adam commented on a move by Mayhem: "Dumb, dumb, dumb! Gramps….Where's Pops?"

"He's away a few days," Mayhem said, "doing some detective work in New Hampshire about your mom's death."

"He's fighting his nightmares alone and out of town?"

"He's doing fine. Are you home for good?"

"No," Kendra said. "We're meeting students in Ann Arbor."

"Political junk," Adam said. "Nothing serious." Kendra jabbed him in the back and he winced.

"Sure," Mayhem said. "Militants—Tom Hayden and the Port Huron Statement."

"Students for a Democratic Society," Kendra said. "You know about SDS?"

Mayhem slid a checker piece diagonally. "A movement without bosses," he said.

Adam's finger tugged at a piece in response. "They're planning for the Democratic Convention."

Mayhem pushed a checker piece, his finger temporarily blotting it from sight.

"It's in November," Adam said.

"News sometimes does travel to Canada," Mayhem said.

Adam moved a piece. "You're done, Gramps."

Mayhem scratched a mark on the pad. "So you two are in the SDS?" he said. "Aiming for some sort of socialist world?"

"The capitalist system is doomed," Kendra said.

"Will everyone get free ice cream?" Sarah called out from the kitchen.

"Thinking about all these things, for sure," Adam said. He received another sharp poke from Kendra.

"Did turning the other cheek," Kendra said to Mayhem, "ever lead to meaningful change? Answer me that."

Mayhem and Adam reset the pieces. "Good question that," Mayhem said. Adam moved a piece, keeping his eyes focused on the board. "I'll think on it," Mayhem said.

"Did you know," Kendra said, pointing to one article, "that medical doctors and waiters in Cuba make the same wage?"

Sarah came out of the kitchen and snugged her arms around Mayhem, kissing him goodnight and moving towards the stairs.

Adam waved. "Night, sis."

She paused on the stairs, her eyes on Adam while speaking to Kendra. "It's good to have you here. Adam's other girlfriends all looked like professional models, pretty things. We were hoping he'd find a plain, simple girl." She started up the stairs. "Night, all."

"Goodnight, *child*," Kendra said.

Mayhem considered his options on the board. "Good thing for Cuban waiters," he said. "Wouldn't motivate me to choose medicine as a career."

"But you didn't do well in school, so that would be academic," Kendra said. "Where do I sleep?"

"I'll bunk on the couch," Mayhem said. "You use Aiken's bedroom. Top of the stairs, turn left." She carried her backpack upstairs.

Mayhem counted the strokes on the scratch pad and fingered a dollar out of his wallet for his grandson. "Taking baby from a candy," Adam said. "A candy-ass, that is."

Mayhem rapped his knuckles against Adam's head and Adam jerked away, smiling.

Mayhem stacked the checkers back into the wooden container. "Some people in Ann Arbor advocate anarchy. Might be trouble brewing there."

"I'll walk carefully, Gramps."

When the noises of the house settled, Kendra snuck from her room into Adam's. In the living room below, Mayhem heard the squeak of the floor boards as she crossed the hall.

Adam rose from the bed as she entered the room. He wore shorts and a T-shirt. She still wore her plaid shirt and jeans but now the green ribbon was woven into her hair. "So tall," she said, tugging up his shirt. "Where did you get those shoulders, Mr. Canada?"

"You saw my gramps."

"I'm glad you don't have his politics."

"You here to discuss politics?"

"Here's the deal," she said, running her fingers across his chest. "Are you with the SDS or not?"

"You do the thinking and knowing, I'll do the muscle."

She wriggled out of her jeans, thrusting close to him, rubbing his shoulders. Her shirttail, unbundled, fell to her knees. "Gimme a slice of that muscle," she said.

He tussled with the buttons on her shirt but his fingers jammed up. She knocked his fingers aside and undid the buttons herself. She wore no bra but her breasts were firm, no bounce or sag. She pressed fingers against his chest, working him over to the bed, sitting him down. He removed her ribbon, letting it flitter to the floor. His fingers ran down her neck and over her shoulders and his hands swarmed over her breasts. "See anything you fancy?" she said. He removed his clothes in a rush and she shoved him down and straddled him. She licked his chest, sucked on his nipples and worked her way downwards.

After sex she rolled a joint with one hand and he opened the window a crack, cramming the mat against the base of the bedroom door. They sat cross-legged on the bed, the joint flipping back and forth. She licked at the sweat on her lips. When he noticed her sweat he pulled her forward, licking at the drops, skimming his tongue along the edges of her lips. She sat before him casual, naked, bold, no attempt to hide.

Downstairs, Mayhem lifted himself up from the couch and fumbled into Aiken's liquor shelf, dropping two inches of Canadian Club, chucking four ice cubes, and splashing a few dribs of water into the glass. He sipped away and when the liquor was gone he washed out the glass and tumbled back onto the couch. "Turning the other cheek works well," he said, "but few things work each and every time."

In the morning Adam and Kendra left for Ann Arbor, declining the offer of a ride. "We'll use the tunnel bus and hitch from there," Adam said to Mayhem. "But check on Pops and his nightmares."

"Will do."

When the door closed, Sarah turned to Mayhem. "She's not that pretty."

"The green kerchief works for her."

"It's poop, Grandpa, absolute poop."

Monday, March 11
Concord, New Hampshire

"Where in hell are you black people hiding?" he screamed. Five days in New Hampshire failed to produce one black person for Aiken Day. Concerned, he sought out Chester, finding him in the rooming house kitchen. Chester waved him in. "The secret to steamed cod," Chester said, "is in the soy sauce." He glided a large skillet back and forth over the heating element.

Aiken leaned against the kitchen counter, arms crossed. "No black people work for McCarthy, unless they're wearing whiteface."

Chester ladled three tablespoons of soy sauce into the pan and added rice vinegar and ginger. He waved the aroma into his face. "Ahh." He flipped pieces of cod into the pan, sprinkling brown sugar over the batch, then pepper.

"I gotta approach this from a different angle," Aiken said.

Chester reached for a bottle of wine, a German white, applying his sommelier's corkscrew. The cork exited the bottle with a harsh pop.

"Give me the blasted bottle," Aiken said. "I'll smell it with you if you give me the keys to the Morgan."

"A fair trade, Kemo Sabe."

Aiken drove to the city centre, parked the Morgan and traipsed about, telling himself he needed a feeling for either the campaign or the town, but actually just searching for a black person, any black person. After an hour of wandering about, cold and shivering, he pressed into a coffee shop, butting down on a stool at the counter. *Ask about the McCarthy campaign. Everybody here must be wrapped up in the political goings-on.* The short-order cook put up bacon and eggs for him, toast with marmalade and rich black coffee. Fourteen patrons huddled inside, wrestling with their late breakfast, all of them overweight men. Two waitresses buzzed around them, hustling constantly. *The population in this café, like the city, seems white, no blacks, Asians or half-breeds. So, where would Tanya be hiding? Paris always went on about the thousands of poor blacks being sacrificed in Vietnam. Why aren't blacks rooting like hell for McCarthy, a man seeking to end the war?*

A waitress gestured to Aiken for a refill and he held up his cup. *Do something, Aiken. Try something!* "Excited about this election?" he said. *How lame is that?*

"Oh yeah, I live and breathe it," she said. She filled his cup to the brim and leaned over, inches from his face. She smelled of cod liver oil. "Live and breathe it. You know, if the right man wins, I can retire in thirty years. Or maybe get my hair done." She tapped a finger to the side of her head, brushing tufts of hair aside. "Live and breathe it, pal, just live and breathe it."

The fellow on the stool beside Aiken, stomach bulging over his belt, was chomping into his third order of toast. He roofed the toast thick with strawberry jam before munching. He sprayed tiny bits of food when he spoke, slurring his words. "Got a lot of college kids in town," he said, wiping his lips with his free hand, "knocking on doors for McCarthy."

"Is that working out?" Aiken said.

"Students are well-mannered, clean-cut types, respectful. Not like the drugged-up student hippies who riot and burn flags on campuses. We'd run those darned long-haired freaks out of town on a spiked rail."

Aiken sipped from his cup. "You think McCarthy can end the war?"

"Nah. No president is gonna let the commies run us out of Asia."

"Nah," the waitress said. "Nah! Much better all those fine young boys die. Nah!" *Right, Miss Live and Breathe It!*

"Are there black people in New Hampshire?" Aiken said.

"Oh yeah," she said, "but they keep their heads down, out of sight, hearing stories from their parents and grandparents about lynchings and beatings I expect."

"Ain't none eat here," the man said, "so we don't got to hear blah, blah, blah about two centuries of slavery and all that civil rights crap."

"Mr. Sympathetic," she said. She splashed coffee into his cup, hot brew that surfed over the cup into the saucer.

"Can't see all those coloureds marching about," he said, wiping up the spilled liquid with a paper napkin, "yelling for civil rights, carping on about slavery. My pa and grandpa never owned no slaves."

"Everybody is against discrimination," the waitress said, "but everyone practises it."

"Not in New Hampshire," the man said, "that's down south goings on."

She grabbed his plate away and trashed his toast into the garbage pail behind the counter. "So you in favour of a black family living beside you," she said." That'd be fine, would it?"

His face grimaced at the sight of his toast in the garbage. "So you got a mood, Bertha. Gotta argue about everything."

"The only difference between the way black people are treated in the north and in the south is the weather," she said. "That's what they say, and that's what I think."

The man flung two dollars down onto the counter. "You're spending too much time at religion. Have a snort once in a while. Wake up next to someone you don't know."

"Blacks are meeting at the coloured school," she said to Aiken. She filled his cup again, careful not to splash. "What do you think about McCarthy?" she said.

"Never met him, don't really know him." A cast-off newspaper lay on the counter and he skidded down, plucking it up, bouncing back to his stool. "Do you know anything about the Tigers or Wings? Any trade talks?"

She settled the pot back on the burner and swiped at her hair again. "He has principles," she said. "He tells you the sort of man he is, what his values are. You get that?"

She filled someone else's cup and leaned on the counter near Aiken. "Not releasing political platforms or kissing babies," she said. "How is that gonna work?" At Aiken's request she wrote out directions to the coloured school in Manchester and to a Concord hotel that housed blacks. "Black folk from out of town are trying to jumpstart the black vote."

"That working?" he said.

"No one else is chasing black votes. Certainly not a president from Texas."

Tuesday, March 12
Concord, New Hampshire

On voting day batches of flurries occasionally throttled down the sun, chilling the air. The weather seemed to purge the state of the shrill political campaigning, the campaigns finally limping to an end. Aiken parked the Morgan up in front of a one-story, eight-room motel. Bubbled paint, falling-down window boxes and drooping shutters marked the outside front office. The eight rooms ran alongside a gravel parking lot with a 1949 Ford at the end of the lot, tires rotted dead, window glass blistered, rusting away, encircled by a hoop of weeds.

"I'll wait here, Kemo Sabe," Chester said. "You get the lay of the land."

Aiken paused, staring back.

"Don't worry," Chester said. "When a shit-kicker is called for, I'm your man." *Yeah, the shit-kicker who waits in the car.*

Aiken closed the Morgan's door and started towards the building.

Behind him, Chester cracked his window an inch and as Aiken moved away, said, "Time for a little relaxer." He hauled a baggie and cigarette papers from under the seat. His fingers rocked a cigarette paper back and forth and shook marijuana from the baggie and quickly rolled a joint. "Whoa, monster perfect!" He struck a match against the shifter knob, lit the joint and inhaled deeply. "Ahh."

The door to the front office was unlocked and Aiken opened it slowly, entering the small lobby and finding a large, muscular black man there offering no greeting, no gesture. *And here's me without the Webley.* "Hi," Aiken said, "I'm searching for a friend of mine, Tanya."

That comment brought concern to the man's face and he straightened, stepping towards Aiken. "Tanya don't have no grey-rabbit friends." His fist shot out, a piston exploding into Aiken's chest, driving him backwards. Aiken smacked against the wall hard, his breath whooshing out. Percy spun him about and batted him through the door, shoving him towards the Morgan. Aiken stumbled and fell to the ground, jabbing out his hands to halt the fall, feeling the gravel and snow grind into his skin. The office door slammed shut and he heard the deadbolt thumping in. He waved to the Morgan but the windows were fogged up. When he collected his breath, he crawled on all fours, inching his way to the car, hands scouring the gravel and ice, knees squeaking with effort, chest revolting in pain. He opened the door and the acrid smell from inside burst into him.

Chester stashed the joint, smashing it into the door frame, letting it drop out of sight. "Engine's smoked up," he said. "We should hire a tune-up or fry up a new motor…some fixing up definitely needed." The state of Aiken's clothes suddenly surprised him. "What in hell happened to you?"

Aiken wheezed out the words while leaning against the car on his knees. "Lost an argument about Tanya." He slumped down into the driver's seat and started the car, craving heat. He folded over the steering wheel, waiting for the heat to filter in. The heat seeped in slowly, miserly increments keeping him cold; the pain in his ragged palms increased. "Curse English sports cars and send them to hell," he said, "with their goddamn sewing-machine engines."

"Weird smell," Chester said. "Engine in this car has always been weird."

Aiken's hands tingled, his palms a red-grey puzzle of blood and gravel chunks. He yanked open the car door, reaching outside, bending down and scooping up snow from the ground, packing it into a snowball and keeping it between his hands as long as he could stand it. He felt the first traces of heat from the car.

Ten minutes later he opened the boot of the car and found the tire iron. *I have located Tanya but I have one big hurdle to climb.* He hefted the tire iron, slapping it against his leg a few times. *This whacker might replace the Webley.* He retraced his steps to the office door and Chester followed. "I'm with you, Kemo Sabe," Chester said. "I got your back." He held up a fistful of ballpoint pens.

"Ballpoint pens?" Aiken said, "This pecker is huge and mean, *Moon Doggie.*"

"These pens will soothe the savage beast. Trust me, they never fail. They are instant ice-breakers." *Sure, the naked-girl pen backup. What a goddamn relief!*

Aiken rattled the front door of the motel, recalling the sound of the deadbolt snapping in. He walked the perimeter, circling the building, tapping the tire iron against his leg, seeking some sort of gap or opening. A side door to the office contained square glass panes and he shifted his position, ready to punch in a pane, but before he could do so the same man opened the door for him. "How about a re-match," Aiken said. He held up the tire iron.

"You're no friend of Tanya."

"Truthfully," Aiken said, "I never met the woman, so yes, it was a lie."

Chester reached around Aiken and held out a pen. Percy accepted it. "Turn it upside down," Chester said.

Percy flipped it upside down. "A naked girl on a pen…Don't you got no girlfriend? The real stuff is better." Chester grabbed the pen back.

Connie Harlan slipped out from behind Percy. "We got ourselves a grey-rabbit epidemic," Percy said.

"This gentleman is Aiken Day," Connie said. "Let him in."

The three men followed Connie down the hall. "The man who was beatin' on you," Connie said over her shoulder to Aiken, "is Percy Turner."

The passageway was blistered by peeling wallpaper and missing chunks of plaster and lit by one light bulb dangling next to an ancient fly strip. At the hallway's end, Connie cracked open the door, allowing Aiken to peer into a room. A woman, face down, scribbled into a book. She glanced up.

Christ! She's alive. Aiken pushed at the door but Percy put a hand on his shoulder and Connie blocked him, snapping the door closed. "But we buried her," he said.

"Wait, mister. She's in hiding."

"Why would she hide from me? Get out of the goddam way." He shoved against the door but Connie pushed back. "She's coming home with me," Aiken said. "Paris!" he called out, pushing at the door.

"Cool down mister, this is important."

Aiken turned to Connie. "Tanya," he said. "So we buried Tanya? Her family just trying to avoid the cost of funeral were they? Too cheap to pop for a casket?"

"My cousin, Tanya," Percy said, but he dropped his hand. "Don't be talking about her, grey rabbit."

Connie put her hands on Aiken's chest. "Paris has been hurt—shot in the stomach and shot the head and she's got a memory problem. You have to understand that before you see her."

"What sort of memory problem?"

"The girl doesn't remember things, that sort of memory problem."

"Things?"

"Things like being married to you and having two kids…and her name, stuff like that."

"That's fucking nonsense," Aiken said. "I'll see my wife now. He brushed past Connie, shoving into the room, shooting quickly to Paris, gathering her up into his arms, kissing her neck.

She resisted, arms thrusting back against him. "Leave me be, mister."

In that brief second her aroma struck into Aiken's memory lode: spring days with blueberries and cream and chilled white wine. But looking into her face, he saw distress. *Eyes wide and wild: she's afraid of me.* Aiken released her. "Paris…"

Connie dragged at his shoulder. "Maybe we should go a bit slower, mister?"

Paris touched fingers to her scar, sitting down, drawing the journal tight to her.

"She doesn't know me," Aiken said. He stumbled back and sagged into a chair. "It's me," he said quietly. "It's me Paris."

Connie dragged a chair across from Paris, shoving in so close to Paris that their knees touched. "We can try again, mister."

Paris wore slacks and a sweater; Connie wore churchgoing clothes from her canvassing. Paris scribbled, squinting up at Aiken again, a brief glance only.

"Paris," Connie said, "listen up, girl. This man is your husband, Aiken Day. Do you remember him?" Paris turned away and Connie shrugged at Aiken.

"Paris, we've two fine children," Aiken said, "Adam and Sarah." Paris kept scribbling. "Mayhem is your pa," he said. "A fine dad. He taught me baseball. He raised you in Chatham but you followed me to the Division Road School near Kingsville." He pushed his chair close and wrapped his hands over hers and the scribbling ceased. She squinted and held his look for the first time. *You were a skinny black girl in a white school and you made me fall in love with you.* "You swooned at my blue eyes. Do you remember saying that? You called me Blue-eyes," She peered into his eyes but suddenly pulled her head back. He let his hand drop away and the scribbling resumed.

"Paris, dear," Connie said, "do you remember your name?"

The scribbling stopped. "I'm away from home just now," she said, "travelling in the preaching life." She stuck out her hand towards Aiken. "My name is Vernon Johns but I did not catch yours."

"My name is Aiken Day," he said, "and I fell in love with you in 1938." She examined his face, focusing on his blue eyes, but she did not reply.

Percy and Chester slunk into the room. Percy positioned himself against a wall, leaning back, arms crossed, and Chester seated himself in the chair next to Connie. Aiken introduced the parties, ending with: "…and this is my wife, Paris."

Chester stuck his hand out towards Paris but she cupped fingers over the scab on her forehead. "I'm Vernon Johns," she said, turning away.

"Vernon Johns," Chester said. "Sure, Vernon Johns." He twisted about, canvassing the silent faces in the room. "I'm tapping into this wavelength," he whispered to Aiken. "I totally get it, Kemo Sabe. Wiretaps?" *What?* Chester rose slowly, bending over the table lamp, speaking into it: "Jack Frost here."

What? "It's amnesia," Aiken said, almost yelling. He twisted to Connie. "Let me speak to her doctor."

Connie's face contorted and she bit her lip. "We should discuss this." She led the three men out the door. As they threaded out, Paris resumed scribbling. They tramped back down the uninviting hall and filed into another bleak room with a box spring and mattress shoved into a corner. Several chairs bunched about an ancient table and each person took a seat.

"She doesn't have a doctor," Connie said, "because the FBI is hunting her."

"And probably you as well," Percy said to Connie, but she shook that comment off.

"She needs a doctor," Aiken said, "maybe a specialist." Percy left the room.

"It's too risky," Connie said. "Last year's Detroit riot jump-started the FBI. They're running scared and shooting to kill."

Percy returned with two beers, caps off, passing one to Aiken. Aiken accepted it. *Now this thug wants to be friends?* Percy passed the other beer to Chester. "Maybe, grey rabbit," Percy said to Aiken, "her memory problem is that you're just not memorable. You know, sorta easy to forget." *Friends? Guess not.*

Aiken drained the beer in one straight chug and passed the bottle back. "Well, I have no memory problems and I remember everyone who sucker-punches me."

Connie shoved between them. "She's coming home with me," Aiken said. "She's not dead. She's bloody well not dead, and anything else we can fix. We've time to fix it."

"Mister," Connie said, "you don't appreciate the danger."

"I can care for my wife and keep her safe, thank you very much for your efforts."

"There's gonna be killings," Connie said. "The FBI peckerwoods have a list and Paris is on that list." Chester tilted a pen upside down, then right side up, repeating the gesture over and over again. "And," Connie said, "she's not inclined to go anywhere with a white man she doesn't remember."

"You know Paris's father?" Aiken said, "Mayhem Chase."

"I know the reverend."

"I'll need to know what he thinks."

Aiken phoned Mayhem from the motel lobby. "Paris is alive," Aiken said. "We buried someone else." The silence before Mayhem replied lasted so long that Aiken wondered if they'd been disconnected.

Mayhem wept. "Praise the Lord for this fine news."

"But she's suffering memory loss," Aiken said.

"Bring my daughter home."

"Do you know someone named Vernon Johns?" Aiken said.

"Most famous preacher about. They broke the mold after Vernon. He's passed on now."

"Did Paris know him?"

"Spent a summer with him when I slept with a whiskey bottle."

"She must have been impressed."

"He was an impressive man."

"People with Paris," Aiken said, "are Connie Harlan and Percy Turner. Know them?"

"Connie's people are hardworking folk."

"They think Paris is on an FBI list."

Mayhem paused a few seconds. "I've heard rumours of a list and I hoped it wasn't true."

"Tell Sarah that her mom is alive, and pass the word to Adam, if possible."

Aiken hung up, unsure of what to do. They collected in the room with Paris. *She still scribbles away, oblivious to everything.* Chester continued to flip a pen up and down, not locking his eyes into those of anyone else.

"I'm taking Paris with me," Aiken said. "If I call the police they'll back me up."

"Sure, because you're white," Connie said.

"White rules," Percy said. "White men always rule. Did you ever know it otherwise?"

The tire iron slapped against Aiken's leg, tapping in some unconscious, undefined tempo. Aiken pulled the bar upright. "Well today, white certainly rules," he said. "She's coming with me."

Chester abruptly flung the pen aside and cleared his voice. "The FBI is chasing someone on a list, Aiken, someone here in Concord. Agent Harry Fortune told me so."

Aiken lowered the bar.

"She's on that list," Connie said.

"I just bumped into him," Chester said, "only by accident."

Aiken looked to Connie. "Those peckerwoods intend her harm," Connie said. She paced the room, stalking it. Paris scribbled faster. "They're running scared," Connie said. "The whole country runs scared."

"I'll keep your wife safe," Percy said.

"And if she gets out of control," Aiken said, "you can always sucker-punch her." He watched Paris scribbling away. "For God's sake, what is she writing?"

"Gibberish," Percy said. "Just words and nonsense. No proper thoughts."

"And you majored in English grammar," Aiken said, his voice rising, "while doing time in prison. Maybe read *Madame Bovary* while locked up in solitary."

"Yelling ain't called for," Connie said. "She writes prattle, just prattle."

Someone rapped on the door and a small woman in a patterned dress plattered in ham sandwiches, with pea soup and crackers for Paris, dropping everything down on the table in front of Paris, stroking her face gently.

"We've called every voter who owns a phone," she said to Connie, "and helped out those without rides." Connie squeezed against the woman's shoulder. "Everything's been seen to," the woman said. She placed a newspaper down and tapped a finger against the front page. "This may be of interest," she said, passing the paper to Connie. Connie scanned it. "They expect McCarthy to do well against Johnson," she said, "so this election could make a difference."

"And maybe pig-shit is tasty as hell," Aiken said.

Paris's face tightened at Aiken's comment. She pondered Aiken's words, failing to cup fingers to her scab. "Tasty pig-shit," she said. "I've heard that before, but I can't use it for a sermon. However, it is familiar."

"It's time to skedaddle," Connie said. "We can't do anything more here but we need her safe."

Silence skulked about the room. Finally Connie spoke up. "What's it going to be?"

"You've got to give me something," Aiken said.

After a few seconds Connie removed a notebook from her handbag and wrote numbers on a page. "My mother's phone number," she said. She tore off the page and shoved it at Aiken. "I call her every day and you can leave a message with her and I'll get the message that day or the following. We can keep her safe."

***

At the Concord rooming house the TV blared. A young female student hunched over on the couch focused on the election results. Aiken ignored her. "Throw the bags into the car," he said to Chester. "Get me out of this goddamn rat-hole."

"Well, she's alive," Chester said, "protected by a monster bodyguard. That's consolation."

The student jumped up and slung her arms around Aiken's neck. "McCarthy's only a few hundred votes behind Johnson," she said. Aiken shoved her away.

"How about one last meal in New Hampshire, with decent wine," Chester said.

"Get me out of this rat-hole."

"McCarthy will make a difference," the student said to Aiken.

"And maybe pig-shit is tasty as hell."

The soft look on her face changed, chopping into anger. "We need a saviour," she said.

We need a head transplant for my wife—That's what we need.

Thursday, March 14
Kennedy Compound, Hyannis Port, Massachusetts

The Bay of Pigs fiasco landed the survivors of Brigade 2506 in Cuban prisons. In November of 1962 Bobby Kennedy was advised that many of those Cuban prisoners were malnourished, some approaching death; he set himself the task of saving the 1,113 survivors, enlisting people in his quest, gathering the ransom demanded, the $11 million of goods—ten thousand items, including drugs, medicines and baby food, items in short supply in Cuba. He arranged for IRS tax exemptions for companies who donated. He personally pleaded with and convinced Cardinal Cushing of Boston to help raise funds. The survivors arrived home for Christmas Eve the same year. John Kennedy, however, kept his own searing lesson from the Bay of Pigs and shared it with Bobby. "Beware of the generals," he said. "Some military opinions aren't worth a damn."

It was out now: Bobby would seek the presidency. Today was the only day the family sanctioned for revelry in the decision, before the actual campaign work began, but even in celebration some people worked, contacting, planning, discussing and strategizing. Servants circulated in the main house, carrying hors d'oeuvres, oysters and artichokes stuffed with shrimp and crab meat, and offering warm pastry canapés filled with heavily creamed mushrooms. Champagne flowed. Dozens of glasses toasted the occasion.

Bobby's family was present—his brother, his sisters, spouses and children. The occasional congressman milled about; two senators and three governors held forth. Salinger was there with his cigar actually lit, newspaper tucked under his arm, reading telegrams from politicians across the country offering support, some serious, some bullshit, some just polite but most rather calculated, in the way of politicians. The phones rang constantly: calls blowing in from people about the country, calls threading out to possible supporters. Potential gurus abounded, sharing possible campaign strategies; tactics were floated, and debated. What worked for Ike? What killed Goldwater?

Kennedy greeted Salinger, draping an arm around his shoulder. "Thought you quit, Sal."

"Big day, Bob." Salinger waved the stogie. "Been waiting a long time for this day." Salinger followed Kennedy into the sun room. When they entered the room, JBM stood up.

"JBM," Kennedy said.

"Senator."

"We'll be butting head to head with McCarthy in Indiana," Kennedy said, "for the whole ball game. We lose Indiana and we pack up and crawl back home."

"We can't lose," Salinger said. "We've waited too long."

Kennedy put a hand on JBM's arm, grinning. "Find a Hoosier to map out the Indiana strategy." JBM's smile beamed its way skyward. JBM was the only Hoosier currently on board.

Salinger dumped the *New York Times* on a side table. "Westmoreland is requesting another two hundred thousand men for the war, Bob. We should craft a position."

Kennedy recalled his brother's advice. "Westmoreland's a general with a bad plan," he said. "If he can't win a war against a backward nation using half a million soldiers, the war can't be won."

Salinger relit his cigar and puffed at it until it glowed once more. JBM lit a cigarette while Bobby paced back and forth. "But the flip side…," Kennedy said. "The ghettos need the money now being spent on the war." He reached out, touching JBM's shoulder. "Work on Indiana," he said.

JBM stubbed out his cigarette. "You've got it, Senator."

Kennedy pumped JBM's hand, wringing it up and down before he left the room.

"Chevy," Salinger said, "man of the people."

"Cadillac," JBM said. "Pure class."

Thursday, March 14
Detroit, Michigan and Windsor, Ontario

The wind ramped up, funnelling across his porch, clustering Aiken's hair into salt and pepper tufts, dancing snow flurries about him. The door was unlocked and he entered the house tentatively, preparing his story about Paris. Chester followed him inside, lugging suitcases, straining with the effort. Mayhem came out of the kitchen drying a dinner plate with a tea towel, rubbing it carefully in circular motions. "Where's my daughter?" he said. His hand flattened, hiding most of the plate.

"Whoa," Chester said, dumping down the suitcases. "That's the father-in-law? Mr. Mack-Truck-shoulders?"

Sarah wandered out of the kitchen, steering close to Mayhem, slinging an arm about him. "Where's Mommy?"

Aiken bit his lip, pursuing words, failing to find them. "Well, she's safe…doing her political stuff."

"Where exactly?" Mayhem said. "And why isn't she home so a doctor can fix her memory problems."

"Well," Aiken said, "safe, I think. She's doing politics with Connie Harlan. They're keeping things quiet and below the radar. We'll get a doctor for her."

"Kennedy's entered the race," Mayhem said, "So they'll be working for Kennedy."

"Sure, Kennedy."

Sarah stepped towards Aiken. "How do you know Mommy's safe?"

"Your mom survived sit-ins and barricades. She has memory problems, not knowing stuff. That'll fix itself up in time."

Sarah cried. "You didn't bring her home." She ran upstairs.

Aiken climbed after her but paused after a few steps and returned to the living room, opting to wait before offering her comfort. "There must be more to this Vernon Johns story," Aiken said to Mayhem.

"When you vacationed in Stalag 8B, I fell into the booze."

"So you said."

"I couldn't get rid of those killings on the beach. Paris hung out with Connie Harlan." He draped the dish towel in halves, then quarters and left it on the dining room table, squaring it to the table edge, taking a chair. "Connie's uncle was Vernon Johns."

"That's it? A summer vacation with a preacher."

"Paris was pregnant but didn't realize it, missing both you and me and not in a good way. She had no mother to lean on."

"Pregnant?"

"Like you didn't have something to do with that."

"What was so special about Vernon Johns?"

"He was a man," Mayhem said, "a great man who blows through once in a hundred years."

The following morning, Aiken found a note from Sarah on the kitchen table: *I will bring Mommy home. Don't worry.* Aiken kicked Mayhem awake on the couch and showed him the message.

"Drive to the bus station," Mayhem said. "Grab her before she leaves Windsor. A young girl shouldn't be alone in Detroit." Aiken and Chester grabbed up coats and flung them on as they ran out of the house, cramming into the Morgan. They bee-lined the car to the bus station in downtown Windsor, screeching to a halt in the parking lot, the car skidding on the wet pavement. Aiken ran about the station calling her name then burst into the woman's washroom, surprising two women fussing in front of the mirror, and raced back out, jumping back into the Morgan. "Get us to Detroit," he said.

Inside Detroit's Greyhound bus terminal Pokeface motioned to the girl with him, his cut-out carrying the drugs, bone-skinny to the point of starvation, a fourteen-year-old addicted to heroin. "I'm meeting someone," he said. "We may be doing a deal. Park it on that bench and don't even twitch your ass." She plopped onto the bench. Sweat beaded across her brow and her limbs shook. She clasped her arms together to hide the shaking.

"Can you give me something sweet?" she said, "Just a bit."

"Park it," he said.

Sarah Day entered the station and Pokeface caught sight of her. "I might be expanding my whore-pack," he said. "I'm gonna give you a whore-sister."

Sarah sat down on the edge of a bench, leaning back, swinging her legs back and forth while humming quietly. Her small suitcase bounced up and down on her lap as her knees alternately spun up and down. A teenager perched on the same bench three feet away. He nattered on, words falling away uselessly, torn sleeves showing needle tracks. She tried to watch him out of the corner of her eye. He mumbled on, not knowing whether he was alone or surrounded by hundreds.

***

The Morgan spun down city streets. Just off Fort Street the bus station hove into view, riot-city central, with row upon row of burned-out buildings surrounding the terminal. Behind the bus station the Statler Hotel dominated the skyline, a hotel whose eighteen floors remained mostly unfilled after last year's riot.

"Piece of trivia for you," Chester said. The Morgan rumbled but did not blot out conversation. "In 1926 Harry Houdini checked in at the Statler, but his final checkout took place at Detroit Grace Hospital where he died from a ruptured appendix." Aiken glanced over at Chester but said nothing.

Chester chuckled. "He never settled up his room charges."

"What?" Aiken yelled. "What the hell are you trying to say? In English!"

"My point is," Chester said, "this hotel and this area are close to checking out. After a riot nothing survives."

"Twelfth Street bothered Paris," Aiken said. "You think Twelfth Street was the American good life? You think the riot was palaces being burned down by angry princes and princesses?"

Chester nosed the car up to the side of the concrete loading docks of the terminal, sliding the car into neutral, shutting it down, yanking on the handbrake.

"The riot didn't improve things for anyone," Aiken said. He motioned towards the people huddled about the doors of the building. "Wretched souls, to say the least."

The people he gestured to offered the only sign of life in the area. The building's granite exterior was a gloomy grey, the adjacent Cunningham Drug Store's burned-out interior slashed grim on one side, while on the other, the loading docks, cracked and split, housed weeds, broken bottles and assorted garbage. "The car may not be here when we get back," Chester said.

"You got your charge card?"

"Of course."

"Then what's the damn problem? You just buy another one."

"No problem, Kemo Sabe, just a tad nervous at our surroundings."

They climbed the stairs and Chester read from the wall. "What in hell is a Motherfocker?" he said. "Have the standards of graffiti-writing fallen so low?"

The people sitting or prowling about were mostly aging men, with few women and no whites. Several of the men quivered in the cold, stamping their feet, scarves wrapped tight. Most asked for money, pleading hunger, while stinking of alcohol. Aiken gave out the coins he had, sharing them about. Chester pulled Aiken aside. "They all reek, major up-chucking reek."

"Paris called it the 'pong of poverty.' Poor people smell. Food and booze march in front of shampoo and perfume."

"Soap is cheap, Aiken."

"Paris would answer that despair is cheaper." Inside the terminal he saw Pokeface talking to Sarah, hovering over her. When Sarah saw Aiken she immediately jumped up and raced towards him, throwing her arms about him, hugging him until he pried her arms loose. Pokeface motioned for his cut-out to remain where she was and sauntered over to Aiken.

"My daughter," Aiken said to Pokeface.

"I'm not going home, daddy."

Her eyes! They're Paris's eyes. Something more: she's determined, the way Paris was.

Sarah pulled away from him. "I'm not going home," she repeated, "I'm going to keep looking for Mommy." *I can help her out or I can stand aside.*

Pokeface flipped open his coat so Aiken could glimpse his weapon. "Never got that money, Pastyman. Still waiting on payment."

Aiken fumbled out his wallet and emptied it, turning over forty dollars.

"Still short, Pastyman."

Chester slipped off of his coat and held it out. "Genuine leather, lined with silk," he said. "Cost a fortune." Pokeface accepted the jacket and spun it about, flipping it back and forth, smoothing his fingers down the silk lining. He gave a short nod, accepting the deal, crooking a finger to his cut-out, who jumped up and gathered in the coat from him. Pokeface left. His cut-out followed behind him, hugging the coat against her body for warmth.

"You just met Pokeface," Aiken said to Chester, "the Duke of Detroit, part of the city's new royalty—an en-tren-prin-oor who sells whores and heroin."

"While wearing my coat," Chester said. "It's like he's family, a young brother wearing my hand-me-downs." Aiken swung arms about his daughter, clasping her tight, lifting her off the ground.

"We can join with Senator Kennedy," Sarah said, "and find Mommy." *I'm not gonna tell her about the list.*

Her face gritted in determination. "We need Mommy home."

Meeting up with Sarah might fix up Paris. "Come back with me tonight," Aiken said. "Tomorrow we'll search for your mom together."

She hugged him again. Tears bundled about her eyes.

Chester waved his piece of plastic about. "Charge card Chester to the rescue—I'll book some airline tickets."

Sarah slung her arms around Chester, squeezing and squeezing him.

"Only we'll visit the school," Aiken said, "and pick up some books and lessons from your teachers."

"Poop," she said. But her face brightened the terminal.

"Warm up the car," Chester said. "I'm missing my coat."

"You should've bought a V-8," Aiken said. Your car won't warm up until August unless you mail it to Jamaica."

"Stop at a coat store."

***

Aiken advised Connie's mom of their plans to travel to Kansas. "I've noted what you said," the woman replied, and rang off.

Mayhem provided Aiken with advice: "Joining muckety-muck university egghead types in a campaign," he said, "ain't going to lead you to Paris or Connie Harlan. They'll be in the trenches, talking to local blacks, working on the ground, not in strategy sessions or licking stamps or making sandwiches. "

"Gotcha. Ignore eggheads."

"They'll work the ground, the way a bloodhound works the ground."

Sure, working the ground when she's not out plowing it behind the mule as Vernon Johns. "Any word from Adam?"

"He'll be fine," Mayhem said. "I'll keep asking about him but you keep a close eye on Sarah." Aiken thought about Pokeface approaching his daughter in the bus terminal. "Count on it."

"Paris is on the list," Aiken said. "Things are complicated."

"Just do the right thing, bud, just do the right thing."

Sure. Keep an eye on Sarah but if time permits, help Paris with the plowing.

Sunday, March 17
Detroit, Michigan

At 8 a.m. the Morgan slowed for US Customs after exiting the tunnel. Chester reeled down the driver's side window and chilled air blew in. Aiken fiddled his wallet for his and Sarah's birth certificates. Sarah sat quietly behind him. The officer spit to the side then bent over, almost folding in half, placing his gloved fist on the convertible top while glancing inside the car.

"Greetings," Chester said.

"Where are you heading, sport?"

"Airport," Chester said. "We intend to fly to Mexico and meet with their president. Gonna sell some of these little suckers." He held up a pen and speared it towards the officer. The officer accepted it. "Now flip it upside down," Chester said.

The officer removed a glove, rolled the pen up and down and grinned. He repeated the process two more times. "Clothes…no clothes…clothes…no clothes. Man, that is one helluva pen."

"Beaners love 'em," Chester said. "Keep it. I insist."

The officer opened his jacket and stuck the pen into his shirt pocket but noticed Sarah in the back seat. "The coloured girl with you?"

"Yes, my daughter," Aiken said.

The officer looked back at Sarah. "She don't look like you."

Sarah leaned forward. "The Children's Aid give me over to this here man and his wife." Her arm shot out and her fingers landed on Aiken's shoulder. *Give me over?*

"So you're living with a good family now?" the officer said.

"Yasser. It's almost like being white."

Yasser?

The officer directed his questioning to Aiken. "So you some sort of do-good social worker?"

Get away, border guard. Don't ruin a good praying day.

"Exactly, Officer," Chester said. "He's a dog-fart do-gooder. Here, have another pen."

As the Morgan exited customs, Chester turned to Aiken. "Conversation with a dick-wad Cossack is an art form," he said. "Never tell the truth and stretch your lie as much as humanly possible."

Sarah reached from the back seat, placing a hand once more on Aiken's shoulder. "People believe what they want to believe," she said. "Move them just a little bit at a time."

"With these stinking pens," Chester said, "a man can move through life with limited social skills."

Imagine that! Someone mistaking me for a dog-fart do-gooder!

Monday, March 18
Kansas City, Kansas

Kennedy spent the night in the guest quarters of the governor's mansion and Salinger arrived there at 6 a.m. to meet with him. They kicked around parts of his upcoming speech before Salinger raised the real concern he wished to address.

"Bob," he said, "make like a politician. Make small talk with people, put them at ease. And for Christ's sake, ask the governor to support you."

"I'm not good at small talk," Kennedy said. "Never been much good at it. And I don't feel comfortable making political deals for support."

Salinger hesitated before replying. "You did the political horse-trading for Jack and you excelled at it."

Fleeting pain tap-danced across Kennedy's heart at the mention of his brother, as it always did. "That was my job then," he said, turning away. "I don't see that as my job now."

"Just take a shot at it."

"I did it for Jack."

"Can you at least try?" Salinger said. "This election is not yet won. McCarthy has the lead after New Hampshire."

Rather than answer, Kennedy changed the topic. "How're Kansas students going to receive me?"

"War anxiety blankets the campus. That'll help."

At 7 a.m. Kennedy sat down to breakfast with the governor, and thirty minutes later to a second breakfast at the student union. He counted neither meal as a success. He offered no small talk, offered no concessions contrary to his feelings, and cut no political deals to advance his candidacy. I'm a political Popeye, he thought: I yam what I yam and that's all what I yam.

***

At 8 a.m. Chester chose Hertz from the rental agencies at the airport and rented a full-size Chevrolet. "I booked us into the hotel where Kennedy's staff is staying," he said.

Aiken threw his kit bag and Sarah's suitcase into the trunk. "How do you know where they're staying?"

"I made a small donation to the campaign using my charge card."

"A small donation?"

"Well, small compared to the American national debt."

"Thank you, Uncle Chester," Sarah said. "We love you for that."

Chester pulled Aiken aside. "Don't worry, Kemo Sabe, in a separate deal with the hotel I'll have access to the hotel's monster wine cellar and their somewhat adequate kitchen. We'll feast while we hunt. I'll manage the food and wine." *I never doubted that for a minute, Tonto. Not even for a split second.*

The cathedral-like stone structure of Ahearn Field House at Kansas State was built to seat 12,200 frenzied people watching the Wildcats torment their basketball opponents while beating them senseless. This day, over 14,500 students and faculty filed into the hall to hear Kennedy speak. They crowded into stairwells, crouched under the press tables, perched on rafters and bunched shoulder to shoulder. The temperature in the building jumped to sixty degrees by 9:30 a.m. Aiken, Chester and Sarah wormed their way into the packed room and gradually moved through the crowd sideways and back until their they rammed up against the rear wall. Aiken rustled up a chair and helped Sarah stand on it for a better view.

Look at the starched white shirts and nicely ironed blouses. Kansas students are all dressed conservatively. Male students sport short hair and the girls are wearing skirts and cardigan sweaters. No miniskirts and no freaky long-haired hippies. This is what students should look like. I might move here.

Aiken watched Bobby Kennedy enter the room, observing the students stomp and whistle, cheering when they saw him. He saw a slight, attractive man, tousled brown hair hardly under control, wearing a rumpled suit with a tie loosely knotted, face crinkled but hospitable. Kennedy threaded his way through the crowd, making his way to the podium, pausing there, acknowledging the welcome, waiting for the crowd to quiet. The introductions began. Kennedy waited off to the side on a chair scribbling notes on his prepared speech. More to kill time than to make corrections, Aiken thought. He must know the speech by now. Aiken sank back against the wall and Sarah dragged him down and kissed him.

"Thank you for this," she whispered.

A student on the left of Aiken held a sign that said GENE FOR INTEGRITY. A female student on the other side of him held a sign that said KISS ME BOBBY. *Not so many black faces and definitely not the one we're looking for.*

Kennedy opened with a few small, self-depreciating jokes, and then slammed into the audience, quickly pivoting to the issue of Vietnam: "The course we are following is deeply wrong. South Vietnamese men buy their deferment from military service while American Marines die in battle. It's not acceptable." His voice jumped out, a trumpet yelling: "Send South Vietnamese soldiers into battle and bring Americans home."

The field house rocked with applause. The temperature in the building was now at 70 degrees. A black face on the other side of the room caught Aiken's attention and he tugged Sarah's arm, dragging her off the chair, slicing through the crowd, losing sight of the figure almost immediately. Sarah plucked at his arm. "What did you see, Daddy?"

Kennedy's voice rose again: "I'm guilty and you're guilty because this Vietnam War has been waged in our name."

Aiken paused, sucked in by Kennedy's compelling voice.

"Will we destroy South Vietnam in order to save it?" Kennedy said. "Is this what you want?"

The temperature in the field house continued to rise. Sweat now streamed down Kennedy's face, glistening on his cheeks. *He's a prizefighter in the ring, slugging it out, trading blows with an invisible opponent.*

Sarah jerked at Aiken's sleeve. "Do you feel what he's saying?"

"He's sincere," Aiken replied. But he remembered the sight of a black figure and he forced his eyes to sift back and forth across the building, seeking Paris. A few black faces sprinkled the crowd, but none he recognized.

"We must end the bloodbath in Vietnam," Kennedy said. "We must negotiate a peace with the National Liberation Front."

The field house blew apart with applause. People jumped up and they waved; they shouted and cheered and stomped their feet.

"Was it Mommy?" Sarah said.

"No, but maybe her pal, Connie Harlan."

"Where?" Sarah lunged forward but Aiken hauled her back. "Be patient. We'll catch up with your mom."

Students, chattering and excited about Kennedy, streamed out of the building as Chester herded Aiken and Sarah back to the car. Chester consulted maps and eventually found the hotel. The two-room suite with living room had Dom Perignon waiting, chilling in an ice bucket, with two champagne flutes perched on either side of the bucket. Eighteen-year-old Scotch, The Glenlivet, shone on the bureau, positioned near two crystal whisky glasses.

"Poop! More alcohol," Sarah said.

Thanks be to God.

***

At 11 a.m., at the same Hertz car rental station Rizzuto requested the government rate, showed his official ID and signed the papers without reviewing them. He chose a Ford, stowing his duffle and four-foot-long leather case into the trunk. Harry Fortune placed his suitcase on top. "We missed the time for Kansas State," Fortune said. "We'll pick up Kennedy at Kansas University, at the Phog Allen Field House."

"What I live and breathe for," Rizzuto said, "mixing with long-haired freaks and foul-smelling draft dodgers."

"That's Berkeley," Fortune said. "No draft-card burners in Kansas. Kansas universities have very conservative student bodies. That smell is farm sweat."

"All universities smell of ripe horse manure."

They found their way to the Field House. Kennedy tweaked his speech from earlier, remembering what went well and what not so well. He struck the students hard and often about the war but he also stressed his position against poverty. He received another delirious ovation, wave after wave of applause. Within a few hours Bobby Kennedy had won over the better part of thirty thousand skeptical, conservative, Kansas university students.

When the crowd at the field house dispersed, the two FBI agents positioned themselves at the main exit, hunting for black faces. "Listening to this crap about tossing in to the commies bites my ass," Rizzuto said. "Good men dying overseas and we hear this Kennedy horseshit." Fortune did not reply.

***

At 8 p.m. Aiken said, "I'll pop down to the lobby and hunt up an ice machine."

Chester, observing a full bucket of ice, raised an eyebrow but kept silent. Sarah set aside her homework and clicked on the television. Aiken picked up his small travel bag. *And I'll try to liquor up someone on where the black folk hide out.*

Monday, March 18
Kansas City, Kansas

The lobby was empty but for the clerk asleep behind the desk, his chair tilted back against the wall, his feet propped over a second chair.

Faint clacking sounds carried from a typewriter in an adjoining room out to the welcome desk. Aiken found a local newspaper crumpled up on a bare wooden chair and a well-thumbed *New York Times* jumbled up on the front counter. He collected both papers and dropped into a chair. *We'll wait a spell and watch who drifts by.*

At 2 a.m. Connie Harlan, wearing a tan trench coat, entered the hotel lobby but quickly spun about when she saw Aiken. He threw the newspapers to the floor and caught up to her and grasped her arm.

"Where's Paris?"

"She's not ready. Give her more time."

"I saw you working for Kennedy."

She struck with her fist, banging it into his chest. "Two peckerwood FBI agents rented a car and are out combing the city for her." She wrenched her arm away. "Stay away for now. It's too risky."

Aiken tugged her elbow. "My daughter needs her."

She jerked away. "Get shut from me, peckerwood." She opened the door. Wind whipped her hair, teasing little sprouts about. "Don't lead those FBI agents to her. They intend her harm."

When the door closed behind her, Aiken roused the night clerk, jabbing a finger into his chest.

"What the hell?" the man said.

"Any black women booked in here?"

"Don't rent to niggers. They meet with the Kennedy people but we wouldn't have 'em in here. Hotels must have standards." He closed his eyes.

The clacking from the adjoining room suddenly irritated the hell out of Aiken. Moving into the adjacent room Aiken encountered a lone man hunched over a small table, finger-tapping at a typewriter.

"You gonna bang that bastard all night?" Aiken said.

The man glanced at him but continued typing. Tears blistered the man's face. *He's crying.* The fellow plastered up a smile.

"Jason Bartlow Morgan," he said. "Everyone calls me JBM...it's JBM here making this racket, disturbing you to hell and gone." He brushed at a tear but more tears dribbled down his cheeks. He waved a hand, a waffling, nonchalant sort of wave. "Usually I'm a speech writer for Bobby, but I'm writing a news story now...a story not be published or believed for at least ten years, maybe never by some."

He looked rumpled to Aiken, wearing a faded navy-coloured, sleeveless wool sweater vest, with a white shirt showing frayed cuffs, cuffs folded over. Plain brown glasses wrapped around his face and he squeezed the stub of a squalid cigarette between his fingers, still clacking away at the typewriter with his right index finger, stabbing away as he spoke. "No one will fucking publish this," he said. "Not the *Times*, not the *Post*, not the *Journal*, not the Texas toilet paper company." He dabbed his eyes one last time. "I don't believe it, and I believe in Santa Claus."

Aiken lifted a chair close, plunked down in it and opened his bag, hauling out a bottle of Canadian Club. He plunked it down next to the typewriter. JBM spun the bottle about, tilted it up and read the label.

"Canadian?" JBM said.

"Guilty."

"I don't like nosy or noisy people."

"I never fart out loud."

"Fair enough, Nanook." JBM reached into a satchel and removed a bottle of Jack Daniels Old No. 7.

"Bourbon?" Aiken said.

"Tennessee whiskey. Anyone not from Canada would know the difference."

"Any black women in this hotel?" Aiken said.

"Not a welcoming centre for people of any colour, save white." JBM cupped the Canadian Club while pointing to the Jack Daniels. "Try a bit of this," JBM said, "while I swallow the melted hockey pucks."

Aiken sipped. My God! Bring back the beach at Dieppe and those bloody Nazis. *Is there a Jack Daniel's Old No. 8 and does it cause permanent blindness?*

After an hour of silence, JBM capped the Canadian Club. "The US Army ran amuck," he said. He clacked the typewriter in time with his speech. "Charlie Company," click; "First Battalion," click; "20th Infantry Regiment," click; "Eleventh Brigade," click. "These American men, our brave soldiers, massacred an entire village in Vietnam."

"My God."

"The village of My Lai. Five hundred Vietnamese civilians—men, women and children executed a few days ago. Women gang raped and mutilated…unarmed people."

"This is awful."

"The Army brass will hush it up."

Aiken twisted the cap back on the Jack Daniels.

"The wheels fell off Bus America," JBM said. "Vietnam fucked over the country's moral compass."

Seeking some way to console his newfound friend, Aiken searched in his emotional cupboard, finding it sparse, almost empty.

"I need Bobby Kennedy," JBM said, "far more than he needs me." He tapped at the keys randomly a few more times. "America needs him."

"Surely this story will hit the *New York Times*."

"About the time the sun explodes."

"You travelling to Indiana with Kennedy?" Aiken said.

"With Bobby all the way. This evil war must die."

"The other campaigners?"

"Some will head to Nebraska, some to California, but me to Indiana." JBM resumed pecking at the typewriter.

Where in hell will the black crusaders go?

Monday, March 18
Memphis, Tennessee

Mayhem Chase checked into a motel on the outskirts of town, requesting room number seven, the only room with a bay window. The clerk, a man with a deep purple hue and a spider-like birthmark around his right eye, took Mayhem's twenty and gave back a five. "Here for Martin's meeting at the Mason Temple?"

"I am."

"Ain't seen you in a while. Been sick? Too busy to help the cause like in days gone by?"

"When a man possesses a quiet and peaceful life and a good family, he might forget about those who don't."

"I hear up in Canada there's no separate washrooms for whites and blacks."

"If that's the only test, it's a perfect place to live."

***

Approaching the Mason Temple hall, Mayhem observed police cars blocking off the street at either end. National Guard armoured vehicles revved their engines and guardsmen and police officers broke open weapons, checking their loads.

Twelve thousand people crowded into the hall, packing the room to the rafters, many hanging or sitting on the rafter beams. The people shone black and brown, the occasional white face usually set apart by a pallid clerical collar. Mayhem Chase strode through the front door of the auditorium, sifting through the crowd, rubbing shoulders, acknowledging the occasional person. Martin Luther King Jr. arrived a few minutes after Mayhem.

The room hushed. King's square shoulders swung gracefully as he walked, substantial muscles present, muscles hard as a brick but not overpowering, trim mustache, dark suit and white shirt finished off with a subdued tie. He meandered through the crowd, slapping at people and rubbing shoulders, stopping to greet Mayhem. Chatter in the room increased. "Mayhem Chase," King said, "Good to have you back in the fray, Reverend."

"Lots of police outside," Mayhem said, "angry men with guns primed and loaded. Could be some buckshot coming our way."

The buzz of the crowd picked up even more. King bent close to him. "If we waited until the police weren't angry, we'd wait until the Second Coming." King moved on, slowing for occasional greetings, looping to the stage eventually, joining others already there. He waited for the crowd to silence, and a stillness settled in. He spoke up, making his position clear in few words: "If the City of Memphis refuses to settle," he said, "we shall cause a general work stoppage."

In spite of the police presence outside the hall, the gathered people of Memphis sent out cheer after cheer. Feet stomped and the clamor and noise refused to end, wave after wave cascading and pumping up more and more applause.

"I'm coming back to Memphis on Friday," King said, "to lead a march through the center of town." The noise and excitement resumed. The room shook to the ceilings.

Mayhem observed the yelling and cheering. "Has everyone forgotten the beatings and shootings of past times?" he said to the young man next to him.

"Old man, the time for killing is coming close. Non-violence is for old ladies."

After the meeting people filed slowly out of the hall, workers at the front monitoring the exit, slowing people down, keeping the exodus slow but steady, sending people in ones and twos past the police barricades with no large group to provoke a police response. King motioned to Mayhem and they exited together.

Leaving Memphis, the King caravan, now including Mayhem Chase and the ever-present news cameras, drove on, stopping at Marks, Mississippi, the poorest county in the entire country. Mothers told King of their poverty, of having no blankets to warm their children, of a diet of only pinto beans, of not sending children to school because of their nakedness. King collapsed to his knees, weeping. "God doesn't like this," he said, his voice rising.

"We can't leave everything to Martin," Mayhem said to the person closest to him.

King remained on his knees. "God does not like this."

Mayhem knelt down, his knees grinding into the ground. Tears flushed down his cheeks. "No, God sure in hell does not like this."

Wednesday, March 27
Kansas City, Kansas

Aiken entered the hotel suite, threw his coat on the bed and rolled his eyes at Chester, signaling that he had not found Paris. Chester turned back to the game of checkers. He selected a red piece, setting it down with precision. Sarah bent over the coffee table, considering her response. "Two wins each," she said. "This is the rubber. Did you have any luck?"

"Some leads and ideas." *But no wife.*

"Face it," Chester said, "most Kennedy workers in Kansas have vamoosed. We aren't gonna locate your gal in this state unless she's been shot and the body dumped at a police station."

"Don't say that, Uncle Chester."

"Just kidding, sweetie."

"Not good kidding," she said. "It's poop kidding."

"You're right—sorry, hon."

Aiken phoned Mayhem Chase at home, eventually connecting with him in Memphis. "She's not here," Aiken said. "The campaign people split up."

"Find out what states they're working," Mayhem said. "I know preachers up and down this country who are tapped into local politics. We'll run her down."

"But in the meantime?" Aiken said. "Sarah needs her mom."

"Come to Memphis, Aiken."

"What for?"

"Sanitation workers strike."

"Garbage pickers? Really?"

"I sat out too long," Mayhem said, "and you've been dead since Stalag 8B. We can both beat the drum a bit louder."

I gave at the office. Aiken folded his body to shield the phone, lowering his voice but not so quiet that Sarah didn't hear. "So it's more civil rights crap?" he said.

"Daddy…"

Oops!

She stomped up beside him. "Let me speak to Grandpa." He held on to the phone, keeping it tight to his chest.

"Give me the phone, please."

He gave over the phone and busied himself, spilling ice cubes in a glass and shaking in three inches of Canadian Club, plopping into the chair, waiting for the row he felt was coming, marshalling his arguments. *Bloody déjà vu or what? She's changing into Paris in front of me.* Sarah listened to her grandfather and put the receiver down when finished. Instead of saying anything or making any argument to her father, she removed her suitcase from the closet and snatched clothes from the dresser, pitching garments into the case.

"You can drive me to the bus station," she said to Aiken. "Or I can walk." *Shades of your mom.*

"Ah, Aiken," Chester said, "what we have here is…a situation." He stacked checkers into the wooden container.

"The march In Memphis," Sarah said, "is the sort of thing Mommy might do. You know—the civil rights *crap* you hate."

"She might," Aiken said.

"I'm going to help Grandpa," she said. *And like your mom, you're not really asking for permission.*

"It's only a six or seven-hour drive," Chester said. "We could make it today." Aiken's face frosted over and Chester reacted. "If you agree, that is. Only if you agree, Kemo Sabe. You decide."

They drove to Memphis but the trip generated new records for muddy silences. Locating Mayhem's motel proved easy. Aiken rapped on his door and Mayhem embraced him.

"King is in Memphis," Mayhem said. "I'm here to support his march." Sarah rushed up and jumped into Mayhem's arms. "Marches are not for children," he said to Aiken. "What are you thinking?"

"She can wait in the room with Chester."

"I could march," Sarah said.

Aiken dragged her close. "You wait in the room, sweetie. Your grandpa and I will locate your mom if she's here."

"More checkers," Chester said, placing an arm about her.

"Poop."

Aiken phoned Connie's mother and left the motel phone number with her. "Tell her I'm in Memphis for a garbage strike," he said. *But I'm not sure why. Am I for or against garbage?*

Thursday, March 28
Memphis, Tennessee

A broad alliance gathered in support of the Memphis garbage strike, a coalition assembled by hundreds of black preachers; the crowd milling about numbered twenty thousand and included the one thousand sanitation workers, black school teachers, white trade unionists and forty priests and nuns.

Whirring sounds above him made Aiken look up. "Police helicopter," he said to Mayhem.

Mayhem pointed to other copters circling farther away, giving the police machine lots of room. Men in those aircraft slung down, hanging out with their cameras, film already streaming. "News people in those copters," he said. Mayhem constantly greeted people he knew. Paris knew these folks, Aiken thought. People she marched with. King closed on the two of them and slapped Mayhem's shoulder before rushing off to confer with other organizers.

"Martin looks tired," Mayhem said, "going from this to that and on again with no space in between."

"He seems good at it."

Mayhem pulled Aiken close and lowered his voice. "There are people here," Mayhem said, "that Martin would prefer not to be here."

"What? White guys like me?"

Mayhem pushed him away. "No, not white guys like you," he said. "Young black men not embracing non-violence; militants seeking confrontation."

The first few rows of marchers were all black people. King led the parade, sandwiched between Ralph Abernathy and H. Ralph Jackson.

Mayhem Chase marched in the second row and Aiken joined in fifteen or twenty rows behind Mayhem, but already casting about for Paris. The marchers were steady, the talking quiet with a few making conversation, some speaking out of nervousness. Police officers and national guardsmen ringed the route, men who spanked batons against their legs, anxious men with clenched fists.

Aiken's eyes wandered back and forth among the marchers, paying attention but not paying attention, seeking to locate his wife or Connie Harlan. A slim black man marched on the other side of Aiken occasionally bumping shoulders with him. "I'm tougher than I look," the man said.

"Sounds like a victim talking."

"What?"

"I was in the war," Aiken said. "Spent time in a camp but never marched in this sort of thing before, so I'm new to this."

The man smiled, a nervous, twinging effort, and Aiken thought he should say something comforting. "My wife did this sort of thing," Aiken said. "I should've done this before now for my kids."

"I wasn't old enough," the man said. "You know. I would have joined up though."

"Truth be told," Aiken said, "I wasn't smart enough. This is my first civil rights demonstration."

"So you said."

The procession marched slowly in the beginning; the marchers stayed steady and quiet and the police kept their distance. "We might escape being tear-gassed," the man said. *Or ass-bitten by police dogs.*

"But it ain't done yet," the chap said. "It ain't nowhere done yet."

A man sporting an Afro several rows behind King kept a two-foot length of pipe alongside his thigh so it wasn't so noticeable. Other young men punched forward from the ranks, picking up speed, carrying pipes or clubs or bricks, and this group gradually overtook the leaders of the parade, ignoring King, who waved them back.

The militants scurried in front of the march. The Afro-man pitched the pipe through a liquor store window. Others raced to the window, pounding away until the glass was chopped away; men jumped inside. Young men smashed other store windows. Cries of "Black power!" rang out. The core marchers stayed together and continued walking amid the screams and breaking glass. Along the storefronts, looting began.

Aiken saw people hustling King away but he couldn't locate Mayhem. He started to run. Police whistles blew and police lobbed tear gas and Aiken ducked around a police officer swinging a billy club at him. He ran past men hurling bricks, stones, bottles and sticks, attacking the police and guardsmen. Two nuns clung to each other. Gunshots erupted sporadically. Aiken skirted a tear gas canister, his eyes stinging. Aiken's companion ran alongside. The young man tripped, falling to the ground, and Aiken bent to help him up. He rose slowly, unhurt but dazed. He struck at Aiken and sped away. Aiken continued searching for Mayhem but as his breath ran out he slowed down, loping through the crowd and trying to comprehend the bustle, the furious turmoil, finding no sense or pattern to anything. He swung past the Clayborn Temple. Marchers sought refuge there, trying to escape the police and the tear gas. He strode on, hunting for the broad shoulders of Mayhem Chase, prowling Memphis streets amid the turmoil.

He found Mayhem squatting on a street curb, blood drooling down his forehead, pooling in his eye. Aiken dropped down on his knees beside him and used a sleeve to dab at the blood, but Mayhem waved him off, sitting quietly while blood continued to dribble down his cheeks. "It's pretty much over," Aiken said. "It ended badly. But they rushed King away and he's safe."

"Martin will take this violence personally," Mayhem said. "That's the character of the man. He takes everything on. It's his strength but also his weakness."

Mayhem struggled up with Aiken's help and they walked the streets back towards their motel. After a few blocks the frenzy died away to faint sounds only.

"Did you have a good time?" Mayhem said. "For your first civil rights demonstration I wanted you to have a good time."

"Hectic as hell," Aiken said, "but I managed to get a few autographs."

Inside the motel room Mayhem flopped down on the bed, pressing a cold compress over his hurt. Aiken switched on the television for the newscast. "The city has declared a state of emergency," the newscaster said. "Police arrested one hundred and fifty people. One black man was shot to death." He smiled at his colleague. "What's in store weatherwise, Ted?"

Mayhem clicked the set off. "That is a killing they won't investigate," Mayhem said. "Another uppity black man getting his just desserts."

The phone rang and Aiken answered, hearing Connie Harlan on the line. "How's Paris?" he said.

"Not much change."

"Our daughter needs to see her."

"It can't hurt, mister. I'll see to it."

During the evening news King appeared on TV, upset but as focused as ever. "Americans are infected with racism," he said. "That is the peril. Paradoxically, they are also infected with democratic ideals, which is the hope." *Right! The hope of "democratic ideals." And maybe pig-shit is tasty as hell.*

Sunday, March 31
Indianapolis, Indiana

The trip from Memphis to Indianapolis ate up nine hours in slick, flurry conditions. The hotel clumped down on the outskirts of the city, faded in character, meagre in trappings. The tires scrunched on the snow-packed gravel driveway.

"Sure this is the right address?" Chester said. "It's kind of run down."

Sarah spoke up from the back seat. "It's obviously a hotel where black people are allowed to stay."

Professor Connie Harlan answered the door and turned to Paris, who was seated at a table, scribbling in a notebook. "We've been waiting for you, haven't we, girl?"

The unit contained a decent-sized living room and two bedrooms, doors ajar with carved up furniture strewn about. Paris paused her pen, glancing up from her note-writing, dimpling her cheek with the pen, but said nothing. Sarah and Chester followed Aiken into the living room. Sarah crossed to her mother's side quickly, jumping into Paris, throwing arms about her neck. Paris did not respond but did not resist either.

After a few seconds Sarah's eyes glanced down to Paris's jottings. "What are you writing, Mommy?"

"A few scribbles for a possible sermon."

Connie took Paris by the arm, leading her to the couch. "Rest here, girl." Paris sat down and Connie gently guided Sarah to the floor in front of her. Connie placed a hairbrush in Paris's hand and piloted it through brushing motions. Sarah crossed her legs and Paris slowly stroked her daughter's hair. Connie motioned for Aiken and Chester to follow her into one of the bedrooms.

"Gentlemen," she said, closing the door behind her, "we'll wait, hoping the mother-daughter bond kicks in." They heard Sarah giggle in the other room.

In the evening the three of them, still in the bedroom, watched President Johnson give his State of the Union speech. Thirty-five minutes into the talk, Johnson released his bombshell: "I shall not seek and will not accept the nomination of my party for another term as your president."

"Political doings by a monster dick-wad," Chester said. He left the room, returning with a bottle of wine and crystal glasses. He popped the cork and they toasted Johnson's announcement.

"This is historic," Connie said.

"It's just political crap," Aiken said. "Whoever replaces him will be the same."

"No," Connie said. "Johnson is evil. He sent five hundred thousand soldiers into Vietnam and forty thousand died." Chester filled the glasses again. Connie clinked her glass against Chester's. "Ghettos burn," she said, "and colleges are in revolt." She sipped again. "One hundred thousand men fled the country to avoid the draft." She tilted the bottle aside, realizing that it was empty. She left the room, returning with her own bottle of wine, giving it over to Chester, who twisted off the cap for her. She filled the glasses once more.

"Johnson dropped more bombs on South Vietnam than the allies did during World War II," she said. "He napalmed a hundred thousand innocent peasants." The two men sipped without responding. She slumped down into her chair, rotating it about, the casters grinding. Her elbows folded onto the desk and her head slowly fell onto her arms. A slight snore sounded.

Aiken grabbed up her bottle.

Chester pointed to it. "I was polite," he said. "Monster polite. "It's dick-wad domestic! I am seconds away from a serious rash."

"I've some Canadian Club in my bag," Aiken said. He opened the door to the living room, peering in, observing Sarah still sitting cross-legged on the floor and Paris still fussing with her daughter's hair, twisting ribbons into it.

"Your name is Sarah," Paris said.

"That's right, Mommy." Sarah pointed to Aiken. "Do you know who that man is?"

Paris stared at Aiken for several seconds. "He's one of the white men."

Thursday, April 4
Memphis, Tennessee

Martin Luther King Jr. arrived in Memphis to preach to a capacity crowd at Mason Temple.

In the first row was a janitor who cleaned a white schoolhouse. He had worked all his life and was now eighty-two but looked fifty. He was counting on change brought by King, change so that his sons and grandsons would not have to push a broom and suffer slights in a white school. And maybe his youngest would survive Vietnam and return home to his family.

The janitor sat beside a waitress. She worked in a whites-only restaurant but was not allowed to dine there. She had three children, children whose teachers taught from age-old textbooks donated by sympathetic white school boards.

Reverend King stepped up to the stage and crossed over to the podium. He waited six minutes until the applause finally died down. He spoke for twenty-three minutes and then reflected: "I don't know what'll happen," he said, "but it really doesn't matter now." His face softened. "Because I have been to the mountaintop, I won't mind."

The congregation responded with an "amen."

"Like anybody," he said, "I would love to live a long life. I'm not concerned about that now…. I'm not worried about anything."

The lines in his face softened even more. A more relaxed look stole across his face, lingering. "I'm not fearing any man."

Thursday, April 4
Indianapolis, Indiana

At the seedy motel on the outskirts of the city, Paris slept in one bedroom, and in the small living room Connie skimmed over the latest *New York Times*, swapping sections with Aiken. Chester and Sarah conferred over food choices.

"Give over the sports section," Aiken finally said. "Like you give a shit about the Yankees or Rangers."

Connie threw over a few pages. "I'm getting why your wife has forgotten you."

Chester and Sarah set out on a shopping mission, leaving for an hour. When they returned, Sarah bustled into the room carrying two paper bags. Chester carried a bottle of wine in an ice bucket, balancing it on top of a two-burner portable electric hotplate.

"Why do we build our own kitchen," Aiken said, "with a McDonald's down the street?"

"Plebeians may voice an opinion," Chester said, "but patricians rule."

Grub is grub. Aiken skimmed the paper for news of the Detroit teams.

"We'll prepare brunch," Chester said. "Notice that, given the time of day, I use the correct culinary term." *Give it a rest. Go buy a bag of burgers.*

Chester and Sarah stirred into action, ramping the chest of drawers into a kitchen counter, popping the burner into play, simmering a broth, butting two desks together as a table, flapping a brand new tablecloth into place, adorning the cloth with two spanking silver candelabras, sparking the candles, and producing proper sterling silver soup spoons. They slung the chairs about, setting dinner places with linen napkins.

At 11 a.m. Chester called everyone to order and hustled them into seats. "We're having creamy carrot and leek soup," he said.

"Leaking soup?" Aiken said, "Couldn't afford steak? Charge card finally hit the ceiling, Tonto?"

"And this," Chester said, removing a bottle of wine from the ice bucket, wiping away the clinging, tiny particles of ice. The bottle glistened. "This is a 1964 Sauvignon Blanc Chasan from the South of France."

A bottle of rats-ass white wine.

Chester applied his sommelier's corkscrew and the cork popped. He rolled it about in his fingers, pressing it to his nose, sniffing it for several seconds. "I smell white fruits, maybe apples or pears." He sipped it and lowered the glass. "Definitely pears. Breath in the bouquet, Aiken."

"Thanks, no."

"Have you no finer sense of smell?"

"I can taste the difference between a glass of white wine and glass of kerosene and that's the only skill a man needs in life."

"And I'm sure you could do that," Chester said, "at least six out of ten times."

"Before we begin," Sarah said, "we give thanks." She said grace, held the spoon in front of her and gracefully dipped into her soup. "It's delicious, Uncle Chester, absolutely delicious. Leek soup has always been a family favourite." *Whose family?*

"I'll wager Robert Kennedy is not sucking down leek soup right now," Aiken said. "He's probably chomping into a steak with gallons of mushrooms smothering its ass."

"Daddy."

"Sorry, smothering its *butt.*"

"Robert Kennedy...," Paris said. "Kennedy." She tasted the word, pronouncing each syllable slowly: "Ken-a-dee."

After dinner Paris clasped her hands in front of her. "It's Bobby's time," she said. "It's Bobby's time and we must welcome Bobby and we should be early as a sign of respect."

Progress! We're back to the sixties at least. Shoot the mule before Paris makes a U-turn.

Connie snatched her coat and scooped up Paris's as well. "Right on, girl, now you're talking some sense. We'll go listen to Bobby Kennedy."

Thursday, April 4
South Bend, Indiana

Jason Bartlow Morgan dragged himself, his suitcase and his typewriter up the ramp of the private airplane for the trip to South Bend. He shot a greeting bow to Kennedy, seated in the first row of seats, and moved to the second row where he whispered to Salinger, "Only three weeks into the campaign and there's traces of grey in the senator's hair."

Salinger whispered back. "Yeah and his hands are raw from shaking everybody and his damn dog."

"And stress lines across his face."

Salinger nodded. "Saw that."

In front of them, Kennedy stood up, undid the buttons of his top coat, sliding it off and sat back down. He folded the garment over his lap.

"…the coat?" JBM said.

"Yeah, it's John's."

Kennedy turned and gestured, indicating that JBM should drop down beside him. People who were still boarding bumped into him as they shunted past, and he tumbled into the seat.

Kennedy motioned JBM close because of the sound of the revving aircraft engine. "What's your home State of Indiana all about?"

"Your briefing papers," JBM said, "describe Indiana as 'anti-politician, anti-government, anti-taxation, anti-big-city and *anti-Catholic*.' Not so many years ago the KKK paraded openly in the State."

"I read all that. Give it to me in a nutshell, please."

"Be strong on civil rights, but stronger on preventing disorder in the streets."

"As of today," Kennedy said, "you run through all my speeches with those two themes in mind."

"Will do, Senator." JBM surrendered his seat to Salinger, who moved forward to sit beside Kennedy. "Cadillac," JBM whispered in Salinger's ear as they crowded against each other. Salinger blew cigar smoke at him in response, plunked into the seat just vacated and tossed his cigar stub out the plane's door as the pilot ramped it up.

"We planned John's campaign months in advance," Kennedy said. "Nailed down everything, every last paragraph and every last comma."

"Yeah," Salinger said, "but flying by the seat of your ass bites better. More fun."

"The expression is 'seat of your pants.'"

"Only in mixed company, Senator. Only in mixed company. We own the original 'seat of your ass' campaign."

Kennedy banged a fist against Salinger's knee. "'Seat of the ass,' it is."

The plane taxied and they buckled seat belts. "Can Johnson end the war?" Salinger asked.

"Whoever wins the presidency inherits a war that is depleting America's resources." Kennedy wiped his forehead, dragging fingers to his temples.

"When the war ends, what then?"

Kennedy rubbed his cheeks and his eyes dropped down. "Atonement," he said. "The country must atone for this war by rescuing America's poor."

* * *

In South Bend Kennedy's speech at Notre Dame was entitled "Feeding America's Hungry."

"In the most affluent country in the history of the world," Kennedy said, "children in the Mississippi Delta and on Indian reservations starve. The children have bloated bellies and diseased sores on their bodies."

The students responded with enthusiasm.

"Good reception," Salinger said.

"He's the brother of the first Catholic president," JBM said, "speaking in the cradle of the Catholic establishment in an anti-Catholic state. If he pissed down their backsides, they'd applaud."

From Notre Dame Kennedy flew to Muncie, pitching a similar speech at Ball State University. "Become outraged at poverty," he yelled out. Ten thousand students reacted with thundering applause.

Before the clapping died Salinger punched JBM on the shoulder. "Well they ain't no bunch of Catholics," he said.

A grin tattooed across JBM's face. "He's becoming the man."

Thursday, April 4
Muncie, Indiana

Martin Luther King Jr., Nobel Peace Prize winner, died before his fortieth birthday. Using a Remington 760 Gamemaster .30-06 rifle, a forty-year-old white man, James Earl Ray, fired a shot that struck him down. King was pronounced dead at 7:05 p.m.

As Kennedy re-boarded the plane in Muncie, Salinger advised him of the shooting.

"Dead?" Kennedy said.

"Don't know yet."

Kennedy collapsed into his seat. The newsreel from Dallas with the fatal shots to his brother played over in his mind once more, as it had so many times in the past. It's Jack in Dallas again, he thought. "Can we help his family in any way?" he said to Salinger.

"I'll ask, Bob."

Arriving in Indianapolis Kennedy learned that King was dead and that the assassin was white. He pressed his hands over his face. An oppressive darkness glided into him. "A senseless killing," he said. He tugged at the lapels of his brother's topcoat, gathering it tight, struggling against the gloom. The cooling inside him deepened, chilling him beyond repair, making him ache for his brother. He thought about Dallas and was once more consumed with grief.

The Indianapolis police chief anticipated rioting and advised Kennedy to cancel his appearance. "It's not safe for you or your wife," the chief said. Kennedy shook him off but decided to send his wife ahead to the hotel. He ushered her into the car without speaking. She was silent, in prayer, rosary grasped tight, praying for the family of

Martin Luther King Jr. He did not interrupt her prayer but kissed her on the cheek and pressed the car door closed. The Dallas newsreel played again in his mind. As they drove him to the rally, he scribbled notes, attempting to banish the newsreel, trying to busy his mind, to shift it away from the evil of that Dallas day.

At the Indianapolis Broadway Christian Center, people waited for the arrival of Bobby Kennedy. Several hundred people milled about, the crowd mostly black. Paris sat in a chair off to the side of the hall, resting quietly, close to Connie Harlan. Chester and Sarah snuggled next to each other in chairs in front of the stage, whispering, with Sarah occasionally bursting out in laughter. Aiken waited at the back of the hall watching his wife and daughter, eyes travelling back and forth between them. Paris suddenly stood. Connie rose as well. Sarah and Chester stood and followed, as did Aiken. Lemming-like, many in the crowd filed out of the building.

When Kennedy arrived at the center the crowd was upbeat, not realizing that King had been assassinated; they simply waited for the person who might become president. People helped Kennedy climb up onto the deck of a flatbed truck. He drew his brother's coat close and immediately began speaking. He advised the crowd that Martin Luther King Jr. had been assassinated in Memphis by a white man. Aiken missed his first words and did not grasp the situation. Somebody cried out. People sobbed.

Paris cast blue eyes about, searching, seeking someone or something. She stared into the face of someone familiar, a white man. She raised her arms, letting her hands fall and rest against his shoulders. "Do I know you," she said. She drew closer and saw his eyes up close, those eyes. "Aiken," she said, "they shot Martin. A white man did it."

She fell tight against him and he strung his arms about her, embracing her, squeezing her.

"We're married," he said. "I'm your husband."

Tears splashed down her cheeks. "Yes we are, Blue-eyes, but they shot Martin." *Holy shit! I'm Blue-eyes again.*

The crowd quieted but the sobbing bubbled forth, gradually increasing in volume. Tears smudged Kennedy's face, temporarily unmasking the lines of worry. He tugged his brother's coat tight again, as tight as he could, speaking over the wailing. He spoke of Martin Luther King Jr. in hushed, respectful words.

And then he said, "For those of you who are black and filled with hatred and distrust against all white people, at the injustice of such an act, I can only say I feel in my heart the same kind of feeling." His face sagged and he wrung his fingers into his brother's coat, trying to wrest comfort from the physical connection with his brother. "I had a member of my family killed," he said, "killed by a white man. But we have to make an effort in the United States. We have to make an effort to understand, to go beyond these rather difficult times. I look to one of the Greeks, Aeschylus, and his poem:

'Even in our sleep,
pain which cannot forget
falls drop by drop upon the heart,
until, in our own despair,
against our will,
comes wisdom,
through the awful grace of God.'"

The end of the poem triggered more tears from Kennedy, teardrops that quickly soaked his face. He released the grip on his coat, his fingers white from the clasping.

Aiken pulled Paris close and she sobbed against him. *This is not some bullshit politician.*

"What'll happen to our children," Paris said, "without Martin to lead us?" Aiken drew her closer, seeking to offer comfort in a day widowed of comfort.

After Kennedy's eulogy, silence engulfed the crowd save only for the sounds of weeping, and these sounds increased. No one could stop weeping. Paris teetered and Aiken quickly slung an arm around her, keeping her upright, steadying her.

"Bobby Kennedy does God's work," she said, falling back. Aiken caught her and held her up, supporting all of her weight. "Thank you, Blue-eyes," she said. "I'm feeling poorly."

He squeezed her tight.

Connie, her face wet from tears, stumbled over to Paris. "There'll be guns and gasoline out tonight," she said.

Sarah noticed her father supporting her mother and closed on them. "Are you sick, Mommy?"

"Call a doctor?" Aiken said.

"Go back to the motel while I dig about for a friendly doctor," Connie said, "but it may be a while."

He touched Paris's forehead, running his fingers over the fading scar, feeling heat. "She's on fire."

***

Bobby Kennedy slumped down in the back seat of the car, keeping his hands over his face as he travelled back to his hotel. His brother's sturdy wool coat failed to dispel the cold and the unending tears draining down his face chilled him deeper. "Hatred is attacking the American soul," he said.

Suddenly he craved his wife, needing to pray with her.

Thursday, April 4
United States of America

America exploded and a night of black rage ensued. In Washington a woman forced her three children to the floor as soldiers ran past her home chasing looters, shooting at them. In Baltimore an angry young man flung a stone at the line of officers moving towards him and was shot, crumpling to the pavement, dead before he hit the ground. In Chicago, fires forced an elderly man from his basement apartment and he wandered, confused.

In the motel Paris slept and Aiken checked on her frequently, wiping sweat away from her forehead as it beaded. Chester clicked the television on and motioned Aiken over. He sat on the couch and Sarah bunched down beside Aiken holding his arm, refusing to let go. Stokely Carmichael raged in front of a gathered crowd of black men.

"If you don't have a gun, go home….When the white man shows up, he's coming to kill you...Go home and get you a gun and then come back, because I got me a gun."

The camera spun back to the commentator: "Another death has been reported in Cleveland," he said.

"That's code," Aiken said. "A cop just shot a black man."

Sarah shifted closer to him, her arms squeezing him tight. "I'm scared, Daddy."

"It's Detroit again," Chester said. "They're burning down everything."

"In Detroit," Aiken said, "they mostly burned out shop-owners who gouged them—grocery shops, liquor, clothing and drug stores."

"But they shot at cops."

"Hits at white power," Aiken said. "White institutions will be left alone. No one torches a factory or a sports arena."

"What else, Kemo Sabe?"

"They won't target hospitals or universities, and the suburbs are safe."

"How can the suburbs be safe?" Chester said. "They're so white they're bound to be a target."

"In the white Detroit suburbs last year," Aiken said, "people spent the night waiting for black rioters to attack them, boarding up windows, buying more ammunition, waiting for attacks that never came. Black rioters burned down their own squalid homes."

Paris woke and they squirrelled the television into her room and she watched the news. Sarah snugged down beside her. "I'm afraid," Sarah said. "Is Adam safe?"

"He's safe," Aiken said, "He's in a university."

On television President Johnson pleaded for restraint. "Some will heed him," Paris said. "Many won't."

Sarah pressed closer to Paris, clinging tightly, and eventually the girl fell asleep.

* * *

In Chatham, Ontario, Mayhem Chase quit his home in despair at news of King's death and walked the quarter mile to his church to pray. He found an aging woman weeping on the steps. "Come in darling," he said. "We can pray together."

"But you knew him, Reverend Chase. You must have a special grief."

"We'll pray together," he said.

Other parishioners wandered to the church in ones and twos, seeking comfort. Mayhem pushed aside his own grief and his personal thoughts of King to deal with the suffering of others, knowing that King would have conducted himself in the same way.

* * *

In Windsor, Percy Turner waited while his mother and her sister prayed over the cemetery stone that read "Paris Day," where his cousin Tanya was buried.

* * *

Later, in Detroit, Turner filled a Coke bottle with gasoline, poked a rag into it, lit the rag and flung it against a police car. The car swerved and its occupants bailed out, drawing weapons, ready to fire. "We gonna run short of Coke bottles tonight," Turner said. He disappeared into the crowd and several young black men trailed after him.

* * *

At Columbia University a group of students struggled to overturn an empty police car. Kendra joined in but the car refused to budge. She turned and called to Adam. "Lend a hand, big guy." He moved in, placed his hands under the bumper and the students tried once more. Adam strained, muscles tightening and drops of sweat appeared on his forehead. The car rocked, then lifted and finally flipped. The bumper had cut into him and splashes of blood lined his hands. A squad of eight or ten police officers in riot gear rounded the corner. Kendra led the students against them and Adam trailed after her. One student was clubbed down and then a second was knocked to the ground right beside Kendra. Adam charged in, knocking into an officer as he swung at her. The cop's truncheon slammed into his shoulder as Adam slung him around and threw him. The students ran. After two blocks Adam and Kendra found a place of safety against a brick wall. Adam leaned back, seeking to catch his breath.

"That was fantastic," she said.

Adam rubbed his shoulder and wiped his bloodied hands on his pants. "About as much fun as a root canal."

They left their place of safety and found that the melee had evolved into a looting spree in nearby shops, but Adam held back, grabbing Kendra's arm. "King wouldn't loot," he said.

"Those people have nothing in their lives," she said, "nothing because of white racism, so their looting doesn't concern me." She jerked her arm away. "I'm glad for it. The system is corrupt and must be destroyed."

"I'm not for looting," he said.

"Then you don't understand the problem, Mr. Detroit."

***

Connie Harlan phoned relatives to confirm their safety, and afterwards settled back to organizing for Kennedy, calling fence-sitting folk, emphasizing that King's death could best be avenged at the ballot box and the only real alternative was Bobby Kennedy. After each person signed on, or seemed to, she arrived at the part she hated. "The campaign costs money," she'd say. "Can you help us?" After a pause they might commit a dollar or even five, and she always said, "I thank you on behalf of Senator Kennedy." But every dollar committed weighed darkly on her because she knew that person would give up something to honour that commitment. "I hope you're the real thing, Senator," she said, more than once.

When she finished her night's work, she slipped into a flannel nightie and crept into bed. She thought about Martin Luther King Jr. and his family, and began sobbing into her pillow, crying herself to sleep.

***

In their shared motel room, Harry Fortune finished the last of the pizza. Rizzuto poured himself another shot of bourbon, splashed a few ice cubes into the glass and dropped back in his chair with his feet propped up on the bed. "I'm telling you, Miss Pussy," he said, "the coons will be pissed off tonight. I'm glad I'm not in Detroit."

"Holy crap, man," Fortune said, "they've a right to be."

"Not saying either way, Miss Pussy, just saying I'm glad I'm not working Detroit tonight. The coons will be out for blood and going after coppers. And a lot of those black fellas learned to shoot in Vietnam."

* * *

In their motel room, Aiken finally switched off the TV, tired of the scenes that played and replayed. "They're marshalling soldiers and National Guard units across the country," he said to Chester. "They'll be killing more black people before the morning sun."

Paris struggled to rise, careful not to wake Sarah. Aiken slid to her side, noting the sweat rising to her forehead. "Don't stretch about so much," he said. The scar was gone now, a tiny scab only. She no longer touched at the area with her hand. "We must do something," she said. "We must help." She continued fussing about.

"Please rest some," Aiken said.

* * *

Late in the evening Bobby Kennedy met with ten leaders of the black community at the Mariott Hotel in Indianapolis. The janitor arranged the chairs and stayed late for the meeting, waiting to pack them away again and finish cleanup. Angry at King's death, the leaders showed skepticism toward this white man peddling hope. The janitor peeped down at his watch, wondering if the buses would still be running.

One of the leaders accused Kennedy of belonging to the white establishment. "That's ironic," Kennedy said. "White businessmen accuse me of being too friendly with black Americans and cut back on their campaign donations."

The janitor decided to spend the night in the hall on the cot pulled from the storage room.

After venting their anger, the leaders pledged to support Kennedy. The group left the room and the janitor swept up debris and collapsed the folding chairs one at a time. "Idiots," he said. "Who else we got?"

***

In Chicago, Mayor Daley phoned the chief of police. "Shoot to kill the bastards," he said.

Tuesday, April 9
Atlanta, Georgia

On a muggy, broiling day they lifted King's coffin onto an ancient farm wagon to be drawn by two mules for the five-mile trip from the church through Atlanta to Morehouse College.

Before he left her, Ethel straightened Kennedy's tie, fussing with it, and placed her hands on his shoulders, stroking him, squeezing hard, brushing her tears aside. He opened the car door for her and she slid into the back seat in that elegant way he loved, but she twisted about, keeping her feet on the ground, so the door remained open. "How awful for his wife and for his family," she said. He leaned over and put a hand on her knee, thinking there was more to be heard. "It's a dangerous time," she said.

"Shall we build a castle and hide behind the moat?"

"No. No, you have to do this."

She swung her legs inside the car and he marvelled at the sexual nature of the unscripted move. She clasped her rosary. He pressed the door closed.

Senator Robert F. Kennedy walked behind the wagon, as did rich and poor, famous and unknown, some fifty thousand people in all. Mayhem Chase lurched along, fighting back tears at every step.

Black people waited in front of their homes, lining the route, handing out glasses of cool water to the marchers. Kennedy became the focus of the crowds, and people cried out to him in their grief. Mayhem, a few dozen people behind Kennedy, observed the attention and respect people conferred on the young senator. "King's mantle,"

Mayhem said to someone he did not know, "landed on Bobby Kennedy, a slim white man."

"Yeah, he become the man," his new friend replied.

"Yeah, he became the man."

Wednesday, April 10
Washington, D.C.

A day later, news people trudged behind Kennedy as he walked through the ruins of Washington's black ghetto. Paris and Aiken watched him on television. "Don't see McCarthy in a ghetto," Paris said. "Only Bobby does ghettos."

A black woman approached Kennedy; he slowed to speak to her. She dragged a kerchief from her hair. "Is it you?" she said. Kennedy reached out, grabbing her outstretched hand. "I knew you'd be the first here, darling," she said. She held the cloth to her face and wiped at tears. "Thank you, sir."

Aiken clicked the television off. "We'll keep a low profile for now," he said. "Do some resting and healing, just like the doctor said."

"You understand," Paris said, "while resting and healing I'll be helping Connie round up black votes for Kennedy."

"Probably no holding you back."

"When you were lost to me I gave birth to Adam and he sustained me while you were imprisoned. I held him close when I thought you lost. But after you came back it was my time to go to war. My people were imprisoned just as much as you were. Only my war was a different kind of war with no guns but still danger. But it was our way, Aiken, yours and mine. We knew we had a duty. You don't get to heaven by sitting on the sidelines."

"There are personal costs in going to war. You know that."

"Everything has a cost." She sat down in his lap and wrapped her arms about his neck. "What'll you be doing?"

Aside from worrying about you? He thought about her question. "I'll help out JBM. Chester can stay and help Sarah with her lessons."

"Why Blue-eyes," Paris said, "you do surprise a girl. You, helping Kennedy's campaign? And him a politician?"

"Just helping JBM, that's all."

When they were alone, Paris wrapped him tight. "I've ringing in my head, Aiken. It's not going away."

Shit! "It's just my heart, sweetie-pie, trying to telephone over to your heart. That's all. It'll fix itself up in time."

Tuesday, April 9
Indianapolis, Indiana

Over the chair beside the shower stall, Kennedy arranged his pajamas carefully next to the towels and adjusted the shower taps slowly, as if this would minimize the sound and his wife could remain abed sleeping. The pipes knocked, spoiling his effort, and he waited for the warmth to appear. When the water had heated he stepped inside, letting the spray cloak him, and it sparkled him fresh, bouncing energy into him for the day ahead. When Ethel heard the pipes, she rose and put on a housecoat, organized his woolen suit, a striking silk tie that she had purchased, a sensible shirt, underwear and woollen socks. "Cherry trees in bloom in Indiana," she said, "do not rule out a frosty or even unfriendly day."

***

Robert Kennedy spent the last part of this day campaigning at Terre Haute. The national press followed his movements, and numerous film clips of him aired on the nightly newscasts, showing his hair blowing and twirling in the wind and his arms waving or stretched out, reaching forward and shaking every hand in sight. The campaign tilted to a different hue and Kennedy sensed it before others. America was fearful and people craved calming. People pushed towards him, trying to touch him, as if they could erase the cities aflame with rioters and killings, as if normalcy would be restored, as if fears would be banished.

He ended the day finally in a downtown area of the city, a dirt-poor scratch of boarded-up storefronts, scruffy tenements, broken windows and flourishing weeds. Dirt-poor America, he thought, and this is where the black population is consigned to live. There is abject poverty amidst the richest country in the world.

A man in a clapped-out Chevy slowed his car and dropped down his window, calling out, "Coon-catcher Kennedy! Out trying to catch coon votes, are you?" The car sped off.

In the front seat of Kennedy's car, Salinger twisted about. "Bob, don't worry about that guff," he said. "Put it behind you."

JBM, driving the car, also turned back to Kennedy. "Ignore racists," he said. "It's why you're running."

Later Kennedy, still rattled, offered up a speech, a wobbly affair. At the back of the room, Salinger perched on a chair beside JBM. "First speech in Indiana's a bust because of some racist idiot."

"It ain't over yet," JBM said.

The following day, still in Terre Haute, Kennedy breakfasted with a group of 150 well-to-do women. He fidgeted with his food, pushing it back and forth, not feeling his best, waiting to give the women a short speech. 'Coon catcher,' he thought. Is everything in this country about race? Can't people see the poverty and what it does?

Salinger stayed off to the side with JBM, both praying that someone would challenge him. "Please, someone attack him," Salinger whispered. "He always rises to a challenge." JBM nodded.

But the women in Terre Haute felt no inclination to attack the handsome man sitting nervously before them, pushing his food about.

"This opportunity is slipping away," Salinger said.

Kennedy noticed the silence then and realized the women were waiting for him. He stood and spoke for a few minutes and answered the polite questions but quite suddenly diverted and addressed instead the poor in America. "They're hidden in our society," he said. "No one sees them anymore, an invisible, small minority in a rich country."

At the back of the room, Salinger slumped down in his chair, knowing the speech was heartfelt but not right for this audience.

"I am stunned," Kennedy said, "by the lack of awareness towards the poor and their problems."

"Bob," Salinger said quietly, "please bail out. The plane is on fire."

"We pay all these taxes," Kennedy said, "and develop these programs to help, and yet the programs don't reach them, the taxes go to other things and every year their lives become more hopeless."

Salinger put his hands over his face.

"And we wonder," Kennedy said, his voice rising, "what's wrong with these people after all we did for them."

The women clapped politely, smiling at the handsome visiting senator from the state of New York. Salinger plucked a cigar from his inside coat pocket and shook his head at JBM.

"That's why we bust our ass for him," JBM said.

"But it would be nice," Salinger said, flaring a match, "to pick up a few votes along the way."

***

In the late afternoon Aiken cabbed to the Kennedy campaign headquarters. In a small back room he found JBM perched behind a desk, wearing his sweater-vest over a white shirt, sleeves flapped up as always, pounding on a typewriter, cigarette hanging from his lip. *Norman Rockwell should paint this guy.*

"It's me," Aiken said.

"Nanook?" JBM said without glancing up. "Nanook! Is it really you?"

"No farting out loud," Aiken said. "I owe you that." Aiken opened his satchel and yanked out a quart bottle of Canadian Club, placing it on the desk. JBM reached into the desk drawer and removed a beaten-up cup, rustled about further and produced a scratched-up water glass. He rubbed his finger around the rim of the cup, then the glass, scouring them, blowing into each one before setting them on the desk.

A bloke who favours sanitary drinking vessels. God, I like that in a man.

Aiken slopped three fingers into each container and JBM waved, splaying fingers, indicating that Aiken should choose. Aiken seized the cup. *It shouts: more character...choose me, choose me.* "It's the little decisions that define a life," Aiken said.

"Indeed." JBM sipped from the glass while striking keys absentmindedly with one finger. "I find myself craving Canadian whiskey," he said. "This melted hockey-puck junk has a tang of its own."

"Who doesn't like it? Maybe the occasional rabid nun..."

"But why are you here?" JBM said. "A sudden interest in American politics, Nanook?"

"I need to help Kennedy." *Because it's a white, white world, just like Paris has always maintained, and I have two black, black kids.*

"Read some newspapers for a bit, I gotta finish this up."

After JBM had tapped the final few words to his speech-writing effort, Aiken shoved the bottle of Club into his satchel. Two blocks away they climbed up two flights of stairs to JBM's room. The bed was unmade; clothes dangled over chairs and towels huddled about the floor. A wet dishrag hung from a floor lamp.

"Housemaid's day off?" Aiken said.

"I can guide Bobby's campaign in this state because I am a Hoosier," JBM said. He popped the cap off a bottle of Old No. 7 and dripped two fingers into each of two glasses, giving one over to Aiken.

"You're a vacuum cleaner?"

"Hoosier, Hoosier.... Grew up in this state. People from Indiana are Hoosiers."

"And this makes you the sparkplug behind Kennedy's Indiana campaign?"

"You learn very little from rich assholes," JBM said. He sucked on his cigarette, smoke spiraling in the air. "Learn nothing from them in fact, maybe the price of an imported Mercedes Benz or BMW, or maybe how to buy a fancy diamond bracelet for the girlfriend stashed on the side. You gotta talk to barbers and cab drivers and waitresses to learn what makes a town tick. Carpenters and bricklayers are good."

"What did you learn?"

"This is the question for Indiana: how do you motivate the black vote and the white vote for the same short white guy who's perceived as a stranger in a state that mistrusts outsiders?"

"You going to give over the answer or should I guess?" Aiken sipped on the Jack Daniel's. *A true American mystery: Why doesn't Old No. 7 dissolve the bottle it's in?*

"White people," JBM said, "are scared witless about violence in the cities, while blacks worry more about schools and jobs. Bobby's speech must scream out: 'Violence in the streets will fucking well not be tolerated.'" JBM lit a cigarette off the burning stub of the current one, puffing and sucking until the new one caught. "Later in the speech Kennedy targets blacks and minorities: 'Everyone gets a good paying job and a proper education.'"

"What does he say about the war?"

"He says no more spending money on this stupid war. Spend that money here in Indiana.'"

Aiken nodded.

"Why are you here, Aiken?"

"I heard Kennedy speak about King," Aiken said. "I believe he might make things better for my family."

"How do you propose to help the senator?"

"Maybe knock on doors or pass out flyers, or stuff envelopes."

"Do you know Camus?" JBM said.

"A Kennedy staffer?"

"No. Camus said, 'There will always be suffering children. That guy.'"

"He doesn't sound real upbeat."

JBM threw aside a pair of boxer underpants from an easy chair and pushed Aiken into it. "Camus is a French philosopher," he said, "so in Canada they call him 'Ca-moose.'"

"Okay," Aiken said, "a Canadian reference." *Not as pithy as Rocket Richard but it'll do.*

"Ca-moose essentially says: 'embrace the absurdity of life'. He's referring to the myth of Sisyphus."

"Sisyphus," Aiken said, smiling. "A campaign worker?"

"The American version of Sisyphus," JBM said. "We shove a 1965 Cadillac up the mountain every day and it rolls back down afterwards."

"Is this some sort of breakaway Pollyanna philosophy?"

"My point, Aiken Day: we'll be happy as hell on the way up, toiling for a righteous cause. We believe in Bobby. But my special spin, the JBM version, if you will, is that at the top of the mountain, we pause and reflect."

Aiken kept his face blank, seeking comprehension. *Christ, it's worse than trigonometry.*

"We break tradition," JBM said. "At the top of the world we wait, zippers down. We stand up proudly and urinate over the rose bushes, Aiken. We persevered for Bobby, standing beside him on top of the world."

Peeing for Bobby? Can I assume there are illegal drugs in the Cadillac? "And after you push a two-ton Cadillac up a mountain? What then? We just stand there in the pee?"

"Well, the next day we climb out of bed and push the Cadillac up the hill again." *Is the engine malfunctioning and the warranty expired?*

"We fight racism," JBM said, "and poverty and rampant evil."

"Like Superman," Aiken said.

"But we don't have to wear those goddamn blue tights." JBM fell silent and dropped to the floor, crossing his legs. Finally he said, "I have a special project."

"Tell me."

"After the Newark and Detroit riots Bobby pushed for a documentary showing the life of a poor black. 'Show the sound, the feel, the hopelessness,' he said."

Aiken emptied out of the chair, squatting down, crouching across from JBM.

"It would be perfect," JBM said, "for a person with contacts, say a man with a black wife and her friend Connie Harlan."

"How do you know about them?"

"Newspaper journalist, here, Nanook. I investigate for a living."

"I might be interested." *I'd have to buy a camera and some film and plead with Paris for introductions.*

"More important," JBM said, "licking envelopes fucks with the taste buds, spoils the whisky."

A documentary for Bobby? "I'm interested," Aiken said.

"I'm out of smokes, gotta scoot out and buy more. Let's call it a night." They trudged down the two floors and stood outside the entrance. The wind was up, occasional snow flurries batted about and they both buttoned coats close, pulling collars tight. "Bobby wants this project," JBM said. "Help us out, Aiken and help yourself out."

JBM left the hotel pursuing smokes and Aiken watched him until he was out of sight. *Nanook is damn interested. Plus that would score big points with the missus. Two birds!*

Wednesday, April 10
Indianapolis, Indiana

Connie Harlan and Paris Day organized their command headquarters, preparing for the battle to turn out black voters for Bobby Kennedy. Stacking the motel furniture aside, they commandeered some beat-up wooden slatted chairs and a lengthy fold-out table with wobbly legs. The table held lists, pages and pages containing the names of preachers and other influential persons in the black community, people who might sway other people.

Paris added a dash of cream to her coffee and replaced the pot on the burner. "I'll have a cup," Aiken said. She sat back down at the table, fussing with the pages, not hearing him. He slid in tight to her, keeping his voice low, seeking to soothe. "Still some ringing today?" She nodded, and flipped through the lists, penning a name as it occurred to her, sipping at her coffee.

Aiken poured himself a cup, leaving it black and sugarless. "Did you think about Bobby's documentary?" he said. Both Paris and Connie paused in their work. Chester and Sarah moved close.

Paris pushed her pages aside. "You're looking to interview black people for a documentary and use it for political purposes, even though you've never been interested in either filmmaking or politics."

"Do you think the idea is stupid?" Aiken said.

She turned and jotted down another name. "Not sure."

"Change of pace, for sure," he said.

"So," Connie said, "you need victims of the system, mister." She stood and angled her hand on her hip in jaunty fashion. "Not like me, the attractive coloured gal who graduated Harvard *magna cum laude*?"

And who modestly refuses to brag about it.

"You're seeking obvious victims," Paris said. "Not the subtle effect on the black race of two centuries of racism."

"He's hunting for the dog-fart bleak ones," Chester said. "Put an emphasis on the bleak." *As opposed to putting emphasis on the 'dog-fart.'*

Sarah plopped into Aiken's lap. "I could do the filming. I could push the camera buttons."

"Sweetie," Connie said, "for now, you help your mom and me."

"I'll just ask questions," Aiken said, "and see what I see, hear what I hear. I have no agenda."

"I'll some make phone calls for you," Paris said. "On a test basis. We'll see how serious you are." She scribbled another note on the page in front of her.

Connie picked up the sheet of paper, observing the latest addition. "Just stay out of our way, mister," she said to Aiken. "Go skedaddle about on your own. We have our own matters to attend to. Kennedy needs the Indiana black vote to turn out for him."

***

In the early afternoon, Aiken tapped Chester on the shoulder and Chester guided the car to the curb. Together they approached three black teenagers on a street corner in downtown Indianapolis.

"Talk to you fellas?" Aiken called out to them.

One man stepped a pace forward, pointing at the camera, his hand resting on the bulge under his shirt. "What's that for?"

"Making a movie about people," Aiken said. "Just asking questions, that's all, nothing serious." He clicked the camera on and lifted it up, focusing on the young men.

"I don't know anything," the teenager said.

A police car slowed down across from them, pale faces shining behind squad car windows. "Ask the cops," the youth said. Aiken kept filming. "Ask them why they're checking us out for just standing on a corner. Shoot that on your camera."

Aiken lowered the camera. "What do you think about the election?" Aiken said. "You know, Kennedy against McCarthy."

The youths wandered off without answering. "Dick-wads," Chester said. "We should've asked him if he suffered from bleakness, or maybe if he can tell us where the bleak people live."

Aiken stowed the camera away.

"Maybe we should knock on some doors," Chester said.

"Or maybe we should wait for Paris to arrange something."

***

In the evening JBM and Aiken walked the few blocks to JBM's room. Aiken carried a bottle of Canadian Club in a paper bag. The room remained in disarray and they jostled clothes aside to sit down. Aiken plopped down into the chair and JBM crunched down on the bed. The bedsprings creaked.

"Nanook, the man is fired up," JBM said. "Bobby has gained some sort of insight into Indiana people. He is hitting his stride at exactly the right moment." He beckoned to Aiken. "Give over the Club for a taste of Canada."

Aiken passed the bottle over.

"This documentary business," Aiken said, "is a work in progress. The first day was not a real success."

"Living creatures leave their mark, Nanook. Dogs piss on poles. Women nurture children and men write poems or start fights in prison. If you do this, it will be your mark."

Aiken set his glass aside. "What does it mean if you've got a ringing in your head that doesn't go away?"

JBM leaned forward and considered his friend. "It means you've been in the ring too much," he said. "You've been in the battle once too often."

Tuesday, April 23
Indianapolis, Indiana

The clanging of the phone shocked Aiken awake and he fumbled with the receiver, trying not to wake Paris. She was already awake. He pressed the phone to his chest. "Head ringing?" he said.

"Only a bit."

Aiken shoved the phone to his ear. "Yup."

"At the turn of the century," JBM said, "hoboes rode the trains, dodging railway police, always on the bum."

Aiken held the receiver tight to his chest, checking the alarm clock for the time. "It's 6 a.m. for Christ's sake and I don't care about hoboes." Paris shook herself upright, found her housecoat and shuffled towards Chester's kitchen area. "I'll put the coffee on," she said.

"Hoboes," JBM said, "concocted a mythical train called the Wabash Cannonball."

"What?"

"At the death of each and every sorry tramp, the Cannonball magically appeared and transported the departed bum to his reward."

"Are you into the Old No. 7?" Aiken said. "Cap the bottle and go back to bed."

"The myth became a song," JBM said, "recorded by Dizzy Dean, Blind Willie McTell and countless others." JBM sang: "'She's mighty tall and handsome, and she's known quite well by all. You can set your watch to the Wabash Cannonball.'"

"Going back to bed now," Aiken said. "Have a good life."

"They wore top hats when they campaigned," JBM said. "The voters in front of them wore cloth caps. Do you fathom the subtle messaging there?"

"Someone's wearing a top hat?"

"Every campaign whistle-stopped. Both Roosevelts used trains. Wilson, Harding and Taft rode trains. Dewey and Truman insulted each other from the backs of trains."

Aiken swung his legs out, sitting up, his feet shuffling back and forth, probing for his slippers. "Okay, I'm awake. What're you babbling about?"

"You and I," JBM said, "will ride the Wabash Cannonball with the next president."

"Explain."

"Kennedy's campaign is resurrecting the Wabash Cannonball for a one day, hell-bent-for-leather, screaming dash across north-central Indiana, and you will be there." The phone clicked off.

After a cup of coffee Aiken sorted through the dresser drawer allotted to him, choosing his cleanest shirt, flapping the grey flannels in an effort to banish the stains and wrinkles. He wrestled into a wool V-neck sweater, shoved his arms into his sports coat and sat down on the edge of the bed, clutching his pants. Paris slid down beside him, giving him a mug of coffee. "You don't think you'll need to wear pants?"

"Overrated, Missy." He explained about the Wabash Cannonball. He smelled or perhaps sensed her Milky Way aura again, her creamy hint of better things on the horizon, the scent drifting into him whenever they closed on each other. His arm wrapped about her. "I don't have to go."

"Of course you do," she said. "We must help Bobby."

He pulled on his pants and stuck a mickey of Canadian Club into a small carry case while she sipped coffee, watching him. "Are we at risk of over-packing?" she said.

He rounded up JBM from his hotel room and together they found their way to the rail station. JBM opened up his leather satchel to reveal a quart bottle of Old No. 7. Aiken showed him the Canadian Club and JBM plunged it into the satchel. Aiken heard a clink as it hit JBM's bottle. "Train might break down, Nanook."

"Exactly," Aiken replied. "Might be miles to the nearest liquor store."

The Wabash Cannonball entourage contained five cars and JBM briefed him about the itinerary. "The train halts at Logansport," JBM said, "then travels on to Peru, Wabash, Huntington and Fort Wayne."

"And?"

"And Bobby speaks at every stop from the back of the train."

They climbed the iron steps and Aiken peeked into the last of the cars, the car reserved for Kennedy's family. Ethel occupied her children with games. In the second-last car, an animated Kennedy, sleeves rolled up, tie loosened and brown hair flopping, discussed his speech with two staffers. Seeing an unfamiliar face, he wandered over and introduced himself to Aiken. "Bobby," he said, sticking out his hand and shaking Aiken's. *His eyes are cold, steel-blue but cold. Eyes created to break hearts.*

"This is Aiken Day," JBM said. "He works for us. He's helping me out with a project."

One of his aides held up a sheet of paper and Kennedy moved away, tossing a smile at them as he left.

Aiken followed JBM into another car where the reporters gathered, the festive atmosphere in this car different from the others. Muffins, donuts and pots of coffee were available, along with shots of Scotch or bourbon.

JBM pointed to the bottles of alcohol. "We replenish these repeatedly."

"Journalistic evaporation," Aiken said.

"Exactly, they need their minds limber."

At each city local bigwigs boarded the train, travelling with Kennedy to the following stop where other bigwigs replaced them.

"He meets with all the pooh-bahs," JBM said, "but more important, it conserves his energy for the big finish at the campaign's end."

At Fort Wayne, Aiken sprung out a side door and joined the crowd to listen to Kennedy. A lively banjo player jumped up the crowd. When Bobby and Ethel appeared, the applause lasted for several minutes. Kennedy now wore a navy-coloured suit, tie perfectly knotted. Ethel wore a simple, knee-length black dress with a round collar and a simple strand of pearls. *What an elegant woman.*

Kennedy introduced her. The crowd applauded with renewed vigour.

The young girl beside Aiken jumped up and down. "This is so exciting," she said. "Bobby is *so* divine."

Aiken soldiered on, speaking to a white-haired man, a wobbling man, hobbling along on a cane. "Are you a Kennedy fan?" Aiken said.

A pained expression crossed the man's face. "Waiting to see," he said, "obviously." *Obvious to whom?*

Kennedy started off on a light note, indicating that he, his wife and ten children would go on welfare if he lost this election, so voting for him actually made economic sense for the country. This brought laughter. He charged into his message: Rioting in the streets would not be tolerated. But we must help the poor; the money being spent on the war should be spent here in Indiana.

JBM sidled up to Aiken. "Did you take note of the enthusiasm, Aiken Day?"

"I did."

"People relate to him, they embrace him."

"Will it translate into votes?"

"We shall see, Nanook. We shall see."

At the end of Kennedy's speech a baby cried and his parents bore the child away, although Kennedy asked them not to. "Could I have silence," Kennedy said. The crowd quieted. Kennedy tugged at his hair. "Camus once said there will always be suffering children in this world. But perhaps we can make a little less suffering, and if we don't help them, who will?"

He reads Ca-moose? Bobby Kennedy reads Ca-moose.

"They love him," JBM said.

And I'm making a bleak documentary for him. It will be the bleakest goddamn thing ever.

Friday, April 26
Indianapolis, Indiana

They slept with the doors to each room propped open, and people moved about as if the suite was a single unit and as if they were all one family. Aiken sat up in his bed and plopped his feet on the floor, resting, preparing for the day. He saw Chester already cramming the two tables together, making ready for breakfast. He watched Chester whip out the tablecloth and flap it, snapping it twice. "Once again," Aiken said, "every meal does not warrant a tablecloth."

Chester paused in his efforts and called over. "What we have here, Kemo Sabe is a situation." He plopped down beside Aiken on the bed. "Relatively few things separate us from animals, Aiken."

Here we go again.

"Animals spit and fart but did you ever observe a dog or cat pat their lips with a napkin or use a finger bowl?"

"No."

"I thought not." Chester rose and flapped the white tablecloth over the joined tables.

"The tablecloth is nice," Connie said, coming into the room. She stuck her tongue out at Aiken. *You keep pushing my wife into the dangerous world of civil rights. When my wife is fixed up, you are history, babe. I'll mail you to Cuba—export you to the commies.*

Paris emerged from the bathroom and Connie elbowed in. Paris noticed the tablecloth and grimaced. "Speed up the cooking, Cheetah, we gotta tumble out the black vote for Bobby."

"Crêpes Suzette and champagne warrant a tablecloth," Chester said. The cooking commenced. He folded the crêpes into quarters.

The first few he dropped in front of Sarah, pushing a bottle of Quebec maple syrup towards her. He put the remaining crêpes into a frying pan and sprinkled caster sugar over them. The crêpes gradually assumed the colour of amber-coloured caramel. He reduced the heat, adding orange juice, lemon juice, Grand Marnier and butter, and re-melting the caramel. He flipped the first efforts onto a plate, setting it before Paris.

She started eating, chomping down with vigour. "Very tasty, Cheetah," she said. Chester's body dipped in a bow. "But they'd taste the same," she said, "without the tablecloth, and be done faster."

Chester turned away. "Blasphemy," he said, "blasphemy from people who should know better."

Chester set the wine glasses out and popped the champagne, filling each flute. Sarah sipped from Aiken's glass and wrinkled her face. "Do I have to play checkers with Uncle Chester today?" Paris glanced at Aiken, throwing the decision to him.

"Come with me today, sweetie," Aiken said, "and watch Senator Kennedy speak at a medical school."

"That'll be unfriendly territory," Connie said, sitting down. Chester held out a napkin for her and she whisked it across her lap. With her knife and fork she sliced her crêpes into tiny pieces before placing each bite into her mouth with finesse. She left the champagne glass alone, but after consideration slid it towards Aiken. *Whoa, peace offering! Cuba trip goes on hold.*

"They always schedule Bobby in front of hostile audiences," Paris said, "people who normally wouldn't vote for him." Aiken drained his glass and reached for the one Connie had offered him.

"Why?" Sarah said.

"Because Bobby's a born scrapper," Connie said, "and when people tangle with him, he shines, he absolutely rises to the occasion."

***

In the auditorium of the Indiana University medical school, 453 people waited quietly. No groundswell of applause greeted Kennedy as he rose to speak, just scattered polite clapping. They posed several questions to him and Kennedy responded to each one. Then he paused for a few seconds. "I understand the tone of these questions," he said. "I look around this room and I don't see many black faces. You students are the privileged people in this country."

"His back is up," JBM whispered to Aiken. "Cock-a-doodle-do."

"It's easy to sit back," Kennedy said, "and say it's the fault of the federal government, but it's our responsibility too, not just our government's. It's our society that spends twice as much on pets as on our poverty program. It's the poor carrying the major burden of the struggle in Vietnam. You sit here as white medical students while black people carry the burden of that war."

The sole black student in the audience cried out, "Don't forget me."

"I see you," Kennedy said, "but you sure stand out here."

The students applauded him at the end of the encounter. *It's not enthusiastic applause but it's more than polite. It's respect. They respect him.*

After dinner Aiken and Sarah collected up their gear and visited a black family, a meeting arranged by Paris. The depressingly small house sparkled with cleanliness. The woman, her skin raisin-coloured and wrinkled, was slight in frame, maybe in her late thirties, and four children aged three years to twelve years frolicked about. The children wandered wherever, kibitzing with each other as the adults interacted. The boy tried to attract Sarah's attention but she ignored him, focusing on the business at hand, working the camera. The woman tipped a teapot, gracefully filling a cup of tea for Aiken. An older woman, hair wrapped in a headscarf, rocked behind them, knitting, silently taking the occasional break from her knitting to sip from her teacup. Centered on the wall above the rocking chair was a photo of President Kennedy, a magazine cover, Aiken guessed, but carefully framed and hung.

Sarah worked the videocoder, ignoring the young boy and gestured for Aiken to start. Sarah pushed the machine so close that the woman pulled her head back. "What would make your life better?" Aiken said.

The woman thought about the question before answering. She pulled the mic close and Aiken almost lost grip of it. "Better schools for my children and good jobs when they was done learning."

Aiken asked about the photo of Kennedy. "When they arrested Martin," the woman said, "on those trumped up charges, President Kennedy called Martin's wife. He didn't have to do that. And while he was alive, young black people enrolled in white universities, the good schools with proper books and rooms."

"And Bobby Kennedy helped with that," Aiken said.

She sipped at her tea. "I know that, darling," she said. "And I knew it long before you did."

Aiken debated whether he should leave money. In the end he decided it was more likely to offend than not. As the door closed behind them, Sarah said, "Where was their daddy?"

Friday, April 26
Indianapolis, Indiana

Harry Fortune opened the motel door at the knocking and discovered a large man blocking out most of the daylight. "Your office in Detroit," the man said, "says we should help out you two fine FBI-ers. Figure maybe you can't locate your own asshole without no map, so you sure ain't gonna collar no black woman on the lam in Indiana." The Indianapolis police officer was burly—whack-'em-up sort of burly—slab muscles mixed with layers of fat, large ham-hock wrists that no handcuffs could ever wrestle in. He wore a cheap suit that failed to hide his shoulder-holster bulge. "We gonna stir up a black speakeasy for you, maybe obtain some sort of lead on that fugitive gal. What's her name?"

"Paris Day," Fortune said.

Rizzuto pulled on his suit coat. "How in hell are we supposed to find a coon living among other coons in a city we don't know? Let's go, Miss Pussy—we can follow the local fuzz-balls around for a while. Learn how to really munch down donuts, maybe watch him kick an old lady down a staircase. I hear they're good at that."

A second story walk-up housed the speakeasy, a former living room and dining room carved into one unit with a homemade wooden bar at one end and a row of ten or so bottles of liquor on a shelf. Fortune and Rizzuto followed the cop inside. Eight black patrons sat among three tables with a skinny, russet-coloured fella behind the bar; a man who suddenly took to polishing the glass in his hand, relentlessly. All the patrons froze, most slowly placing their hands on the table. Rizzuto braced himself against the door, leaning tight against it, sliding his hand inside his coat, wrapping his fingers around his pistol grip. Fortune moved in and stood next to him. "And you without your piece," Rizzuto said.

The Indianapolis cop pointed at one man still grasping a beer. "You, boy, stand up."

The man rose slowly, leaving his beer on the table but holding his hands out, keeping them visible.

"Did I ever arrest you, boy?"

"No sir, you never did. I ain't done nothing."

"Guess I never could tell youse apart."

The cop motioned that the man should sit back down and turned back to the bartender. "Jonesy, we're chasing a black gal, named..." He looked to Fortune.

"Paris Day," Fortune said.

"That's it, Jonesy—Paris Day. We're real interested in locating this woman. She does political shit."

"I could check about."

"I'm sure you could, Jonesy. And I know that you will, boy."

Monday, April 29
Columbia University, New York

The Students for a Democratic Society and the Student Afro-American Society occupied five buildings at Columbia University. Adam and Kendra climbed to the first floor of Hamilton Hall, joining a few other students. She settled in front of the expansive windows and he slouched close to her, edging an arm about her shoulders. On impulse he moved his hand down her back until it rested against her spine, then slid it down a few inches lower. She pushed it away, but did so gently.

"White students are separated from black students," Kendra said. Adam shrugged and she explained, "Scared white politicians are nervous about Harlem exploding, so they negotiated a deal. Black students can leave but not the whites."

"So we join the black group and bail out of here."

"We wait and we learn," Kendra said. "White politicians won't stay scared forever. Cops will be attacking black people right soon." They remained and watched the police spreading out, assuming control of the campus. Adam shoved towards her, intending to comfort her. "Don't," she said. "I like sex like any normal person, but I'm not in need of consoling by a guy needing to feel manly."

Adam turned to the scene below them. The first tear gas canisters clanged against marble steps, bouncing off stone walls.

"They should tear up their shirts," Kendra said, "and soak the strips and wrap their faces. Stupid white students are begging to be gassed. "

"Some of the students are just lying there," Adam said. "Passive resistance, trying to make a statement."

The police dragged students from the building, and clubbed everyone, even the students offering no opposition. "I'll tell you what statement those white students are making," Kendra said. "They're saying: Pigs! Come and stomp my ass into the ground, beat me senseless." She turned away from the scene below them. "We'll choose the time to meet pigs in battle," she said. "But we'll need weapons that kill."

"Whoa."

Adam turned back to the scene below. Police officers swung clubs, bashing students until their arms tired. They rested a minute or so and resumed swinging.

"They're clubbing unconscious students," Adam said.

"I could pop a few Molotov cocktails down there and burn a few cops. Fat, greasy porkers would flame nicely."

"Whoa, I'm not into killing. Not every cop is bad."

"When white porkers question you," she said, "they call you by your first name."

"So?"

"It's a euphemism for 'nigger.'"

"My dad calls me Adam."

"But your dad," Kendra said, "is not an old white man."

"No," he said, after a silence of seconds. "I guess not. Did you never have a white man help you with your jump shot or your curve ball…or anything at all?"

"I'm not up for condescending whites helping me with anything."

Adam watched an officer clubbing an unconscious student and pounding his face into an unrecognizable bloody pulp. "Holy shit! That's just mean and ugly. That guy will never get his face back the way it was."

"Who cares about white students?" she said. "It's black against white now. So we don't trust any grey cats."

He swung away from the window and the scenes of violence. "You said you liked the sex?"

"Doesn't mean anything. It's a bodily function. It keeps you healthy and strong."

"Something one does for the revolution," Adam said, "like eating and drinking to stay healthy—screwing for the cause."

"This conversation is over."

The screams subsided as police cuffed and hauled off students. She watched the scene down below and saw the red streaks on concrete left by bleeding students. "LeRoi Jones said it best. 'Up against the wall motherfucker, this is a stickup.'"

Monday, May 6
Indianapolis, Indiana

Paris rested in a chair by the bed, a blanket shrouding her legs. Occasionally she stirred to sponge the sweat from Aiken's forehead with a hand towel. When he mumbled and shook about, she woke him by pressing the cloth against his cheek. His nightmares fled and he jumped into present tense. "Are you feeling okay?" he said.

"We are a matched pair of dray horses if ever there was."

She put the coffee to percolating while he repaired the bed, finishing with hospital corners as he had been taught to do in the Essex Scottish. They sat with their coffees, quiet with each other, the silence comfortable and welcoming, sipping slowly. He drained his cup and she filled it again. "Two sickies," he said. "Two broken souls."

"There's a nine a.m. appointment for you." She pressed a piece of paper at him with the address.

"The ringing?" he said.

"Comes and goes," she lied, "gone at present."

They sipped in the absence of noise, a silence in the absence of anticipation, a dearth of expectation, feeling each other's presence for the first time in many months. Their knees touched, unnoticed, undetected.

Chester busied himself in the kitchen, clanging pots and pans in a jumble of noise. Aiken rinsed his cup, setting it on the counter. "No breakfast for Sarah and me today," Aiken said. "An early appointment, so we'll catch a burger later on."

Chester banged the frying pan down and tore off his apron, flinging it to the floor. "A burger? You're farting out on eggs benedict and choosing a burger? Did they teach you nothing at Stalag 8B? Maybe that breakfast fuels you for the entire day."

Aiken rose, his knee falling away from his wife's, and suddenly the sweats swept over him. He was transported back to Stalag 8B. *Towards the end, after Stalingrad, we got one cup of thin soup for the whole day.*

As they packed up their equipment, Sarah said, "Is Uncle Chester mad?"

Got a soufflé pan stuck up his ass. "Nothing to do with us, honey. His *Joy of Cooking* book has gone missing and he's having a small problem with his sauces. You know how chefs are." *A fricassee fuckup has fried his brain.*

At 8 a.m. they parked the rental, and Sarah heaved the camera up slinging the strap around her shoulder. The stucco-sided apartment building needed paint and the propped-open front door admitted them readily.

Exposed buzzer wires torn out of the wall indicated a bankrupt intercom system but the unlocked inside door admitted them. "Apartment six," Aiken said, moving down the centre hallway. He knocked twice on a door. The varnish had long since faded into a peeling mish-mash. A middle-aged woman, copper-coloured, with straggly bits of hair spouting out of a bandana, opened the door. She wore a cotton blouse and faded skirt with black shoes, shoes polished to sheen. "My wife, Paris, called you." He pointed in Sarah's direction. "My daughter, Sarah," he said. The woman shifted outside the apartment, drawing the door shut behind her, denying them entry.

"Come here, child," she said, gathering her arms about Sarah, hugging her, speaking quietly. "Is this white gentleman really your pa?"

"Yes ma'am," Sarah said, "He's my daddy."

"Paris didn't mention you was white," the woman said, "but it so much explains why she works so hard about some things."

"What do you mean?" Aiken said.

"She won the pot of gold, honey. Rainbow-chasing worked out for her. So, she got some big-time guilt. Bet you got a nice home in a pretty, white neighbourhood and your child here gets a proper education." The woman hugged Sarah again and invited them both inside. A young boy left the kitchen table where he had been scratching in a notepad, working with a schoolbook. The furniture consisted of a bed against one wall, a table and four kitchen chairs. The linoleum-covered countertop running along the other wall contained a sink with goose-neck tap, a single tap handle, a small row of cupboards above the sink with no cupboard doors, and dishes not matching but stacked neatly. The boy closed the book, nodding respectfully to the guests. *No plush couch to park your ass on, and no hot water, but goddamn the kid is doing homework before school.*

The woman plopped down into a chair and invited Aiken to sit in the one facing her. Sarah kept apart and began filming. Aiken held the microphone for the woman to speak into. "Paris said you and your son were in Newark last year," he said.

"We visited family in July," she said.

"During the riot," he said.

"Yes."

"Was it dangerous?"

"The looting and week-long fires made you careful," she said, "especially if you had a child with you."

"Can we talk about the looting?"

The woman reached out and tapped the camera. Aiken pulled the camera from Sarah, placing it on the floor. "Just help me learn," he said. "No recording."

"The looting and burning kept on all day, all night," she said.

"Did you loot?"

She remained silent for a moment. "I did."

"Did you think it right to do that?"

"It wasn't right but it wasn't wrong. They burned the stores that robbed black people for years."

"But the small stores...stores owned by real people, sometimes immigrants, and merchants, not rich companies."

"People looted to get even with the Man. Whites rob us of rent and food and jobs. They steal education from our children." She reached to the table, grabbing up her son's textbook to show to Aiken. "This book is twenty years old." Looking to Sarah, she said, "How old are the books in her school?"

"New books," Aiken said.

"Furnace in my child's school don't work sometimes. Send them home those days." She covered her face.

"Thank you," Aiken said, "for teaching me."

The woman suddenly grabbed the camera off the floor and put it back into Sarah's hands. "Git this going, child. I'll say these things for you. These things should be said."

Sarah started filming and Aiken began again. "You visited Newark last year..."

After they left the apartment, Sarah twisted Aiken about. "Where was their daddy," she said. "Aren't there daddies in the ghetto?"

Tuesday, May 7

Indianapolis, Indiana

At 5 a.m. the alarm clock jangled them awake. A crank of the shower knob sent hot spray bouncing off Kennedy's face, drilling down onto his chest, soothing his muscles. After wrapping up in his housecoat and fuzzy slippers, he slumped down on the bed and thrust out his hands in a new morning ritual. Ethel delicately patted them dry with a towel, noting the blood crusts. She dabbed Penaten cream over them and gently swabbed it in, the antiseptic, parsley-like smell unusual to him but not unpleasant. His outstretched hands stayed steady, not flinching, and beads of sweat dappled his brow.

Afterwards he flipped on the chair-side lamp and read a few passages from *The Greek Way* by Edith Hamilton. He reviewed previously underlined passages from the dog-eared pages. He reflected on her belief in the "calm lucidity of the Greek mind," taking comfort from the thought. After several minutes, relaxed and focused, he carefully closed the book, steeling himself for the day that charged towards him. "The final run," he said.

"Is there even a tiny chance of keeping your hands in your pockets today?" Ethel said. "Maybe shake a few hundred less hands?" They both smiled at her comment.

***

At 6 a.m. Aiken found JBM at campaign headquarters. The rooms bustled with people. "Finally, the last damn day," Aiken said. JBM buckled at the knees and knelt down over the wastebasket, vomiting into it. Aiken stared at him. "Whoa, hard night?"

"How heavy is a Cadillac?" JBM said.

"Five, six thousand pounds?"

"Try a million pounds."

"Stomach troubles?"

JBM stuck up his fingers in Aiken's face, counting. "Bobby needs the Negro vote in Gary and Indianapolis to turn out big time."

"Paris is working her butt off," Aiken said.

"The counties along the Ohio River that identify with the Confederate states must vote for him." Another finger dropped.

"Well..."

"The Slavic workers in the industrial cities must roll out in record numbers." Another finger fell. "The racists who previously voted for George Wallace must vote for Bobby." Another finger trickled down. JBM raised his voice, almost yelling: "He must get both the *anti-Catholic vote and the Catholic vote.*"

"How does that happen?"

JBM plunked down at his desk chair and booted the wastebasket away. "And he's a senator from New York with a strange accent."

"This is shittiest pep talk in history," Aiken said. He rummaged in the desk and found two glasses. He poured three fingers of alcohol into each. "Do you think Bobby has a dangerous cancer," Aiken said, "A serious type, the sort to rot his penis off?"

A shocked expression sliced across JBM's face. "God, no. Why would you say that?"

"Good, I wanted this conversation to end on a positive note." Aiken downed his drink. After a few seconds JBM did likewise.

JBM grabbed his coat. "Grab hold of your side of the bumper, Nanook," he said, "and take us to the airport so we can kick some ass."

***

Connie Harlan woke at 6 a.m., having slept in Gary at the home of another canvasser. Someone prepared a thermos of tea, already cooling, and three ham-and-lettuce sandwiches, and threw them at her at the last minute. Percy Turner showed up in a borrowed car. She stuck the thermos and sandwiches on the back seat, promptly forgetting about them. She reeled off the first address to Percy. "This fellow is wavering," she said. "But he's voting for Bobby if you have to beat on his ass."

"No problem," Percy said. "But do you think black folk are gonna vote for a grey rabbit after a white man killed King?"

"Kennedy's the only horse we got."

"Sure, if they vote at all."

At 6:30 a.m. Paris Day, still in Indianapolis, made the first of hundreds of phone calls. If a person requested a ride, she noted the name and location. One of the seven men on her list who owned a car would respond. She pleaded with undecideds, stressed the importance of the election. She used two catchphrases, *Bobby put black students in Old Miss*; *Bobby needs your vote*, until she worried that the phrases might be cancelled from the language for overuse.

Chester coached Sarah on the ancient art of canapé making. "What do we do with all the crusts we cut off?" she said.

"I mail them to Chinese people who are starving. Swear to God."

Paris overheard that comment. "Play checkers, Cheetah!" she said. "The people in China are fine!"

Chester mouthed the words to Sarah, "A little tense today."

Aiken and JBM hitched a ride to the airport and waited for the candidate. Kennedy's standout shaggy mane was immediately visible as he emerged from the car. People swarmed him. A mother held her baby up to him and he paused, cradling the child in his arms, but instead of kissing the child he rubbed his fingers about her face in gentle caresses, finally pressing his fingers to the child's fingers before passing her back. People pushed towards him, needing to touch him, and he endured it, shaking hands endlessly, disappearing at times as the crowd bustled around him. *He's healing them. Maybe they can forget John and Martin. He's taking on everyone's troubles.*

A slim young girl offered Kennedy a bouquet of flowers. He bowed and accepted them, but when the crowd closed in against her he cradled her into his arms, protecting her, seeing her safely back to her mom. Aiken and JBM boarded the plane with Kennedy, flying to Evansville for an airport rally. The receptive crowd bordered on rambunctious. Kennedy rendered a short speech. The party boarded another flight to Fort Wayne, and Kennedy huddled with JBM, scribbling a few notes.

A boisterous crowd greeted Kennedy at the Fort Wayne courthouse, campaign madness overtaking everyone. They escaped. JBM directed them to factory gates and they skewered the schedule with impromptu stops. "Screw the schedule, Nanook," JBM said, "this is Bobby on fire." *Even working stiffs hover about him, waiting to shake his hand, needing to caress him. His hands must be dead.*

The party arrived at the airport two hours late. "He has the full measure of Indiana now," JBM said. "The worker drones are done—finished. It's all on Bobby now." The campaign flew to South Bend but Aiken and JBM rented a car, driving back to Indianapolis alone. JBM, his work done, puddled sleepily into his coat, leaning into the vehicle's doorpost, suddenly the mute malingerer.

Kennedy's trip from South Bend to Chicago provided multiple stops for cheering crowds. He travelled through white areas and black areas, back and forth, rendering speech after speech. The trip, normally three and a half hours, lasted nine hours. As he entered the plane for the last trip, he grasped the door handle while waving to the assembled people. He tumbled into a seat as an aide mopped blood off the handle in one smooth, practised effort and pocketed the bloodied handkerchief without showing it to others.

At Kennedy campaign headquarters people waited quietly alone, or waited in bunches. Scattered lists of names now cluttered the room. Yesterday the lists were priceless; now they were worthless. Banks of phones no longer fought over and sweated over remained silent, untended. Wine bottles littered the campaign centre, some empty, some half-full. Empty beer bottles and damp sandwiches clung to paper-covered tables. A tie strangled a coat hook, and a suit coat lay on the floor for trampling. JBM rocked in his chair, legs and feet hooked over his desk. Aiken leaned back in his chair, noting that JBM's shoes needed a shine, that his pants cried out for proper pressing, that sweat stains streaked under the arms of his shirt. Aiken used the cup, JBM the glass, and the bottle of Old No. 7 seeped in silence towards empty.

At 11 p.m. the results were announced: Kennedy's 42 per cent to McCarthy's 27 per cent. McCarthy even finished behind the favourite son candidate, Governor Branigin. The room exploded. People shouted, stamping their feet, reaching for the good stuff, the chilling bottles of champagne, the bubbling alcohol transporting in frenzy, vaults of toasting and backslapping springing forth and kisses abounded. Celebrations bounced to the room rafters.

"We pushed him to the mountaintop," Aiken said.

"Indeed we did," JBM said. "Savour the moment." His face warped, smile sagging. "The Cadillac is tilting," he said, "ready for its roll back down the hill." *But not yet, don't fumble and piss down your pant-leg until it actually begins the backwards slide.*

JBM raised his glass and Aiken tapped his cup against it. After finishing their drinks they pulled on coats and scarves, leaving the bustle of the campaign headquarters behind them. The chill in the night air was friendly, welcoming. "Fuck them all, "JBM said. His voice blew frost, captured in the air. "We pushed him to the top. We pushed Bobby to the fucking top of the mountain."

***

Kennedy and his wife arrived at their hotel after midnight, too late to join the campaign celebration but too ragged to socialize in any event. He plopped into the chair and she doubled the quilt back, readying the bed. "Indiana is history," Ethel said, "but what a wonderful accomplishment for you." He did not reply. He sat bolt upright in the chair, asleep, his hands swollen and weeping blood.

Thursday, May 9
Watts, Los Angeles, California

Across from the hotel, three black teenagers bunched together. They wore black leather vests, jeans and sneakers. They wore matching cloth bandanas, and their bulging waistlines silently screamed out: we are armed; be wary of us; don't mess with us. They waited just off the curb, promenading, lest someone think them afraid or even concerned about passing traffic.

Chester parked the rented car in front of the hotel and stared at the three men across the street. "You sure this is the address," he said. "Those three dick-wads appear dangerous and the front door of the hotel has bars on it."

"Why don't you skedaddle to the Ritz," Connie said. "Your crêpe pan would be more at home there."

"This is it," Paris said.

Connie dragged herself and a file folder out of the car. "Welcome to the ghetto."

"I'm with Uncle Chester," Sarah said. One of the three toughs shot a middle finger at them. "It's not safe."

"Get used to the ghetto," Paris said. "We'll be working here."

Percy Turner stepped out from the hotel and removed a few pieces of luggage from the trunk of the car, stacking them by the curb. "Boys over there are Bloods," he said to Paris. "They have seven or eight gangs between them and control half of the black housing projects in Watts."

"Who controls the rest?" Connie said.

"Crips. We'll meet their boy later. Meet together and we got a killing."

Connie passed over an envelope to Percy. "A thousand dollars ain't going to go far with those gangs, mister."

"It's not money. We paying respect," Percy said. "We'll be able to sell your grey rabbit candidate without being harassed." He crossed the street and held up the envelope.

A gang member on the side accepted the package and pushed it into a pocket, but the one in the centre, the boss man, gestured towards Paris. "Know that woman," he said.

"Paris Day," Percy said.

"Feds want her dead and offering money."

"Friend of mine. Might be death money to anyone trying to collect that money."

"Know that."

"And you know me."

"We don't deal with the FBI, just passing along a warning," the boss man said. "No charge for warnings."

Percy jerked his head up and down, conveying his thanks. He crossed the street. "It's done," he said to Connie.

The three men slunk away, slowly, sauntering. "They act like they're in charge of the world," Connie said.

"They live high but they'll have dirt spread over their face before long," Percy said. "Always a younger, tougher guy in the ranks wanting to be the boss man."

Paris waved at the luggage, speaking to Chester. "You take care of the luggage and go through Sarah's lessons with her."

"It'll be hell uncovering a decent Bordeaux in this area," he said. He threw his bag down. "Did that even cross your mind?"

* * *

Paris and Connie arrived back at the hotel in the early evening. Chester had secured two rooms with a small kitchen between. Bags of groceries lined the table; dirty pots and pans adorned the countertop.

He sat quietly with a half-full bottle of white wine perched in front of him. Paris dumped her sweater on the couch. "How did the homework go? The math?"

"Your brilliant daughter can now bake a soufflé. She is primed and ready."

"Cooking?" Paris said. "She did cooking today? How about math or grammar?"

Chester held up his hands as though conducting an orchestra. "I will demonstrate." He twisted to Sarah, "Preheat?" he said.

"Three-hundred-and-fifty degrees," Sarah said.

"White sauce?"

"One cup."

"Egg whites?"

"Four."

"Egg yolks?" Chester said.

"Three."

"Parmesan cheese?"

"Seven teaspoons, no more."

"Bake?" Chester said.

"Twenty-seven minutes."

"And what sort of wine would you serve?" Chester said.

Sarah tapped a finger to her cheek before answering. "I think a Chardonnay, Uncle Chester."

"Which arm would you drape the napkin over while dispensing?"

"Left."

"That's the math lesson?" Paris said.

"She's a natural Einstein," Chester said.

Friday, May 10
Beatrice, Nebraska

In the afternoon the Kennedy entourage visited the Beatrice State Home for the mentally handicapped. Only two newsmen followed Kennedy into the building, most opting to remain in the car with their flasks and muddled conversations of baseball trades. Salinger and JBM followed the two reporters; Aiken trailed behind.

Inside the foyer the group converged on the warden. "Can I show you the wards?" he said.

"No," Kennedy said, "but you can show me the children."

In the first ward a hydrocephalic child lay on a mattress. The child's head was extra-large, basketball size. Kennedy lay down beside him and rubbed the child's stomach. The newsmen flinched, taking no photos, backing up, giving the two a private space. Kennedy visited with other children on the ward, children making no sense with their words or others who couldn't cease crying. He cuddled and stroked cheeks. He held them close. One child chewed at his fingers and he did not resist. The visit lasted two hours.

Outside the building Salinger hauled JBM aside, cramming into his space. "We'll never get that time back," he said. "Why did you arrange this? Mentally retarded kids don't vote."

"Nothing to do with me," JBM said. "Bobby set this up."

Kennedy approached the two. "What have you two cooked up for Nebraska?" he said.

"McCarthy and Humphrey," Salinger said, "are both Midwestern people. They speak the language of farmers, so we've got to tailor our message and cut back on the poor people stuff."

Kennedy looked to JBM for his input. "We stick with the one we brung to the dance," JBM said.

"Nebraskan farmers," Salinger said, "don't want to hear about housing on the reservations or ghetto problems."

Kennedy's arm gathered in Salinger. "We'll leave the speeches as they stand, Sal." Kennedy led him by the arm and walked him back to the first car. He opened Salinger's suit coat and removed two cigars from his inside pocket. He rummaged Salinger's coat pocket for matches. The two of them huddled into the back seat of the Cadillac. Kennedy lit the cigars. Smoke wisps seeped out the windows and the back window clouded over.

JBM whispered to Aiken, "Sal won the consolation prize."

***

On May 14 Kennedy won the Nebraska Democratic Primary with 51.7 per cent of the vote. McCarthy captured 31.2 per cent, Humphrey 7.4 per cent and Johnson 5.6 per cent.

The campaign split up after Nebraska. JBM and Aiken flew to California, the remaining team members, including Kennedy, to Oregon. As they settled into their seats on the plane, JBM said, "Marginalized people still have an advocate in Bobby Kennedy. Thank God."

"Will that play in California?" Aiken said.

"The real question, Nanook, is this: will it play to the million registered bedsheet-white Democrats in Orange County?"

Saturday, May 18
Los Angeles, California

As a young boy Richard Nixon applied himself with bulldog tenacity to all things academic, whether or not he possessed any innate aptitude. An astounding memory allowed him to succeed.

His aide coughed politely. "A group of six coloureds are still waiting for you, sir."

"A coloured group?" Nixon said. A practising Quaker, he recalled and recited words from another Quaker, the poet John Greenleaf Whittier.

"De Lord dat heap de Red Sea waves
He jus' as strong as den;
He say de word: we las' night slaves;
Today, de Lord's freemen."

Nixon could have recited all of the stanzas from the Whittier poem but chose not to.

"I don't quite know what to make of that," his aide said.

"It's a Civil War poem in the Negro vernacular," Nixon said. "Well received at the time."

"But maybe dated now?"

Nixon tugged the curtain cord and the drapes winched open with a whirring, grinding sound. The outside seeped in. "A bleak, overcast day, not pretty, a day that hardly showed up at all."

"The Negroes?" his aide said.

He gestured to his aide to show the group in. Six people entered the room, four men and two women.

"Welcome, ladies and gentlemen," Nixon said. The senior gentleman, leaning on a cane with a hand-carved ivory handle, gray hair carpeting his pate, said, "It is good to meet you, sir. Coloured people always meet with candidates to learn their positions on social policies."

Their concern, Nixon knew, centered on racism and civil rights, and he counted to ten before giving his rehearsed response. "I grew up in a small Quaker town in California," he said. "Our family was not rich but not abnormally poor. I wore clothes handed down from my older brother when such things were common in families."

He gestured to his aide and the man produced a glass of water. Nixon sipped, counting to ten, before continuing. "We had servants," he said, pausing for a five count, "black, Mexican or Indian, who shared our table for both dinner and discussion. There was a complete and utter absence of racial or religious bias at my mother's table." He paused again. "Everyone was respected and listened to, and that remains an integral part of who I am."

Paris Day spoke up. "My name is Paris, sir."

"What is your question, my dear?"

"You will face off against George Wallace."

"Quite possibly."

The senior gentleman spoke up. "Mr. Wallace is said by some to be a racist."

Nixon had the ability to reinforce an argument while apparently denying it, and he used that facility now. "I will not say that Mr. Wallace is racist," he said, "although I understand why many do. I just do not know enough about the man to condemn him of such terrible deeds or thoughts."

"If you don't carry the southern states," the senior gentleman said, "you may not win the election." Nixon nodded.

Connie Harlan raised a hand. "My name is Connie, sir. To use the words of Mr. Wallace himself, sir: you cannot be 'out-niggered' in the South."

Nixon threw out his rehearsed answer. "One does not do right in the long term by doing wrong in the short. As a Quaker, I will do what is right."

"Will Senator Thurmond," Paris said, "be your surrogate in the southern states?"

"Senator Thurmond will support me if he so chooses, as, hopefully, will many others."

"Allow me to quote Senator Thurmond," Paris said, flipping open a sheet of paper. "'All the laws of Washington and all the bayonets of the Army cannot force the Negro into our homes, into our schools, our churches and our places of recreation and amusement.'"

Familiar with the quote, Nixon paused as though taking it in for the first time. "The lesson from that quote," Nixon said, "may be that Senator Thurmond is against federal intrusion into matters best dealt with at a local level."

Paris waved the paper at Nixon. "You don't think that's a racist position?"

"I cannot peer into a man's heart and discern evil or racist intent."

"You will side with Strom Thurmond," Paris said, "so white southerners will assume that he'll keep the niggers down and stall any civil rights legislation."

Nixon slowly rose. "Thank you for coming," he said. "I'll reflect on our conversation."

After the group left the room, his aide said to Nixon, "How do you convince racist people to vote for you without losing the black vote?"

"The woman, Paris, guessed the truth," Nixon said. "Strom Thurmond's job is to 'out-nigger' George Wallace in the South."

In the lobby, the senior man, a reverend, wrapped his arm around Paris. "Sometimes," he said, "the slow, inch-at-a-time measures bear the best results."

She broke out in sweat suddenly and waited for few seconds before speaking. "Nixon has adopted a racist strategy to win," she said. She tugged at the reverend's string tie and it untwisted, rolling into limp laces. "That's my inch for the day."

"We accomplished little today," the reverend said.

"We know Thurmond is in bed with Nixon," Paris said, "so if Nixon is elected there will be no civil rights legislation from Congress and no enforcement of existing civil rights laws."

He tapped his cane up and down. "Yes, we should assume that."

"So that's two inches for the day in my book," Paris said. She flicked a finger at his black string tie, rolling it over onto his suit lapel.

The reverend wrapped his arm around her shoulders once more. "Rude as the devil but never dumb," he said. "Don't agitate yourself so, child, or your injuries will open up."

She pressed fingers to her temples and sweat dribbled down her cheeks. She shook her head as if to clear it. "Kennedy is our last chance," she said. "If we don't elect him it will be twenty years of ghettos on fire and white police shooting down black men."

Wednesday, May 22
Los Angeles, California

Paris, still in her pajamas, worked the phone in their room, digging up contacts from a long list. Aiken read the *Los Angeles Times*, occasionally trying to engage her in conversation. He failed; her answers mechanical and short as she focused on her chores. He left the room, taking himself down the hall to JBM's room where the door was propped open. Still wearing his housecoat, JBM clacked away, cigarette drooping from his lips, smoke spiralling above him and he muttered the occasional curse. Aiken knew that he worked in his room to avoid the campaign frenzy blasting the headquarters, floors below. JBM waved Aiken in, pointing to a thermos of coffee. Aiken grabbed up a cup.

Paris suddenly realized that Aiken was no longer in the room. She scrubbed up thoroughly and changed into a dark skirt and white blouse. She knocked on JBM's open door, gliding inside, waving to both men. JBM ground out the stub of his cigarette and waved back. Paris snuggled down on the bed, bumping against Aiken, the springs squeaking. She glided her arm under his, probing for his fingers, resting her head on his shoulder.

"Ringing?" he said.

"No."

"Liar," he whispered.

JBM propped back in his chair and his hairy legs threaded out from the plaid housecoat. "The politics in this state are complicated beyond measure," he said. "The fault lines bite you in the ass, Nanook."

Paris nestled her fingers in Aiken's, her fingers clenching tight, causing him to glance at her and raising concern about her.

"We got blacks against whites," JBM said, "migrant farmworkers against landowners, poor people against rich assholes, young people against old farts, order versus dissent, past versus the future. Try writing a speech that covers all that."

"Our cleanup hitter shows well," Aiken said.

JBM's face bunched into quizzical and he thought for a few seconds. "You're right, Aiken. We got Bobby. Everything else will tumble into place." He picked up the first page of the speech and read it to himself, scribbled a few comments and set the page aside, turning back to the typewriter. His fingers bounced along the keys, quickening, and the clacking increased in volume. "I'm gonna nail this sucker yet."

Aiken and Paris left JBM pecking away. Inside their room, she snaked up alongside him, kissing him on the lips. "We could make this into a good praying day," she said.

"Seeing my sweetie dressed to the nines and making a comeback is already a good praying day."

She slung her arms around his neck and whispered to him, "We could make it an even better praying day."

He drew her in tight; she rubbed against him, nibbling his neck. "Order some wine," she said. "You can have sex with a hot black woman and it won't cost you a dime."

"How are your wounds?"

"We'll just be careful, Blue-eyes."

He wiped a finger across her forehead, noting that the scar was completely gone. "How's the ringing?"

"Disappeared…vanished…. We'll order the wine later," she said. Her arms tightened around his neck and he kissed her, fumbling with buttons, dragging her blouse off, guiding her onto the bed.

***

She showered first and while he showered she slipped into one of his shirts. Room service delivered the wine, and after the waiter popped the cork for her, she added a tip to the bill. She filled two glasses. Sitting cross-legged on the bed, she sipped wine. "I should be campaigning for Bobby," she called out to Aiken. "This is so decadent." Aiken rolled out of the bathroom with a towel about his waist, rubbing his hair with another, and bent down beside her, kissing her cheek.

"You committed," she said. "You bonded with Bobby."

"Going along for the ride, that's all." He kissed her cheek again.

She slapped his chest. "You lie, Aiken Day. You like the man."

He tugged at the towel about his waist. "Take that back," he said, "or I'll drop this towel and send you into a black sexual frenzy."

"After the war you came back, Blue-eyes. You just didn't make it all the way back. The documentary will rescue you."

Aiken shoved in beside her, breathing her in, gathering strength from her strength. "So far the bleakest thing about ghetto life is the lack of fathers."

"Fathers leave the home so the family qualifies for pogey," she said. "Don't get me started on the damage done to black families by three centuries of racism." She pressed fingers to her temples and drops of sweat appeared.

"More ringing?"

She smiled at him. "Nope. What did you expect after ringing my bell the way you just did?"

What good is a husband if he can't suck up the occasional lie?

Friday, May 24
Los Angeles, California

Aiken parked the rental car in front of a row of side-by side, seen-better-days apartments. He marshalled his gear together, for the first time noticing the damage to the car parked behind him. The car was a foreign job, he thought, expensive…maybe one of the fancy German cars currently kicking the guts out of Lincoln and Cadillac. A basketball-sized hole broke up the windshield. Behind the hole in the windshield, the tattered front seat was splatted maroon, deep maroon—dried blood, he thought.

A door twenty feet away squeaked open. "You Aiken Day?" the woman said.

"I am." The middle-aged woman beckoned him inside, using quick, culling motions with her hands. "The car?" he said as he slipped past her.

"Rich white men shouldn't be in this neighbourhood," she said, "even chasing a fancy, high-stepping yellow whore." *Memo to self.*

Inside the apartment a musty smell greeted him. Two-by-fours were crossed and nailed to the two windows, forbidding fresh air. Once inside, she propped a two-by-four strut against the doorknob, sealing them in. *Is this the smell of fear?* The woman was overweight yet supple and graceful, showing the agility of a former high school jock as she moved. She settled into an aging rocker, fingers plucking at her apron, smoothing it down. Two young black children frolicked in the room, squealing and racing about. "Mind yourselves," the woman said. They ignored her and their rough-housing continued.

"Children can be a handful," Aiken said.

"They're good kids, honey."

"Other children?"

She waved down at the children once more before answering. "One in the army, one in jail."

"Kids seem happy?" Aiken said.

"They're children. Happy in the ghetto disappears at twelve."

After the interview, the woman opened her door and stuck a finger to his chest. "Wait a bit, honey. I'll have a look-about."

She hooked her fingers around a broom and swept it back and forth while her eyes scanned every doorway, every street corner. "Scoot," she finally said.

***

Aiken ran the film from the previous week and Chester and Sarah watched the three interviews, the scenes thrown up against the pale hotel room wall. Afterwards Aiken waited for comments. "Just getting the hang of things," he said.

"Nothing unusual about these stories," Chester said, "just ordinary welfare stories. No drama, no extraordinary bleakness."

"Bleak prospects for the young ones," Aiken said.

"Hire actors," Chester said. "Spot them in wheelchairs and make them sob and cry. The laughing kids behind those moms were having a wee old time."

"They didn't do homework," Aiken said.

Chester filled two glasses with white wine, placing them alongside a cheese tray. "Who likes homework?" he said.

Sarah cried. After a few seconds she said, "You don't get anywhere, Uncle Chester, if you don't do homework." *You certainly don't climb out of the ghetto.*

***

In the evening Paris dragged him outside the hotel and Chester followed. "Got a surprise," she said. "Found a nice little panel van for storing all your film and cameras."

Aiken stitched an arm around her and squeezed. The beige van had a few traces of rust around the fenders. "You bought a van for Bobby's documentary?" he said.

Chester paced a circle around the vehicle, peering down at rust spots. "This piece of crap must be twenty years old," he said. "Twenty years old is perfect for a bottle of wine or a blonde mistress, but a van?"

"It's old so Aiken can take it across the border without paying duty."

"You can't import new cars into Canada," Aiken said. "No one knows why. Something to do with ice and snow and Mounties on horseback."

Paris opened the back door of the van. The sides of the van held shelves and drawers. She flipped up a small access flap in the floor. "For a pistol and some shells," she said. "A white fella in the ghetto," she said, "might need an edge."

Aiken thought about the car with the shotgun-shell windshield. *Chester: I might be needing the Webley back.*

Thursday, May 30
San Joaquin Valley, California

At 7 a.m., with JBM bunched beside him, Pierre Salinger rapped his knuckles on the door to Kennedy's suite. Ethel, wearing a silk housecoat with her hair already done, ushered both men in. "Emergency breakfast meeting?" she said. "Bacon gone missing? A sudden shortage of toast?"

Salinger shrugged an apology. "Sorry to bother the senator this early," JBM said.

Ethel nestled down in one of the two armchairs. Kennedy strolled out from the bedroom. His fingers clasped a package of throat lozenges and, plopping down into the other chair, he popped a lozenge into his mouth. The sickbay smell of the lozenge braced into him. He squinted up at the two men and his expression said, "What?"

"Cancel the trip, Bob," Salinger said. "Orange County voters matter most." His fingers dipped into his suit coat and emerged clinging to two cigars. "And skip Oakland. Those angry blacks will piss down your back." He waved an offer of cigars about but no one accepted. Kennedy dropped another lozenge into his mouth and smelled the same antiseptic odour.

"The whites of Orange County watch the news," Salinger said. "Don't let those voters observe you in front of cheering migrant farm workers or ghetto blacks."

Kennedy peered up at JBM.

"Your base needs to vote big time," JBM said. "And blacks and Chicanos love you. They are your real base. You can't hit it out of the park without them."

Kennedy, his voice hoarse, whispered, "Any other points?"

Both men shook a "no."

"People have to be part of it," Kennedy said. "We'll do the train ride and Oakland blacks can piss down my neck."

"He said your back," Ethel said. "They may miss your neck."

At the door Kennedy corralled JBM. "Bring your documentary man. The contrast between cheering Chicanos and the Oakland people says something about America."

***

The day carried sunshine and pain for Bobby Kennedy; the day carried sore hands and blistered knees for Chicano farm workers, sweating, crouching in half, in the San Joaquin Valley fields. Two folksingers warmed the crowd up with "If I Had a Hammer." Inside the Pullman, Kennedy waited for the folksingers to finish and wrapped his fingers around his throat, praying for relief from the pain. His wife pushed into the car with a bowl of chocolate ice cream oozing with chocolate syrup. "Eat this," she said. "It'll soothe your throat." He shovelled ice cream down and started to thank her. "Don't you dare say a word," she said. "Save it. You'll need every word you can muster today."

He squeezed her close. "I'm a lucky man," he said, "blessed in so many ways."

"Don't talk," she said. He felt his leg against her leg, and his shoulder against her shoulder, and the closeness gave him comfort. He ate more ice cream, easing the pain in his throat.

Outside, most people waiting for Kennedy wore field garments; the ones with time to fancy up sported white shirts and dark pants, church-going attire. The others wore bibbed overalls, worn thin, threadbare jeans or thin cotton trousers. The younger male Chicanos fancied T-shirts; displaying muscles earned in the fields rather than in LA exercise clubs, the older men wore plaid shirts, folded up sleeves, and everyone showed dark arms, tanned faces. The older women, even those fresh from the fields, wore long skirts, but the younger women showed cotton slacks and white blouses. Handwoven straw fedoras, panamas or planters, dotted the crowd, each brim edged with a fancy striped cotton band.

Kennedy appeared at the back of the Pullman, grabbing the wrought iron railing. The crowd roared. The women kept their hats on, locking the sun from their faces, but men held theirs before them, respectfully, shaking and waving them up and down to complement the clapping and cheering—a sea of thrashing, flapping sombreros— as Kennedy spoke.

Aiken panned his camera once across the crowd but dropped it to his side. "No bleakness here," he said to JBM. "Chicanos are perfectly happy with Bobby Kennedy."

"They love him," JBM said.

"Stab someone," Aiken said. "Or shoot someone with family. Drum up some bleakness somewhere, anywhere."

"I'm on it. I'll machine gun a family for you, maybe two. Shoot these happy fuckers to smithereens."

***

The whistle-stopping ran late, over an hour late. Kennedy arrived at the Oakland church at 11:15 p.m. for a meeting scheduled for 10:00 p.m. Several hundred Bay area activists and black leaders, including a few militant Black Panthers, milled about. Paris Day and Connie Harlan huddled together at the back of the room. "Some of these people," Paris said, "are hell bent on confrontation."

"We'll watch our man," Connie said. "A little test can't hurt."

As Kennedy walked into the church, a fellow shouted, "So good of you to find the time, rich fella."

Salinger placed a hand on Aiken's camera. "We shouldn't film this bitterness. No purpose to it."

Kennedy overheard the exchange. "You film away, Mr. Day. These people have something to say and I'm gonna listen."

The first question to Kennedy established the tone. "How rich are you?" a short woman asked.

"I'm rich enough so that I can choose to be here or not," Kennedy said, "and I choose to be here."

"You're part of the white establishment," she said.

"I'm close enough to know the problems and offer a solution: we must end the war and address poverty in this country."

A voice called out: "What do you really think about black people?"

The question knocked Kennedy down a bit but after a few seconds, he responded. "I like some. Some I don't. Same goes for white people." He paused. "I haven't decided about you yet." Laughter flooded the room.

At 1 a.m. the yelling ended. People threaded out and Aiken crossed the room to Connie and Paris. "They roasted him alive," he said.

"He did well, mister," Connie said. "He held his own, didn't back down none and didn't promise what he couldn't deliver."

Paris put an arm around Aiken's waist. "She's right, Blue-eyes. These people will vote Bobby into the White House."

Saturday, June 1
Los Angeles, California

On May 28 Eugene McCarthy, with a well-organized campaign effort, won the Oregon primary, the first time someone outpolled a Kennedy in twenty-seven elections. Coupled with McCarthy's defeat in Nebraska, the California primary loomed as critical for each candidate. The two teams agreed to a televised debate. McCarthy, the college professor, a glib and agile speaker, showed up without preparation. Kennedy, a mediocre student at Harvard, crammed hard, his team bombarding him hour after hour with potential questions.

Print reporters occupied the first two rows of seats in the studio of KGFO-TV, host of the debate. Paris Day and Connie Harlan slipped by those rows and Aiken followed. "A somewhat private club," Paris said, referring to the reporters. "White, male, and middle-aged."

"And cynical to a man," Connie said. *Potbellied also springs to mind.*

Most of the seats were occupied, the staffs of both candidates flooding the chairs, and a bustling excitement bounced about the walls. A conversation hum crunched into the room but the room reeked of anxiety. Save for a few of the more jaundiced reporters, everyone hoped their soldier would do well and strike down the opposition, swinging the election towards him.

Aiken found folding chairs for Paris and Connie, settling them against the back wall. He fetched Paris coffee in a paper cup. "Go sit with JBM," she said.

McCarthy entered first, calm, relaxed, chatting with the journalists, appearing every inch the distinguished senator, a soul who would present well as president. Kennedy arrived after McCarthy, followed by his wife and Salinger. Booting someone aside, Salinger found a chair for Ethel. Kennedy appeared apprehensive. His hair, somewhat floppy, telegraphed to people that he was disorganized. He nodded politely to people but spoke to no one. With the entrance of Kennedy the room hushed and people sorted out, leaving conversation groups, shifting about, finding places to sit. Aiken joined JBM, wedging against a wall twenty feet from the dual podiums, the focal point of the debate.

Each candidate assumed a position behind a podium and greeted one another with a curt nod, borderline respectful but unfriendly. *Two gladiators waiting to duel to the death in the Coliseum.*

"Gentlemen," the moderator said, to an absolutely dumb-quiet room, "first question: How do we bring peace to Vietnam?"

McCarthy gripped the podium and raised his right hand, grasping the lapel of his suit coat, and reflected before responding. "Include the National Liberation Front in any new South Vietnam government," he said.

Blemishes of sweat spotted Kennedy's face; studio TV lights banged down, emitting fierce heat. He chopped a hand down and immediately retorted, "I wouldn't enter a coalition with Communists before we begin negotiations. That's not good tactics." *Bobby throws a left jab, a glancing blow to McCarthy's jaw; McCarthy staggers back but stays on his feet, still in pursuit, needing a knockout to win.* Murmurs danced across the audience and reporters scratched notes.

The moderator directed a question to Senator McCarthy. "You have criticized Senator Kennedy," he said, "for the decision to send twenty-two thousand US troops to the Dominican Republic."

McCarthy accepted the question, twisting to face Kennedy directly. "A person retaining a senior position in a government," he said, "bears a responsibility for the actions of that government."

"That decision was President Johnson's," Kennedy replied, "and he made it in April of 1965. I left his Administration in 1964." *McCarthy, not having prepped properly, takes a blow to the body, staggers but remains upright, still in the fight but somewhat shaken.*

"Gentlemen," the moderator said, "please give me your views on public housing."

McCarthy, the professor, the former candidate for priesthood, reflected on the vexing moral and philosophical question that had long tormented him. "Putting better housing in the ghettos," he said, "perpetuates a practical apartheid. We've got to distribute the races throughout the city."

Kennedy lunged out: "Senator McCarthy will fix the ghetto by moving ten thousand black people into Orange County."

Silence cocooned the room, a stunned quiet. After a few seconds reporters scrawled and scribbled. *Bingo: McCarthy hits the mat, bleeding from his nose. We have a new heavyweight champ!*

After the debate Aiken jammed against the flow of people leaving, seeking Paris. While most of the audience was in motion, she remained in her chair, Connie sitting alongside. Her face showed stress, lines of age not normally present. "You're a little wobbly," he said, coming to her side.

"Just a bit of ringing," she said, "but the debate reminded me of a conversation with Richard Nixon." Standing up she wavered slightly. Aiken thought she might buckle and he steadied her, touching her elbow. "Drive me back to the hotel please," she said.

***

At the hotel, Chester and Sarah, seeking an update, set aside their game of checkers. Paris brushed by them, opening her suitcase, stuffing clothes into it.

Seeing what she was doing, Aiken pushed close to her. "What's up, sweetie-pie?" he said.

"It's time for Sarah to resume proper schooling," she said. "A girl should know more than what wine goes with grilled cheese sandwiches. And suddenly I feel like cooking and cleaning."

"But the election?" Aiken said.

"And lying down," Paris said. "I intend to do some serious lying down."

"Cooking, I get," Chester said, "but cleaning?"

"Back to basics," she said, "back to basics." She swiped at her eyes with a tissue. "I caught a cold or something." She wiped her eyes again.

"I'm with you two girls," Connie said. "I gotta find some employment."

"I'll drive you to the airport," Aiken said.

"There's a taxi stand downstairs," Paris said. Connie hefted her bag up and left the room.

Sarah picked up her suitcase but dropped it back down. "What about the election," she said. "We worked to elect Senator Kennedy as President."

"Aiken will work on it," Paris said, "by finishing his documentary on bleakness." She tugged at Sarah's arm, gently shoving her towards the door. Aiken and Chester picked up bags and suitcases and carried them down and outside to the waiting taxi. Connie sat inside the taxi, the back door of the cab open, waiting. Sarah hugged both Chester and Aiken.

When the cab fled out of sight, Aiken said, "I don't understand. The election ain't over yet."

"Let's hunt up a decent meal," Chester said, "and some quality wine. Don't try to figure a woman out. It's enough to know that when you turn the pen upside down, her clothes drop away."

"Bobby bloodies McCarthy's nose," Aiken said, "and they all jump ship."

***

Moonlight shot into the hotel suite, swaying in through the windows, but neither man thought to switch on the room lights. In the dimness they shared the bottle of Crown Royal nestled between them, dropping in the occasional ice cube to their glasses, cubes plucked from the bucket in front of them. Curtains ruffled in the breeze and street smells snuck into the room, growling aromas from the city of Los Angeles. The street noises were quieting, the sounds of the day dying.

The whiskey tasted sour to Aiken, dead-crow flat, as if the alcohol in the bottle was just dim gossip, a mere rumour of potency.

Chester hated silence and babbled occasionally but Aiken hunched down without speaking, not hearing Chester's words. Finally he recapped the bottle. "Bobby scared the white people of Orange County," he said. "He used the threat of blacks moving into white neighbourhoods to win the debate, to crush McCarthy, but it was similar to Nixon's 'southern strategy.' That's what bothered Paris."

"Dog-fart thinking," Chester said. "Even Jesus blasted out the occasional fart in the manger, scaring the hell out of the three kings. That didn't mean he couldn't walk on water when he put his mind to it."

Let me guess, Tonto: you got this from a hippie Haight-Ashbury church sermon—Walking on Water after Jesus Farts.

Monday, June 3
Los Angeles, California

At 4:30 a.m. Ethel rubbed her husband's hands with cream. "Only a politician's wife acquires this particular skill," she said. Kennedy responded with his first smile of the day, a quiet, loving flicker. She dabbed cream on his nose and when he smiled again she wiped it away, returning the smile. She removed a stack of handkerchiefs from his suitcase, pressing them into her purse. "The day is upon us," he said.

"You sound tired," she said, "wearied down to your soul."

"Not to worry. Final hours—the end is almost upon us."

Breakfast for the Kennedy team, at 5 a.m., consisted of coffee and toast. Staff members heaped additional jam and marmalade on the slices, seeking extra energy for the day. California weather warped about for the day: sunshine erratic, the day bristling cooler, clouding over, spitting out in downhearted bleats at times. The campaign courting votes spun into its final day. McCarthy and Kennedy ran close in the polls, each seeking a win to validate their candidacy.

JBM approached Kennedy, offering a suggestion. Kennedy snapped at him. "It's too late to fiddle with phrases."

Salinger flicked a finger towards JBM, who bent close. "He's dead on his feet," Salinger whispered. "His reserves are gone."

"I'll juice him up," JBM said. He grabbed a phone and dialled, then spoke quietly into the receiver.

Kennedy's team flew to San Francisco. Two Kennedy staffers waited on the tarmac, both wearing rented coolie costumes, hunching beside a rickshaw. "Cadillac broke down, Senator," JBM said.

Kennedy plopped down on the plane's landing steps, laughing until tears dripped from his eyes.

Kennedy's motorcade danced through Chinatown, springing towards Fisherman's Warf. He spoke briefly to a small crowd, *Italian-Americans for Kennedy*. The team flew to Long Beach and he shook hands with six thousand ramped-up supporters. His wife held out a handkerchief to him; he wiped with it, passing it back to her, and she crumpled it up, hiding the blood stains. When speaking to the crowd, his tongue betrayed him, bumbling his words, mixing his phrases. Ethel gave over a second handkerchief, noting for the first time the tremors in his hands. She lied to him: "Almost done."

They motorcaded through Compton, Watts and Venice. In Watts, wave after wave of people swarmed the convertible; Salinger and two staffers hooked together, keeping Kennedy from being dragged into the crowd. Kennedy shook every hand that reached out for him; he accepted a third handkerchief from his wife. The crowd swarmed at the car. Kennedy reached down and grabbed a young black child up, pulling her into the vehicle to keep her from falling under the car. He tapped on the driver's shoulder and the vehicle slowed to a stop. Salinger slapped his own face. "Pointing out that we are running behind," he said.

"How old are you," Kennedy said to the girl.

"Five." She held up fingers.

"Five," he said. "You appear older, maybe twelve." She grinned at the fiction. "Go to school?" he said. Her head wagged up and down.

"Know your momma's name?" She said the name.

Salinger turned to a staffer. "Go find her parents," he said, "before we spend the rest of our life here."

At the El Cortez Hotel, before his speech, Kennedy failed to recognize JBM. A few minutes into the speech Kennedy's knees caved and he crumpled down on the floor. JBM yanked the plug from the TV crew equipment, preventing them from filming Kennedy's lapse. In the washroom, Kennedy threw up. He stumbled up, making his way to the hall, tumbling down beside Ethel. Andy Williams cradled the microphone, preparing to sing. Kennedy said nothing. After the concert the team boarded the plane. Ethel shoved him into a seat, draping her shawl over him, wagging a finger, warning anyone from speaking to him. Kennedy slept fitfully, sweat dripping from his face. In LA, rounding up their children, they escaped to a Malibu home, waiting for the judgment of Californians. Kennedy slumped into the bed, instantly asleep. Ethel tried to wrap his hands in ice, trying to reduce the swelling, but it was mostly unsuccessful. She undid and removed his shoes and wrestled off his suit coat and pants. "Another skill a politician's wife should possess," she said, dragging a sheet over him and tucking him in. "Tearing off your husband's pants when he's passed out."

Tuesday, June 4
Los Angeles, California

In a city suburb a short, dark young man with bushy hair waited outside the San Gabriel Valley Gun Club. One of the employees of the club, a teenaged clerk, unlocked the front door, and the twenty-four-year-old immigrant from Jordan rammed inside, crossed to the desk and printed his name on the gun club register, scratching a signature.

"Early bird," said the employee, but the young man ignored the comment and shoved past him, choosing the closest shooting range. "Fetch you a morning coffee?" the employee called after him. The young man bent about, staring at the employee for a few seconds before assuming the proper stance of an experienced shooter. He fired rapidly, round after round of .22 calibre bullets from an Iver-Johnson pistol. The employee read the scribbles, deciphering the name: *Sirhan Sirhan.*

Tuesday, June 5
Malibu, California

In Malibu the ocean fogged coldness into the shore, quilting down quiet, numbing the sounds of the rocking waves and gulls, muting them, allowing Kennedy to sleep in. Inside the beach house none had to be told to keep things on the downside; people padded about in slippers and bare feet, children playing quiet games that Ethel organized. When Kennedy swung his legs down off the bed, she heard the squeaking coils and attended to him within moments, bringing a small metal cooler and rosary beads, placing the cooler near the chair, keeping the beads close. She pushed back drapes and cranked open windows.

Outside, the sun unexpectedly cracked through the fog, filtering small morsels of light into his room and carrying with them the ocean smells of brine, sand and driftwood, aromas that stung his senses awake. Alive on a glorious, God-given day, he thought. Gulls flapping by the window squawked a welcome. "How peaceful after the last few days," he said, bouncing over into the easy chair. She flipped the bedsheets down, neating them up automatically, perching on the bed when satisfied with its condition. "I recall Andy," he said, "but not what he sang."

Her face sprung up into an easy smile, almost impudent. "You didn't snore while he sang, and you drooped down sleepy-quiet for Rosemary Clooney."

Now his tease: "Rosemary showed up?"

"I expect a long campaign," she said, "but today we rest and repair." She reached out, wrapping her fingers about his wrists, gently rotating them. Scuffs and scratches crusted each hand. "Must you shake every hand reaching out to you?" He did not respond to her comment, understanding a tease, rather than a criticism.

"Flesh heals," he said. She pressed against the cooler with her foot, butting it to the chair, below his knees, placing the prayer beads on the bed before she started. He made the sign of the cross and placed his hands on his lap. She removed white Bristol towels from the cooler, packing them with ice, pleating them about his hands, securing the towels with strips of yarn. He kept his hands on his lap, balancing the towels of ice, and she knelt and started the rosary, beginning with the Apostles' Creed: "I believe in God, the Father almighty, creator of Heaven and earth…"

He leaned against the chair back, his unspoken words and thoughts silently tracking the soothing choruses spoken by his wife. Wellness leached into him, soothing his mind, and icy coolness comforted him. After the prayer they stayed quiet. A few minutes later she removed the ice packs, placing everything back into the cooler, neating things up once more.

At breakfast the family quieted, bowing heads. The moments of silence before Ethel said grace swept the family together, closing them off from the outside world. After grace the buzz quickly resumed but Kennedy tapped a spoon on his cup three times. His children waited for him to speak, quieting down again. "In this wonderful beach home," he said, "we should appreciate how blessed we are. In Mississippi, an entire family lives in a shack the size of this one room. The children are blistered with sores and their tummies stick out because they have no food." He undid the napkin then and draped it across his lap. "Each one of you is capable of doing something for your country, of fulfilling your obligation to this country." He paused, examining each child's face closely, seeing that they understood. "But now we should eat." The family dug in. They swallowed up ham and eggs, fresh rolls, juice newly squeezed and gallons of coffee for the adults. The children burst forth with opinions, becoming animated and vocal, arguing, pleading or teasing. Kennedy listened to the exchanges between his children, not taking sides in their arguments.

At 11 a.m. JBM arrived at the beach house and Ethel pulled him inside with a quick half-hug. Kennedy, wearing swim trunks, swarmed JBM with a greeting as warm as Ethel's. "Hectic day yesterday," Kennedy said.

"It's in the bag."

Kennedy pointed to JBM's clothes: sports coat, dress pants and tie, slightly wrinkled dress shirt. "We're at the beach," he said.

JBM removed his wire-rimmed glasses. "Bottom end of the wardrobe, Senator."

"Well you look nice," Ethel said. "More than nice."

One of his sons beckoned and Kennedy waved back. "Beach time, JBM," he said. JBM slung his jacket over a kitchen chair, pulled off his shoes and socks and trailed the Kennedy offspring outside, all bursting towards the beach. Kennedy won the race to the water, diving in first, followed closely by his twelve-year-old son, who plunged in a few seconds behind him. The ocean brine stung Kennedy's tortured hands but it brought relief to them as well. He stood in the surf, flashing his hands to Ethel, twisting them back and forth.

"All ready for more touching," she shouted out.

"Still time for more healing," he called back.

JBM sat cross-legged in the sand, his pant legs rolled up, his glasses perched up, his shirt unbuttoned, revealing an undershirt. His bright red tie, coiled up, nested in the sand, a de-fanged silk cobra. He noticed Kennedy's son suddenly plunging under a wave, dragged down by the undertow. He jumped up, feet crushing his tie, running into the surf, but he stopped short, seeing Kennedy sweep the child in, carting him to safety. The two of them, father and son, waded through the wobbling, bubbling surf. Kennedy kept his arm around his son and they pulled up when they reached JBM. "God designed you as a hero," JBM said. "I would have drowned both your son and me in the effort."

Kennedy took JBM by the arm and pointed to his drenched trousers. "But you tried, JBM. That's the heroic part. The doing comes later…and is not a test of character." His clan emptied from the beach and straggled towards the house, and Kennedy dragged JBM along in that direction, still gripping him by the arm. "Let me buy you a cup of coffee for that heroic impulse," he said.

Once Kennedy left to change clothes, JBM phoned CBS for their early projections. Back in the living room Kennedy found JBM gripping a bottle of Scotch, fingers pinning two glasses together. Kennedy called Ethel into the room and JBM hustled up a third glass.

"The network says voting is close, very close," JBM said. "But you've a decent shot and might prevail."

JBM tumbled a few inches of Scotch into each vessel; they clinked glasses and sipped. Ethel tucked an arm about her husband's neck, kissing him. JBM fumbled in his jacket's pocket, removing some loose pages. "I've made some speech notes."

"Give me your notes," Kennedy said. "Stick around and watch the returns with us." Something tweaked in JBM's face. "That look?" Kennedy said.

"The networks have their crews at the Ambassador Hotel."

Ethel shrugged to Kennedy. "We'll mosey over to the Ambassador," Kennedy said, "into harm's way once more."

Tuesday, June 5
Los Angeles, California

The Kennedys arrived at the Ambassador Hotel to receive the voters' decision in both South Dakota and California. They entered through a side door, unannounced, unnoticed. The hotel elevator clunked, grinding upwards. Kennedy and his wife shifted to the rear, the children bunching in front; Ethel fussed at his suit coat, flicking imaginary lint away. "You're much improved from yesterday," she said. "All healed up."

"Time with you and family," he said, hauling her to him, ignoring the children in front of them, clutching her tight, longer than normal, holding his body against hers, reminding her that she was not only a woman, but his woman. He kissed her cheek. "And time with those blasted ice packs."

"Plaster the smile on," she said. "Touch people in that Bobby Kennedy way." He grinned at that, squeezing her tight, running his fingers down her back, patting her bum. The elevator doors clanked open on the fifth floor at 7:15 p.m. The children burst from the elevator, slamming into the campaign room, swarming into an already crowded scene. Inside the room, frenzy battled panic, the scuffle too close to call. Tables of phones lined one wall; TV sets another, a makeshift bar a third.

"Holy crap. Are those phones working yet?" Salinger yelled.

"One is," JBM replied.

"One damn phone!" Salinger yelled. "Great! Call someone's mom and ask her to cook up a pie."

JBM shambled over to the bar and removed two beers from a bin in which dozens of beers were chilling. He popped the caps, crossing back to the phone technician, who still fussed with wires, quietly swearing. JBM tapped the tech person's shoulder, gently pulling the man about. He shoved a beer at the man, pressing it into his hand. "Gotta ask you a question, pal, but have a sip first." The fellow swallowed beer, standing, leaning back against the table. "You think the Dodgers can go all the way this year?" JBM said. "I see some skimpy skills." Several feet away, Salinger dumped Scotch into a glass and added a few ice cubes, trying to maintain his composure.

The tech sipped from his bottle, peering down at the jumbled wires before answering. "They can and I know the son-of-a-bitchin' problem." He fixed the phones quickly. Salinger, sweat dripping from his face, chomping firmly on his cigar, thrust through staff members to reach Kennedy. Kennedy gathered him in, sweeping an arm about his shoulder, tapping a finger against his chest.

"Don't pat his bum," Ethel whispered to Kennedy. "It'll start rumours in the press."

"Do you plan to personally control the Scotch all night?" Kennedy said.

"A reporter poisoned by Scotch is guaranteed to generate bad press." Salinger tapped cigar ashes into his palm while searching for an ashtray; finding none he dumped them to the floor. He removed a second cigar from his inside pocket. Kennedy accepted it, ripped the packaging off, and Salinger struck a match. Kennedy puffed it aglow.

"Thoughts on California, Sal?"

"Too soon to call, Bob."

The elevator doors thumped open and the first of the news people toddled out. Salinger pointed. "Work them, Bob. Let me run the room." Kennedy beckoned to the first news person, dragging him into a quiet bedroom for his first interview. Salinger waved, gathering the phone staffers in close to him. "Digest every phone call," he said, "in ten words maximum. I'll forward the calls. Are there any questions?" No one responded. Two phones rang at once. Someone dialled up the volume on NBC as it reported a precinct result.

The elevator doors banged open again, ejecting Aiken Day. The odour of dead pizza, butted cigarettes and half-empty glasses of beer greeted him. People milled about and gestured, hand signals he did not understand. People gobbled slabs of pizza while working, sipping from Coke cans or plastic cups. Half-eaten slabs of pizza lay abandoned on desks; a stack of empty, greasy, crushed pizza boxes banged against empty beer crates and Coke containers. Aiken parked himself in a corner. JBM noticed him and wandered over to him, slipping past people absorbed with their jobs. "How fares the battle?" Aiken said.

"If it goes well," JBM said, "I'll scream and grab someone's ass. If it goes badly, I'll cut my throat." *We'll pray for the ass-grab then.*

The liquor flowed in greater quantities and the noise level increased. Television sets blared and people tried to hear results while performing tasks. One of the phone workers spoke to Salinger and he yelled to the room, "Quiet all!" People turned televisions down. Salinger jumped to the bedroom door, banging on it. Kennedy opened the door. "We won South Dakota," Salinger shouted. "We beat the vice-president in his home state!"

Screaming and clapping erupted but after minutes the room quieted for Kennedy. "You people were responsible," Kennedy said. "This is a victory for all of us." He bounded back to the bedroom to continue an interview with a reporter. Within seconds the room buzz jumped up and the volume of television sets dialled back up. The phones once again screamed for attention.

The California results dribbled in. The suburbs voted first and the results leaned towards McCarthy. Staff members tried to minimize those results. TV sets in the room, still tuned to different channels, blared totals, competing with each other for attention.

The night wore on. Print reporters interviewed Kennedy. He also answered questions in front of television cameras, repeating answers already given. He accepted the phone calls filtered through Salinger. Salinger directed some phone calls to Ethel, and later to

Kennedy's sisters. When a phone call rang off, the phone sounded again, often within seconds.

At 10:30 p.m. JBM beckoned Aiken over. "Hispanic and black neighborhoods turned out big time for Bobby," he said. "He's picking up speed." Later someone wearing headphones scribbled on a pad, holding it up to Salinger. He screamed for silence. "We won California!" He raced to Kennedy and threw his arms around him, lifting him off the ground. "We won, Bob. We won."

People rushed the bar, toasting and toasting and toasting again, backslapping and hugging, some dancing about. The noise crushed all conversations. Staffers cried. The phone calls subtly twisted in nature. With Kennedy's California election victory, Democrats from across the country re-thought positions and alliances. People offered congratulations but some offered support, lining up behind Kennedy.

Salinger held two short glasses and his other hand displayed a bottle of Johnny Walker Black. "You killed in the ghettos," Salinger said, "the only white man trusted there."

Kennedy accepted a glass and sipped, smelling the peaty aroma. But it suddenly tasted harsh to him, and his face lines bleaked up. "If I'm the only white man trusted in the ghetto," he said, "America has some serious problems, more serious than we thought."

JBM dragged Aiken to the windows, yanking the drapes apart. "What do you see?"

Aiken scanned his eyes down at the scene. "The city lights of Los Angeles?"

"Look farther."

"Is it Watts?"

"Nanook, I can see the White House."

Tuesday, June 5
Los Angeles, California

JBM spoke into Aiken's ear, overriding the noise in the campaign room. "Bobby will speak to supporters downstairs. Move now and we'll score a ringside seat." They left the suite together, riding the clanking elevator down to the first floor. The music clatter from the Embassy Room banged into their ears when the elevator doors opened. Two thousand Kennedy supporters twirled, spinning to the music, skipping about the room in conga lines, chanting slogans, screaming to be heard.

Aiken jerked JBM's arm. "Do they know Kennedy won both California and South Dakota?"

"Everyone knows. President Johnson knows. Santa Claus and the Easter Bunny know. Brezhnev knows, the Pope knows." JBM swayed with the music, joining a conga line, dancing away from Aiken. A young girl carrying a champagne bottle bumped into Aiken, slapping fingers around his arm. "He's coming?" she said.

"I heard that," Aiken said. She lurched away.

At midnight Kennedy and his wife entered the room and the screaming broke out immediately, lasting several minutes. They mounted the small stage together, Ethel close, a heartbeat behind. Kennedy rendered an unscripted, rambling speech, thanking everyone in no particular order, tossing out names as he thought of them. Winding down, he said, "I also gotta thank my dog, Freckles." He paused, pulling in his wife. "And I gotta thank my wife, Ethel." He paused again. "I should've thanked her before Freckles." Laughter bounced across the room. He continued speaking, discarding the light approach, and people quieted. "We must address the divisions between black and white, rich and poor, young and old…and we must end the violence in this country. Above all else we must end the war."

Aiken, from the back of the room, filmed his talk, filming the enthusiasm, filming the lively bodies popping in and out of his camera frame.

No screams, just applause and clapping greeted these words. Kennedy waited until the clapping drained away. "We are a great country," he said, "an unselfish country, a compassionate country, and I intend to make that my basis for running. My thanks to all of you, and now it's on to the Chicago Convention and let's win there."

He left the stage amid sustained applause, his arm about Ethel, helping her down. She twisted over one of his hands. "All healed?"

"Ready for the touching," he said, leaving her, moving into the crowd. Kennedy exited the hall through the kitchen, shaking hands with the staff, patting shoulders or elbows, touching people while glancing behind him for his wife. Rosie Grier, former pro football lineman, hovered beside her, his job to watch out and protect her. Bobby flipped a short wave to her, still reaching out to people, moving towards the scheduled news conference. Ethel was fifteen feet behind him when Sirhan Sirhan pumped bullets into Bobby's head with his .22 calibre pistol.

The gunshots rang out and Kennedy crumpled to the floor. People screamed, jumbling against one another, trying to escape. Men wrestled the shooter down and Grier smothered the weapon with his huge hand, tearing it from the shooter. Bobby's crumpled body lay on the floor as if sleeping, his head oozing blood. Ethel reached him, kneeling beside him, cradling his head in her lap. Bobby said her name twice, so softly that only she heard. "I'm with you, my baby," she said.

***

One hour later outside the Ambassador Hotel Aiken and JBM shared a bottle, passing it back and forth between sips. The liquor soured in

Aiken's mouth and scratched his throat going down but he continued drinking. Tears streaked JBM's pale face, the bottle shaking when he touched it.

"He might live," Aiken said.

"With his brains splattered on the floor? It's Jack all over again. He's dead and the country's fucked. Everything gets fucked."

"He's not dead yet."

JBM sipped from the bottle again. "Now I feel nothing but despair. When they killed Jack, I thought, 'Well, there's always Bob.' Now there isn't Bob. His brains are slopped on the floor and he's dead, or soon will be. There's nothing. Nothing! No hope, nothing…"

"I never thought I'd push a Cadillac for anyone, "Aiken said.

"Any other Cadillac rising to the top of the hill will find piss, more piss and gallons of putrid shit, a world of black gas and festering purple pus."

"But the documentary," Aiken said. "He wanted that."

"Who's going to review the thing and who's going to sell it to Congress? Everything is dead." JBM yanked the bottle up and flung it against a stone pillar. The exploding glass popped crystal chunks in a five-foot radius, tinkling smaller sparklers even beyond that. JBM shook Aiken off and wandered into the night, leaving him alone. *I'll sell it to Congress if no one else will.*

Three cabs lined up outside the hotel and Aiken dropped down into the back seat of the first one. The cold interior of the cab shivered him. He dumped the camera on the floor, dropping it on empty cigarette packages and a flattened condom. "Take me to the closest hospital," he said.

"You sick?"

"Nothing urgent, nothing contagious."

"Bigshot politician got shot up in the hotel," the cabbie said. "You missed the action."

"I heard that." *Maybe he's not dead. Maybe JBM is wrong.*

The headliner in the car was torn, with fabric hanging down, and a discarded newspaper rested on the seat beside him. The streets outside showed damp and bare, with few vehicles, and the traffic lights flashed in ways he couldn't comprehend, so he left it to the driver to fathom their unusual patterns. There's a lot of litter on the streets, he thought, more garbage than should be. "Tomorrow must be pickup day," he said.

At the hospital Aiken waited with the crowds, the weeping crowds, mostly black and Chicano, everyone crying or pretending not to. Pierre Salinger stumbled out of the hospital and Aiken waved him down. "A bad goddamn day, Mr. Salinger," Aiken said.

"It's Aiken Day, isn't it? JBM's friend doing the documentary?"

"Yes sir. I need to know. Please tell me."

Salinger tapped at the camera slung over Aiken's shoulder. Aiken pulled it up, clicked it on, focusing on Salinger's face. Tears tumbled down Salinger's cheeks when he tried to talk but he wiped them away, composing himself, pausing until he could speak, waiting to catch his breath. "After eighty-two days of campaigning for president," Salinger said, "Senator Robert F. Kennedy was shot and approaches death in the hospital behind me. He's dead, still breathing, but dead. He will not survive. He will cease breathing in one hour or ten hours as God wills."

He waited, composing himself once more. "It is, as Mr. Day has pointed out, a bad day for America. But this is not a bad day for Bob. The senator will die at peace with himself, at peace with his family, at peace with his efforts and at peace with his God."

Salinger paused again to compose himself. "Don't weep for Bobby Kennedy joining his brothers Joe and John in heaven. Weep for America."

Saturday, June 8
New York City

A slow-moving funeral train carried Bobby's body from New York to Washington. Two million people lined the 226-mile route. Inside the train rode eight hundred people—family, friends, politicians and celebrities, mostly white. Ethel, together with Bobby's oldest son, Joe, circulated with the guests, comforting people, Joe touching people in the manner of his father. The railway ran chiefly through poor neighbourhoods, past legions of black faces. From inside the train, Aiken filmed the disadvantaged people, Bobby's people, standing on factory rooftops, on top of cars and along the tracks. People held up signs. Most signs said *Goodbye Bobby.*

Thursday, June 13
Windsor, Ontario

Harry Fortune and Agent Rizzuto crossed under the Detroit River in a cab. They ditched the cab after customs clearance and they hiked up Ouellette Avenue for about a mile. Rizzuto carried his large leather bag, the wide strap allowing him to shoulder the container. Fortune carried a sack of diet Cokes and store-bought sandwiches, all chicken-on-white, Rizzuto's choice. "I thought they placed these assignments on hold," Fortune said. "Some sort of hiatus."

"Officially that's true," Rizzuto said. "Every time someone kills a pussy Kennedy, politicians worry about black uprisings."

"So?"

"This one is off the books." At the intersection of Ouellette and Erie Street they paused for a red light. "It's between you and me, Miss Pussy. You understand?"

"Absolutely. Between us."

"I've never welched on an assignment," Rizzuto said. "Fuck the politicians."

"What's the plan?"

Rizzuto pointed to a six- or seven-storey office building across the street. They crossed and rode the elevator to the top floor and climbed to the roof. The Medical Arts Building, a mostly empty office complex, overlooked the intersection of Erie Street and Ouellette Avenue.

Rizzuto dropped the leather bag down and popped the clips, flipping the bag open. "Everyone names their weapon," he said. He put his hand on his crotch, moving it up and down suggestively.

"Every serious weapon has a name." He removed the rifle from the container, embracing it before holding it out for Fortune to view. "This is 'Gregory Pecker.' Understand, Miss Pussy? After the actor in that Mockingbird crap."

"Atticus Finch."

"Exactly, this is my Gregory Pecker."

"What's the plan?"

"Paris Day walks her girl to school. I pop the youngster first. Mom freezes. I give momma two seconds to grieve and pop her too."

"The kid's like thirteen."

"Save shooting her when she follows in her momma's footsteps."

Rizzuto lifted binoculars from the case and passed them over to Fortune. "You spot." Fortune took the binoculars, the pebbled material of the glasses feeling cold under his fingers. He unwound the straps, fiddling with them, not raising the glasses to his eyes.

"They'll drift in from the west," Rizzuto said, smiling, "shuffling down Erie Street. I like to splat them in an intersection, fuck up the traffic and scoot away in the bustle."

"'Shuffling'?"

"Pickaninny humour. Not everything is graveyard serious, Miss Pussy."

Paris and Sarah rounded the corner of Victoria Avenue, strolling without haste down Erie Street. Peering down from above, Fortune recognized the two figures. Sarah was skipping back and forth in front of her mom. The binoculars dropped down, straps jerking them about Fortune's neck. He turned to Rizzuto and took out his pack of cigarettes, tapping two cigarettes out of the packet, offering one to Rizzuto. "A quick smoke before the job?" he said.

Rizzuto accepted the cigarette, setting the rifle down, butting the cig to his lips, waiting, expecting a light. Fortune bent forward and clicked the Zippo several times, sparks flying. Rizzuto's face changed. A nerve quiver raced down his cheek. He wrenched about, convulsing. Fortune yanked the revolver from Rizzuto's shoulder holster, dropping the pistol to the ground, slinging his arms about his partner's waist, straining, struggling with the weight, shoving him against the railing. He set his feet down firmly, straining, pushing hard and finally he pitched Rizzuto over the edge.

A split second later Fortune heard a quiet thud. He waited for a response or outcry. Hearing none, he leaned over and saw Rizzuto's body spread-eagled on the ground below, one arm outstretched. He retrieved the rifle and flung it down, aiming for the body. The rifle hit with a snapping sound, missing the body by inches. Rizzuto's body appeared to be reaching for his weapon, in death.

Fortune picked up the revolver and tucked it into his waistband. "You lost your piece to Miss Pussy," he said. "Gregory Pecker wilted, failing to penetrate."

Minutes later, Paris and Sarah passed the intersection, heading towards Patterson Collegiate, unaware of the body in front of the Medical Arts Building.

***

At Detroit Metro Airport Fortune approached the first ticket window, breathing in and out repeatedly, trying to bounce away the nerves that suddenly attacked him. "Print me a ticket to Haight-Ashbury?" he said.

"'Frisco," the young girl said. "One way or return?"

Harry Fortune lost his composure. "Holy crap!" he yelled. "Why would anyone return to Detroit?"

Friday, June 14
Windsor, Ontario

The small house on McDougall Street between Giles Boulevard and Erie Street butted in claustrophobic nearness to other homes, squatting alongside the other undersized houses in the middle of the Windsor area where black people lived, where their living was tolerated. Percy Turner poked the doorbell and waited. He wore a white T-shirt and jeans, hunching over to minimize his size. He opened the storm door and banged his fist against the inside door until it opened. Connie Harlan swung the door back. Her tangled hair flopped about, tufts drooping loosely; her flannel housecoat flapped open, scarcely concealing her bare breasts. "What's this," she said? "Am I hosting a Jackson Prison reunion?"

"I could use some introductions or some names," Turner said.

"Come back at a decent time."

"It's past noon, Miss Harlan."

"Git away. Windsor zoning by-laws don't permit ex-cons in public."

"The miracle man, Kennedy," he said, "gonna end ghettos and save the black folk."

Pain slashed across her face, contorting it to ugly. "Bring yourself in," she said, gripping her housecoat, looping the ties closed. He followed her into the kitchen. Her hands trembled while she poured two inches of cheap whiskey into a glass. She put the glass to her lips but before downing it she glanced over to Percy.

"Too early for me," he said.

She sipped from the glass.

"Did you get a teaching job?" he said.

"No openings…hiring white teachers only." When she finished her drink she crossed to the sink, rinsed her glass and stowed the glass and bottle in her cupboard. Swivelling about, she leaned back against the counter. "Hair of the dog," she said.

He gave a nod. "Sure."

"Lost Kennedy," she said, "and I'm slowly losing my best friend." He waited. "What kind of names you hunting for?" she said.

"Heard about west coast groups not bothering with voting and politics…serious types."

"How serious?"

"Weapons, guns, bombs…real serious types."

She shrugged. "Why not?" She found a pencil and piece of paper and scribbled a name and address. "Go to these people," she said. He poked the note into his jean pocket.

"Thanks Ms. Harlan. I owe you for getting me out of Jackson."

"We're even, Percy." When the door banged closed, she removed the glass from the cupboard and wrapped her hand around the bottle.

Friday, June 14
Watts, California

On his first day Aiken found that the mousy motel clerk would fetch a mickey of cheap bourbon for ten dollars. His suitcase lay in the corner of the motel room, unopened since his arrival. The dripping noise from the toilet no longer bothered him; the pathetic, peeling and browning wallpaper no longer offended him. The squatting phone on the ten-inch-square end table kept mostly quiet, untended. When it sounded that morning he answered on the first ring, just to end the clanging. "I've arranged more interviews," Paris said to him. "Bleakness on demand."

Aiken dropped his legs off the bed, stretching upright. *Bleakness! I'll give you bleakness, girl. Park your ass in a concentration camp for three years and watch your buddies die. That's fucking bleakness.*

He cradled the phone in his arm while pouring two fingers of alcohol into a dirty glass. Guessing at the reason for the pause, Paris said, "The drinking under control?"

He rubbed stubble from three days of beard growth and pushed the glass aside, taking the receiver in hand. "No time to drink," he said. "Spending my days in church. A bunch of good praying days are constantly striking me in the ass."

The conversation moulded into silence but neither sought to end the contact.

"You patched up?" he finally said. "Back to normal?"

"White wine and Camembert," she said. "Living the good life. Cooking and cleaning soothes the soul."

"Sarah?"

"She's young. She'll be fine. The tragedy of Kennedy pales alongside a teenager worried about fitting in, clothes and pimples."

"Adam?"

"She misses you, Aiken."

A pause. "Adam?"

"No word," she said. "But he's strong and smart. You did a good job with both of them."

"How's Mayhem?"

"Mule has his faith, Aiken. He'll always have his faith."

Mule? "You said 'mule.'"

"I said 'Mayhem.'"

"But he's okay?" Aiken said.

"After a while," she said, "you just realize you've done all a person could."

Aiken emptied his glass. "I'm searching for Bobby's bleakness."

"Go interview the people I called for you, Blue-eyes."

"Yup." He rang off.

"I'm feeling warm," she said, before hanging up, talking out loud, to herself. "Maybe I should do a few notes for Sunday sermon."

Aiken dumped alcohol into a glass and drank. The brownish liquid spun down his throat, burning—a coarse, swampy taste. *To find bleakness you just need a mirror and a firm grasp on reality.*

Sunday, June 16
Watts, California

At 8 p.m. Aiken parked the van in a driveway next to a store with boarded-up windows. He checked the building number against the one on his piece of paper. The numbers matched but the building appeared empty. He threw his camera gear together, locked the vehicle and banged on the door a few times. It opened, but just a slit. The slight brown man peering out at him waved a pistol. "Yeah?"

"My wife phoned you. I'm Aiken Day."

"She never said you was white bread."

"She possesses a mean sense of humour." Aiken showed him the bottle, a mickey of Canadian Club. The man beckoned and Aiken followed him inside, greeted by a sooty smell, not unpleasant, a burning log-campfire smell.

The room had not functioned as a store for eons. The aging shelves held boxes of bullets and shotgun shells. Behind the shelves the walls were fire-scorched. Both the shotgun and rifle stacked against the front wall carried traces of barrel rust. Aiken figured the room at twenty feet by sixty, the back wall sandbagged floor to ceiling and a cardboard box to the side jumbled full of pistols. Cordite, Aiken thought, that's also mixed into the smell.

The man pointed to the scorching. "Jewish lightning."

Aiken uncapped the bottle. The man produced two chipped glasses; they hunched down at a two-foot-square table, squatting on scuffed-up chairs. Aiken poured two inches into each glass. "Ice machine is conkers today," the man said.

Aiken sipped from his glass. The first burning flashed by, leaving the pleasant charcoal tang. "Sometimes they go conkers."

They sipped slowly, and after the glasses emptied Aiken grabbed the camera off the floor, switching it on and pointing it. "What are the sandbags for?"

"This is the Watts Pistol and Shooting Club. We getting ready for the revolution."

"How does one get ready for a revolution?"

The man waited before answering. "We train young coloureds in shooting, show them how to make homemade bombs, help them dig up guns. When the revolution shows up we'll be ready to stand up to the Man."

"The Man?"

"The Man has the police and army on his side and we preparing for the day."

"What will happen on the day?" Aiken said.

The man broke his pistol, blew into it and snapped his wrist, cracking the weapon shut with a sudden, harsh crunch. "Whites and blacks…they'll commence to killing each other."

Aiken switched the camera off, set it down and splashed another shot for each of them. The man chugged his down, wiping his lips before speaking. "Who you gonna be shooting on the killing day, white bread? You gonna be killing your people or your wife's?"

Tuesday, August 20
Chicago, Illinois

Folks call Burnside, Chicago, a version of Detroit's 12th Street, "the Triangle." The name springs from the railroad tracks bordering it: the Nickel Plate Railroad on the east, the Illinois Central on the west, the Rock Island on the south. European immigrants drifted into the community after World War II, abandoning it to blacks as the steel mills closed and jobs disappeared. Aiken Day parked his van in front of a beaten-down home off East 93rd Street. The woman answering the door wore a faded-to-grey white slip and fuzzy slippers. "Paris Day called about me," Aiken said. She slapped on a housecoat. After tightening it, she motioned him inside.

In the one-room apartment, three young children clustered in a circle behind her and the youngest, a baby, stumbling towards her, began to cry. "I've no money for milk," the woman said. "My man, Otis, grabs my pogey for boozing." Aiken reached into a pocket and took out a twenty-dollar bill. She grabbed it. "You watch my children, mister. I'll be right back."

"Wait!" he said, "I can't care for your kids." The door slapped shut behind her. The baby screamed. He picked up the child, rocking him back and forth, patting the child's back at the same time. One of the other children clasped an arm around Aiken's knee, head-butting so hard that he almost lost his balance. As Aiken rocked the child, the crying slowed, rolling into sobs. *Please hurry, Mom.*

The door opened and a sizable black man entered the room. *Crap. Now what?* The newcomer's bib overalls revealing a stained sweatshirt; the smell of booze drifted across the few feet between them. "You holdin' my son," he said. Aiken offered the child to him, holding the child out, but the man made no effort to gather the child up, so Aiken kept on with the rocking. The sobbing sounds continued.

"Put the kid down."

Aiken set the child down and the screaming started up again, kicking up into screeching.

"Where's my woman?" He staggered towards Aiken, noticing the camera gear on the floor, kicking at it. "What're you doin' with my woman?"

"Asking questions, making a film," Aiken said. "Maybe you know my wife, Paris Day?"

"Gonna shoot naked pictures. Maybe use her on the floor, make her whimper?" The man clenched his fists, causing Aiken to tense. *Do they make them any bigger? I'm gonna throw the first punch.* Aiken shifted to his left, raising his left hand in a fist, and the man backed up, circling. *My God, he's done this before.*

The apartment door swung open and the woman, clutching a grocery bag, sized up the situation. She inserted herself between the two men, setting the bag on the table, then moving to the kitchen counter and slipping her fingers around a frypan. Keeping her back to them, she removed a five-dollar bill from the bag. When she faced them, the bill flashed high in her left hand; she pulled the frypan up, waving it high in her right, the pan winking as she flicked it back and forth. "Your choice, Otis?"

He slouched down a few seconds, considering. He snatched the bill, wobbling to the door. "Don't be here when I'm back," he said, shoving the words in Aiken's direction.

The door thumped behind him, the whacking sound generating an eerie, cloaking silence. The woman held up dollars and coins to Aiken. He declined but she rammed them into his chest, insistent, so he accepted, stowing the money in his pocket.

"He's a good man without booze," she said. *Aren't we all?* She pointed to the camera.

Aiken spent three more days filming in the Triangle, breathing in the choking, rank smell of fear in homes, dispensing money, a small bill at a time, each person he filmed sending him along to someone else.

Martha, with four children in the home, confided to him. "I should have learned in school, got a trade." She sucked on a succession of unfiltered cigarettes, rising occasionally to check on children in the bedroom. She cuffed at the youngest child, pulling him in to her. "You make do," she said. The radio murmuring in the background spilled out gospel music. "There's gangs…. Keep the children away from gangs but they got to go to school. You hope to keep them safe." She emptied milk into a bottle, fiddled on a nipple and plunged the bottle into the child's mouth. Sucking sounds spilled out. "Outside, you keep your eyes down. You don't give offense to a gang member."

Aiken found grandmothers depending upon social security, raising children and grandchildren and extra children taken in, surviving on meagre budgets, washing and wearing clothes forever, mending, passing them down, cotton print dresses and worn cotton jeans the only clothes in sight.

A weeping woman admitted him to her apartment. Seven people sat on folding chairs or leaned against walls. A dead teenager stretched out in the living room on a wooden table, sheet covering his chest, eyes open, string-bean legs hanging down forty-five degrees, dangling in death. "He's in a better place," the woman blubbered, "in the Lord's hands. No gangs in heaven." She ushered Aiken inside. "I'll do witness," she said, standing before her dead child. In the kitchen a young girl offered turnip soup to Aiken. He declined. He kept his camera down, not seeking to intrude on their grief. A teenage boy, features similar to the dead one, motioned Aiken aside. "We don't have money to burn him." *Burn him? Cremate?* Aiken gave over all the money in his wallet.

The woman called him back into the living room. "You film this, mister. You film until you run out of film. The gangs killed my child."

"Yes, ma'am," Aiken said, switching the camera on. *No gangs in heaven. Here on earth: something else.*

Thursday, August 23
Democratic National Convention, Chicago

LSD: a drug that affects consciousness, raising it. If everyone dropped LSD the world would pivot to bliss, the argument went, Earth would turn into an Eden paradise where raindrops ruled and each snowflake became a miracle admired. The Yippies announced a plan to unload LSD into Chicago's drinking water during the convention.

Adam and Kendra rode a Greyhound bus to the downtown station in Chicago. Coming off the bus the heat knocked into them, along with the city stench of asphalt and gelling sweat, of strewn garbage and droning flies. Knapsacks dragged against their shoulders, sweat dripping as they sludged their way to the Chicago Civic Center. In addition to her backpack Kendra carried a small flour sack of rocks, throwing-sized rocks. Sweat stains branded the arms of Adam's khaki shirt, a wet-paste adhesive clinging to his skin. They circulated among the few hundred long-haired types already gathered. Yippies circled about them, handing out pamphlets, papers ink-smearing to the touch, papers urging revolution.

"Yippies are clowns," Kendra said. "Give me a street fighter any day."

"Room in the world for everyone. Relax a bit, killer." He set his knapsack on the ground and she lowered hers, keeping the rock sack in hand.

Ten uniformed officers milled about the hippie crowd along with a few undercover agents, the covert crew conspicuous by their age, military bearing and short hair. The officers and agents were somewhat relaxed in a crowd of non-threatening young people. A station wagon drove into the square, tailpipe splatting. Seven yippies piled out of the car engaged in laughing and giggling fits, one yanking down the tailgate. Three of them hauled a squirming, wriggling pig out of the vehicle, muscling the creature about, struggling him down in front of the Picasso sculpture. Two yippies held the pig down, soothing the animal, attempting to relax him. The police officers milled about, unsure of how to react.

The yippie leader read a statement to the crowd on behalf of the pig: "I, Pigasus, hereby announce my candidacy for the presidency of the United States." The crowd laughed and applauded and yippies led the crowd in chanting: "Vote pig, vote pig." The police reacted, moving in, arresting the seven station-wagon yippies.

After taking custody of the seven, officers rounded up the pig, sparking squeal after squeal from the animal. "Damn," Adam said. "The pigs are arresting the pig." He shouted, "The pigs are arresting a presidential candidate." The crowd chimed in with similar sentiments, exploding in catcalls and barbed comments. The police officers left with the seven, but also with the pig.

"That pig will squeal on everyone," Adam said to Kendra, who did not reply. "That's so over-the-top cool." Kendra scooped down, adding another stone to her rock bag. They slung their backpacks up again, following others, trudging the few blocks to Lincoln Park.

In the park, people offered up joints, an endless stream of marijuana butts threading back and forth. Adam plopped down, banging a few tokes, sucking in the harsh blast of marijuana, letting it smack into his lungs. Kendra dropped to the ground, crossing her legs. She ignored the joints passing about her. A girl cradled a Gibson guitar, strumming casually, plucking simple chords at first, long blonde hair teasing down to her waist, paisley print dress clinging to an ample body, sturdy black army boots tapping rhythm. The Gibson quieted, but after a few seconds it struck up again. People sang along to "San Francisco," following her supple voice.

Kendra jabbed a finger at Adam. "Chicago ain't about getting stoned."

He waved her off. "Kendra, relax and enjoy life," he said. "Sit beside me. Sit with me, sweetest."

"Singing protest songs and smoking grass is hippie bullshit."

"Relax, Killer, the time for demonstrating draws near and you can heave a few rocks."

"Drugs and music solve nothing," she said. "I need a proper weapon." She kicked at her rock bag. "Better weapons. I'm gonna hunt up some other types." She left her bag with Adam, quickly falling from his sight and merging into the crowd. More people gathered, huddling about the guitar strummer. Other musicians performed after the army-boots woman, still others replacing them in turn. Civil rights songs and songs protesting the war kept on hour after hour. Pleasure sticks of marijuana flew back and forth nonstop.

The sun crested, the heat mellowed and the music still swarmed on. Kendra plopped down beside him. "So your joke," she said. "'The pig will squeal.'"

"Yeah."

She slowly opened her jacket to reveal the butt of a pistol. She drew the material back over it, sealing it away. "I'll make a few pigs squeal."

Wednesday, August 28
Democratic National Convention, Chicago

Chicago hosted one hundred divergent anti-war groups, drawing together in revolt: draft resisters, flower children, socialists and communists, along with Marxist splinter groups and long-haired freaks just out for a good time. The Mayor ordered the entire Chicago police force of 11,321 men on twelve-hour shifts. The governor called up 5,650 members of the Illinois National Guard. Seventy-five hundred regular army troops waited on standby alert. One thousand intelligence agents from the FBI, CIA, army and navy disbursed about the city.

For the first few days police and demonstrators clashed in Lincoln Park, the police arresting many and slapping people up and down by the score. On this day—a muggy day, the smell of marijuana whiffling into the rotting-cabbage big city smell—the forces of law and order beefed up against the demonstrators in Grant Park. Police helicopters patrolled the air. Police snipers crouched on rooftops. Police officers muddied licence plates, taped over car numbers and removed badges and nameplates, intending to leave no footpath to their door.

Adam and Kendra joined fifteen thousand other protesters. The park swelled with endless noise: people strumming, people singing, people empowered, arguing about the fate of the world.

"Keep to the back," Adam said, "until we get the lay of the land."

"As in 'sit the back of the bus'?" Kendra said. "I don't think so, Mr. South Detroit."

"It's going to be a Columbia beat-up again."

"Not this time," she said. She rubbed the bulging pistol.

"I could hold that for you. Keep it safe."

"Get your own."

The music and singing ceased and the person in charge of the microphone called for people's attention. Police helicopters whirled above, dropping down, hovering, blades howling, bushes whipping.

"I'm gonna make a white pig squeal," Kendra said.

"Look over," Adam said. "National Guardsmen are joining the ranks of police."

"More targets."

"They're coming for us."

The speeches by the protesters began. "Always the stupid speeches," Kendra said. "Yappity, yappity, yappity…. Dig me a hole and blow me into it."

Police officers, each one wielding a truncheon, travelled in lockstep towards the park, moving across the street pavement, wading slowly into the park. Someone pitched a rock and suddenly a flight of rocks and bottles rained down on the police. Police officers trenched forward slowly, flinging canisters—tear gas spewed in out green putrid rivulets, the acrid smell choking, blistering up tears. Kendra retrieved a canister and flung it towards the charging officers. Others followed her example, pitching canisters back. She removed her weapon, gripping the pistol tightly, pointing at the ground, hiding it behind her leg. Adam grabbed for the gun but she shoved him away.

The police rushed, attacking, swinging clubs, wading into the protesters with batons, smacking down everyone. Screams broadcasted fear and pain. Police whacked and beat, hit and hurt. A few students threw rocks or bottles but most broke, fleeing. As demonstrators flew past her, Kendra surged forward and Adam followed. She raised her weapon and fired at a police officer twenty feet away and he plunged to the ground.

Three officers raged at her in response, piling on top of her, drubbing blows, grinding her down. The gun sprang free, kicked away. One officer struck her in the face. "Bitch, bitch, bitch," he yelled, pounding blow after blow. Adam jumped against the man, grabbing his helmet, slapping it off, fingers grabbing at the cop, trying to rip his face off, fingers tearing against cheeks, needing to rip a head from a torso, trying to wring his neck like a chicken's. Something struck him on the back of his head; he felt blows pounding into his back. He swung at a short cop. He yanked on Kendra's arm, failing to free her, and finally kicked a cop between the legs. As the man dropped, Adam seized his nightstick. He flailed away at faceless bodies in front of him. Kendra broke free and lurched away.

The police behind Adam began cuffing people, carting them off to waiting police vans. He caught sight of the green bandana and stumbled through to her. The kerchief still clung to her head, limping down one side to her cheek, a bloodied cheek. "Do you have my gun?" she said. He shook his head, noticing the cut on her forehead. "That's gonna scar up," he said. He observed squads of police officers flanking the protestors, pinching them in. More tear gas canisters clanged, spewing ugly dark lines of smoke. Lines of officers filtered out, carrying Mace, spraying the gas, clubbing anyone they encountered. As the clubbing began, the police, crazy-like, became an out-of-control mob. The Michigan Avenue massacre began.

When the police line closed to within a few hundred feet of her, Kendra fired a rock, missing. She searched the ground for other ammunition, finding none. The police swarm whacked away and bodies bounced down. Kendra waded into the swarm, attacking, punching, scratching; Adam followed. A burly officer whacked his nightstick against her shoulder, swinging at her again, a glancing blow that struck her forehead. Adam swung a fist at her new assailant, stumbling as the blow connected, falling as a billy club struck him from behind, feeling the blow, feeling other blows against his back and head. He lost consciousness and felt nothing as they kicked his body about, twisting him about for handcuffing. He lay on the searing pavement, aware of nothing. After handcuffing Adam the officer banged his billy stick against Adam's head, again and again, until the stick, drenched in blood and sweat, slipped from his hand.

***

Adam stumbled, limping out of the cell.

Mayhem stared at the crusted-over cuts on his face.

"No need to comment," Adam said quietly, glancing towards the police officer. "No need to give them that satisfaction."

Mayhem nodded and put his arm through Adam's arm, shouldering some of the weight.

"Kendra bailed me out?" Adam said.

"No."

"But she called you?"

"Someone recognized your name on a list two days ago. I came directly after raising the money."

Adam stayed silent for a few seconds, leaning hard into Mayhem. "She's moved on," he said, "gone into killing mode."

Mayhem shifted his weight and moved them forward. "It's happening more and more."

Monday, September 2
Windsor, Ontario

Mayhem entered the house without knocking and Paris waved in greeting. Standing at the ironing board set up in the dining room, she squirted more water on a wrinkled blouse, resuming the chore, sliding the iron back and forth in slow, deliberate movements. He noted her clear forehead, blemish-free, scar vanished. A notebook lay open on the kitchen table and Mayhem picked it up, flipping pages. "There's scribblings here," he said, "some bible references."

She ignored that and reached over, closing the journal.

"Adam home?" he said.

"No, he's back to school, determined to make some sort of team."

"Sarah?" Mayhem said.

"Anyways, I don't have food for him yet. He eats like a mule."

"Moose. You always said he ate like a moose."

Paris continued to work the iron back and forth. Sweat dappled her brow. Mayhem covered the notebook, tapping his fingers against it but leaving it unopened. "Vernon Johns owned a mule," he said.

"Yes." She pressed the iron firmly but gently, with purpose.

She wavered slightly, a faint tremor, but Mayhem noticed. She tumbled backwards and Mayhem caught her before she collapsed completely.

"Let's help you to the couch, child." He propped her up and helped her stumble to the living room. "You rest a piece," he said. Paris slid down on the couch and Mayhem swung her feet up. He unplugged the iron. The scorched blouse had a dead-fireplace smell, stinging his nostrils, but the odour masked something else. He followed the new smell into the kitchen. The black lab lay in a puddle of urine. He gathered up the dog, shoving the creature outside before mopping up the mess.

In the dining room Mayhem read the journal, flipping page after page. "She's leaving," he said. "She's drifting back to Vernon Johns." Paris slept, but she made wrenching, jerking motions in her sleep. He called Aiken's hotel in California and left a message for him.

Thursday, October 10
Windsor, Ontario

On Victoria Avenue Aiken and Mayhem tuned in the radio for the seventh game of the World Series between Detroit and St. Louis. Aiken popped two beers. "The smart money is on the Cardinals," he said.

Mayhem sipped from his beer. "Good thing we ain't smart."

Upstairs Paris lay in bed covered with a single sheet, flipping the pages of a *Vogue* magazine, flipping pages one page at a time without reading, not understanding the images before her, a glass of wine untouched on the night table beside her. When she reached the end of the magazine, she flipped it over carefully and began again, turning each page over with dogged purpose.

The ballgame ended at 4:06 p.m. Detroit won its third World Series. "Can you believe that," Mayhem said, "the Tigers won it."

Aiken dumped their first two beers, too warm to consume, into the kitchen sink, and opened a second cold beer for each of them. "Why aren't we delirious?" he said. He clicked the radio off. The living room wallpaper appeared faded to him, craving refreshment; the flooring worn, outdated and ugly. They sat quietly, melancholy swarming into them.

"Paris isn't doing so well," Aiken said. "Mixes things up when she speaks."

"The doctor?"

"Did some tests but said the brain is a funny thing."

Mayhem grabbed Aiken's shoulder and squeezed, and tears slithered down his face.

"Too technical for you?" Aiken said. Mayhem wiped at his cheeks and sipped his beer, waiting. "The head-bang turned some brain matter into Jell-O."

"Squishy stuff," Mayhem said.

"Yeah, squishy stuff."

Upstairs, Paris rolled over another page.

Friday, October 11
Windsor, Ontario

Aiken answered the banging on his front door. Two boxes were stacked in front of Chester and his hands floated over them, guarding them. "Where you been?" Aiken said. "Haven't seen you…"

"Since he was killed. Yeah. It makes you rethink everything."

"What did you rethink?"

"These cartons are a farewell gift to my Kemo Sabe." His fingers touched down, tapping the top carton. "A case of white, a case of red. Promise me you'll take in the bouquet."

"You're going away?"

"I felt lost after Kennedy. And a position opened up in the naked-girl-on-pen business."

"What sort of position?"

"Father's placed me in charge of manufacturing. Ask me anything about ballpoint pen production or how you make girls drop down their pants on a pen."

"In charge?"

Chester lowered his voice, hauling Aiken close and speaking quietly, conspiratorially. "Father suffered a small heart attack, or a stroke, or some medical thing. He raises his hand once for yes and twice for no."

"And you're in charge of production?"

"Yeah."

"Charge Card Chester has a real job?"

"Doesn't seem so important after the Kennedy campaign, but I needed find something after all that excitement. Remember?

Me…setting up a gourmet kitchen in a flea-trap motel in a foreign country while the fate of the world was at stake."

"You're gonna sell pens?"

"But I'm knocking together a kitchen for the factory, several hundred square feet, stainless steel pieces, multiple ovens, and I'm off to France and on to Italy to buy a few vineyards. Delicate whites and bold reds."

"Your father agreed to this?"

"I waited until his arm tired."

Tuesday, November 5
Windsor, Ontario

The elbow patches on the doctor's drab sports coat cried out for mending. His serviceable brown trousers, somewhat too long, hung down over worn shoes with laces half-knotted. He led Aiken outside of the bedroom and Mayhem followed both of them down the stairs and out to the porch.

"What did the tests show?" Aiken said. "Why did you send her home from the hospital?"

"There's part of her brain that's damaged, jelling up, shutting things down."

"An operation?"

"She's under eighty pounds and shedding weight rapidly. She wouldn't survive surgery." The doctor stuck his stethoscope back into his black satchel, snapping the bag tight. "She'll revive," he said, rubbing Aiken's shoulder, bending over, speaking for him alone. "Or she won't. I can't say more. You should say a prayer but prepare for the worst."

After the doctor departed, Mayhem huddled close to Aiken. "What did he whisper to you?" Aiken put an arm around Mayhem's shoulder, guiding him inside towards the kitchen and the liquor cabinet. "They won't be operating."

Mayhem's face sagged. "So it's with God now."

"Yeah, it is." *But some days God is busy elsewhere and don't give a rat's ass.*

***

In the bedroom silence Aiken reached back and threw up the double-hung. The bedroom curtains quivered, the cool draft shooting in from the failing days of Indian summer. Aiken's family collected in fear, distressed by Paris's fading strength, her words dispensing anxiety. She drifted into sleep and the family slunk quietly down the stairs to the living room. The drab overcast day buffed little sunlight into the room. Aiken switched a lamp on, but it did little to dispel the gloom. He rubbed his fingers along the lampshade, fingering the dust. "Time for dusting," he said.

"Did you call Connie Harlan?" Mayhem said.

"No answer," Aiken said. "Maybe she's out of town." He sagged down into the easy chair. Sarah slouched down onto its arm, squeezing Aiken's shoulder. Mayhem dropped onto the couch. Sarah burrowed down beside Aiken, nestling as close to him as possible.

"Do we pretend mom is Vernon Johns?" Adam said.

"We correct her," Aiken said. "She deserves honesty from her family."

"We don't upset her," Mayhem said. "She's fading, but upsetting her might speed things on."

***

In the afternoon Sarah climbed the stairs to the master bedroom. Seeing her mother awake, she settled into the kitchen chair that now was a permanent presence in the room. She grasped her mother's hand, causing Paris to take note of her, and Paris stared intently at her daughter. Sarah shut the journal, moving it aside. She withdrew a hairbrush from the drawer of the nightstand. She moved the chair away and swung her mother's legs over the edge of the bed, compelling Paris to sit up. She wrapped her mom's fingers around the hairbrush and sat down on the floor between her mother's legs.

Paris flashed the hairbrush and ran fingers through Sarah's hair. "You're Sarah," she said. Sarah welled up, tears flooding out suddenly, silently staining her cheeks. Paris dragged the hairbrush through Sarah's hair, a gentle motion, gaining in strength as she continued stroking.

***

"You had us worried," Aiken said to Paris. He perched on the edge of the bed. Sarah huddled beside him, an arm draped around Aiken's back, her fingers unknowingly scratching at him, digging into his flesh, unfelt. Paris raised an arm and lowered it, her eyes following the rolling of her limb, the twisting of her wrist and hand. "My strength dwindles," she said, "my preaching days are numbered." She raised her arm and it flopped down, lifeless, and she stared at it, her face bleaking up. Tears appeared—raindrops in a human form, Aiken thought. *My wife is leaving me.*

Sarah nudged him, jabbing fingers into his back and Aiken responded by lying down, pushing in beside Paris, stringing his arm around her shoulder. She gently cast his arm aside. "We've met before," she said, turning, inspecting his face, boring onto his eyes.

Aiken retrieved her journal from the nightstand, put it in her lap, and placed a pen between her fingers. "Vernon," he said, "Why don't you and I toss around some ideas for a sermon?" He wrapped his arm around her and this time she left it in place. Sarah left the room, tears bubbling down, and when she closed the door, she broke down completely.

In her last moments her family drew together. Paris bounced, stumbling through the haze, and banished the gibberish, embracing each of her family in turn, clasping tight to Aiken last of all. "Goodbye, Blue-eyes," she said. "You've left Stalag 8B."

She slept, ambling into death quietly.

Thursday, November 7
Kingsville, Ontario

Few people attended Paris Day's final goodbye; it wasn't widely published. "Why are we burying Mom in a Kingsville cemetery?" Adam said. His melton and leather coat, purple and grey, the colours of the University of Western Ontario, emphasized the bulk of his shoulders. Snowflakes floated about him, the skies spreading whiteness over the bleakness.

"It's easier than explaining a second burial in Windsor," Aiken said. His coat, open to the waist, displayed a white shirt, but he showed no signs of feeling the chill.

"Who did we bury in Windsor?" Adam said.

"A woman named Tanya."

"So people might be praying over the wrong body?"

Mayhem buttoned his wool coat tight. "Praying brings its own reward," he said, pressing an arm around his grandson. "God listens and sorts through everything so prayers aren't dumped into the trash because of human mistakes." *And maybe pig-shit is tasty as hell.*

They left the funeral men still digging and hacking at the hard ground. Sarah linked her arm through her father's and they traipsed through the cemetery, scooting by stones and wilted flowers, frost nipping at them and chilling their noses.

"Do you dream of Mom?" she said.

"I remember everything about her," Aiken said, "but I don't dream of anything. My dead friends at Dieppe and Stalag 8B now leave me alone. They leave me in peace."

"Mommy expected you to finish Bobby's film."

"I know that, honey."

At 11 a.m. they lowered Paris into the ground and quickly left, leaving the funeral people to finish the throwing-dirt part. Back in Windsor Aiken opened a forty-ounce bottle of Canadian Club and tossed the cap into the kitchen garbage can. Sarah retrieved the cap, rinsed it off, and plucked the bottle away from her dad, screwing the cap back on. "You and Grandpa go shoot some rabbits for dinner," she said. "Do something without alcohol."

* * *

Aiken and Mayhem drove slowly down Highway 3 at noon, heading through Cottam, cutting off at Division Road and parking inches away from the county ditch, close to a farm known slightly to both of them. They plucked their twelve-gauges from the trunk and loaded the weapons. Each man pulled a few extra shells from the cartridge box.

Aiken gripped the trunk lid and snapped it shut. "What now?" he said.

Mayhem checked his load again. "Same as me—keep moving forward."

"Forward to where."

Mayhem shifted the shotgun into his left arm, cradling it. "Do Kennedy's movie."

They hauled the dog from the back seat floor but she wobbled outside, stumbling when free from the car. Across the ditch she balked at the bent-over wire fence and they lifted her over. When they were well into the field she stretched into her lope, crossing back and forth in front of the two of them, back into her game. She flushed pheasants but the two men ignored the birds. She gamed on, poking up a jack, but her legs played out in the chase and she dropped to the ground. They propped her up but her legs collapsed once more. Aiken hoisted her up by the hips but she tumbled down again.

"First thing that dies in a Lab," Mayhem said, "is the legs."

"She's just tired." Aiken said. He scratched fingers behind her ears, massaging her neck, and her eyes telegraphed a message into him: *I like the attention.* He lifted her hindquarters up once more, squaring her legs straight, but she crumpled to the ground when he released her.

Mayhem waited, shotgun butted to the ground, grasping it like a shepherd's staff. "She's done," he said. "No going back, Aiken." Aiken removed his coat and laid it out and they lifted the dog onto the coat. Aiken shivered once but the chill of the day suddenly played away from him, unrecognized, unknown to him. Sweat stung his brow.

"Do we need a vet to put her down?" Mayhem said.

Aiken rubbed the dog's neck again. Her neck veins pulsed firm and her furry nape showed. Her eyes pleaded with him: *Give me one more shot. I can flush a bird or run down a jack.* But her legs lay flat, limp-shit flat, power departed. *Heart alive, body gone. Why do you look at me like that, Gus?*

Her legs quivered.

Bobby, with your body gone…where is your heart now?

"Let me do it," Mayhem said.

Tears dribbled down Aiken's cheeks. "My dog, my chore," he said. "Push her up a bit."

Mayhem thrust the coat under her neck to make her comfortable, but her head rested against field stubble. Aiken leaned his gun barrel down, pressing to an inch from her head and fired. They waited, taking care of the business of death, allowing her blood to drain into the earth, but the frosted ground puddled the blood, so they dragged her off a bit to keep the coat clean. After the blooding finished, they bundled her up in Aiken's coat and carried her back to the car, placing her into the trunk. Aiken shivered but he left his coat around her.

"Where you gonna bury her?" Mayhem said.

"Near the roses?"

"Good, yeah, next to the roses is good."

Monday, November 18
Detroit, Michigan

From the Tunnel Aiken pointed the Chevy down 12th Street, cruising past block after block of burned out homes and sacked businesses. He parked the car, trudging through ruin after ruin, charcoal shells, wreckage upon wreckage, seeking some sort of sense or reason to the destruction. People's lives exploded and died here, he thought, a great defiant act after which dismal lives crumpled into more despair. Trinkets of life remained, scrunching underfoot, burnt or crushed: scorched photographs, broken china, sodden clothing, everything discarded, everything soiled. The smell enveloped him: the putrid odour of rotten spuds; sometimes a dead-carcass stench. And rats, out of sight at first, then timid gaining in boldness. Squeaks blared at him, the intruder, as rodents squirrelled out from underneath the trash, challenging visitors, hissing, squealing, back in charge once more. A sense of dread swarmed him, driving bleakness into him, slinging him back to Stalag 8B.

* * *

In the early evening they watched geese circling above, forming up for the trip south. Aiken's Chevy was parked twenty feet from the Detroit River, in the city park near the university, the Ambassador Bridge towering above. Across the water Detroit lights slowly began twinkling on.

"From this side," Aiken said, "Detroit appears the same as before the riot." He plucked the last two beers from the cooler in the back seat, passing them to Mayhem.

Mayhem worked the opener for both. "I'm still unsure of the reason for this get-together," he said. He examined the label on the beer bottle. "American beer. You on a diet?"

"I spent an hour in Detroit," Aiken said, "searching for bleakness, groundwork for the documentary."

"A lot of bleakness shillyshallying about?"

"Block after block of homes burned down to cinderblock with no signs of re-building." He held up a cheap charm bracelet, scorched. "Some child doted on this," he said. He twisted off one of the charms, holding it up to Mayhem.

"A charm from the Michigan State Fair," Mayhem said, fingering the item. "Are you filming Twelfth Street for Bobby's film?"

"Don't think so," Aiken said. "People consumed Bobby, not buildings."

The empty cooler sloshed when Aiken dropped the Chevy in gear. Mayhem placed a hand on Aiken's shoulder. "Go down on Brush Street," he said. "Film the whores working there. There is no bleakness like the bleakness of the black whores of Detroit."

Tuesday, November 19
Oakland, California

A slightly built man, the interviewer possessed curly black hair and a neatly trimmed mustache and goatee. He wore dark glasses that gave him the air of an intellectual. He motioned Percy Turner to a seat, pointing to the only other chair in the room. The poster on the wall behind him showed a man in a dark beret with a rifle in this right hand, a spear in his left, sitting on a bamboo chair with the chair's wide round mesh framing him.

The interviewer pointed to the poster. "Huey Newton…our founder."

"Know that," Turner said. He sat down in the chair, resting a briefcase on the floor.

The interviewer read from a slip of paper: "Whenever any government becomes destructive to these ends, it is the right of the people to alter or to abolish it, and to institute a new government." His eyes shot up to Turner, inviting a comment.

"I'm here ain't I?" Turner said.

"Know where those words are from?"

"Declaration of Independence. Jackson State Prison gives over plenty of reading time."

"I nccd to know—can you kill a man?"

"I wasn't in Jackson for parking tickets."

"The briefcase? You bring a lunch?"

Turner kicked the briefcase towards him. "Documents on the FBI collected by Paris Day and her friend Connie Harlan."

The interviewer opened the briefcase up and dragged out files, sorting through the pieces of paper, pausing to read occasionally.

After ten minutes he glanced up at Percy. "Welcome to the Black Panthers."

"Who do you want me to kill?"

Wednesday, November 21
Windsor, Ontario

The clicking and whirring of the projector downstairs woke Aiken and he wrapped a housecoat about him, stumbling down the stairs to the living room. Sarah perched on the edge of the couch, elbows on knees, reviewing rough cuts from his footage of Watts. The images bounced around, black faces speaking of pain or disappointment, grim flickers on his living room wall. Tears rolled down her cheeks. "So sad," she said.

"You spent two hours last night watching film cuts," Aiken said. "And it amazes me that your body still retains liquid for today's tears." He clicked the projector off and hustled her into the kitchen, pushing her into a chair, filing slices of bread into the toaster. The two slices popped and he scooped them up. He held one up in front of him, sniffing at it. "As Chester might say: a fine bread-like bouquet, somewhat reminiscent of a decaying watermelon in Alsace-Lorraine."

She accepted the toast from him, spreading jam on each slice, munching in. "Thank you, Daddy." He reached out, wiping a chunk of jam from her top lip. He held his finger up, showing the lump of jam. "Such a gracious eater," he said.

From the porch he flipped a goodbye wave as she left for school. When she trundled out of sight, he collected the rough cuts, bundling the film canisters into several cardboard boxes, stacking the boxes, loading the negatives into the van.

* * *

In the early morning hours, in downtown Detroit, few whores trafficked up and down John R. and Brush Streets, most staying indoors, holding back, some recovering from hangovers, many high on drug hits, but each and every one dreading the habitual meanness that approached them.

At noon Aiken parked the van on a short street near Jefferson Avenue but waited inside the car, radio on WXYZ with the volume low, turning the vehicle on occasionally to charge the battery but also to bounce in a bit of heat. Eventually he ventured outside. Wind blew off the river, but the temperature held at a few degrees above freezing, the wind light, possessing little biting effect. In an effort to appear less threatening, he wore jeans and a well-worn air force jacket, with his pant legs jammed into his Kodiaks. *What does the average white John wear? Bib overalls with the crotch cut out?*

He checked the ten folded-over twenty-dollar American bills in his inside pocket, money to sweeten the pot for any woman nervous about sharing her story. *Goodbye savings account.* He sorted through his equipment, making sure everything was ready to go, dumping it into a canvas duffle, stowing the bag in the back of the van. He intended to keep the camera out of sight until he made contact, until he sweet-talked some working girl into an interview.

He watched several women parade past the van. He thought that they could be prostitutes. At 2 p.m. he approached a woman wearing an imitation fur coat with a gold spangled top peeking out. She slowed as she shambled towards the van. She wore a short black skirt, butt-tight, and white vinyl boots bunched up to her knees. He gave a short, tentative wave, hoping he wasn't flagging down someone's secretary.

"Whatch you want, honey boy," she said, "a handsome white man like yourself."

"Just hoping for some talking," Aiken said. He slipped out the first twenty and she perked up at the sight of money. She edged closer to the van and he reached into the back to his duffle, removing the camera.

"What's that for, honey boy?"

Aiken withdrew the second twenty and added it to the first. "I'm just hoping to ask you some questions. I'm making a film about Detroit."

"I shouldn't talk to you."

Aiken removed the third twenty.

"My man could hurt me," she said, "if he doesn't like it."

Aiken shrugged, bending the money over, making like he was putting it away.

"Maybe for one more of those Jackson's," she said, "he wouldn't care, honey boy."

Aiken added the fourth twenty into the others and passed them to her, dragging the camera out, cranking it up. "How did you start up in this business?" he said.

She waited before responding, finally shaking her head in an irritated toss. "At first they in love with you," she said. "You know, my man, that is."

The camera clicked away but neither person noticed the sound.

"'You the prettiest thing,' he say. He give you things you never had." She stuffed the bills into her blouse. "A nice pearl necklace, a good warm coat, real fur." She dipped down, then up, playing to the camera, apparently feeling okay about the filming. "Driving in a fancy car with him, eating good at restaurants, and him loving you all the time, he loves you up more than once a day."

She teared up and cleared her throat. "And you in love with him finally. And then you doing it with another man for him, 'cause you in love with him, 'cause he tells you to do it."

She turned away from the camera. "Then others," she said. "He makes you do them." Anger shot across her face. "Then he takes things back. Takes the necklace back." She stuck her fingers into the collar of her coat, poking a finger through a hole. "This ain't real fur," she said. "And it ain't warm. Now, if you don't make enough money he gives you a beating."

She stopped speaking and stared downwards. Aiken prompted her: "You have children?"

"Pregnant girls in our line of work get punched in the stomach. Punched a lot."

Someone grabbed Aiken from behind, spinning him about, flinging him to the ground. The whore ran. Pokeface picked up the camera and jerked out the film, flinging it to the ground. Aiken climbed to his feet slowly, dusting the snow and dirt off his jeans. Pokeface wore a long dark leather coat with a white scarf tucked about his neck, a striking contrast that blasted out his blackness.

"We did business before," Aiken said.

"You're messing in my business, Pastyman." Pokeface flipped open his coat and removed his gun from a shoulder holster. Aiken jerked a step back but Pokeface jumped forward, slapping him in the face with the gun. Aiken fell to the ground but struggled up. Pokeface slapped him a second time and Aiken hit the ground hard and stayed down. When his body hit pavement, Pokeface straddled him and pounded his pistol repeatedly against Aiken's face.

"Stay out of black people's business, Pastyman."

Aiken lost consciousness.

Pokeface walked to the front of the van. With an angry, jerking motion he snapped the radio antenna off. He removed the gas tank cap and flicked it away in another brisk motion. He jerked the scarf from his neck, snapping it once. Using the aerial he poked the cloth down into the gas tank. He set the scarf afire using a monogrammed gold Zippo and pulled back about twenty feet.

The gasoline in the tank exploded, consuming the van in flame. Heat blasted for several seconds, and the heat warp hitting Pokeface brought a smile to his lips. Aiken's hair flamed briefly. When the flames dialled down a little, Pokeface kicked Aiken's body over, locating and pocketing Aiken's stash of money, twisting a ring off his finger and removing his watch. Slapping imaginary dust from his coat, Pokeface brushed his clothes off, buttoning up his coat and resumed his business, the business of selling black whores to white men with money. White men who carried no cameras, who made no record.

* * *

The Detroit police officers broke official policy, crossing the border to bring Aiken to his Victoria Avenue home. He waved to them and they left. He managed the walkway but stumbled on the front stairs, and the noise carried to Sarah, inside. She set the arithmetic assignment aside and opened the curtains to peer out. Seeing Aiken she rushed outside. Black scorch marks stitched his face and the right side of his head carried singed hairs and bloodied patches of white-red mottled skin. The bandages on his face, slipping down and about to fall off, displayed crusted clusters of dried blood.

Sarah helped him inside and led him to the couch. She raced back to the kitchen, wet a towel, returned to his side and dabbed at his face. He tried not to flinch. She finally set the towel aside. "I'm just hurting you more," she said.

"I found the bleakness," he said, "but I lost Bobby's documentary." He sank back in the couch, his eyes closing, drifting back to the beach at Dieppe. German soldiers cautiously made their way down from the headlands, gathering up the survivors to send them to the Stalag 8B concentration camp, shooting the occasional soldier who resisted and shooting some who didn't. Sweat beaded on Aiken's brow.

Sarah dabbed gently, trying to avoid the blemishes of blood plastering his face. She sobbed and wrapped her arms about him. The bloodied cloth fell to the floor.

Acknowledgements

I cannot stress how much the following free-lance editors improved this work: Marie-Lynne Hammond; Marnie Lamb and Greg Ioannou.

www.ingramcontent.com/pod-product-compliance
Lightning Source LLC
Chambersburg PA
CBHW020838020726
47497CB00005B/1154